When You Wish Upon a Star

A Twisted Tale

WHEN YOU WISH UPON A STAR

A TWISTED TALE

What if the Blue Fairy wasn't
supposed to help Pinocchio?

ELIZABETH LIM

DISNEP · HYPERION

Los Angeles • New York

Published by Disney • Hyperion, an imprint of Buena Vista Books, Inc.
No part of this book may be reproduced or transmitted in any form or by any means,
electronic or mechanical, including photocopying, recording, or by any information
storage and retrieval system, without written permission from the publisher.
For information address Disney • Hyperion,
77 West 66th Street, New York, New York 10023.

Printed in the United States of America
First Hardcover Edition, April 2023
1 3 5 7 9 10 8 6 4 2
FAC-004510-23048
Library of Congress Control Number: 2022037968
ISBN 978-1-368-07754-5
Visit disneybooks.com

SUSTAINABLE FORESTRY INITIATIVE
Certified Sourcing
www.sfiprogram.org
SFI-01681

Logo Applies to Text Stock Only

For my sister, Victoria,
for the love, the music, and the laughs

—E.L.

PROLOGUE

The Blue Fairy wasn't supposed to listen to wishes tonight, and especially not wishes from the sleepy little town of Pariva. But there came a twinge in her heart as she flew across the low-roofed houses and narrow cobbled roads, and her conscience begged her not to ignore it.

It was well into the evening, and many of the houses were dark, their inhabitants gone to bed. Candlelight lit only a handful of windows, and the Blue Fairy saw eager faces peek out of the open frames. Adults and children alike cried into the empty streets, "Look up! The Wishing Star is bright tonight!"

And so it was. It shone so brilliantly that its light eclipsed the stars around it, and even the moon.

"Hurry, hurry!" the Blue Fairy heard a girl cry. "It'll

be gone if we don't hurry up and make a wish! I've always wanted to see the Wishing Star. Finally, it's here!"

With a smile, the Blue Fairy descended upon the roof of Pariva's old bell tower, her silver slippers landing on the cracked clay tiles with the gentlest tinkle. The bell tower was empty, but even if it hadn't been, no one could see her. She was invisible, as all her kind could be when they wanted. Such allowed her to go about her business and perform the necessary duties without being seen.

Now more than ever, she was grateful for that ability. Oh, she knew it was silly to feel that way. After all, there wasn't anyone in Pariva who would have recognized her even if they could see her. And yet, that twinge in her heart sharpened.

Pariva was a small village, unimportant enough that it rarely appeared on any maps of Esperia. Bordered by mountains and sea, it seemed untouched by time. The school looked the same as she remembered; so did the market and Mangia Road—a block of eating establishments that included the locally famous Belmagio bakery—and cypress and laurel and pine trees still surrounded the local square, where the villagers came out to gossip or play chess or even sing together.

Had it really been forty years since she had returned? It seemed like only yesterday that she'd strolled down Pariva's narrow streets, carrying a sack of pine nuts to her parents' bakery or stopping by the docks to watch the fishing boats sail across the glittering sea.

Back then, she'd been a daughter, a sister, a friend. A mere slip of a young woman. Home had been a humble two-storied house on Constanza Street, with a door as yellow as daffodils and cobblestoned stairs that led into a small court-yard in the back. Her father had kept a garden of herbs; he was always frustrated by how the mint grew wild when what he truly wanted to grow was basil.

The herbs went into the bread that her parents sold at their bakery. Papa crafted the savory loaves and Mamma the sweet ones, along with almond cakes drizzled with lemon glaze, chocolate biscuits with hazelnut pralines, and her famous cinnamon cookies. The magic the Blue Fairy had grown up with was sugar shimmering on her fingertips and flour dusting her hair like snow. It was her older brother, Niccolo, coaxing their finicky oven into working again, and Mamma listening for the crackle of a golden-brown crust just before her bread sang. It was her little sister Ilaria's tongue turning green after she ate too many pistachio cakes. Most of all, magic was the smile on Mamma's, Papa's, Niccolo's, and Ilaria's faces when they brought home the bakery's left-over chocolate cake and sank their forks into a sumptuous, moist slice.

After dinner, the Blue Fairy and her siblings made music together in the Blue Room. Its walls were bluer than the midsummer sky, and the windows arched like rainbows. It'd been her favorite room in the house.

The memories made the Blue Fairy's heart light and heavy all at once. Instinctively, her gaze fell upon her old house. It was still there, the door a faded yellow and the roof in need of repair. No one was at the window making a wish upon the star.

With a deep breath, she turned away from her childhood home and concentrated on the rest of the town. Still standing on the roof of the bell tower, she leaned forward and touched the end of her wand to her ear so she might hear the wishes being made below:

"Oh, Wishing Star, please help my little Maria do well in school."

"Dear Wishing Star, I'd like for my Baci to have a whole litter of puppies. Nine of them, that look just like him—all healthy and happy, of course."

"I wish for my shop to have more success."

So on, the wishes went.

Several of them caught her interest, but the Blue Fairy couldn't answer them. Pariva was not a town where she was permitted to grant wishes. Another fairy would listen to the hearts of those who spoke tonight and would heed the pleas of those they deemed worthy.

A white dove appeared at her side, settling its wings as it landed on her shoulder. It made a gentle purr, urging her to leave.

"Don't worry, my friend," she replied. "I know what time it is."

She'd already overstayed the hour, and she'd be missed if she lingered any longer. "Farewell, dear Pariva," she murmured. She raised her wand, preparing to depart—when one last wish caught her ears.

"Starlight, star bright, first star I see tonight . . ."

Quickly the Blue Fairy drew a circle with her wand, creating a magical window through which she could observe the speaker more closely. He was an old man kneeling upon his bed, with a spry black kitten at his side while he gazed wistfully up at the stars. His voice was not one she knew, but the sound of it—with its gentle inflections and earnest way—was familiar.

"I wish I may, I wish I might," he continued, "have the wish I wish tonight."

His name rushed back to her in a breath.

Geppetto.

Forty years had turned his hair entirely white and aged

his face beyond recognition. But his kind blue eyes and even his nose, round and slightly ruddy, were the same.

Geppetto turned to his pet, a young prince of a cat with sleek black fur and white paws. "Figaro, you know what I wish?"

Figaro shook his head.

"I wish that my little Pinocchio might be a real boy. Wouldn't that be nice? Just think!"

Geppetto's smile was warm and bright, but the Blue Fairy had always had a gift for seeing into one's heart. She could sense the loneliness lurking behind his eyes; he had no company but for his cat and the goldfish in his workshop— no wife, no son or daughter, no siblings. Pariva's children delighted in the toys he made, but their laughter filled only his days. His evenings were almost entirely empty.

Still smiling at the idea of having a son, Geppetto tucked himself back into bed. Within minutes, he was sound asleep.

The Wishing Star faded from the sky, and the Blue Fairy started to lower her wand. It was time to return home. Another fairy would see to it that Pariva's wish-seekers were well taken care of, she told herself.

Yet she couldn't go.

Seeing Geppetto had released in the Blue Fairy a flood of emotions—compassion, pity, and a flicker of guilt—and she paused in her step. Her gaze fell upon the wooden puppet sitting in Geppetto's workshop. Her chest squeezed. She knew she ought to leave. She wasn't supposed to be there at all, honestly, but she couldn't bring herself to go.

Her dove tilted its head inquisitively, and the Blue Fairy made a tentative smile.

"Well, why not?" she said to the bird. "No one will know."

Before she might think better of it, she waved her wand and became a soft beam of starlight, traveling swiftly into Geppetto's home.

She entered through an open window and waited until Geppetto and his cat, Figaro, were fast asleep before she unfolded from the light.

There she stood, in the middle of Geppetto's workshop. She'd visited before, so long ago it felt like a dream. The walls were the same; the low ceiling and the long wooden table to the side, cluttered with tools and pots of paints and brushes and sketches, too, but she would not have recognized it otherwise.

Toys sat on every shelf: wooden horses with legs that wobbled and elephants with flopping ears, tiny families in boats that sang when they were wound up from the side. There were clocks, too. Clocks whose hands pointed at stars, clocks where angels standing on clouds trumpeted the hour, clocks with bunnies and sheep running out of a barn when the time struck noon and six. Ships with red-dyed sails hung from the ceiling, and toy soldiers watched over the workshop from a high shelf just below the ceiling.

So much had changed, but the smells were familiar: pine wood and paint and gentle smoke from the hearth and snuffed wax candles. Geppetto had always loved working with wood, and the Blue Fairy's heart warmed to know that after all these years, that hadn't changed.

"You were true to your word," she murmured, taking in the dancing couples and music boxes. "Your promise to bring joy to all those around you."

A cricket hopped onto one of Geppetto's shelves and settled into an open matchbox. The Blue Fairy smiled to herself. Even it felt welcomed in this cozy little workshop.

She paused then before Pinocchio, the wooden boy Geppetto had spoken of in his wish. The puppet was leaning against the wall, newly finished and paint still drying.

He was tenderly crafted, simple compared to some of the other toys in the room. But the care in every detail, from the soles of his brown shoes to the gentle lift in his eyebrows, made the Blue Fairy want to reach out and hug the young toy. He was Geppetto's masterpiece.

There was a certain mischief to his round eyes, and his

innocent smile had echoes of Geppetto's own. Had he been a real boy, he could have passed for the old toymaker's son.

A real boy.

The Blue Fairy inhaled a deep breath. It was not within her power to grant such a wish. But her conscience would never forgive her if she left now. If she ignored the pain emanating from this noble man who had brought more than his fair share of love to the world—who could bring even more, if given the chance.

The first lesson she had learned as a fairy was to follow her conscience. To let it guide her.

"Good Geppetto," she murmured, "you have given so much happiness to others. You deserve to have your wish come true."

Magic gathered in her wand, sparks glimmering from the star at its tip. She pointed it at Pinocchio's feathered hat. "Little puppet made of pine," she said, "wake."

A silvery crown of starlight burst from her wand, shimmering across Pinocchio's body.

"The gift of life is thine," said the Blue Fairy.

The light swelled until it encompassed all of Pinocchio. Then, once it faded, Pinocchio wriggled to life, sitting up on his own. He rubbed his eyes and looked around before fluttering his hands.

"I can move!" he exclaimed in astonishment. The young

puppet covered his mouth with his hands, his wide eyes blinking as if he didn't know where the sound had come from. "I can talk!"

The Blue Fairy chuckled as Pinocchio rose unsteadily to his feet.

"I can walk." He took a few steps before he fell down onto the table once more.

"Yes, Pinocchio," said the Blue Fairy kindly. "I've given you life."

"Why?"

"Because tonight, Geppetto wished for a real boy."

"Am I a real boy?"

The Blue Fairy paused, not wishing to dampen his happiness with the truth, but she wouldn't lie to him. She chose her next words carefully. "No, Pinocchio. To make Geppetto's wish come true will be entirely up to you."

"Up to me?" Pinocchio echoed.

"Prove yourself brave, truthful, and unselfish, and someday you will be a real boy."

"A real boy!"

The Blue Fairy smiled, ignoring the wave of unease rising to her chest. She couldn't bring herself to tell the young puppet that she might not be able to grant Geppetto's wish in earnest. Turning Pinocchio into a living, breathing wooden boy in itself had been no simple feat, and it would surely come with consequences. And Pinocchio becoming a *real* little boy would be another matter entirely. But whatever the cost, she would bear it—and she would see his journey through.

I will find a way, she thought. *Geppetto deserves this happiness. And Pinocchio deserves to be real.*

She looked around, trying to figure out a way to quell the worry that still nagged at her. Even with a good father such as Geppetto, a wooden boy was bound to find himself in trouble. Especially one as new to life as Pinocchio.

A conscience. Pinocchio would need a conscience.

The Blue Fairy eyed the workshop and spied the humble cricket who had been eavesdropping on their conversation. She had a soft spot for crickets. Doves, too.

Pinocchio would need help—why not a cricket?

This one would do fine, the Blue Fairy knew in her heart. After a pleasant introduction, she knighted "Sir Jiminy" to be Pinocchio's official conscience.

Then she renewed her attention on Pinocchio. "Remember, be a good boy. And let your conscience guide you."

As Pinocchio and the cricket waved farewell, the Blue Fairy exited Geppetto's workshop in the same soft beam of starlight with which she'd come. But she lingered outside Geppetto's house, listening to Jiminy warn Pinocchio about the world's temptations.

The cricket chirped about learning right from wrong, and taught Pinocchio how to whistle when he needed Jiminy's help.

She chuckled, and the unease in her heart faded. Pinocchio would be just fine.

Now all she had to do was find a way to fulfill the whole wish. Surely her fellow fairies would be sympathetic to Geppetto's cause. She'd bring it up with them as soon as she could, at the next monthly meeting on the Wishing Star.

She shot onto the rooftop of Geppetto's workshop, reassuming her fairy form to take one last look at her old friend's home. She didn't know when she'd have another chance to come back. Then she spun, about to make for the Wishing Star that had disappeared behind the night, and a shadow fell over her.

"Still making promises you know you can't keep," mused a woman from behind. "Some things never change."

The Blue Fairy recognized the intruder immediately. Slowly she turned, and as her eyes met the Scarlet Fairy's, her famous poise and serenity faltered, and her lips parted with disbelief.

"Speechless, I see," said the Scarlet Fairy. She lowered her arm, letting the slender red wand in her hand click against the roof. A round ruby sparkled at its head, bright as fresh blood. "Well, it *has* been a long time."

"So it has." The Blue Fairy tried to search the Scarlet Fairy's face for signs of regret or remorse. For any feeling at all.

It shouldn't have surprised her that she found nothing.

She raised her chin, refusing to let the Scarlet Fairy's appearance ruffle her. "I do intend to keep my promise to Pinocchio."

"And make him a real boy? Pray tell, how?"

"He is a good lad. I'm certain the other fairies will see so, too. They'll find that Geppetto deserves some happiness, and Pinocchio will be a worthy addition to the world. They will grant me permission to give Geppetto his wish."

"But what if Pinocchio *isn't* worthy?" The Scarlet Fairy lowered her lashes. "You assume he'll be unselfish, brave, and truthful, but . . ."

"But what?"

"But he's a puppet." The Scarlet Fairy toyed with a strand of her dark hair, as if she were twisting the strings of a marionette. She paused meaningfully. "He has no *heart*."

Suddenly understanding what the Scarlet Fairy meant to do, the Blue Fairy's pulse quickened in alarm. "Please. Don't—"

"Interfere?" the Scarlet Fairy said with a laugh. "But that's my duty. My *responsibility*. How ironic, Chiara, that after all these years, it's *you* who should falter from your responsibility. Then again, I shouldn't be surprised. You aren't as loyal as you make everyone think."

The Blue Fairy flinched, both at the insult and at the sound of her birth name. "Now, that isn't true—"

"Once your hopeless little fairies see what a wicked boy Pinocchio is," the Scarlet Fairy went on, ignoring her, "you'll have to turn him back into a pile of wood. How sad old Geppetto will be then."

"You wouldn't!"

The Scarlet Fairy's lips curved into the ghost of a smile Chiara had once known and loved, except it was all wrong. There was no cheer in it, no warmth. No mischief. It was cold enough to freeze the Lyre Sea.

Forty years had wedged a world between them.

The Blue Fairy half closed her eyes, missing the days when the Scarlet Fairy spoke to her without vitriol, and she replied with dread. "Unless what?"

"Unless we make a wager," mused the Scarlet Fairy. "Or are you too good and righteous to partake in a harmless little bet?"

"Coming from you, I doubt very much that it will be harmless."

"It could be very beneficial for your dear Pinocchio," the Scarlet Fairy said. Before Chiara could respond, she went on, "If you win, I won't tell the fairies about what you've done here tonight, and I'll even help you turn Pinocchio into a real boy."

Surprise made the Blue Fairy look up. "You'd help me?"

"*If* you win," confirmed the Scarlet Fairy. "But if you lose . . ."

Chiara went silent, knowing that the price would be high. She'd been caught in a trap, and she knew it. If she left now to tell the others, the Scarlet Fairy would embroil poor Pinocchio into an awful plot, and everyone on the Wishing Star would unanimously vote that Chiara lift her spell. There would be a good chance she'd lose her wand and wings and be cast out from the fairies forever.

How did we become like this? she wanted to ask aloud. *Can we go back to the way things were?*

But she already knew what the Scarlet Fairy's answer would be.

Hiding her disappointment, the Blue Fairy eyed her companion coolly. "Name your terms, sister."

CHAPTER ONE

Forty years earlier

Ask anyone in Pariva, and they would have agreed that Chiara Belmagio was the kindest, warmest girl in town. Her patience, especially, was legendary. Then again, anyone who had grown up with a sister like Ilaria Belmagio—local prima donna in both voice *and* demeanor—and still considered her to be their best friend had to be nothing short of an angel.

Chiara was newly eighteen, having celebrated her birthday a month earlier, in June, and she was the middle child of Anna and Alberto Belmagio, beloved owners of Pariva's only bakery. In short, she had modest ability on the harpsichord, favored blackberry jam over chocolate, and loved to read outside under her family's lemon tree, where she often helped children with their arithmetic homework and nurtured nests of young doves.

Like her neighbors, she knew each name and face of the 387 people in Pariva, but unlike most, she took the time to make anyone she encountered smile, even grumpy Mr. Tommaso—who was a *challenge*. And she took pleasure in it.

When people wanted to talk, she listened. That was how she learned of the dreams and hopes of everyone in town. Many dreamt of leaving Pariva, some to seek fame and fortune, others to find adventure or even romance. But never once did Chiara ever desire to leave her hometown. Never once did she covet such things as fine dresses or invitations to grand parties in Vallan. Still, that didn't mean she was without dreams.

Hers was a simple one, compared to her sister's of becoming an opera singer or her brother's to master their parents' rye bread and serve it to the king one day. A silly one, Ilaria would say, if she knew.

But Chiara never spoke of her dream. Unlike most folks in town, she never looked out for the Wishing Star to wish that it might come true—she was too practical to believe in miracles that came from wands or wishes, and she certainly didn't believe in fairies. She didn't believe in magic, either, at least not the sort of magic in the stories her papa had told her and her siblings when they were little, about fairy godmothers who could turn pumpkins into carriages and magic wands that could change stones into diamonds.

The magic she believed in was of a different sort. The sort that cheered a pall of melancholy, that fed a hungry belly, that warmed a cold heart. She believed in kindness, in compassion, and in sharing what fortune she had—with those who needed it.

Ironic, of course. For little did she know it, but Chiara Belmagio was about to meet a fairy.

It was a blistering August morning. Too hot even for Chiara, who typically loved the sun. She was outside in the garden, pruning violets and bluebells to take to the bakery. She liked giving flowers to their customers; it always made them happy.

"Mamma and Papa sent a messenger," called her older brother, Niccolo, from the back door. Careful to stay under the shade of the roof, the young man had one foot out in the garden, and one foot remaining in the house. "You've the day off. No one's buying bread in this heat."

Chiara bunched the flowers into a bouquet and rubbed her hands on her aprons. "Are Mamma and Papa coming home, then?"

"They're going over to Mr. and Mrs. Bruno's after they

sell off Papa's sandwiches. Bet they'll be there all afternoon playing cards." Niccolo turned back for the kitchen. "I made juice. Orange and lemon. Come inside before Ilaria drinks your share."

Ten more minutes outside under the torturous sun, and Chiara decided to take her brother up on his offer. She was parched. Her scalp burned, and her skin was so warm she felt almost feverish. As she retreated into the house, she doffed her hat and wiped the perspiration that pooled at her temples. Her fair blond hair clung to her temples, and the blue ribbon she always tied around her head was practically drenched.

The promised glass of juice awaited her in the kitchen, and she drank quickly, savoring the tartness of orange and lemon on her tongue. "Ily?" she called, entering the hall. "Nico?"

Beyond the kitchen, in the Blue Room where her family gathered while not eating, she heard her siblings. Sixteen-year-old Ilaria, primarily, wheedling their brother to take out the boat. Chiara stopped just outside the door, not wanting to interrupt.

"Will you stop being such a slug, Niccolo, and take pity on your poor, favorite sister for once? All I'm asking for is just an hour at sea. You always love taking out the boat—"

"I don't think I've ever called you my favorite sister,"

replied Niccolo, turning the page of his book. His dark brown hair fell over his eyes. "That honor belongs to Chia."

Ilaria ignored the insult. "The house is a furnace. If I stay here any longer, I'll perish."

"Then go outside for a walk."

"Outside isn't much better. You know how sensitive my skin is on days like this. I'll peel and burn—I need fresh sea air."

"Fresh sea air is still under the sun, sister," Niccolo pointed out. He dipped his head back into his book. "I told you, the water's dangerous. There's talk of a giant whale in the sea. It's already capsized four fishing boats."

"Giant whales." Ilaria rolled her eyes. "I bet if they were mermaids you'd be clamoring to go for a sail. Even if their siren song made us crash against the rocks."

"There are no mermaids. Only a whale."

"So you say." Ilaria leaned against the chipped blue wallpaper, the back of her hand to her forehead. Chia knew the look well—the prelude to a dramatic swoon. At the age of seven—when Ilaria first decided she would become a world-famous opera singer—she'd begun practicing the art of swooning. By now she was a master.

Unfortunately for her, Nico wouldn't fall for her tricks.

"You kill me, brother," Ilaria said, going ahead with the swoon anyway. "I shall die of heat and suffocation."

"Go ahead. Usually it's consumption, lovesickness, or utter boredom that are going to kill you. Heat and suffocation should be amusing. Are you going to sing a twenty-minute aria now as you die?"

Ily glared. "I sense a mockery being made of me."

"You make it too easy."

With a scowl, Chia's sister folded her knees under her skirts and began to slump gracefully down against the wall. In about three seconds, she would wilt into a well-posed puddle on their grandmother's knotted rug.

One, Chiara counted.

Ilaria fanned herself with her hand.

Two.

Ilaria tugged at her collar.

Three.

Ilaria collapsed with an elegant thud. A beat later, Niccolo lowered his book and rose from his seat, walking leisurely to his sister's side. "No song this time?" he teased.

When she didn't reply, he dropped his book squarely on her stomach, and her eyes snapped open.

"Why you—you could have broken my rib!"

"Hardly," said Niccolo dryly, retrieving his book, which was small enough to fit in his pocket. "You've cried wolf far too many times, little sister. Did you really think I'd believe you?"

Ilaria rolled up, twisted toward the mirror vainly, and touched up her crumpled hair. "You'll regret this when I'm famous."

"Your death scenes are already famous—in this house."

Chiara chuckled, giving away her presence just outside the room. Niccolo glanced over his shoulder, and his frown released into a smile. "See, even Chia agrees. Maybe she can accompany your swan song on the harpsichord."

Ily threw up her arms and appealed to her sister. "Every day, he mocks me. How am I related to this uncultured boor!"

"It might be wise not to call our brother an uncultured boor," said Chia evenly. "Especially when you're trying to ask a favor of him."

"Ignoramus, then," amended Ilaria without a hint of contrition. "Chia, I have to get out of here." Her dark green eyes rounded with a plea. "Please, help me?"

Chiara pursed her lips as she studied her sister. Side by side, she and Ily didn't look much like sisters, and their temperaments too were as different as night and day. Chiara was bright like the meaning of her name, with sun-kissed golden hair—the color of uncooked pasta, Nico liked to tease—that curled at her shoulders, and eyes as blue as the jays that perched along their roofs come spring. She was kind and patient and warm, while the only angelic thing about Ilaria was her voice. Mischief and cunning made the younger Belmagio daughter's green eyes glitter, and she shared the same dark chocolate hair as Niccolo and their mother. But what both girls did share was the heart-shaped blush on their cheeks when they were happy, the way their heads tilted to the left when they were quizzical, and the way they sighed—as Chiara did now, with resignation.

Why not, her heart told her. After all, like Niccolo said, the bakery was closed and didn't need flowers, her parents were playing cards with friends—and most of all, it would make Ily happy. Chia loved seeing her sister happy.

But how to convince Niccolo to take them out?

"Think of my voice, my future!" Ily went on. "It hurts just to breathe, the air is so thick."

"Smell this, then," said Chiara, passing her sister a small bouquet of the flowers she'd plucked outside. She made a curtsy. "For the prima donna of Pariva."

"Are you sure you want to encourage that ego of hers?" said Niccolo.

Chiara knew what she was doing. While Ily sniffed the flowers, Chiara seated herself at the harpsichord and coaxed out the opening chords to her sister's favorite aria, "The Nightingale." As she predicted, Ilaria couldn't resist joining in on the music. Without even realizing it, Ilaria started singing the first stanza, which mimicked a lost nightingale chirping as it searched for its home.

Music always cast a spell over the Belmagio household and eased away any discord between the siblings. The three had spent many afternoons in their youth making music together, Niccolo joining on his violin. By the time Ily had sung through the whole song, even Niccolo had forgotten his irritation at Ily and was clapping. Just as Chia knew he would.

Chiara joined in on the applause. "You see?" she said to her sister. "A little heat has no chance against a voice as powerful as yours. Which means when your auditions come around, they'll be a breeze."

Ilaria grinned. "Only because *you're* at the keys, Chia."

"Well, I'm not going anywhere. I'll be your accompanist as long as you need me." Chiara paused, turning slowly toward Niccolo as she flexed her fingers. "Though now *I* am a bit warm."

It was true. Sitting at the harpsichord by the window had made Chiara's skin heat. She raised her glass of juice for one last sip. "If Niccolo won't come, maybe *I'll* take the boat out for some fresh air."

Ilaria gasped in delight. "You're a bona fide saint." She hugged Chiara. "Thank you, thank you!"

"You can't take the boat out by yourselves!" Niccolo exclaimed.

"Why not? If you won't go . . ."

Their brother grimaced and tugged on his collar, the way he did when he was about to give in to something. "I told Ily already I don't think it's safe—"

"Because of the whale?" Ily snorted. "Who'd you hear this from, the sailors on the docks? You really believe there's a giant beast large enough to swallow entire houses?"

Niccolo flinched. "Monstro. Everyone says he's real."

"Then maybe we should look for him." Ilaria knew better than anyone how to pull her brother's strings—when she put her mind to it. How to pull anyone's strings, really. That was her talent. "Unless . . . you're afraid."

"Afraid?" Niccolo spluttered, though from the way his shoulders tensed, it was obvious that he was. "*I'm* not afraid of a big fish. I'm afraid of putting my two sisters in danger."

"You talk as if we're delicate lilies wilting under the sun," said Ilaria. "We're—"

"Grateful for your worry, Nico," Chiara interrupted. "How about we only go for an hour, and stay close to the coast? If the water starts to become too rough, we'll come back straightaway." She cast her sister a meaningful look. "Ilaria will even help row."

Niccolo gave Ily a narrow look. "I'll have to see it to believe it."

"It's a promise," said Ilaria, making a crossing motion over her heart. "Honest."

Niccolo sniffed. But he was tempted; Chiara could tell by the way he tilted his head, considering. "I guess there's no harm so long as we keep in sight of the coast," he said slowly. "I'll bring my telescope in case there's a Monstro sighting."

Ilaria let out a triumphant squeal and pushed Chiara toward the stairs. "Hurry and get your hat, Chia. Can you pack some sandwiches, too?"

"And pistachio cookies?"

Ilaria winked. "You read my mind."

Simple as that, Chiara's plans were changed. Fate had stepped in and ordained that she should go sailing with her siblings.

It was to be a decision that would change everything.

CHAPTER TWO

Geppetto blamed the heat for muddying his senses, and for making him slip out of the workshop in the middle of the afternoon for a row around the coast. It wasn't like him to take off to the sea, especially in his father's cherished but moldy shrimping boat.

At least he wasn't the only one with the idea. Back at the docks, Niccolo Belmagio was untethering their family boat while his sisters, Chiara and Ilaria, hopped inside.

"Looks like they're going for a sail, too," Geppetto murmured. Had he waited twenty minutes, he might have gotten to say hello to them.

He laughed at himself. "Even if you had," he admonished, "you'd be too shy to speak with them. To make friends." Oh, Niccolo had always been pleasant to him; they were the same age—nineteen years old—and had gone to school together, and there was no one kinder than Chiara, but Ilaria . . . Ilaria probably didn't even know he existed.

Geppetto's laugh died in his throat. He could never admit aloud, not even to himself, that it was Ilaria he wanted to speak to. Well, it was Ilaria he wanted to *hear*. Her voice, round and resonant with a singer's richness, was his favorite sound in the world. It was music to his ears, and simply thinking of it made a clumsy smile spread across his face. Without realizing it, Geppetto started humming.

The sound filled the silence between his oar strokes, and finally he succumbed to the ache in his arms and set the oars aside for a moment's rest. He was a competent enough sailor, thanks to the frequent trips to sea he and his papa used to take before his mother had passed away two years earlier. What he wasn't—was a rebel.

Taking the shrimping boat out without permission, leaving in the middle of the day when there was still work to be done—it had to be the heat that had stolen his senses. He could hardly believe what he'd done. He'd regretted it the moment he'd jumped into the boat.

But the current was strong, and when he tried to turn back, it pushed him the other direction—into the wide and open sea. He glanced back, watching his hometown shrink against the horizon.

He took an uneasy breath. "I guess I should just enjoy it."

Folding his arms behind his head, Geppetto leaned against the side of his boat and gazed at the sky, marveling at how far and blue it unfolded. When was the last time he'd just stared at the clouds? All day and evening, he worked as Pariva's sole luthier, repairing instruments. Papa's fingers had become swollen with age, so he increasingly relied on Geppetto to keep the workshop running. And Geppetto did, dutifully.

He didn't have the courage to refuse.

Nor did he have the courage to open the trove of dreams he kept stowed in his heart. Secret dreams, like the one that had led him out to sea today.

"That's all they will ever be," he murmured to himself as he watched the sea. A ripple disrupted the still water. "Dreams. Papa will never understand."

The ripple ballooned, and Geppetto thought he glimpsed the flash of a black tail far in the distance. He sat up, the rush of fear in his gut telling him he should pick up his oars right away and row back toward shore.

But then the breeze picked up and a gull squawked and he realized how silly he was being on this perfect day.

"It's probably just a seal," he said, laughing at himself. "Don't be such a coward, Geppetto."

With a sigh, he picked out the pencil he had tucked behind his ear and fumbled for the sketchbook he'd brought. He might not have the courage to tell his father about his dreams, but he certainly wouldn't run away from a seal. Still humming to himself, he flipped past sketches—a father and son hiking the base of Mount Cecilia, an old woman feeding pigeons along the old fountain in the middle of Pariva's town square, a young couple strolling around the bell tower at dusk—until he found a fresh new page. In a series of crisp, confident lines, he drew a seal's tail, and he readied his pencil for more as the ripples grow closer and stronger.

Everything seemed to go perfectly still.

Then the water beneath his boat suddenly lifted, and the sea turned black as night. Geppetto stopped humming, but it was too late.

Two wrathful green eyes lifted out of the sea.

And Geppetto found himself face to face with a monster.

CHAPTER THREE

"Fine," Niccolo finally conceded, when the Belmagio siblings had made it out to sea. "This was a good idea."

"Didn't I tell you so?" said Ilaria as she basked in both Niccolo's compliment and in the breeze. She tugged at the red ribbon in her braid and let her hair fly loose. "This is how summer should be spent. Much better than having to be in Mrs. Tappa's shop selling hats to old fuddy-duddies. Or chopping pistachios with Mamma right next to the oven. Why so quiet, Chia?"

Chiara smiled. "I'm enjoying the view."

And what a beautiful view it was. Mountains to the north, with a clear vista of Mount Cecilia—its snowcapped peak so high Chiara couldn't tell it from the clouds—and endless blue sea to the south. The weather was perfect there, the day's heat muted by the generous breeze from the water and the sun's glare mellowed by the shadows from the mountains.

"We should've brought cards," complained Ilaria, who couldn't stay still for longer than a few minutes. She picked up Nico's telescope. "How about a game? One minute each with the spyglass, two rounds. Whoever sees the biggest fish is the winner, and losers swim one lap around the boat?"

"I don't think you want to be taking a dive in that dress, Ily," Niccolo retorted. "Besides, your head's so full of air you might float away—and what would happen then?"

Ily punched their brother in the arm.

Nico nearly dropped his oar. "Hey!"

"It could be fun," Chiara said, mediating. "Though let's not have winners and losers, shall we?" She took the telescope from Ily and turned it to the water, taking in the wrinkles in the otherwise still sea. Strange; they seemed to be getting stronger, and the water darker. Squinting to take a closer look, she followed their trail all the way to the curve of the earth beyond the sea. On the edge of her lens, an enormous black tail cut through the water.

With a gasp, she shot up to her feet. "A whale!" she cried.

"You can't win already," Ily muttered, not grasping the danger.

But Niccolo's eyes widened, and he seized the telescope to look. "Stars Almighty, it's Monstro!"

"I want to see," said Ilaria, grabbing at the telescope. But no sooner did she speak than Monstro reappeared, his tail lashing out of the sea like a mighty whip. As it hurled down, waves rolled across the sea so far that even the Belmagios could feel the creature's power.

"Have you ever seen anything so enormous?" Niccolo was flush with adrenaline. "Just the size of his tail—it's bigger than all of us combined."

"We've got to get a closer look," Ilaria urged.

"Are you sure that's a good idea?" said Chiara, holding her hat as a sudden wind gathered.

"When will we get this chance again?" Ily needled Niccolo. "Come on, just a little closer. We're miles away as it is."

Their brother didn't need the encouragement. He was already steering the boat in Monstro's direction.

"We're getting awfully far from the coast," cautioned Chiara. "Remember what the sailors said . . . that Monstro is—"

Before she could finish her words, the wind disappeared. The waves flattened, and the water went still as it had been before. Too still.

"He's gone," Ilaria breathed, shooting up to her knees

for a better look. Indeed, the whale was nowhere to be seen. She slapped the side of the boat. "Look what you did, Chia. We missed him!" As her balance faltered, she sat back down with a moan. "All that for nothing. I think I'm getting seasick."

"Rest," Chiara said, moving to the side so her sister could lift her legs. While Ily lay down, she propped her arms on the edge of the boat. The water was as blue as before, as if nothing had happened. Bluer than the sky, really, and the cornflowers and bluebells that Mrs. Vaci sold in her chocolate shop. Chiara's favorite color.

Chiara dipped her fingers into the sea, letting them skate across the water as Niccolo took a break from rowing. It was still warm, but the air had cooled. The ripples that she created were black—like the dark water earlier. Was she the only one who noticed that?

The hairs on the back of her neck bristled, and her stomach churned with dread. Something wasn't right. There was evil in the air; in the sea, too. She didn't know how she knew, but she could feel it. She clenched the telescope and scanned the horizon.

To her far left drifted the remains of a boat. Planks of wood floated among a trawl net and a plain white sail.

There, amid the debris, flailed a pair of human arms. "Help! Help!"

Chiara gasped. "There's someone out there!"

"Someone out where?" Ilaria echoed. "I don't see anyone."

Chiara wasn't listening. She kicked off her shoes. Every second marked the difference between life and death, and she had none to waste. Her knees buckled at the sight of the waves ahead, some thrashing so powerfully they sounded like thunder. There it was again: that cold prickly feeling in her stomach.

Danger. Wrath. Fear.

It should have made her hesitate, but Chiara sensed something else beyond the darkness that gathered in the sea. Her heart had always been sensitive to the needs of others, and what she felt now was so familiar that her entire being latched to it like a magnet.

Hope. It was feeble and dying, like a candle being held against the wind. Still fighting, but without much longer until it became nothing.

I'm coming, she thought to it.

She dove off the boat.

CHAPTER FOUR

The water was the perfect temperature for a dip, but that was quite possibly the last thing on Chiara's mind as she swam. The currents were against her, trying to push her back toward her brother and sister, so she kicked harder, ignoring their shouts and screams.

"Chia, come back!"

"Chia!"

The water and wind swallowed Nico's and Ily's cries, and soon Chiara was utterly alone. Never before had the world been so silent yet deafeningly loud. Water thrashed and roared in her ears, yet amid it all, she could hear her heart thumping in her chest, her breath growing shallower.

A cracked piece of wood coasted past her, traveling at

alarming speed. It nearly crashed into her head, and Chiara swerved only at the last second.

Go back, her body screamed at her. If she went on, there was a high chance she would get caught in the tides and drown.

"Help!" cried the young man again. "Help!"

There's a chance you'll die, her conscience agreed, *but there's also a chance you might save him. If you give up now, there will be no chance for the boy. Only death.*

That was all the convincing she needed. She threw aside her fears and pushed even harder. Salt stung her eyes, and seawater choked her throat and burned up to her nose. The pain quickly became unbearable, yet as the water roared in her ears, Chiara had only one thought.

Faster. She had to swim faster.

Keep a steady rhythm, she told herself. *Don't panic.*

But Chiara was only human, and she was nothing compared to the sea. Soon she could feel herself losing against the tides, and for every kick forward, the sea pushed her back five strokes. She was losing him. She was losing herself, too.

Chiara blinked, struggling against the seawater brutally flushing her eyes. They instinctively closed, leaving her in the dark. Her legs at least kept kicking, but her muscles were on fire, and her strength was near the end of its reserves.

Over there, came a voice in her ear. It wasn't hers; it was a woman's voice that she didn't recognize. *Just a little more. You can do this, Chiara Belmagio. Keep fighting.*

The voice sounded like a friend. Chiara trusted it, and its intensity gave her the strength to force her eyes open. Sunlight painted her world white before granting her sight again; another blink, and she saw him.

The young man who had shouted for help. He looked unconscious, and his arms were wrapped precariously over a floating log.

With all that she had left, Chiara swam until she reached him.

He was from her village; that she knew right away. The luthier's son. Not someone she often saw in the town square, but were she not half-drowned, his name would have come to her immediately.

She struggled to keep his head above the water. His mustache was soaked, and his skin was so cold she couldn't tell whether he was alive. "Stay with me," she said hoarsely. "You're going to be all right."

It felt like a lie, even though she didn't mean it as one.

What now? she thought desperately. She couldn't swim him all the way back to Niccolo's boat. Even if she wanted to try, she couldn't see it; she knew her brother and sister were looking for her, and she couldn't risk swimming in the wrong direction. And there was no way for her to try to revive him while they floated in the sea, one fierce wave away from death.

The seconds ticked, each an era. Now that she wasn't swimming, the water felt colder than it had earlier. Chiara's teeth chattered uncontrollably. She was hot and cold at the same time, her muscles weeping as she cycled her legs to stay afloat. *Focus,* she told herself as she bobbed out of the water, shouting for help.

She might have cried when she spied Niccolo and Ilaria. Even her sister was rowing, for the first time in her life—a fact made obvious when, in the excitement of finding Chiara, she stopped and accidentally dropped the oar in the sea.

"T-t-take him first," Chia said, pushing the luthier's son into Niccolo's arms.

She waited until he was safely aboard before accepting Ilaria's outstretched arms.

"Don't you ever do that again!" Ily cried, hugging her fiercely. "I thought you died."

"C-c-careful," Chia tried to tease, but her voice came out as a series of hacking coughs, "you . . . you might get your favorite dress wet."

"At least you'll be alive to help me wash it."

Chiara would have laughed if she could, but she was exhausted. She let her head fall back against the boat, hardly able to move. She was still shuddering, and her teeth still chattered violently.

"Drink some water," urged Ily. "Here, take my—"

"Give . . . to him," Chiara rasped, pointing at the luthier's son. Niccolo was pumping the young man's chest in vain.

Ilaria twisted; she'd forgotten the half-drowned young man. "He's not even awake. Nico's helping him. I want to be with you."

Chiara choked. "Ily . . ."

"All right, all right." Ilaria angled back toward the luthier's son and took his chin, sweeping aside his mustache. "Hey, don't die on my watch, all right? I'd never hear the end of it from Nico and Chia."

As she dribbled fresh water through his lips, the young man's eyes fluttered. "My word," he murmured, half-consciously. "A fairy! The most beautiful fairy I've ever seen in my life."

Ilaria giggled at Chia. "I like this one. Even half-dead, he knows beauty when he sees it."

Consciousness returned to the young man, and his eyes went round. "Oh, my!" he cried, springing upright. His body was a step behind his mind and wasn't quite ready to rise yet—resulting in his breaking into a fit of coughs.

As he spluttered, seawater dribbled from his sleeves and splashed onto Ily's skirt.

"Watch it!" Ily moaned, holding up the outer layer of her skirt against the sun. "It's all wrinkled."

Niccolo yanked Ilaria behind him and caught the young luthier before he teetered off the boat. "Easy, easy," he said. "Breathe in, out."

"Here, have more water," Chiara offered. She crawled to the young man's side, covering his hand with hers. Thank heavens it was a warm day. Already some color was returning to his cheeks.

"Thank you," he said, catching his breath. "Thank you."

"You're old Mr. Tommaso's son!" said Niccolo at last. "Geppetto."

"Yes, yes, I am," said Geppetto dazedly. "And you are?" He squinted in Nico's direction and his fingers went to his nose, where his missing spectacles left two reddish imprints. He scrabbled about the boat, searching, and explained, "I can't see much without my glasses. I must have lost them."

"I would bet that you lost them," said Niccolo, laughing. "You nearly drowned. But better that we fished you out and not your glasses, wouldn't you say?"

"Niccolo Belmagio!" Geppetto cried, recognizing him at last. "I thought it was you getting onto your boat earlier. It's a good thing you saw me. I'm indebted to you."

"Thank my sister, not me. Chia's the one who saved you."

Dipping his head, Geppetto turned to her and practically bowed at her feet. "Thank you, Chiara. If not for you, well . . ."

"Call me Chia," she said. "All my friends do."

"Chia," repeated Geppetto. Just then, the boat tilted over a rough current, and Geppetto stumbled over a trawl net. As he struggled to regain his balance, he grabbed Ilaria's arm—then immediately recoiled.

"Awful sorry, Miss Ilaria." Geppetto reached for an imaginary hat on his head before remembering he didn't have one. He repeated, "Awful sorry."

"Sorry won't make my dress dry," Ilaria lamented.

"We save a fellow, and all you care about is how wrinkled your dress gets." Niccolo clucked his tongue at his youngest sister. "To think, Geppetto thought you were a fairy. He must really not be able to see without his glasses."

"Hush, you." Ilaria slapped Niccolo's arm. "He said I'm a fairy because he thought I'm pretty." She leaned closer to Geppetto and batted her lashes. "Don't you?"

"Well, I . . . I . . ." Geppetto averted his eyes to the bottom of the boat. "Yes, Miss Ilaria."

"See?" Ilaria tilted her head triumphantly. "Though come to think of it, we never got around to introducing *my* name."

It was true, and Chiara hid a smile. Young Geppetto's face had gone from being seasick pale to tomato red.

There came a tender ping in Chia's heart. *He likes her,* she realized.

That ping in her heart turned into a warm buzz. She was familiar with the feeling, even though she couldn't pin down what it was. But when she listened it, often good things happened. Like saving Geppetto. And right now, it was telling her that the young man and Ilaria would be wonderful for each other.

I agree, Chiara thought. On the other hand, Ilaria had lived her whole life in Pariva and probably had never known Geppetto existed before today.

I'll have to help change that.

"Pariva's a small town," said Chia helpfully. "It's really Ily you should be thanking, Geppetto. If she hadn't asked us to come out today, we wouldn't have found you."

"Thank you truly," said Geppetto to Ilaria. "And I'm sorry about the dress."

"I was going to wear it to my audition in Nerio," Ilaria said coyly. She crossed her arms, pretending to be displeased. "Now it'll have to be pressed again."

Niccolo rolled his eyes. "If you knew you needed that dress for an audition, why wear it out to sea in the first place?"

"Are you accusing me of lying?"

"It wouldn't be anything new."

"Why, you—"

"Ily," Chia interrupted, "I'll help you press your dress before your audition. It'll look as good as new."

With a harrumph directed to Niccolo, Ilaria sat beside her sister. "I hope so."

"I'm terribly sorry," said Geppetto again, looking more distressed about Ily's dress than he had been about nearly drowning. "If I could afford it, I would offer to buy you a new one. . . . Miss Ilaria, you have such a beautiful voice, I would never forgive myself if I hampered your efforts toward . . . toward . . ."

"Becoming the most famous prima donna in Esperia," Ilaria finished for him. She leaned forward with interest. "You've heard me sing before?"

"A few times last summer," he confessed. "Ms. Rocco's house is next door to my father's workshop—"

Ily gasped. "You've eavesdropped on my singing lessons?"

"I couldn't help it," Geppetto said bashfully. "I like opera."

"You do?" That made Ilaria's face light up, and she stuck out her tongue at Niccolo. "See? Someone here likes opera."

Niccolo rolled his eyes and resumed rowing.

Hastily, Geppetto picked up a spare oar to help. As he cut into the water, he asked Ilaria, "Will you sing again this summer?"

"Unlikely," she replied, evening out the folds in her skirt before she placed her hands primly on her lap and crossed her ankles. "Mamma says it isn't ladylike to sing out in public. And ever since that tavern opened, she thinks it's less safe."

"I hadn't thought about that."

"That's enough, Ily," said Niccolo between breaths. "You can seize the conversation later. We haven't asked what happened to this poor fellow."

"No, no, it's all right," Geppetto insisted.

But Niccolo went on, "How did you end up capsizing your boat?"

Geppetto inhaled. "I don't even know what happened.

I was looking at seals, then it wasn't a seal. It was a monster. A—"

"Whale," said Niccolo. "Monstro."

"Monstro?" Geppetto repeated, confused. "What's that?"

"You haven't heard the stories?" Niccolo sighed. "Oh, Geppetto, you really need to get out of your father's workshop more. And not just to listen to my sister sing."

Impressive, how quickly Geppetto's face turned red again. Chiara supposed it was good for his circulation.

With a smile, she passed him one of the sandwiches she had packed while Geppetto and Ilaria defended the importance of listening to opera, and her brother resumed rowing them all back to Pariva.

Everything was well, and as the new friends sailed back toward Pariva, no one noticed the sinister clouds of magic that oozed out of the distant sea.

CHAPTER FIVE

Ilaria saw the fairy first. It was past nine o'clock, and she was late to Mrs. Tappa's for her morning shift, but the old lady was probably still asleep in her bed above the shop. Besides, Ily was the prettiest girl in town, and she modeled Mrs. Tappa's hats every time she went out. The lady would never fire her.

Rather than hurry, she strolled into the garden and crouched beside Mamma's prized rosebush. After snipping three of the loveliest roses, she plucked a bright red bud from the bush and plaited them all into the hat she'd borrowed from Mrs. Tappa's display.

The hat was an ugly thing, woven of brown straw the color of horse dung. But the roses would help, and a sprig of rosemary from Papa's herb garden, too, to make it smell nice.

"With any luck, this will sell today," Ily said to herself, admiring how she'd made over the hideous hat. The more hats she sold, the more money she'd make, and she was aching for a new dress. She hadn't had one in over a year, and she couldn't bear the thought of going to auditions in Nerio and Vallan in one of her chocolate-stained gowns and torn gloves.

Vallan, especially. An audition in the capital was the final round, and she'd get to sing for her idol, Maria Linda. She had to make an impression from head to toe.

But I'm getting ahead of myself, she thought with a sigh. *I haven't had a lesson in over a year since Ms. Rocco died.*

As she admired her reflection in the window, a soft bloom of light floated behind her, gliding along the roof of the Belmagio residence. Ilaria ducked behind the rosebush, but her eyes followed the light. It was a shimmery violet she had never seen before, and when she looked hard enough she could almost make out tiny wings fluttering within. About half the size of her fist, it was too large to be a firefly, but no bird could emit such a powerful light.

Her heart leapt as she realized.

A fairy!

She held in a squeal of excitement. What was a fairy

doing here? Maybe she'd heard the wishes Ilaria had made, night after night when she stared out her window searching for the Wishing Star. Maybe she was here to finally make Ily's dreams come true.

The light slipped through an open window into the house, and certainty welled in Ily's chest. Unable to contain her excitement any longer, she raced inside, quietly tiptoeing up the stairs after the fairy.

When she was halfway up the stairs, Ily rose to her toes. The fairy was hovering in front of her doorknob, its light fanning over the bronze handle. Like magic, the door creaked open, and Ily hastened up another two stairs.

Until the fairy left her room and swooped up the stairs into the attic. To Chia's room.

Ily halted in her step. *Chia's room?*

Her sister didn't believe in fairies. Her sister didn't believe in magic.

What could a fairy possibly want with Chia?

The corners of her lips tugged down into a frown, and Ilaria turned back downstairs. She should get to work. Mrs. Tappa liked her, but at this rate, she'd be half an hour late. Even for her, that was beyond the pale.

And yet . . . how would she be able to concentrate on work if all she could think about was why a fairy was visiting her sister?

Throwing aside her cares, Ilaria crept up the stairs to Chia's room in the attic and pressed her ear to her sister's door.

Sure enough, she heard the fairy's voice. It was a rich and resonant alto, but she could hardly make out what the fairy was saying. Soft bells muffled her voice—as well as Chia's. As if they knew Ilaria was eavesdropping.

With a grumble, Ilaria lifted her ear from the door. By now she was burning with curiosity and wanted nothing more than to waltz inside, pretending she didn't know Chiara had a visitor. If it'd been anyone else except a fairy inside, she would have. But she had respect for fairies. The stories warned that while they were kind and generous and fair, if you offended them, they wouldn't hesitate to teach you a lesson. Like her mother, in a way.

Mamma would have made an excellent fairy.

Ilaria knelt by the door and peered into the keyhole. Her view was a partial one, but she could see Chia speaking to a lady dressed in purple from hat to shoes. Correction: a lady dressed in purple from hat to shoes, *with wings*! Wings that cast silvery reflections on the wooden parquet, wings that sparkled like a slice of moonlight upon the sea. Wings that made the fairy's feet barely touch the ground.

That confirmed everything: Ily couldn't hold back any longer. "Chia!" she cried out, pushing into her sister's room.

There was no one inside. Chia and the fairy had disappeared.

Ilaria clambered to the window, but there was no sign of them outside. She hurried down the stairs to the kitchen, the Blue Room, the parlor. No one there, either.

She combed a hand through her hair, baffled.

Letting out a loud sigh, Ilaria grabbed her hat from where she'd left it by the rosebushes. She ought to start for Mrs. Tappa's shop in the square, but maybe—just maybe—she ought to wait at home a little longer.

Wherever Chia and the fairy had gone, she'd find out soon enough. Her sister never kept secrets from her.

Chia would tell her everything. She always did.

CHAPTER SIX

"Still don't believe in fairies?" said the Violet Fairy as she and Chiara emerged in the middle of Pariva's market square.

Chiara drew a startled breath. She whirled, taking in the familiar sight of Mangia Road. There was Mamma and Papa's bakery in the northeast corner, where she was due in minutes to deliver an account of their finances and spend the rest of the day helping Papa make sandwiches. And there was Mr. and Mrs. Vaci's chocolate shop, the local fish-monger, and the market, where clusters of tomatoes hung on bright green vines across a rusty yellow wagon. A pocket of children ran around the fountain, likely playing hooky from class.

"How . . ."

"Magic, Chiara," the Violet Fairy replied. "Obviously.

Come, time's more precious than magic, and you're standing about as if you've inhaled a whiff of stardust." The fairy chuckled. "You did, in actuality, and I'm pleased you aren't heaving. That's an important requirement for a fairy-to-be."

Chiara hardly heard a word. She was in a daze, unable to believe that the woman before her—the Violet Fairy, she'd called herself—was actually, well . . . a fairy!

But how else could she explain everything? Only minutes before, a beam of purple light had sieved under the door into her room. Chiara hadn't thought anything of it until the light swelled, radiating from floor to ceiling. Then *poof!* A woman about Chiara's height materialized, with cropped brown hair that curled below her ears, full ruddy cheeks, and chestnut eyes that shone when she spoke. She'd called herself the Violet Fairy, and she'd waved her stick in the air with a flourish.

And here they were, in the middle of Pariva's main square.

Chiara fumbled at the thin shawl over her shoulders. She was sure she'd left it at home; same with the wicker basket under her arm—the very one she carried when she went out on her errands. At her side, the Violet Fairy chuckled at her astonishment.

None of the folks bustling by seemed to notice them suddenly appear. Normally, the nosier townspeople would have stopped to ask whether the Violet Fairy was visiting from Elph or Nerio. Yet no one gave her a second glance.

That surprised Chia more than anything.

"They only see you," said the fairy as if reading her mind. "So try not to move your lips too much while you're talking, or else they'll think you're mumbling to yourself."

Chiara stared as the townspeople cheerfully waved at her.

"It *is* magic," she breathed. "You really are a fairy."

"Not so loudly." Mischief twinkled in the fairy's eyes. She leaned closer, "Your neighbors are what made you believe, not the traveling light or the magic wand?"

"Everyone knows everyone's business in Pariva," said Chiara sensibly.

"Well, no one else knows mine." The fairy guided her down the cobblestone path toward the pasture. "I prefer it that way. The fewer distractions, the better." The Violet Fairy gestured casually at the statue of three fairies in the center of the square. Simona, one of Ilaria's friends, was there asking the statue when the next Wishing Star would appear in the sky.

"You see? I'd like us to have a conversation without being interrupted."

Fair enough. Chiara inhaled, finally getting her

bearings. She had so many questions. "Why me, of everyone here? Are you my fairy godmother?"

"Do you have a wish you wanted to make?"

The question made Chiara's gaze flit to the ground. "No," she replied. "Not for myself, anyway."

"Then I'm not your fairy godmother." A chuckle. "I will say, it's unusual for someone who doesn't believe in magic to get an invitation, but I'd argue that not believing isn't necessarily a bad thing. You're a practical girl, and you like to get things done yourself. We could use more of that."

"An invitation?" Chiara echoed, remembering what she had called her earlier—a *fairy-to-be*. "From . . . the fairies?"

"Yes, indeed." The fairy waved her hand dismissively. "I'm assuming you've changed your mind about us existing. It's fortunate I've observed before what a bright girl you are. Otherwise I'd be having doubts right now."

The gibe was honest but good-natured, and Chiara smiled. "We don't see much magic in Pariva."

"So I've learned," huffed the fairy. They'd arrived at Pine Grove, a pasture behind Pariva's local school. It was a quieter part of town, at least until the school bell rang and the children ran toward the fields to play. Chiara had spent many afternoons sitting on the grass, naming the cows and sheep that grazed there. Beyond was a grove of pine trees where she occasionally spotted Geppetto gathering wood for his projects.

The fairy guided Chiara under one of the trees and patted her arm. "I suppose I should properly introduce myself. I am Agata the Violet, a member of Esperia's oldest school of fairies. We listen to wishes made in good faith, and we guard the love, hope, and wonder in the hearts of all. You may call me simply Agata."

"Agata." Chiara dipped, making a curtsy out of habit. "I'm pleased to make your acquaintance."

"This isn't the first time we've met." Agata winked, and when next she spoke, her voice became resonant, echoing as if it bounced off a hundred walls. "Do you remember me, *Chiara Belmagio*?"

Chiara gasped. "It was you! You spoke to me when I was rescuing Geppetto."

"I was going to save the lad myself," replied Agata, "until you came out of nowhere. And you needed no magic to answer his calls." The fairy's voice turned somber. "You were close to perishing yourself, Chiara. You knew that before you leapt, but still you went on."

"I couldn't let him die."

"You'd be surprised how many would," said Agata. "But I knew you wouldn't give up. I've been watching you since long before you saved Geppetto."

"Watching me?"

"You have a talent for seeing into people's hearts," the fairy explained, "and for helping them."

"I'd hardly call it a talent," Chiara said. "I've lived in Pariva all my life. Almost everyone here is my friend, and I care about them."

"So you do," Agata agreed. "But you went beyond what most people who care would do. When Mrs. Cousins's husband died, you visited her every day for three months so she wouldn't be lonely. You played cards with her and helped her plant a tulip garden. You even found her a stray kitten to keep her company."

"That wasn't much—"

"When Mr. Vaci's wife came down with fever, you made broth for her until she got better. You feed the pigeons by the fountain with leftover bread from your parents' bakery—the ducks by Pine Grove pond, too—and you tutored little Clarence and Lila with their arithmetic until they got high marks at school."

"Those were hardly good deeds," said Chiara. "I did them because—"

"Because it's your calling," Agata finished for her. "You get a feeling in your gut when you see someone who's sad or lonely or in trouble. You listen to that feeling, and it shows you how to heal their hurt—how to bring joy."

Chiara stared. No one knew about that, not even Ilaria.

They had stopped walking, and Chiara found she couldn't say anything. "How . . . ?"

"Because I feel it, too," replied Agata. "Everywhere I go, and before I was a fairy, too. Let me guess . . . you can sense other people's happiness and unhappiness."

Chiara nodded slowly. Then she remembered, and added, "On the day I saved Geppetto, I thought I sensed something."

"What did you feel?"

Chiara frowned, remembering. "The water . . . it felt cold. Inside it, I felt . . . wrath and danger . . . evil."

"That was Monstro," confirmed Agata. "His strength is overwhelming, even for a seasoned fairy such as myself. Yet even while near him, you could still sense Geppetto's hope. That's how you found him—and saved him."

Chiara's knees went weak, and she could hardly breathe. "Yes, I suppose it is."

"You have great empathy, Chiara. And a powerful conscience. It guides you, doesn't it?"

Was Agata talking about the hum in her heart? "It's nothing special."

"Even so, not everyone is so in tune with theirs that they listen to it. You are, and that's what led me to find you," said Agata.

"I . . . I don't even believe in magic. I mean, I didn't—until now."

"Listen, the wisest fairy turns to magic only as a last resort. That is why I have reason to believe, Chiara Belmagio, that you would make an excellent fairy."

A laugh bubbled in her throat. "Me, a fairy? I don't think so. Like you said, fairies are wise, and I barely know what I'm doing with my life. I wouldn't know how to grant wishes."

"Experience and age have no correlation to the strength of one's heart," said Agata. "Your whole life, you've shown courage, compassion, and kindness."

"There are plenty of others who are kinder than I am, and braver, too."

"Perhaps that is true," said Agata, looking pleased that Chiara was uncertain. "But fate did not lead me to their doors. They led me to yours." The Violet Fairy paused. "I've already proposed your name to my council, and we unanimously agreed to invite you to trial with us. Should you complete your training, we would grant you wings and a wand—should you wish it."

Chiara was stunned. "You *are* serious."

"I don't lie, Chiara Belmagio," said Agata.

"What . . . what would I even do?" asked Chia. "What do fairies do?"

"A good question. Most know us for granting wishes, but that is only a fraction of our responsibilities." Agata inhaled. "The world can be a dark place, dear. Our greatest role is to guide the light wherever we can. It is no trivial task, I assure you, and few are suited for it. But I hope you'll try."

Chiara said nothing. Usually she depended on her heart to tell her what to do, on that tingle in her gut to guide her. But here, in this moment that could change her entire life, any guidance was absent. "I don't know what to say," she admitted. "That's not the answer I'm supposed to give, is it?"

To her surprise, Agata chuckled. "If you had jumped at the chance to wield a magic wand and fly on fairy wings, then you wouldn't have been the young woman I thought you were." Then her expression changed. Her brown eyes filled, but Chiara couldn't tell what had stirred their sadness. "Life as a fairy is more than the ability to conjure magic or wear sparkles and fly on beams of starlight. Far more. It's the chance to make hearts full and make the world a slightly better place."

"If fairies are able to do such wonderful things and bring joy," observed Chiara quietly, "then why do you sound upset?"

"Our job *is* wonderful," Agata admitted. "But it is not

without its costs, sacrifices. I'll explain more at the end of your training . . . should you come trial with us."

The older woman could sense Chiara's skepticism. "Think on it, please, Chiara. I will visit you again in a week for your answer. Until then, I ask that you speak of my invitation to no one. Not your parents, your brother, even your sister. There is wisdom in caution, and humans have fickle memories—especially when it comes to fairies. We'll tell them together about the trial if you should choose to do it. But I wouldn't want a stray comment now to influence your decision. Will you promise?"

Chiara hesitated. In her mind, she was certain she already knew her answer. Grand as Agata's invitation sounded, she couldn't leave her family.

She waited for that warm hum in her chest to affirm her decision, but it was absent. She was on her own.

"Think on it," repeated Agata, this time with a small smile—as if she knew.

Chiara supposed a week of consideration wouldn't hurt. "All right, I promise."

"Good. Until next time, then."

Agata vanished in a fan of light, leaving Chia alone once more.

Her mind wheeling back and forth between disbelief

and excitement, Chia raced home, forgetting for the first time in her life that she was expected at the bakery for work.

Ilaria pounced on her as soon as she returned home. "Where have you been?"

Chia had to bite her cheek so she wouldn't tell Ily everything. No one would appreciate Agata's visit more than her sister, who loved fairy tales and believed in fairy godmothers and wishes that would come true.

But Chia had made a promise.

"What's wrong, Chia? Cat caught your tongue?"

"No." Chiara fumbled. She wasn't good at lying, so she settled for what was technically the truth. "I . . . I forgot the ledger for Mamma and Papa."

"That's unlike you. Did something happen?"

"Nothing important." Chia hastily slipped past her sister and headed up to her room. Any other day, she would have heard the disappointment in Ily's voice and tried to set things right.

But not today.

And so, Ilaria stood alone on the stairs, gripping the railing as her chest tightened. It was to be the first crack in her heart.

CHAPTER SEVEN

A week crawled by, and there was not a peep from Chiara about her meeting with the fairy.

Ilaria went back and forth from being frustrated to being charitable. Every chance she got, she plopped in front of her sister and gave her ample opportunity to bring it up. "Do you think there'll be a Wishing Star tonight?" she asked casually one morning. And, "You know, I'm really starting to love the color purple. I should wear more of it."

But Chiara never took the bait. She merely replied, "The Wishing Star, tonight? I don't know, Ily. Maybe." And: "Purple is a lovely color. I think it'd suit you beautifully." Then she returned her gaze to the blocks of dark chocolate she was chopping to make Mamma's famous chocolate-hazelnut spread and completely missed the scowl that Ilaria sent her way. "Your lunch is on the table, Ily. If you want cookies, they'll be ready at the bakery before noon."

"If you want cookies, they'll be ready at the bakery before noon," Ily mimicked under her breath. "Always so prim, always so responsible. You're my sister, Chia, not my mother."

Resentment made Ilaria scowl, and she tore away from the kitchen, not bothering to ask if Chia needed help. On the way to work, she breezed past Geppetto, picking up fallen tree branches in Pine Grove. When he saw her, he fumbled with the bundle in his arms so he could wave, but she pretended not to notice. These past few weeks, he'd stopped by the bakery every other day to chat with Chiara and Niccolo—they spoke about dull and dreary things, like the ships Monstro had recently sunk and whether the tomatoes in Pariva were in bloom. Every time, Geppetto glanced at her as if he wanted to say hello—just as he was then—but Ily couldn't be bothered. Any friend of Chia's was not a friend of hers.

She arrived at the hat shop ten minutes early, a miracle that unfortunately bore no witness since old Mrs. Tappa was still asleep upstairs. Annoyed that her effort was for nothing, Ilaria went straight to the mannequin in the front of the store and yanked at the hat's pale blue ribbon.

Chiara's favorite color, same as the ribbon she tied around her head every day.

Just seeing it sent Ily a sharp stab of resentment. She wasn't used to being angry at Chia; she couldn't even remember the last time they'd had a disagreement.

But then again, Chia *never* kept secrets from her. What could the fairy have said to her that she wouldn't immediately tell?

Ily thought hard as she tossed the blue ribbon over her shoulder and replaced it with a tight red bow. Chia didn't believe in fairies, so there was no chance that she'd made a wish and the fairy had come to grant it. Or was there?

It was the only answer she could come up with. As for why Chia wouldn't tell Ily . . .

Maybe she made a wish for me, Ily thought, some of her resentment washing away in shame. Knowing Chia, she'd never wish anything for herself.

Could she have wished for Ily to go to Vallan? To study with the great Maria Linda and become the most sought-after prima donna in Esperia?

Don't be stupid, she told herself. *Chia wouldn't wish that. She'd waste her wish on something for everyone, like a good tomato harvest or a cure for the pox.*

Besides, Chiara was acting like she had a secret.

One she didn't *want* to share, was keeping from her on purpose.

The shop door rattled, and Ily nearly jumped to see Chia herself poke inside, swinging her basket. "You forgot your lunch," said her sister. Her cheerful tone made Ily cross her arms. "Are you eating with Nico and me today?"

Ily acknowledged Chia with the barest flick of her eyes. "I'm having lunch with Simona."

"Simona?" Chia held her basket still as she stepped inside. "Are you sure? I saw her a minute ago with Pietro. They're riding to Elph for the day."

Ilaria gritted her teeth. Just her luck that Simona would lunch with her beau. The traitor.

"Is everything all right, Ily? You seem upset."

"What would I be upset about?" Ily repositioned the hat on a mannequin and pretended to fiddle with some pins and flowers. "I've been busy is all. Gia Fusco ordered half a dozen caps for her husband and a dozen hats for herself." An outrageous lie, but she'd already spun it and couldn't stop: "I'll be working nonstop for the next few days just fulfilling her order."

"I see," said Chia. "Shall I bring you cookies, then? We're making the cinnamon ones today. Your favorite."

As if Ilaria didn't know what her own favorite cookies were. "Don't bother. I'm cutting down on sweets."

"They'll be fresh out of the oven."

Curse Chiara for knowing her too well, and bringing her weakness for cookies into their argument. Ilaria waved her sister away. "Have to practice. Since Ms. Rocco died, I have no one to help prepare me or take lessons from . . . and my audition's only a month away."

Chiara's shoulders fell. "Gosh, it's only a month from now?" Her face softened. "I'm sorry, I haven't been helping."

"I haven't asked you to. Besides, you've been busy with . . . who knows what." It was a shameless punch at her sister, and from the way Chiara's face folded, Ilaria knew she'd made a hit.

"Let's practice together tonight. We'll put on a concert for Mamma and Papa after dinner."

"I won't be home till late," Ilaria blurted before she knew what she was saying. "I'm going to . . . to see Ms. Rocco's niece. She said I could use her harpsichord to practice my new aria. Hers is much better than ours."

"I could come with you," Chia offered.

"Her niece wants to play for me," Ily lied. Janissa Rocco was an awful player who attacked the keys as if her fingers were knives, but she didn't think Chiara knew that.

"All right, then," said Chiara, swallowing. "We'll see you when you get home."

At long last, Chia left, and Ilaria bit down hard on

her lip. The pain helped keep her from running after her sister.

Pride had always been her weakness.

Dusk couldn't come soon enough, and Ilaria leaned her head against the wall, praying for the clock to hurry up and strike six. She pressed her palm against the window and looked outside. Mrs. Tappa's shop was close enough to the bakery that she could see her parents cleaning up the store-front and preparing to go home.

As Pariva's bell tower chimed six o'clock, her mother glided out with the day's aprons and cloths tucked under her arm to wash at home.

Ily swore her mother had the eyes of an owl. Mrs. Belmagio instantly caught Ily watching from her shop window and frowned in consternation. An understandable reaction: usually, by this time, Ily would have left work to see her friends or gallivant about town with her latest admirer.

A quick jaunt across the street, and Mamma arrived at Mrs. Tappa's shop.

"You're working late, darling," she greeted Ily. "Chia told me you were going to Janissa Rocco's to practice?"

Ily pretended to uncuff her sleeve. "I'm about to leave."

Mamma paused, and for a moment, Ily was certain she could detect the falsehood. After all, Mamma always liked to tell her: *A lie keeps growing and growing until it's as plain as the nose on your face.*

But no such lecture came from her mother today.

"You've been working so hard lately," Mamma said instead, which only made the ache in Ily's chest sharpen. She helped Ily with her sleeve, then touched Ily's cheek. Mother and daughter had the same dark chocolate hair, though only Chia had inherited Mamma's curls. "Try to be home before dinner, all right? Until then . . ."

Mamma dipped into her pocket for a small pouch. Ily smelled cinnamon right away, with a lace of chocolate.

"Cookies?" she breathed.

"Your favorites. Saved them for you."

Ily couldn't resist them again. She clasped the pouch, warming her palms with the treats. There were only two people she ever felt guilty about lying to. Chia and her mother.

Ily wanted to keep silent, but another lie slipped out. "I'll try."

"I'll see you at dinner, then," Mrs. Belmagio said. "You're going to do wonderfully at that audition."

"Will you come with me?"

"I thought you'd asked Simona or Beatrice—or Chia." A pause. "Is everything all right with you two?"

"Of course it is," Ily lied.

Mamma cocked her head. "You sure?"

"I'm sure."

"You won't be embarrassed to have your mamma with you?"

"Never."

That pleased Mrs. Belmagio, and her cheeks glowed. "I suppose that your father can manage half a day without me." She chuckled as Mr. Belmagio stepped out of the bakery, still absentmindedly wearing his baker's apron and hat before he remembered to leave them back inside.

Ily wanted to hug her mother. She wanted to sink into her arms and cry and have Mamma end the fight she was having with Chia. She wanted Mamma to make everything better again. But she wasn't a girl of seven anymore. She was almost seventeen—a young woman. So she placed the cookies in her pocket, and said in her evenest voice: "Thank you, Mamma."

Once her parents disappeared from the square, Ilaria slid out of Mrs. Tappa's shop and strolled across the street. No one in Pariva ever locked their door, so all Ily had to do was turn the knob, and she was inside her parents' bakery. The smell of yeast and unbaked bread tickled her nose, and a rush of warmth from the ovens—still cooling—swelled to her cheeks.

"Anyone here? Nico?" She waited. "Chia?"

No answer.

The tension she carried in her shoulders released, and she glided past the counter through the half shutter doors into the kitchen. The ovens still emanated heat, and sweat prickled on Ilaria's skin. She didn't mind. She'd spent her childhood within these walls, tossing flour at Niccolo and pouring extra chocolate into Mamma's cakes while Chia kneaded bread with Papa.

The racks by the wall were empty, but crumbs sprinkled the floor, and there was a cake pan left on the counter where Mamma displayed the sweets of the day. The day before had been almond cake with blackberry—Chia's favorite. That day, cinnamon as well as pistachio cookies, the latter perfectly round and pale green, topped with plump pine nuts.

Ily nibbled on one of her cookies as she went up to the south-facing brick wall. She counted the bricks and tapped on one just off the center of the wall, then wriggled it loose. Behind was where Mamma and Papa stored their profits for the week, if there were any.

Five meager oros, sitting on a cracked plate, awaited her.

Ily sighed and placed the brick back. Then she noted the fresh lilies on the counter, the basket of lemons under the table. No one in Pariva was wealthy, and Mamma and Papa often let their customers pay with goods like flowers or fish or salt instead of money. Before she'd taken her job at the hat shop, Ilaria herself had only had three dresses, most of them so worn Chia had helped patch the seams.

"When I'm famous, Mamma and Papa won't have to work anymore," said Ilaria to herself. "They'll have a house on the fanciest street in Vallan, right across from mine. And all of my dresses will have lace on the sleeves and on the collars."

With that, she tucked herself into the back of the kitchen and stood in front of a pan to see her reflection. A girl holding a foolish grudge against her sister stared back at her.

"I can't go home now," she told her reflection. "I already said to Mamma and Chia that I'm at Janissa Rocco's practicing."

The girl in the pan made a righteous face at her. *Then tell them the truth. That you're bored, and you don't want to spend the next three hours holed up in the kitchen. Go home and eat and make up with Chia.*

"No," Ilaria refused, stubborn as ever. She tossed the pan under a table and settled herself in a corner. Her stomach growled, and she didn't feel like singing. But she wouldn't let go of her pride.

At least she had cookies.

It was well past the Belmagio dinnertime when Ily finally came out of her hiding place in the bakery and hurried home. She felt like an interloper as she turned onto Constanza

Street, practicing her lies under her breath. She only hoped there was still food left. Mamma would have saved her a plate. Chia, too.

But as she doubled her pace toward home's yellow door, she heard voices from the window.

"Are you sure this is what you want, my dove?" Mamma was asking.

"I meant to say no," Chia responded, "but something in my heart told me I was making a mistake. So I have decided to do the trial."

Ilaria froze. *What trial?*

"We'll take good care of your daughter," someone with a lilting voice said.

Who is that?

A rush of wind stole away the response from her parents, and Ily hurriedly barged into the house before she missed the rest of the conversation.

She was already too late.

Her mother and father were rising from their respective chairs in the parlor, and Chia was rushing upstairs to her room. Only Niccolo was still sitting. Something smelled a lot like hot chocolate.

Hot chocolate was a special-occasion drink. It was Ilaria's favorite . . . though Mamma always resisted making it during the summer.

"What's going on?" asked Ilaria. "I can't tell whether someone died or we inherited a fortune."

Mr. Belmagio set down his mug. His eyes were glazed, like the sugar he worked with all day. "You missed her."

"Missed who?"

"The fairy."

Ilaria's heart skipped. "The fairy?"

"She said she had to leave. We waited for you as long as we could." Mrs. Belmagio pushed Ily's red mug in her direction. "Your cocoa's gone cold."

It *was* hot chocolate. Usually a treat in the Belmagio house. It meant there was cause for celebration, or a need for comforting. Or both.

"Have you eaten?"

Ily shook her head numbly, forgetting to lie.

"I'll get you something—"

"No," interrupted Ily. Nico and Papa were avoiding her gaze. As if they'd been stricken by news. Only Mamma would tell her the truth. "Will you tell me what's going on?"

Mrs. Belmagio stirred her hot chocolate slowly. "Your sister's been asked to join the fairies."

That was quite possibly the last thing Ily had expected. "What?"

"It's an invitation." Mrs. Belmagio held her mug

unsteadily. "For Chia to study under her at the Wishing Star. Chia's asked for our blessing."

Ily's pulse spiked. Chia, leaving to become a fairy? She couldn't make sense of it. "What a ridiculous invitation. Of course you said no, didn't you, Mamma?"

At her mother's silence, Ilaria's stomach sank. "Didn't you, Mamma?"

"It's a wonderful invitation. And my children are old enough to make their own decisions," replied Mrs. Belmagio as Chia returned to the parlor and appeared in the doorframe.

"I said yes," her sister replied softly. "I'll leave home in two weeks to study with the Violet Fairy."

"You're leaving us?" Ily couldn't believe it. "In two weeks?" She whirled, bombarded by emotions she couldn't control. "Mamma, Papa . . ."

"We've given Chia our blessing," Mrs. Belmagio said. Her father nodded.

"Chiara being invited to join their ranks is a stupendous honor."

So already her sister was no longer Chia but *Chiara*.

"Well, she doesn't have *my* blessing!" spluttered Ilaria.

"Ily!"

"No one told me anything. No one asked me anything."

Chia swallowed hard. "Ily, I'm sorry. I wanted to tell you, but I promised—"

Ily didn't want to hear another word. She raced up the stairs and slammed the door. She threw her quilt over her head, but even then she could hear Chiara's footsteps. They landed just outside her door.

"Ily? Please."

"Let her be," said Niccolo in a low voice. No doubt he thought she couldn't hear through the door. "She'll feel better about it tomorrow."

He was wrong. Ilaria wouldn't feel better about it. Not tomorrow. Not ever.

A pang of disappointment squeezed Ily's chest as the footsteps departed. But Chia came back, alone, a few minutes later. She knocked.

"Go away," said Ily spitefully.

Almost always, Chia listened. But she didn't today, and she came inside.

Her sister had brought an assortment of cookies—cinnamon and pistachio and chocolate ones, too, on a dish with a fresh glass of milk. She held out the plate as if it were an olive branch, but that only irritated Ily further.

"Ily," began Chiara, "I don't want you to be angry with me."

"Who said I was angry?"

"I've known you all your life, ever since you were a baby in diapers and wouldn't stop sucking on your toes. I know when you're unhappy."

"I didn't suck on my toes," she retorted. "That's disgusting."

"Babies aren't disgusting. They're adorable."

"Of course you would say that." Ilaria shut her curtains with one yank. "I've been angry for a week and you didn't even notice."

Chia settled the plate on Ily's desk. She hung her head, looking sincerely contrite.

"Don't give me that look," said Ily. "You always think pastries or music will make things all better. Not this time. I saw you with her. I knew you were keeping something from me."

"Ily. I'm sorry. I wanted to tell you, truly I did. But I promised I'd keep everything a secret until I'd decided."

Ily threw up her arms. "How can you make a promise to a complete stranger—over your own sister? How can you leave me?"

"I haven't promised to leave," said Chia softly. "It's just a trial for me to see if I like it, and for them to see if they like me."

"You didn't even think about my audition," said Ilaria sourly. She wanted to push as much guilt onto Chiara's plate as she could. "If you're leaving in two weeks, you'll miss it."

"I'll help you prepare," Chia promised. "I'll bake you cinnamon cookies every day before then, too—for luck."

"I won't be able to fit into my dress, then!"

"I'll sew you a new one." Chia paused. "I need to take this chance, Ily. There's . . ."

"What?"

Chia chewed on her lower lip. "Sometimes I get this feeling." She touched her heart. "It's like a hum or a buzz, and when I listen to it, it tells me whether something is good or bad. Agata says that it's what led me to her."

"What is it, a fairy sense?" It sounded so silly and non-sensical Ily couldn't help laughing. Who would've thought her sister, who as of a month before didn't believe in fairies or magic, would be talking to her about inner voices and gut feelings? "Not everything's good or bad, Chia. You can't rely on some fairy voice to tell you what to do."

"It isn't a fairy voice. . . ." Chia bit her lip. "It's hard to explain. But . . . I can't help feeling like I need to try to understand it. To go with the fairies, at least for a little while. For myself." She looked up at Ily, as if for approval. "It's only a trial. I won't be gone forever."

Ily's laugh died. All these years, Chia had been at her side, helping her prepare for her auditions and giving all she could to help Ily follow her dreams. How could she be so selfish as to deny Chia the same opportunity? Still, she couldn't help voicing her fear: "What if you decide to stay with them?"

"I'd miss you too much to do that," said Chia gently. "And this—" Without warning, Chia threw a pillow at Ilaria's face.

"Hey!" Ilaria retaliated, and within moments, the two sisters were laughing and fighting at the same time.

"All right, all right," cried Chia when Ily hoarded all the pillows to throw. "Truce!"

Ily grabbed her sister's hand and they fell backward onto the bed, stretching their arms high as they caught their breath.

"What if I really do make it to the Madrigal Conservatory?" Ilaria whispered. "And you become a fairy? Will we still have moments like this?"

"Of course we will."

Chiara meant it with all her heart, and the last traces of Ily's fears and anger faded until they were forgotten.

Neither sister could know that this time, it was Chia's words that were a lie.

CHAPTER EIGHT

In the middle of Pariva's main square was a statue called the Three Fairies. It had been there ever since Geppetto could remember, and from what he knew, since his father's and grandfather's and great-grandfather's times, too.

The children in town liked to touch the fairies' stone wings for luck before their exams, and plenty of Pariva's residents—adults and children alike—often stopped before the statue to ask, "Will there be a Wishing Star tonight?" According to local legend, if a bird landed on one of the fairies within a count of ten, that meant yes.

Geppetto had never approached the Three Fairies with the question before, but for the first time in years, he caught himself *wanting* to.

Three fairies. One was an elderly lady, one a middle-aged

gentleman, and the third a younger woman—about Ilaria's age. They were all smiling serenely, their wands pointed toward the sky—as if a reminder to make a wish. To *believe.*

Their names, their homes, and their pasts were mysteries. Geppetto didn't even know if they were real people, let alone whether they were from Pariva.

"Maybe Chia will find out," he mused aloud.

Chiara Belmagio's invitation to become a fairy was the talk of the town. Mrs. Belmagio had spoken of it to only a few confidantes, but such news could not be contained for long. Within a day, it had spread across the town, and no one could hide their excitement.

Imagine, a fairy from Pariva!

Geppetto wasn't surprised at all that Chiara had been chosen. She'd always had a knack for bringing happiness into people's lives. After she had rescued him from drowning, she'd gone out of her way to befriend him, and he looked forward to when she and her brother visited his shop. Niccolo would tease him about never going out, and Chiara would ask him questions about the lutherie business and recount stories that she had read recently. Their company made the long, lonely hours pass quickly.

The only person he could imagine not being pleased about the news was Ilaria. The sisters were so close. Often when he walked down Constanza Street, taking the long path toward the sea, he could hear the sisters making music together.

He'd hum along, for he recognized every tune. But lately, the Belmagio house had been quiet.

With a sigh, Geppetto sidestepped away from the Three Fairies. There was a crowd of children behind him waiting to approach the statue, and he smiled as they flocked around the fairies.

"I'd like a new toy, please," Bella Vaci told the statue dolefully. "My brother Gus just got a new cat, and it scratched my doll. I'd love a new one."

Geppetto couldn't help listening. From his pocket, he took out a wooden shepherdess and sheep he had carved and painted. When no one was looking, he placed them on a bench near the statue, then started back for home.

Before he left the square entirely, Geppetto glanced over his shoulder. Just as he'd hoped, young Bella had spotted the figurines and picked them up in delight.

"Look!" she cried to her brother Gus. "It's a shepherdess. A sheep, too! See, I told you fairies were real." She held them close. "Thank you, fairies!"

"Let me see," said Gus, reaching out for the toys. When his sister passed them to him, he started running off. "Can't catch me now!"

While the siblings squealed, Geppetto chuckled to himself. He loved watching the children in town. How happy and free they were. Unburdened by responsibility or the worries that there wouldn't be enough food on the table for dinner, or by the reality that not all dreams came true. He knew this wasn't true for all of them, but at least when they played together in the park, they seemed happy. He missed that carefree joy, and he couldn't remember the last time he'd laughed. Really laughed.

He'd grown up without brothers or sisters, and he'd always wished for someone to call his dearest friend—or at least someone other than his distant father to keep him company. But finances were tight, and there was work and cooking to be done, so Papa insisted he come home straight after school instead of getting to know his classmates, like Niccolo Belmagio.

By the time Geppetto's work was done, the hour was late, so he passed his precious spare minutes before bed whittling toys out of spare wood for the village children. But even that displeased his papa.

"That wood's for making violins," Papa said crossly. "Not for carving silly trinkets."

"The piece is too small to make any parts," reasoned Geppetto. "It's just a toy, Papa. The children are so happy when they find my toys around Pariva. They make the

*funniest stories with their imaginations. Matilde pretended
the wooden cow could jump to the moon—"*

"Imagination doesn't feed the belly." His father cut him
off. "You want to talk about children? When I was half your
size, I was already earning my keep in the house. Now, if I
catch you wasting firewood to make useless baubles, you'll go
without dinner, understood?"

Geppetto gulped. "Yes, sir."

Mr. Tommaso was a stern parent, but Geppetto didn't
resent him. After all, it was thanks to his father's training
that he was able to craft the toys he so loved to make. However he could, he saw to it that the children of Pariva had
toys to play with. That they could be happy.

And maybe one day, his own child might be happy.

Geppetto slowed in his step, trying to bury the secret
longing that rose in him: his wish that one day, he might
have children of his own. He'd raise them differently than
his father had raised him. Oh, he knew his father was strict
because he wanted the best for him, and that it had been
difficult to raise Geppetto alone after his mother had died.
But a child needed love to bloom, and Geppetto would have
so much love to give.

"Geppetto, Geppetto!" called a young voice behind
him. It was Bella Vaci. "Did you make this?"

She held up the wooden shepherdess and sheep.

Geppetto couldn't lie. "Yes."

"You left them for me to find, didn't you?" The girl's eyes rounded with gratitude. "Thank you, Mr. Geppetto. I thought it was from the fairies at first, but that you made it—is even better. Thank you!"

Geppetto was tongue-tied, and before he could think of something to say, Bella made a shy curtsy and ran off to join her brother. While she ran, she bumped into a young lady— Ilaria Belmagio!

Out of instinct, Geppetto ducked behind a tree. Usually Ilaria was flanked by her friends Simona and Beatrice, but she was alone today.

She approached the Three Fairies, and Geppetto wished he had the courage to say hello.

Why, hello, Ilaria, he'd imagined greeting her a thousand times. *What brings you here? Are you looking out for a Wishing Star?*

Yes, Geppetto.

It wasn't couth to ask anyone what they wished for, but in Geppetto's daydreams, Ilaria always told him. *I've been wishing to become a singer. Chiara and I have been practicing for ages. One day, I want us to put on a concert for all of Pariva, maybe even start a music school.*

And Geppetto would compliment her on what a wonderful idea that was, and they would stroll together for the rest of the afternoon, chatting about their favorite songs and all the wonderful emotions that music made them feel.

But in reality, Ilaria barely even stopped in front of the statue. She passed it without so much as a glance and headed toward Mrs. Tappa's hat shop.

How sad she looked. She tried to hide it, but her steps had a heaviness about them, and her hands no longer conducted an imaginary song as she walked.

He might not have had Chiara's gift for cheering people up, and the sisters' business was none of his—but he cared about the two of them. Chiara and Ilaria were born best friends.

If there was anything he could do to cheer Ilaria up and help the two sisters reconcile, he had to try. But what could he do?

Geppetto stopped humming.

"That's it," he cried aloud. "That's it!"

He hurried home, his steps light from the joy of a brilliant idea.

CHAPTER NINE

Too soon, Chiara's last day in Pariva arrived.

She lay in bed longer than usual, letting her head sink into the pillow she'd slept on every night since she could remember, and inhaling the faded warmth of the quilt her grandmother had sewn for her when she was born. Sunlight stung her eyes, and for the first time, it hurt.

How could a heart feel so light and heavy at the same time? She couldn't separate one feeling from the other, the heavy sadness and the great hope.

Clouds scattered the sky, and she smelled the possibility of rain. A typical September morning in Pariva—except it wasn't at all.

Chiara dressed and tiptoed down from the attic, careful to avoid the squeaky corners on the steps. She hesitated as she passed Ily's room. In the two weeks since Agata had last come, she and Ily had had an unspoken pact not to mention when she'd have to leave for the trial. But the day had come.

Chia's hand rose, her fingers closing to shape a fist. She wanted to knock on her sister's door, yet at the last second she withdrew. Best not to waken Ily; she was always grumpy in the morning.

Downstairs, Niccolo was drinking coffee in the kitchen, and a smear of milky foam coated his thin mustache. Under his arm was his violin, and he strummed its strings idly until he saw her.

"Saints and miracles," he said brightly. "Everyone's up before you."

"Morning," echoed Chiara. A platter of yesterday's pastries awaited her on the table, bordered by a frame of fresh berries and apples. A far more sumptuous breakfast than they usually enjoyed. "Where are Mamma and Pap—"

"They left. Errands for the bakery."

Chiara raised an eyebrow. "On a Sunday?"

Everything was closed on Sundays.

Niccolo shrugged and tugged the end of his mustache—his tell that he was lying. Chia didn't pursue the truth; she wasn't surprised her parents were up to something on her last day home. "You said Ily's awake?"

"The other miracle of the morning. She's in the Blue Room warming up her voice—or, given the silence, just staring at herself in the mirror."

Chia started, but Niccolo grabbed her sleeve and held out his violin. "Wait," he said. "Chia, I need some help. My G and A strings snapped this morning. Could you get me new ones?"

"Don't you have extra strings? I could have sworn I bought you some last week—"

"I've misplaced them," Niccolo said abruptly. "I need new ones. The sooner the better. I have a chamber music rehearsal with Abramo after lunch, and—here, take my violin to Geppetto."

"Won't you come with me?" Chiara asked as she carefully placed Nico's violin into its case. "It'd be nice to say hello to Geppetto."

"Mamma needs me to rake leaves from the yard," replied her brother. "The old oak across the street's started to shed, and she's worried the leaves will fly over and smother her precious rosebushes. And Papa's basil. Why don't you ask Ily? Or don't. If she comes with you, he'll be so distracted he might accidentally saw my instrument in half."

"Very funny," said Chia, though it wasn't that farfetched a notion. Poor Geppetto was hopelessly infatuated with Ilaria. Whenever she visited, he always found some way to bring up Ilaria. He would say her name as if it were a song, taking extra time with each syllable.

In spite of Chiara's urging, not once had Ily visited him. Maybe today she'd finally come.

Ilaria was sitting at the harpsichord, warming up her voice with a series of hissing and grunting noises, then a stretch of verbalizing nonsense syllables. Every time she struck a chord on the harpsichord, she made a face.

Their instrument was an old one, with three keys missing and dubious tuning on the highest notes. "When I'm famous, we'll have a real harpsichord," Ily liked to say. "A pianoforte, too, since that seems to be the future."

This morning, she didn't complain about the harpsichord's condition. Instead, she cast Chia the barest of glances and said, "Don't you ever wear anything other than blue?"

"It's my favorite color. Just like yours is red."

"I don't wear red every day."

"Red is too ostentatious for daily wear," Chia quoted their mother.

Ily smirked. "If that's Mamma's reasoning, maybe I ought to wear it more. Who knows? Maybe I'll offend the right people and get sent away from Pariva."

Chiara gave her sister a stern look, then decided it best

to change the subject. "Niccolo needs me to get new strings for his violin." She paused. "Do you want to come along?"

"To the luthier's?" Ilaria sequenced her warm-up a step higher.

"You've never come with us to say hi to Geppetto."

"He's *your* friend, not mine. Besides, he falls apart every time he looks at me." Ilaria scoffed. "He might break Niccolo's violin while he's at it."

"Only because he likes you. You should give him a chance. He's far nicer than the other boys you—"

"Nice is what you say to describe a wallpaper color, not a boy. I'm yawning, Chia—it's a good thing you're not a salesperson. Now I've got to practice. My audition's next week."

Ily resumed her scales, but when she'd reached her highest note, Chiara scooted next to her on the bench.

"You could use a friend while I'm away. A real friend, not like Simona and Beatrice."

"What's wrong with Simona and Beatrice?"

"You know what I mean," said Chia. "Let Geppetto be a friend—at least until I'm back."

"*If* you come back." Ilaria's fingers flattened against the harpsichord keys. "Two weeks went by faster than I thought it would. We didn't even get to go sailing again. Or run through the fields like we said we would. Or spend the day in Elph looking at dresses . . ."

Ilaria's voice trailed, and she reached behind the harpsichord to open the window. The smell of lemons flooded inside. It came from the tree just outside the Blue Room, and Chia inhaled, relishing yet another smell of her childhood. She paused, unsure how to answer her sister.

"Anyway, hurry up and get out of here," said Ily, pushing her aside. "It's almost noon, and Mamma and Papa want you out of the house."

"Why?"

Ilaria gave her a dull glare. "I'm not going to be the one to ruin today. Just go." She rolled her eyes and uttered what she knew would make Chiara eager to leave. "Tell Geppetto I said hello."

That made Chiara smile. "Will do."

Chia hurried into the marketplace. All the shops were closed since it was Sunday, but she still savored the familiar sights of summer tomatoes on display and sprigs of lavender for sale and the smell of stinky cheeses drifting out of the market's cracked window. At the far end of the market, beyond the schoolhouse and a few more streets down, was Geppetto's workshop.

Chiara slowed, mindful of every stone under her foot,

every pigeon that flew over her head, every tree that she passed.

The shops were closed, but the townspeople descended upon her almost as if they'd been waiting for her. "There's our Chia! Shouldn't you be at home with your family?"

She raised her brother's violin. "Niccolo sent me off on an errand."

"Inconsiderate of him," Mrs. Ricci said. "You're leaving to become a fairy tomorrow."

There it was again, that wash of excitement and sadness. Chiara couldn't untangle the two. "I'm leaving to apprentice under a fairy," she corrected gently. "We don't know whether I become one in the end."

"I'd eat my rubber tree if you didn't," huffed Mrs. Ricci. Mrs. Valmont appeared at her side and nodded fervently.

"You're the goodest girl I've ever known, Chiara Belmagio. Everyone is going to miss you. We are so proud of you."

"There's nothing to be proud of," said Chiara. "Honestly, I—"

More people were gathering around her. "Don't be so humble, dear. Let yourself beam."

"Yes, be proud! We know so little about fairies and their mysterious ways. To think, the next one is our very own Chiara!"

"Take this," said Mrs. Ricci, tucking a generous sack of olives and chestnuts into her basket. "A taste of Pariva will keep the homesickness at bay. You will think fondly of us and visit, won't you?"

"There's plenty of wishes to be granted here," chimed in Mrs. Valmont's son.

Chiara smiled, because she didn't know what to say. She reached for her money purse.

"Don't you even think about paying," exclaimed Mrs. Ricci. "It's our gift to you. Watch over our little town."

"I'll do my best, ma'am," said Chiara, meaning it. She made a small curtsy. "Thank you for the olives. And the chestnuts."

Mrs. Ricci was only the beginning. Everywhere she turned, townspeople stopped her, filling her basket with wares from their shops and gardens.

"I know what you did for my darling Giulia," said Mr. Passel, stopping Chiara before the fountain in the town square. "I know you meant to keep it secret, but you've helped rekindle her love for painting. She's happy again."

"Art brings her joy," said Chiara simply. "It was nothing."

Mr. Passel nodded. "What will we do without you, Chiara?"

So on it went for the next hour. Chia loved seeing her

neighbors and friends, but she had a feeling they were try-ing to postpone her journey. The way Mrs. Vaci, carrying sacks of chocolates, hurried off in the opposite direction of her house, and Mrs. Valmont with a bushel of flowers, only added to her suspicion. Were Mamma and Papa planning a party for her?

That would explain Niccolo trying to get her out of the house. Ily, too.

Testing her theory, Chia finally deviated from the mar-ket for the path around the square. The townspeople waved as she left, and when she turned back they were all hurrying about their business—definitely odd for Sunday.

With a shrug, she continued down the hill toward the old part of Pariva. It was a longer path that went past the dodgier sections of town, but there was a road ahead that would cut straight back toward Geppetto's home.

"Well, well, if it isn't Pariva's very own fairy," drawled a man loitering outside the Red Lobster Inn, the local tav-ern. She'd never seen him before. A tail of uneven gray hair curled behind his back, and his words were slurred even though it wasn't quite noon. In his hands was a bottle of pungent ale.

The sort of man Mamma called "unsavory."

He tipped his hat in her direction. "Good morning, Chiara Belmagio."

Chiara slowed. Were Ilaria here, she'd have made some tart remark and nudged Chia to move along. But that tingly feeling in her heart bade her be kind to everyone, even this unsavory-looking man.

"Good morning," she responded.

Encouraged by her greeting, the drunkard grinned at her. "Hear there's a party in your honor tonight. Am I invited?"

"If there is, it's my parents' party," replied Chiara truthfully. "I don't know much about it."

"A surprise party, then?" The man covered his mouth with his hand. "I suppose I ruined the surprise. Dear me."

"It's all right. I already—"

"You'll be granting wishes as a fairy," interrupted the man, looking up from his hat. His bloodshot eyes were fixed on her. "Won't you?"

"To the brave, the unselfish, and the truthful," she replied, quoting what the Violet Fairy had told her. "If you have such qualities, your wish upon a Wishing Star will be heard."

"Oh, you'd best hear *my* wishes, little Chiara, or I'll be paying your family a visit!" He flashed a set of bright white teeth. "That pretty sister of yours, especially."

Chiara tensed all over. "It'd be wise not to threaten my family," she warned.

"What will you do, turn me into a toad?"

"If you deserve it," she said.

He snickered. "You don't have it in you."

She wouldn't be cowed, and she gave him her most dauntless stare, holding it for good measure before turning on her heel. The man simply laughed and laughed, the sound bubbling in her ears as she hurried in the opposite direction.

All of her trembled, and she crossed her arms over her body and held herself still. It should have come as no surprise that there would be people who would try to take advantage of her. But to have a complete stranger threaten her and her family left her unsettled.

It won't scare me away, she thought, easing away the fear icing her heart. *The world's not a perfect place, and if I become a fairy, I'll have the chance to make it better.*

She picked up her nerve and continued on her way, trying to focus on how good it'd be to see Geppetto.

CHAPTER TEN

Geppetto was humming to himself. It was a habit of his to make music when he was happy, and he was happiest when he was working on one of his secret projects. A music box, this time. His most ambitious project yet.

He'd only just finished designing it, after two weeks of studying the mechanics of how to construct one. He didn't have any money to buy supplies, so he had built everything from scratch. Thus far he'd constructed a rough cylinder, which was meant to fit into the box just above a metal comb. The plan was that as the cylinder rolled, the comb would tickle the nodes on its surface, and each would produce a pitch that was part of the song he'd selected.

That song, of course, was the Nightingale Aria. Its melody was simple enough for even him to sing, and so memorable that it always took hours to get out of his head. It was a popular tune these days, about a young bird that had lost her way and kept singing until she found her way back home again. Geppetto took the box onto his palm, carefully etching the beginnings of what would become a nightingale carved onto the lid. Then he would paint it, and maybe, if he summoned the courage, he would give it to—

There came a knock on the door, and, worried it was his father, Geppetto hastily threw a cloth over the music box. Then he remembered—his father was upstairs playing his guitar.

"Silly me," he mumbled with a laugh as he opened the door. "Now who could it be?"

Chiara Belmagio stood at the threshold, carrying her brother's violin and a basket loaded with wares from town.

"Why, Chiara!"

"Greetings, Geppetto. Is the shop open?"

Out of habit, Geppetto looked behind her—hoping that he might see Ilaria Belmagio, too. But no younger sister came.

"Yes, yes, we're always open," replied Geppetto. He put on his apron and gestured for her to come inside. "What does Niccolo need this time?"

"He says two of the strings snapped. I think he just

wants me out of the house." Chiara opened the case so Geppetto could take a look. "I don't mind—I meant to stop by anyway."

"Hmm." Geppetto turned, reaching for the cupboard where he kept extra violin strings. As he opened the doors, a small wooden figurine tumbled off its shelf. Chiara bent to pick it up.

"Did you make this?" she said, admiring the thumb-sized cat. "It's beautiful." She rose and noticed the row of similar such creatures Geppetto had carved, sitting carefully behind the box of violin strings.

"They're just chunks of wood," he said hastily. "Nothing special."

"How long do they take you to carve?"

"A few hours, if they're small. A week for a larger piece."

Chiara studied the figurine on her palm. Recognizing it, "This is little Gus's new cat," she said. "You even captured her forked tail."

Geppetto shrugged shyly. "I thought little Gus might like it."

"He'll adore it. Will you give it to him?"

"Maybe," said Geppetto. "After it's painted."

Chiara passed him back the cat, watching as he tenderly returned it to its place in the cupboard. When he faced her again, her expression had turned pensive.

"You should open a shop, Geppetto. A toy shop. I can already imagine what joy you'd bring to the children."

"A toy shop?" Geppetto pretended he'd never dreamt of such a thing. "Oh, no, no. There's no future for a toy maker here."

"Is that you speaking," said Chiara softly, "or your father?"

It astounded him how easily she saw into his heart. No one had said that to him before. Was that why the fairies had come to her, because she could read his dreams and the fears that hindered them?

Geppetto found he couldn't reply. But his actions were telling enough. Without meaning to, he stole a glance upstairs, flinching when the sound of his father's guitar playing came to a halt.

As he fixed his attention on Niccolo's violin, Chiara lowered her voice. "It's what you love," she said. "I can see it in the way you beam about your work, and the way you handle your creations. You don't feel that love when you're repairing violins and guitars."

Geppetto forced a laugh. "Not everyone is meant to do what they love," he said woodenly, as if he'd rehearsed the words to himself a hundred times. He mustered a smile and spread his arms to show his father's workshop. "This is close enough."

Before Chiara could reply, footsteps thudded down the stairs. "Which of the Belmagio girls are you?" growled Geppetto's father. "The fairy or the diva?"

"Papa," said Geppetto, his cheeks growing hot. Papa was in a mood, thanks to the weather. As autumn approached, it was getting colder, and that made his joints ache and his guitar playing clumsy. He didn't like any reminders that he couldn't play or work as well as he used to.

"Papa," said Geppetto again, "she's a customer."

"The fairy, then," Tommaso said. "The whole village is in a frenzy, getting ready for your party."

"Father!" Geppetto said. "It was supposed to be a—"

"It's all right," said Chiara politely. "I already knew." She gave his father a winsome smile that he did not deserve. "Will you be attending, sir?"

"Parties are for gossips and nags," replied Tommaso, "and freeloaders. My son and I don't keep such company." He harrumphed at the goods in her basket. "Besides, it seems like you've gifts aplenty, Ms. Belmagio. What could my humble shop offer a future fairy?"

"You misunderstand, sir," said Chiara. "I don't want any gift—"

"I don't care how you meant it," replied Tommaso. "I suppose your parents will be well looked after, now that their girl's going to be a fairy—but not everyone in this town is thriving."

To her credit, Chiara barely flinched. "Mr. Tommaso," she said warmly, "your son is my friend, and he would be my honored guest tonight. Without him, I might never have met the fairies."

"Geppetto's too poor to have friends. And too busy." His father started for the door and wagged a finger at Geppetto. "Don't you be giving her the strings free just because she saved you!"

Chiara glanced at Geppetto, who wouldn't meet her eyes. Like a turtle, he shrank into his shell and did not know what to say.

This was what he had feared every time Chiara and Niccolo visited. This was always why he insisted they leave the workshop and go for a walk downtown. It wasn't only because of the creaks in the floor, the broken paneling or crack in the windows, or that he had nothing to serve his friends, or even that he was forced to charge the Belmagios for his services even when Chiara had saved his life.

It was because he was afraid Papa would come barging down—as he just had—and frighten away his friends.

"Well, there you have his answer," Geppetto mumbled,

staring at his cat figurine as his father made for the door. "No party for me."

"I'm sure he'll change his mind if I—"

"No, he won't."

Chiara's brows furrowed determinedly, and she started after his father just out the door. "There will be cake," she called. "A table full of cake. Chocolate, so I've heard. No one bakes a better chocolate cake than my mamma."

Geppetto's father donned his hat, bright yellow with a blue band. By now he could have been well down the street, but he stopped midstep. Though he didn't turn around, he was listening.

"Even if you don't come, you must try some," said Chiara brightly. "I'll ask my mamma to save you and Geppetto an extra-large slice . . . though, to be honest, it's best when it's fresh."

The old man let out a grunt, finally whirling to face Chiara. "You trying to bribe me with cake, Belmagio?"

"I would never bribe," said Chiara truthfully. "I'll ask my sister to bring you a slice tomorrow."

"Your sister?" Geppetto's father grunted. "I don't want your sister stepping foot in my workshop, what with those giggling geese she's always with. Gossips, the lot of them."

"Then maybe Geppetto can fetch it tonight," said Chiara. "He can simply stop by."

Geppetto stared at his hands. There was no way his father would fall for this.

"No," said his papa, after too long a pause. Stars above stars, he was actually hesitating. "The whole town will wonder why he didn't bring a gift. Gossips like Becca Vaci and Gretel Valmont will notice."

"Then he *will* bring me a gift," said Chiara.

Now Geppetto spoke up, low and quick. "Chia, we can't—"

"I'd like a wood carving," she interrupted, turning to him. "A figurine, like the one you made of Gus's cat."

"You want a stupid trinket?" Geppetto's father scoffed.

"They're not stupid trinkets. They're beautiful. I'd love one to treasure when I'm with the fairies."

Geppetto's father shook his head as he fastened the top button of his coat.

"Please, Mr. Tommaso," said Chiara. "It would mean a great deal to me."

A grumble. "All right," said Geppetto's father, to his son's astonishment. The old man softened. "The boy's only young once, I suppose, and a party's how I met his mother. If he finishes his work along with your gift in time, he can go. I'll come, too, to make sure he's back before nine o'clock. I won't have him in the company of this town's carousers."

"I understand, sir," Chiara agreed.

The old man's face went stern again, and he let out a harrumph—clearly to have the last word—then left the workshop.

Once his father was gone, Geppetto leapt off his bench. He was shaking. "How did you . . ." He gaped. "He said I can go!"

"All I did was ask nicely," said Chiara, grinning, "and remember that your father loves cake. Baked goods always help turn things around."

Chiara bit her lip as soon as the words came out, and Geppetto couldn't help noticing that her smile faltered. But he wasn't brave enough to ask her about it.

"My stars," he said, hands still trembling as he packed Niccolo's violin back in its case. "The whole town will be there. Maybe I shouldn't go. I'm not much fun at parties. I never know what to say."

"Niccolo and I would love for you to come. You always know what to say around us." Chiara paused. "And Ilaria will be there."

Geppetto hated himself for how his breath hitched.

If Chiara noticed, she hid it very well. "Come for the music, Geppetto. Come for the food and the company. Come because it's my last night in Pariva."

That made Geppetto look up. He blinked, pushing his glasses up the bridge of his nose. "You're really leaving?"

"It isn't called a farewell party for no reason," said Chiara, her eyes filling with mirth. "I'm leaving tomorrow morning with the Violet Fairy."

"I didn't realize it was so soon." Geppetto remembered then that she had asked for a figurine. "What shall I carve you?"

Chiara thought for a moment. "A dove," she said finally. "It's what my mamma and papa used to call me when I was little—because I'd bring peace between Ily and Nico." The nickname made her smile. "And it's my favorite bird."

"A dove," Geppetto repeated, nodding. He raked his fingers through his black hair. "That's simple enough. I should finish it by tonight."

"So you'll come?"

"You're not going to leave until I agree."

"Promise?" She teased, "You can't break a promise, you know, especially not to a potential future fairy."

"Yes, yes." Geppetto nodded. "I promise."

"Good." She tucked Niccolo's violin case under her arm and picked up her basket. "The party starts at seven."

CHAPTER ELEVEN

The Belmagios gave up trying to keep Chiara's party a surprise. A good thing, because by seven o'clock there had to have been at least two hundred people—half the town—crammed onto their property. Guests spilled onto the road, many of them in line to view the long table set up in the courtyard: Mrs. Belmagio's famous dessert spread.

The tower of cookies was high enough to touch the lanterns Mr. Belmagio had hung on the trees, and everyone clapped appreciatively when Mrs. Belmagio and Mrs. Vaci brought in a five-tiered chocolate cake, meticulously decorated with plump crimson cherries and hazelnut frosting. Each layer was shaped like a scalloped bowl, meant to resemble the fountain in Pariva's central square, and topped with a generous sprinkling of bluebell petals.

But what made Chiara tear up were the cards pressed carefully into the cake, each on a sliced piece of cork— messages from every friend, neighbor, child, and elder she had ever known.

We'll miss you. May you spread your light and make all of Esperia bright.

Good luck with the fairies. They'd be fools not to take you in.

And so on it went.

Chiara held the cards to her heart. She hugged the children at her side, who had been reading over her shoulder, squeezing each of them affectionately. She turned to her parents and kissed them on the cheeks. "How lucky I am to have you, Mamma, Papa. Thank you." She faced the waiting guests. "And how lucky I am to have been born in Pariva."

"Don't forget to watch over us when you're a fairy!" Mr. Sette shouted.

"Of course she will."

"That's our Chia!"

Chiara pursed her lips. She knew they all meant well, but she couldn't help feeling a twinge of uncertainty. She was only leaving on a trial; her heart told her she owed herself a chance to see what becoming a fairy would be like, but she hadn't made up her mind about what would happen afterward.

What could she tell them without letting everyone down? "*If* I become a fairy," she said, "I'll do my best to make you all proud."

"Now, let's eat!" her mother cried, wiping at the tears that slipped from her eyes. "Cake for everyone!"

At the announcement, Niccolo and his string quartet filled the merry courtyard with songs, most of which were serenades to woo Sofia Farrio, the young lady he'd started seeing. Mrs. Belmagio wove around the house, chatting with the guests and making sure everyone's plate was full, while Mr. Belmagio ushered people to dance and drink and eat cake. The house and the yard buzzed with laughter, with fond memories of Chiara, with everyone having a marvelous time. Even Mr. Tommaso, who had made a surprise appearance with his son. The stern luthier was helping himself to the promised piece of chocolate cake.

While everyone celebrated, Chiara couldn't shake the feeling in her gut that someone here was far from happy. Someone was miserable.

She spun slowly, holding an invisible compass that guided her.

That was when she found her sister.

Ilaria was parked beside Papa's herb garden with Simona and Beatrice, eating cake. Every few seconds, she threw her head back and laughed, and her face settled into an overly wide smile. Her actress's smile, Chia knew. It only showed her upper teeth. When Ily was genuinely happy, you could see the bottom teeth, too. Her eyes kept drifting off to the side as if she'd rather be anywhere but there.

I need to talk to her, Chia thought.

Squeezing her way through the crowds toward her sister was a herculean effort. Every two steps, someone stopped Chia to congratulate her, and out of courtesy, she couldn't cut the conversation short. By the time she made it to her sister, Simona and Beatrice had already finished their slices of cake.

"What do you mean, you don't know whether she's going to join the fairies?" Simona asked, licking the frosting from her fork. "When she comes back, she'll be a full-fledged one, won't she?"

"She'll be able to grant wishes then," Beatrice added. "I wonder, will we still need to wish on the Wishing Star if we have our very own fairy?"

Simona rolled her eyes. "I know what *you'd* wish for— for Niccolo to finally notice you. Well, you'll have to wish him away from Sofia."

"I wouldn't waste a wish on that." Beatrice's cheeks flushed with anger. "Not everyone's as shameless as you and Ily."

"Ily's kissed half the town," said Simona. "I've only kissed Pietro."

Simona passed her plate to the waiting young man and ordered him to fetch her another slice. Then she turned to Ily. "*You* must be happy. All your dreams are going to come true."

"What do you mean?" asked Ily thinly.

"Why even bother applying to the conservatory when your sister's going to be a fairy? One tap of her wand, and you'll be rich and famous."

"I didn't spend years studying and practicing for my sister to make me famous," said Ily. "I can do it on my own."

"You think so? Let's face it, your voice is pretty, but it's the sort of pretty that's for peddling extra money on the street and lulling babies to sleep."

"And getting boys to kiss you," added Beatrice with a giggle.

Ily glared.

"It doesn't strike the ear as diva material," Simona went on. "On top of that, you're not even a good actress. Last time I saw an opera, Maria Linda made me sob—she was divine."

Ily's fists clenched at her sides.

"Luckily, now you have Chia."

"Your future's all sorted," Beatrice agreed. In spite of what she'd said, Beatrice was just as shameless as Simona, and she tugged on Ily's hand, wheedling: "I can't think of the last time a fairy's visited Pariva, and I look out for the Wishing Star every night. Help a friend, Ily. We've been like sisters ever since we were born. Do you think—"

"No," said Ily coldly. "I don't know if she'll be able to grant your wishes." Ily eyed Chia's approach. "Why don't you ask her yourself?"

Her friends whirled, finding Chiara behind them. It was an awkward situation to arrive in, but Chiara deflected the girls with a pleasant wave and asked, "May I borrow my sister for a minute?"

"It's your party, Chia," said Simona, her words honeyed in a way Chia had never heard directed at her. "You can do whatever you'd like."

"Thank you." Chiara steered Ily into the house. It was crowded inside, too, but not as badly as in the courtyard. "You all right?" she asked her sister as they hiked up the stairs. Piles and piles of gifts covered the staircase.

"It's a like a funeral," muttered Ily, overhearing someone praise Chiara's kindness. "Except you're not dead. Everyone saying all these wonderful things about you, everyone toasting your memory. Doesn't it bother you?"

"A little," admitted Chiara. "But the party's more for Mamma and Papa than for me. Agata didn't tell us what will happen if I decide to become a fairy after I finish my training. Whether I'll get to live at home again and see you often . . . or . . ." Her voice trailed, and she didn't want to think about the alternatives.

"It'll be different when you come back," said Ily.

"What do you mean?"

"Everyone loves you. They always have. But now they want you to love them, too." Ily glanced at the mound of fruit baskets and wrapped sliced meats and homemade soaps and candles that had taken over the staircase. "In case they want something from you."

"Not everyone is that mercenary."

"We'll see."

Often it amazed Chiara how different she and Ily were. She tried to see the goodness in people, whereas her sister was far more cynical. *We balance each other, I suppose.*

She reached for Ily's hand. "I heard what Simona and Beatrice said. You don't need friends like that."

"Then who will be my friend?" said Ily. "You? You're not even going to be here."

"I'll always be your sister," said Chia. She dusted a crumb from Ily's collar. "Now chin up. What would a Belmagio party be without a concert? Let's not let your practicing go to waste."

"I don't feel like singing," mumbled Ilaria.

That didn't sound like her stubborn younger sister.

Ily thrived on attention; she'd practically been born giving concerts. "Is it because of what Simona said?" asked Chia. "Don't listen to her. You've a beautiful voice, Ily. A show-stopper voice. Would I lie to you?"

"You can't lie," Ily scoffed. "Even if your life depended on it."

"See?"

Her sister released a woeful sigh. "No one wants to hear me sing tonight. This is your party, not mine."

"I can think of one person who's here for you, not me."

Ily crossed her arms. "Who?"

"Come with me." Chia guided her sister downstairs to the Blue Room. Inside were dozens of Mamma and Papa's friends. But standing in the corner, studying the design of the lyre music stand, was Geppetto.

Ilaria's shoulders went tight under Chiara's hands. "No, Chia. I already told you, I—"

"He's our friend, Ily. I'm not asking you to marry him, for goodness' sake. But you never talk to him."

Her sister cast her a glare. "Because he literally turns into a tomato every time he's within three feet of me. Maybe I'm the one who's becoming a fairy."

That got a laugh out of both sisters, and Ilaria finally relented. "All right, but only to show you I'm right."

Right she was. Geppetto practically tripped over

the music stand at the sight of Ilaria, and his ears turned bright red.

"Find the music stand fascinating, Mr. Geppetto?" said Ilaria, sending a sidelong I-told-you-so glance at Chiara.

"Oh. Um. Yes. The engravings on the cedar are quite special. It must have been in your family for a long time."

"Our great-grandmother was an accomplished violinist—" supplied Chiara.

"Much better than Niccolo," Ilaria added.

"—and it was a gift to her."

"Well, it's beautifully preserved," Geppetto said, straightening. He backed up until his heels hit the wall. "And . . . and this has been a wonderful party."

"Our family owes its fortune to you," said Ilaria dryly. "If you hadn't almost drowned, the fairies would never have noticed Chia."

"Ilaria!" Chiara exclaimed. "That's an entirely inappropriate thing to say."

"No, no," Geppetto insisted. "I think the fairies would have chosen Chiara even if I hadn't fallen off my boat. It's fate."

"I don't believe in fate," replied Ilaria, crossing her arms.

"Perhaps you should," said Geppetto. "Fate watches over all of us. She's the reason we're here tonight."

Ilaria arched a dark eyebrow. "I never would have taken you for a dreamer. What dreams would a luthier's son have?"

He reddened, stammering. "I . . ."

"I thought so. There's not much potential for dreaming in a dusty old workshop."

"Oh, no. There's an art to lutherie. Making an instrument the very best it can be is a craft."

"You talk as if the instruments are alive."

"They are—when they're played," Geppetto said seriously. "I guess that makes the voice the most natural instrument of all."

The creases on Ilaria's brow smoothed. "I suppose so," she allowed, softening.

Her sister was charmed, Chiara could tell, and she backed away a little to give the two some space to talk.

Geppetto and Ily had much in common. They were both secret dreamers who shared a deep love for music. Yes, Ily was reckless and headstrong, but Geppetto . . . Geppetto was endlessly patient and caring. They would balance each other beautifully. In her heart, Chiara knew they would find their way.

But it helped to give a nudge.

"Speaking of which," she cut in, "Ily's agreed to sing. How about the Nightingale Aria? It happens to be both your favorite."

Before Ily could question Geppetto whether that was true, Chia towed her to the center of the room, where an audience was already beginning to congregate. While Ilaria gathered her poise, Chiara settled on the harpsichord bench and rested her fingers on her opening notes. The ivory keys had begun to yellow with age, but their sound was full and joyous.

She glanced at her sister, taking a breath to cue that she'd begin.

The second Ilaria released her voice, the chatter ceased. People eating cake in the hallway ambled into the chamber to listen, and someone opened the windows so guests outside in the courtyard could hear, too.

"The nightingale waits for a song to go along," Ily sang.

It was a bittersweet aria, whose story Ilaria had mastered sharing with not only her voice, but also with the expressions on her face, the movements of her arms, and the carefully choreographed blocking she performed as she crossed one side of the room to the other. Yet tonight, something was off. Her tone carried more melancholy than usual, and the tempo she led was a beat slower than when they'd practiced. Chia doubted anyone would notice. Ily's pride was in her coloratura, and every moment was still magnificent—each note in the impressive cascades attacked with vim and beauty—as if she were truly a bird chirping.

But behind the technical difficulties of the piece, Ily managed to show her musicality and bring emotion to her voice; that was what cast a spell over everyone who listened.

"Brava!" the guests cheered when the song was over. Applause made the walls vibrate, and Chiara remained at her instrument while her sister curtsied and bowed.

Usually after a performance, the children raced up to Ily and tugged on her skirt adoringly. "Will you sing more for us, Miss Ilaria?" they would ask. "How does your voice go so high? You sound like a bird! Sing another one!"

But tonight, Ily ignored the children as they went up to her. Her mind was on something else, and as she slipped out of the room, the children turned instead to Chiara. They peppered her with questions about the Wishing Star, about wands and wings and other things Chiara couldn't answer. A reminder of how little she knew about the future she was about to undertake.

"I don't know," she replied, to question after question. While she indulged her curious admirers, she kept an eye out for Ily.

Her sister did not return to the Blue Room, and Chiara was getting up to find her—when Geppetto came up to her at the harpsichord.

He smiled at the children and shyly offered them a few little toys from his right pocket: the small figurines Chiara had spotted in his cabinet. The cat with the forked tail, a wooden tiger, and even an elephant.

The children gasped with delight and ran off to play with their new toys.

And as Geppetto approached Chiara, he reached into his left pocket. "I put this on the stairs at first, but it's so small I worried you wouldn't see it." He plucked out a wooden dove and presented it to her bashfully. "I didn't get a chance to paint it, but—"

"It's perfect," said Chiara, cupping her hands to accept the gift. She held the dove on her palm and marveled at how lifelike it looked with its smooth rounded wings and gentle beak. "If I have a window on the Wishing Star, I'll set it on the sill."

That made Geppetto beam. "Imagine that. Something I've made, on a fairy's windowsill."

"I'm not a fairy yet."

"You will be," he said. "Everyone's proud of you, even my papa—though he'd never admit it. Having a fairy come from Pariva, well . . . it's a great honor."

Everyone said that, and Chiara's shoulders fell. "Not everyone is happy," she murmured.

Geppetto furrowed his brow, then guessed: "Ilaria?"

"Is it that obvious?"

"No. But she . . . she sounded different tonight."

Of course Geppetto had noticed.

"Will you talk to her?" Chiara asked.

"Me?" Geppetto said. Without looking, he aimed his hands for his pockets but missed completely. He stared at them as if he'd been betrayed. "I don't know. She doesn't seem to like me much."

"That's not true," said Chiara softly. "I have a feeling you two are destined to be friends. She'll like you very much once she gets to know you."

Geppetto's blue eyes flew up. "You think so?" He cleared his throat. "I mean . . . I don't . . ."

"She could use a friend when I'm not here. A true friend."

Geppetto looked down at his hands again. "I seem to forget how to speak when I'm around her."

"She's nicer than she acts," Chiara encouraged. "Will you be a friend to her—as a favor to me?" When still Geppetto hesitated, Chiara knew she needed the two to come together. She played her very last card, smiling: "I did save you."

A gentleman like Geppetto couldn't refuse. "All right."

"Why don't you go look for her now? She's been in the kitchen a while and everyone's waiting to hear her sing more."

"My father . . ."

"Don't worry about your father." Chia glanced at Mr. Tommaso, who was embroiled in a hearty argument with Mr. Vaci. "I doubt he'll be ready to leave."

Geppetto drew a deep breath, as if gathering his courage. Then he nodded.

"Don't forget to take a slice of cake for him."

CHAPTER TWELVE

It wasn't like Ilaria to slip away during the middle of a party, but she wasn't in the mood to celebrate. She hadn't even been in the mood to sing, but she hadn't wanted to make a scene in front of half the town.

She'd done her best to be charming: she'd smiled, she'd danced, she'd piled her friends' plates with cookies and echoed her sister's praises. But the moment her part on "stage" was finished, she made for the wings. After all, no one had asked her for an encore, and aside from a guest or two offering half-hearted praise for her singing, no one cared about her performance. Even the knots of young men who usually clamored for her attention ignored her. All anyone was talking about was Chia.

Alone and forgotten, Ily fled into the kitchen, kicking out the guests loitering inside.

Once alone, she blew out the candle and sank onto a stool, listening to the forks tinkle against plates in the courtyard, to Nico's string quartet playing in the Blue Room. Chia was still there, probably surrounded by a den of admirers. Ily could pick out her voice through any din; it was rich and warm—with a lilt that instantly made people love her.

But honestly, if everyone loved Chiara so very much, why celebrate her leaving?

That morning, Ily had accepted the idea of losing her sister. Accepted the idea of having her world turned upside down and losing her best friend.

What had been wrong with her?

Mrs. Belmagio tapped on the kitchen window from outside. "Ily? Mrs. Vaci said she saw you inside. Ily?"

Reluctantly, Ilaria got up and cracked opened the window, music and chatter from outside spilling into her quiet refuge. "There you are," said her mother. "We're serving coffee now. Bring some sugar out, please. Cream, too."

How can you smile, Mamma? she wanted to ask. *How can you laugh and dance and entertain half the town when tonight is our last night with Chia?*

She could already hear what Mamma would say:

Because what can we do, Ily, other than show her how much we love her?

Ilaria pasted on her brightest smile. "Yes, Mamma, I'll bring them out right away." But as soon as her mother disappeared into the crowds again, Ily closed the window and dashed out the front door as fast as she could.

No one would look for her. Not Simona or Beatrice or Niccolo. Not even Chia.

Summer evenings in Pariva were brisk, and Ilaria ran to keep from shivering, making for the sea. It was quite a walk, and by the time she reached the shore, the lights of Pariva were a faint blur against the dark of night.

Wind tousled her dark hair, and she undid the chignon at her nape, letting her long locks fly loose. She glanced behind her, but no one had come.

Of course no one had come. The only person who'd paid her any attention tonight was Geppetto. It'd been sweet of him to talk to her, to actually listen to her while everyone else was fawning over her sister.

Are you actually warming up to Geppetto? she asked herself. *It's his fault the fairies noticed Chiara. If he hadn't been out sailing that day, if he hadn't been foolish enough to chase after Monstro, then . . . then . . .*

Her hands squeezed into fists at her sides. Then she wouldn't lose her sister.

Ilaria sighed, knowing it was hopeless to wish she could change the past. She crouched, picking up a handful of pebbles and flinging them angrily into the sea. The water was so dark she might as well have been tossing them into oblivion, but she heard the rocks' splash. Then a louder splash.

Frightened, she stood and took a step back. Shadows had gathered in the water, tracing as far as she could see. "Monstro?" she whispered.

"I'm not Monstro, my dear," responded a woman's voice, low and rich and faraway—it came impossibly from the sea. The voice drew nearer. "But he's a friend. Asleep now, though he'll awaken soon enough."

Ilaria gasped and jumped away from the water. She staggered to turn back for the road, but curiosity nagged her to stay. Putting on her grandest tone to mask her fear, she demanded: "Who are you?"

The water washed up, almost touching her toes. It was a shade of green under the moonlight, something she had never seen before. "Just a passerby."

"You're lying," said Ilaria. A chill raced down her spine. "*What* are you?"

"I'm embraced by the forgotten, the unwanted, the unworthy. That's how you've been feeling lately, haven't you—Ilaria?"

Forgotten. Unwanted. Unworthy.

As Ilaria repeated the words silently, they left a bitter taste on her tongue. Forgotten, yes. Unwanted? Sometimes, when her mother scolded her for being lazy and vain, for shirking her duties at the bakery and at the hat shop.

Unworthy?

She gritted her teeth. Every night she looked out for a Wishing Star, and she practiced hours and hours every day, sometimes until her voice went hoarse.

A shameful thought, which seemed to have been kept deep beneath the fears of losing her sister, suddenly reared its ugly head: why had the fairies never come to her? Why had they gone to Chia—who had no passions, who had no dreams? Was it because Ilaria was somehow *unworthy* of their attention?

All anyone ever did was praise Chiara. Love Chiara.

Even Mamma and Papa preferred Chia, though they never admitted it. All anyone could talk about was Chia.

"How have I ended up with two girls so different from each other?" Papa had said once. "Ily wants the whole world, while you, Chia—you want absolutely nothing."

He'd glanced at Ily, at the bright red ribbons in her hair, the extra lace on her sleeves that she'd painstakingly sewn herself. As if she had no substance compared to her sister. As if she'd been made of dreams that would never come true.

"You've been a shadow to your sister all your life," said the mysterious voice. "Why do you tolerate it?"

The secret spring of envy buried inside her bubbled up. There was nothing special about Chiara. Feeding a few ducks and helping an old woman or two carry their groceries had amounted to a gift far grander than she deserved. Ilaria would have rescued Geppetto from drowning if she'd had the chance.

She'd simply never been given the opportunity to prove herself.

I'll become a famous singer, she told herself. *I'll become the greatest prima donna in the land.*

It was easy telling herself that when she had the loveliest voice in Pariva, but what if she wasn't good enough for Vallan? There were a thousand girls in the capital just as talented as she—maybe even more so. A true star was supposed to shine no matter where she was. Deep down, she feared everyone was right. That all her dream would ever be . . . was a dream.

How was it fair that at the same time, Chiara would get to be a fairy? Everyone knew that fairies lived as long as they wanted and stayed young forever. She'd never have to worry about graying hairs or wrinkles or sagging skin—or her voice losing strength over time. All while Ilaria would age and die, then be forgotten.

"It isn't fair, is it?" the woman whispered, as if reading her mind.

Ily threw a rock at the shadow, but it did not flicker and ripple as the water did. The rock disappeared into the darkness as if consumed.

Spooked, she grabbed another rock and reeled away from the sea. "Geppetto!" she said, spying a silhouette behind the trees. "Heavens, Geppetto. You scared me! Why aren't you still at the party?"

He looked flustered. "I . . . I, um . . . I . . ."

"The docks aren't on the way home for you." She eyed him suspiciously. "Were you following me?"

"No! No."

He was a terrible liar.

"Yes," he confessed. "Your sister was worried about you, so I went to go find you. But when you weren't in the house . . ."

Suddenly the rock in her hand felt heavy, and she let it go. It tumbled down, falling against the pebbles on the shore. "I just needed some air," she lied.

"You didn't even bring a jacket," he said, doffing his. "Please."

"What a gentleman you are, Geppetto," said Ilaria. "Now won't *you* be cold?"

He was wearing only a shirt and a vest.

"I can still work if I catch cold," he said, scratching at his mustache sheepishly. "But you won't be able to sing."

Ilaria's eyes drifted into the sea, where the shadow had spoken to her. It was gone now, but she wondered whether she'd imagined it. She pushed the thought out of her mind and reached into her pockets.

"I forgot my cloak, but I did steal some cookies from the party. Almond and pistachio. Would you like some?"

Geppetto accepted an almond cookie. "The view's better from here," he said, guiding them toward a bench farther down along the docks.

"Shouldn't you be at home?" said Ilaria, plopping onto the bench. "I've never seen you at any other parties. A good boy like you . . . your papa won't like that you're out with me."

"Papa's bark is worse than his bite," Geppetto replied. "Besides, he's still at the party. Chiara talked him into letting me come."

Oh. Ily immediately soured. "All good things are always thanks to Chiara."

Geppetto didn't catch the sarcasm in her tone.

"It's lucky she came by," agreed Geppetto. "Cakes are Papa's weakness. Boats, too . . . but I guess thanks to me, ours is gone." He hung his head. "As soon as I can afford the wood, I'll build him a new one."

"You know how to build a boat?" Ily asked.

"Papa taught me when I was young. He's good with construction . . . he says it's not so different from making instruments. It used to keep his mind off Mamma."

Ilaria remembered that Geppetto had lost his mother many years ago. Everyone had gone to her funeral, though she hardly remembered the occasion—or the lady.

"I'm sorry," she said.

Geppetto stared off into the sea. "He wasn't always the way he is now. Working at the shop was his greatest joy, and he used to travel across Esperia to sell his instruments. But now every other town has a luthier, and business . . . business is failing." He gave a wan smile. "I'm sorry, I must be boring you."

"Have you told Chiara?" asked Ily. "She's going to be a fairy. She could help."

"Oh, no. I couldn't."

"You haven't told her?" When Geppetto shook his head, Ily felt a rush of pleasure. It pleased her that Geppetto had confided in her and not Chia. "Maybe you should travel more. Sell violins, like your father used to. There are plenty of music schools in Vallan."

"Like the Madrigal Conservatory. That's where you want to study, I heard."

Ilaria tilted her head. "You've been asking about me?"

Even in the dark, she saw Geppetto's cheeks turn red. "I . . . I didn't say that."

"I think you have," Ily teased. "You're the only one who noticed I left. You followed me all the way here."

"I was worried about you. You . . . you sounded different tonight. Sadder. Maybe I imagined it. I don't think anyone else noticed."

"But you did." Ily paused. "You said you used to listen to my lessons with Ms. Rocco."

"I couldn't help it," he replied shyly. "Her house isn't far from mine."

Yes, Ilaria knew that. That was how she'd first spied Geppetto, working away diligently at his father's shop.

Ms. Rocco was the closest Pariva had had to a local celebrity. For over twenty years, she had sung in the Accordo, Vallan's opera house, as a member of the chorus. After she retired, she returned to Pariva.

It had taken Ilaria weeks to convince Ms. Rocco to give her lessons. She'd badgered the old lady until finally she caved, and Ilaria had taken a job at Pariva's hat shop—which she loathed—just to pay for her lessons. They'd been her favorite hours of the day, half focused on training her voice and learning the masterpieces by Esperia's composers, and half filled with stories about the lady's youth in the capital, and what it'd been like to sing in the greatest opera house in the world.

"You must go to Vallan," Ms. Rocco had urged her. *"You aren't meant for a place like this, full of milkmaids and fishmongers."*

"My family is here."

Ms. Rocco wrinkled her nose. *"Do you want to work in the hat shop forever, Ily? Listen to me so you won't end up with my fate. You have the voice to go far, my dear, but there will be others who wish to bring you down. Do not let them. Follow your dream, no matter what you have to do."*

Ily had wondered what Ms. Rocco had meant by the warning not to end up like her, but she'd never asked. Then her dear teacher had passed away, and there were no more lessons. Still, Ilaria kept her job selling hats so that she might afford tuition at the Madrigal Conservatory. If she got in, anyway. Her first audition was next week in Nerio. If she passed that one, she would advance to Vallan—and meet Maria Linda.

"She left me all her music," murmured Ilaria, thinking of her treasured cabinet at home, filled with a lifetime's worth of songs she studied whenever she had a moment. "Said it'd be a waste if I didn't use my talent to become great."

"Then you will."

Typically, Ilaria would have raised her chin haughtily and said, *Of course I will*. But maybe it was the melancholy rising to her chest, or the solemn way that Geppetto looked at her, truly believing in her music, that humbled her.

"I don't know," said Ilaria, voicing her uncertainties. "Maybe it's a silly dream. A reverie, like they say in the city. A pastime." She didn't give Geppetto a chance to speak. "She told me I need to pick a new name. Ilaria is too . . . country bumpkin."

"I like the name Ilaria," disagreed Geppetto. "It's lovely."

"Lovely isn't suitable for a prima donna," said Ily with a huff. "Lovely is how you describe a babbling brook or lace that goes on a hat. You don't describe a shining star as lovely. A shining star is magnificent. I want to be magnificent."

"What name will you choose?"

"I already have one." She leaned close enough to smell almond on his breath. "Do you want to hear?"

Under the lamplight, Ily could only make out a hint of how intensely Geppetto was flushing. "Y-y-yes."

She whispered, in her most dramatic voice: "Cleo del Mar."

The words steamed into the cold air, and Ilaria lifted herself, drawing some space between them as she waited for Geppetto's reaction.

"Cleo," repeated Geppetto, tugging nervously at his collar. "That's a . . . that's a fine name."

"The name for a prima donna," Ilaria said, puffing up with pride that he approved.

"It is." A long pause. "But I still think Ilaria suits you better."

What did he know? "Maybe here," said Ilaria, displeased. "But I'd be a fool if I wanted to stay. There's nothing for me here. Only donkeys and sheep." She scoffed. "Not even the wolves come to Pariva."

Poor Geppetto had gone speechless. He opened and closed his mouth, trying to come up with something to say, but Ily took pity on him and let out a sigh.

She said, softly, "Knowing my luck, I'll be stuck here forever."

"That wouldn't be so bad. Would it?"

"It'd be the worst fate ever. Never getting to see past the mountains or what's on the other side of the Lyre Sea."

"But you'd be near your family. And—"

"And what, Geppetto?" Ilaria recognized the lift in his voice. Coyly, she said, "Why, would you miss me?"

It was quite impressive how red Geppetto instantly turned. He blinked and stammered and mumbled, all while looking as though he wished the sea would swallow him whole. "Oh, um . . . who wouldn't miss you, Miss Ilaria? I mean . . ."

"If you call me *Miss* Ilaria one more time, Geppetto, I'll push you into the sea. And unlike my sister, I won't dive in after you."

"Oh." Geppetto's lips rounded, and he nodded, taking the threat seriously. "Yes, *Ilaria*."

"That's better." Ilaria hid a smile. Who would have thought she'd find straitlaced young Geppetto charming? But there was something about the way he listened to her, as if every sound she uttered were gold.

She liked it. More than that, she liked her effect on him. He was obviously in love with her, but it wasn't like the puppy love that the other boys in town showered her with. After a few weeks at her beck and call, they always tired of her. Ily had a feeling Geppetto was different.

Inching closer to him on the bench, she threaded her arm through his. The way Geppetto's spine went straight, she worried it was about to snap. Yet then he drew a deep breath, and he asked, "So what's your favorite opera?"

Ily grinned. Now that was something she could talk about for hours. And for hours they did, until the world grew so still that even the sea made no sound.

"I can't believe you've never heard an orchestra before," Ilaria exclaimed. "And you call yourself a luthier?"

"Tickets are expensive," replied Geppetto. "Besides, hardly any orchestras ever come to Pariva."

"Wait until you hear one," breathed Ily. "One violin sounds nothing like twenty. And with the flutes and oboes and horns—you'll feel like you're in heaven!" She clasped her hands, remembering how amazing it sounded. "I've only heard one once, when Mamma and Papa took me. It was a long time ago. I'll take you to a concert one day."

She blushed, realizing suddenly what she'd proposed. A meeting as such was usually only for young men and women who were courting.

"Maybe my first concert will be yours," said Geppetto quickly, noticing her stricken silence. "Miss Ilaria Belmagio and the orchestra of—"

"No," said Ilaria. "We'll go together." She smiled. "It'll be a grand time."

He smiled back, and Ilaria felt the most unexpected flutter in her stomach when Geppetto looked at her.

"Oh, my," Geppetto said, glancing at his pocket watch. "It's almost midnight! My papa and your parents must be—"

"Asleep by now," Ily finished for him. "Will you walk me home?"

Geppetto extended his arm for her to take, and she took it.

CHAPTER THIRTEEN

The torchlight along Constanza Street flickered, but the road was empty. Mamma and Papa's guests had gone home, and all that remained of Chia's party was a smear of chocolate on the fence and a lone pink glove that had fallen into a bush.

As Geppetto accompanied Ily to her door, the awkward tension she'd helped him forget the last few hours resurfaced in the worried grimace on his face. His expression gave everything away: what did he do now? Did he stay to ensure she entered safely; did he say he'd see her again soon; did he dare reach for her hand and hold it, as he'd been wanting to all night?

Ilaria was tired, but not too tired so shine her most

winning smile at the poor young luthier. "It was a pleasure getting to know you better, Geppetto."

"Um. You . . . you too, Miss . . . I mean, *Ilaria*."

Still smiling, she tipped up her chin and half closed her eyes. "Good night," she murmured.

Unfortunately, Geppetto didn't understand her games at all, and he merely tipped his hat nervously. "Good night."

He turned back for the road, and Ilaria stared after him, blinking with disbelief. Then she shook her head and laughed to herself. Only Geppetto would miss the opportunity to kiss her good night.

What he did do, though, was wave to her from the end of the road. It was a shy wave, but his smile was as wide as his entire face, and it warmed Ily in spite of the night's chill. As did the sight of him quickly whirling to hurry home, muttering something about his papa being angry that he was so late.

Sand and seawater squeaked out of Ilaria's shoes as she entered her home. The party was long since over. All the guests were gone, and not a candle was lit. In the darkness, she toed off her shoes and leaned them against a wall to dry. Then, as she made her way into the hall, a shadow darted out from the parlor.

Fear iced Ilaria's stomach. She thought of the strange

voice she'd heard at the beach tonight. Had she followed Ilaria home?

Without thinking twice, she picked up the closest thing to her: the lyre music stand, placed in the hallway right outside the Blue Room. The intruder *should* have dashed out of the back door in the kitchen and jumped over the fence. But he was greedy and refused to give up the heavy sack over his back. Ilaria charged and whacked him as hard as she could on the back.

He thumped against the wall and dropped, silverware clattering out of his sack—Ily's own pillowcase, stuffed with gifts that their neighbors and friends had brought to Chia's party.

Rage filled Ilaria, and she set down the music stand, breathing hard. Then she knelt and studied the thief's face by the moonlight. She didn't know him, which meant he had to be from out of town. When he grunted in pain, she gave a hard kick to his ribs. "You . . . you scoundrel. Get out of here, you thief. Get out before I—"

"Ily?" Chiara whispered from the stairs. Her sister crept down from her room, holding a lone candle. "Ily, I heard a crash. What—"

Chiara saw the body on the floor, and the anxious crease on her brow turned into shock.

"He was stealing your presents," said Ily, waving a tired

hand at the thief. Chia held her candle over his face. Gray hair and a poorly cropped beard. "Doesn't look like he's from Pariva. Do you know him?"

Her sister actually shuddered. "I saw him by the tavern today."

"Just our luck," Ily grumbled. She dusted her hands and grabbed the man's feet, lugging him out of the door. "He's unconscious. Help me get him out of here."

"You're going to put him on the street?"

"We're definitely not putting him on the daybed," retorted Ilaria; she knew exactly what Chiara was thinking. "He tried to rob us!"

Together, they hauled the thief onto the roadside, and Ily dusted her hands as if she'd just dealt with an enormous rat. "I'm guessing this isn't how you thought you'd spend your last night in Pariva."

"It certainly will be memorable."

Chiara knelt and took out her handkerchief, using it to wipe a smear of blood off the man's forehead where Ily had struck him. Under their neighbor's wan lantern light, Ily was proud to see that a hideous bruise was already forming.

Her sister, on the other hand, loosened the shawl from her shoulders and placed it over the thief.

"For this crook?"

"Have some compassion, Ily. It's a cold night."

Ily rolled her eyes as Chia got up to go back in the house. When her sister wasn't looking, Ilaria yanked the shawl back. Then she followed Chiara inside and locked the door.

Ilaria let out a yawn as she entered her room to sleep. She was certain she'd left her bed unmade, but the wrinkles in her blanket had been smoothed, and her pillows were neatly fluffed. Mamma had stopped making her bed ages ago, and had all but given up censuring Ilaria for her messiness. Ilaria crossed her arms at Chiara. "I don't need you to make my bed."

"I was waiting for you to come back."

"Why?" Ilaria muttered. "Mamma and Papa didn't care enough to stay awake."

"Where were you?" asked Chiara, choosing to ignore her sarcasm. "I was worried."

"I went for a walk by the sea."

"Alone?"

"Certainly not with you." Ilaria didn't regret the barb even when her sister flinched. She wanted it to hurt. She needed Chia to hurt.

"Doesn't matter." Ily jumped onto her bed, instantly creating a ripple of wrinkles. "No one missed me."

"I did."

Chia's voice was soft, and as her candle flickered,

illuminating her face, Ilaria saw that her cheeks were wet. Had she been crying?

Regret pricked at her, but Ily pushed it aside. She crossed her arms and turned away from her sister.

"If you care about me so much, then don't go tomorrow," Ilaria said. It was a test she knew Chia would fail. Still, she dared to hope. "Don't leave with the fairies."

Don't leave me, she almost added.

The mattress dipped under Chia's weight as she sat on the edge. She said, quietly, "How does music make you feel?"

A flash of irritation rose in Ily's chest. "What does that have to do with anything?"

"Just answer."

Ilaria grabbed a pillow and hugged it close. It had been a long night, and she was too tired to be petulant, so she answered, "It makes me feel alive."

"That's how helping people makes me feel."

"It's not the same. Helping people isn't a . . . a . . ."

"A job?"

"You're not a doctor, Chia. You're not saving lives."

"In their own way, fairies do save lives," responded Chiara. "Doctors heal the body. Fairies look after the heart."

Ilaria hugged her pillow tighter. She didn't want to understand. She didn't want to listen.

Chia scooted into the center of the bed and pried the pillow from her sister. "It sounds silly, but there's always been this feeling I get—inside me—when someone's unhappy. It makes me unhappy, too, until I help them feel better."

"That's nonsense."

"Is it?"

Chia was serious, which made Ily frown. "You're saying you can feel how I'm feeling? Like, you can read my mind?"

"I can't read your mind. I can just sense that you're unhappy . . . with me."

Ilaria snorted. "Didn't seem to work for you that week when you were keeping secrets from me."

"I'm not very good at it yet," said Chiara. "And it helps when I'm focused."

"So what is your fairy sense telling you about me now?"

Chia pursed her lips, the way she always did when she was about to say a truth Ilaria wouldn't like. "Right now you're angry. You wish you could come with me."

At that, Ilaria finally let go of the pillow. "I *am* jealous," she admitted. "You get to leave Pariva and see the world. While I'm stuck here."

"Stuck here?" Chiara chuckled. "Next year, you'll be in Vallan studying with Maria Linda, the most celebrated prima donna in Esperia. Before long, you'll be gracing Accordo and the world's greatest opera houses." She tucked a stray brown lock behind her sister's ear. "You're destined for an amazing adventure, Ily. I can't wait to see how far you'll go."

Ilaria jerked her head away and twirled her hair back in place. But when she spoke, her words had only a trace of their earlier bitterness. "You *were* the best accompanist I've had. Pity I'll have to find someone else."

"Yes." Chia poked her arm. "Too bad Geppetto doesn't play the harpsichord. He found you at the sea, I'm guessing. That's why you're back so late."

Ilaria threw her pillow at Chia. "I should have known you sent him after me! You're sneakier than I took you for."

Chia caught the pillow. "I thought you two would get along." She winked. "It's my special fairy sense again."

"Your special fairy sense," Ily repeated. The corner of her mouth twitched, and a smile peeked out of her frown despite herself. "He was nice. He walked me home."

"See?"

"See what?" Ilaria crossed her arms. "I'm not going to marry him. He wants to stay in Pariva forever. I'm getting out of here the first chance I get."

"I'm not trying to play matchmaker," Chiara said, laughing. "I only want you and Geppetto to be friends. You'll need friends who will stay by you through good times and bad. Geppetto would do that for you. He's a good person."

"Unlike Simona and Beatrice."

"Simona and Beatrice don't always have your best intentions at heart. I heard what they said about your singing, Ily. It was unkind, and untrue."

"What if they're right, though?" Ily said, voicing her fears. "What if I *do* need your help? Hundreds of girls will be applying to study with Maria Linda." She sighed. "Girls who've grown up seeing operas at the Accordo and can afford acting and singing lessons. Girls who can play both ingénue and vixen and have four-octave ranges. Girls who can reach a high F without straining."

"Worrying about your competition will make you neither a better singer nor a happier one," said Chiara. "Focus on yourself. Which reminds me." She reached into her pocket for her money pouch, neatly tied with a blue bow. She placed it on Ily's lap. "Here, open it. This should help you buy that new dress you've been longing for and help you settle into a new place in Vallan."

Ily stared at her sister, then into the bag. There had to be a hundred oros inside, over a year's worth of savings.

"Chia!" Ilaria breathed, tongue-tied. "You can't—How did you . . ."

"I saved a little every day from my shifts working at the bakery, and Mamma let me sell some of her flowers. It's hardly enough for life in the big city, but it should help you get started."

Ily swallowed hard, so moved she could hardly speak.

Chia tucked the loose strand of brown hair back behind Ilaria's ear. "It doesn't matter whether I'm gone for one month or one decade. I'll miss everything about Pariva. I'll even miss the smelly fish street on the way to our old school. I'll miss Niccolo and Mamma and Papa. Our mornings playing music together. Most of all, I'll miss you."

I'll miss you, too, Ilaria started to say, but then she noticed that a star had risen above the moon out the window.

"Look!" she cried, pointing outside. "Is that a Wishing Star?"

Chiara squinted. "I think so."

Ilaria pulled her sister toward the window, planting their elbows on the sill. "Let's make a wish. You're still allowed to, right? You're not a fairy yet."

"I think so."

The sisters knelt side by side, and Ilaria mouthed a silent wish.

"What did you ask for?" Chiara asked.

Ilaria grinned. "You should know that if I tell you, it won't come true." She scooted to her sister's side, leaning her head on Chiara's shoulder the way she had when they were children. "You'll just have to wait and find out—like everyone else."

CHAPTER FOURTEEN

The Belmagio household was an uneasy balance of laughter and sorrow as the family nibbled on leftover cake, made lighthearted digs at Ilaria's walk with Geppetto, and danced around the topic of Chia's departure.

"Robbers tried to take our silverware," Ily recounted. She embroidered the truth with some extra details: "They had knives on them, and they were taller than bears! You should have seen their faces when I thwacked them on the head with the music stand."

"So that explains why it's cracked," said Niccolo. "Maybe Mr. Tommaso can repair it. You wouldn't mind a visit to Geppetto, I hear."

Ily glared while Mr. Belmagio chuckled at his children.

Mrs. Belmagio was not in the mood for humor. "You're not eating, Chia," she observed.

"It's rather early for such a feast," replied Chiara.

"Nonsense. Here, you didn't take any of the almond cookies." Mrs. Belmagio plucked her own cookies, toast, and sliced meats and piled them onto Chiara's plate. "I packed you extra bread and cookies in your bag, too. There should be enough for a good week. Who knows what kind of food fairies eat, or if they have to eat at all! But don't forget your meals, my dove. Three meals a day will keep your energy up and bring you sweet dreams."

"I know, Mamma," said Chia softly. "Thank you."

At last Mrs. Belmagio set down her jam knife, her napkin trembling as she dabbed at her eyes and sniffed. "My sweet, sweet girl. If it doesn't work out with the fairies, you come straight back, understood? You're always welcome home. All my children are. Remember that." Mrs. Belmagio smiled her pinched, sad smile—the one that told Chiara that her mother was secretly hoping she wouldn't find her place among the fairies, but felt awful about it.

"It isn't farewell," Chia said, setting down her fork. "It's only a trial for a few months. I'll be back."

"I know," replied her mother. Her voice quavered. "But it's the last time you'll be my Chia, my little dove that

I raised for eighteen years. Whether or not you take up a wand, you'll be different the next time we see you. And we'll be different to you."

Mr. Belmagio had been quiet during breakfast, but now his spectacles fogged. He wiped them on the bottom of his shirt, a habit Mrs. Belmagio always fussed about but overlooked now.

"This is not a path I could have predicted, Chia, but it is the path that has chosen you. No matter where it takes you, remember, home will be here."

"I will, Papa," Chia whispered.

It was nearly time, and the Belmagios gathered in the Blue Room, their hearts never more sad and anxious and proud to hear the clock chime.

Tears pooled in her parents' eyes, and Chiara was crying, too. She turned to Niccolo. "Take care of Mamma and Papa while I'm away. Make sure Papa doesn't lose his reading glasses—they're usually on top of his writing desk. And help Mamma warm her milk: simmer for six minutes."

"I will," promised her brother.

"Be good to Ily," said Chiara to her brother, hating how her words sounded so permanent and formal. "Don't fight too much."

Last was Ilaria, and a lump formed in Chia's throat. Without saying anything, the two sisters hugged each other.

Then Ily blurted, "How long will you be gone exactly? Will you write us?"

Chiara didn't know the answer, and Ily never got a response, because Agata had appeared. The older woman leaned against the clock as if she'd been there all along.

"The Violet Fairy!" Mr. and Mrs. Belmagio exclaimed, bowing in respect.

"No, no, none of that," said Agata, motioning for them to get up. "I'm not a queen. Not even a lady."

She lifted herself from the clock. "As for your question, Ilaria—correspondence between the fairy realm and Esperia is not encouraged."

"Why not?" Ily asked.

Mrs. Belmagio sent a warning look at her younger daughter, but Agata didn't mind the question. "Over the years, we've found that it is best for our initiates to focus on their lessons rather than have one foot at home and one foot in the fairy realm. Chiara will have until the winter to complete her training—five months."

"Five months means she'll be back by my birthday," said Ilaria, making the calculations aloud. "What happens after that?"

"Then she will have a week at home to make up her mind. Either Chiara becomes a full-fledged fairy, or she returns home to the life she led before."

"What happens if she stays—"

Mrs. Belmagio took Ilaria's arm, urging her to be quiet. For once Ily obeyed, but her face twisted into a frown.

"All will be explained in due time," Agata promised. She turned to Chia. "You've packed?"

"Yes," was all Chiara could say.

"If you are ready, will you come with me?"

If I'm ready. Chia wasn't sure she'd ever be ready. It was the heaviest step she ever took to reach Agata's side. She pivoted slowly so she could face her parents, her brother, her sister. "Goodbye," she mouthed, so quietly the sound barely came out.

Agata waved her wand in a gentle arc, and a soft silvery light enveloped them.

"Don't forget us!" Ily called after her. "Don't forget to come back for my birthday."

Chia's throat tightened, and as she nodded, she felt the weight in her stomach anchoring her to home. In a flash, she left behind the only life she had ever known.

They were flying! Chiara could hardly believe it, but the rush in her stomach did not lie. The clouds were closer than she'd ever seen before—they drifted by in a stream of white that she could reach out and touch. When she looked down, her home was a yellow dot against a cluster of brown and red roofs, a patchwork of fields and pastures, a pool of sea, and then a lining of mountains. All too soon, the town she'd known all her life became smaller and smaller until it was smaller than her thumbnail, and then it disappeared altogether.

They pierced the clouds and made deep into the sky. This was where the light became a gauzy cloak over Chiara's vision, and she had to close her eyes.

The rush in her stomach returned, accelerating as they soared higher and higher. But when Chiara finally opened her eyes again, it was over.

Her feet touched upon ground, and a cloud of silvery dust bloomed up to her waist. Her clothes shimmered, and the checkered cotton dress she was wearing became an elegant white gown with a silver cord around the waist.

"Your apprentice gown," explained Agata. She gestured ahead. "Welcome to the Wishing Star."

Before her was a village not unlike Pariva, only every cottage was a different color: rose, violet, mahogany, marigold. Burgundy, magenta, and pearl. Even the flowers in the gardens matched the colors of the houses, and trees made of gold and copper and silver lined the shimmering streets. In the center was a house made of crystal, its windows stained with hearts of every color in the town.

As soon as her gaze fell upon the house, its door opened,

and over a dozen fairies filed outside, each wearing a warm smile.

"Welcome, Chiara," greeted the first fairy. Chia recognized her immediately as one of the Three Fairies in the center of Pariva.

In real life, she was a head shorter than Chiara, but the presence she carried—emanating pride and kindness and courage—made her seem like the tallest person Chiara had ever met. She wore entirely gold, from the bells on her slippers to the gilded leaves sprinkled against her gray ringlets. "We've been looking forward to welcoming you. I am Mirabella the Gold, the mother fairy of sorts, but really just the longest serving on the Wishing Star. You'll find that being a fairy isn't too different from being a girl in Pariva. You'll live in a cottage where you eat and sleep, and you'll find companionship among your fellow fairies."

Mirabella gestured at the others behind her. "For now, you might find it easier to remember our titles rather than our names. I am the Golden Fairy." She curtsied, and the fairies behind her introduced themselves one by one—the Rose Fairy, the Orange Fairy, the Silver Fairy, and so on it went. "Your title you will choose after you complete your training with the Violet Fairy. Do you have any questions?"

Chiara had hundreds of questions, but she settled for the one that nagged at her the loudest. A glance at all the fairies showed her a troupe of men and women from all around Esperia, and of varying ages. Yet all of them had an ancientness about their eyes, as if they'd been on the Wishing Star for many, many years.

"How long does one serve as a fairy?" she asked.

"While you reside on the Wishing Star, time shall pass differently for you," replied Mirabella. "You will serve as long as you wish."

A vague response that only half answered her question. Yet judging from the firmness of Mirabella's tone, Chiara wouldn't get more explanation from the head fairy. At least not right now.

"And each fairy is represented by a color?" Chiara asked.

"My favorite color was always violet," Agata said, "and Mirabella's gold. They started off as nicknames, but they seem to have stuck."

Peri, the Orange Fairy, stepped forward and offered her a friendly grin. "Blue is available, in case you were wondering. Agata told us it's your favorite. We sense the color's been waiting for you."

Chiara was touched. "Thank you."

Peri picked up the hoard of books floating at his side and his smile widened. "If you have any other questions, always feel free to find me in the Archives. Though I doubt there will be much I can answer that Agata cannot. Along with Mirabella, she's one of the oldest fairies on the Wishing Star. She's trained many of us, myself included. You'll be in capable hands."

"Thank you," said Chiara.

Peri smiled amiably. "I was in your shoes once. Nervous, and uncertain what would happen. I'll warn you that our duties are many, and the work can be heavy and nonstop, but nothing will make your heart fuller than to see the changes you will make on each life."

The words did warm Chiara, and she smiled back.

"A wonderful welcome." Mirabella clapped. "The rest of us must depart for Esperia, but Agata will give you a tour of the Wishing Star. We look forward to getting to know you, Chiara Belmagio."

One by one, the fairies wished her well on her first day. Then they lifted their wands, identical silver rods with pointed stars at the tip, and disappeared. Leaving Agata and Chiara alone on the Wishing Star.

"Well, short and sweet as always," her mentor remarked. "You'll find we don't waste time around here. One of my favorite things about being a fairy." Agata snapped her fingers, and every lamp along the road lit.

Chiara stared in wonderment, but Agata had already begun strolling down the starlit road. "Hurry, hurry," the

Violet Fairy trilled. "We have much material to cover, and I have to show you to your house."

My house?

Chia dashed after the Violet Fairy, marveling at how each step on the silvery road emitted a note from her favorite song.

"Our tour will be short," said Agata, "because there isn't that much to see. We spend most of our time in Esperia doing fieldwork—responding to distress calls and granting wishes. Your time on the Wishing Star will be either to rest, eat, research, or consult your fellow fairies." Agata pointed at the crystal building in the center of the Wishing Star. It looked like a modest castle, with two towers on either side and spires that changed color every time Chiara blinked.

"That's the Star Center," said Agata. "When the bell on the tallest spire chimes, it's a call for an official meeting. It's where we meet for official business, and where you may access the Archives. I myself go every morning—the Archives hold records of what every fairy has done during their tenure, and it's where you may research should you have questions about any person in Esperia.

"Once you have your wand, you'll be able to ring that bell on the top spire there."

Chiara looked up, spying a crystal bell that hung suspended over the rest of the building.

"Chime once if you need guidance from a fellow fairy. Chime thrice if you're in a pickle, and every fairy available will find you no matter where they are."

"What sort of emergencies might a fairy encounter?" Chiara asked.

"Now that is a question best answered while on the job," said Agata. "But I'll say that we are not without enemies, Chiara. Oh, don't look so agitated. Come, let's continue on with happier things. Look, there's Mirabella's Wishing Well."

"Wishing Well?"

"Every fairy has one on their cottage grounds," explained Agata, circling Mirabella's. She motioned for Chiara to come closer. "From it, you may see wishes that are being made in Esperia." Agata pointed her wand at the sparkling waters within. "How high its waters flow reveal how much magic you currently have on Earth. Magic is limited, you see. It buds from bravery, kindness, and nobleness of heart. So the more we spread hope, the more magic we have to continue our work. It's a rather sympathetic cycle, I like to think. Just take care not to overexert yourself."

They moved on toward a cottage behind a brook of pink water and trees with marbled leaves and star-shaped fruit. Chiara couldn't stop staring at the otherworldly garden, so much that she barely paid attention as Agata approached an empty field to their right.

"This will be your new home," the Violet Fairy said, waving at the lot.

"My home?" Chiara blinked. "But it's . . ."

Agata's mouth twitched with humor, and from behind her back, she waved her wand in a grand circle. Before Chiara's eyes, a cottage sprang from the ground, with a pale blue door and windows with painted doves.

"Oh, my!" Chia exclaimed.

Inside, the cottage was sparsely furnished, with four wooden chairs covered in blue cotton cushions, a table with hearts carved along the edges, an oven that smelled like chocolate and cherries, and a harpsichord in the corner by the window. But it was everything Chiara could have dreamt of. A home of her own.

"This spot is one of my favorites," Agata narrated. "Absolutely lovely. Look there, you've a view of the Silver Brook, and in the mornings the moon crickets sing most beautifully."

Chiara inhaled. All the smells she had loved most from home—the wild grass, the pine cones from the trees, the fresh loaves Papa baked before dawn, the musty parchment from Ily's music paper. They flooded her nostrils all at once, as if she'd brought them with her.

"It's perfect," said Chiara, clasping her hands. "It looks like it's straight out of Pariva."

"I had a feeling you might say that," Agata said. She spotted a patch of dust on one of the chairs and swept it clean with her finger. "I designed it to remind you of home, but I set down only the basics. Whatever doesn't suit you, change it as you wish. You'll have plenty of time to spruce up the place however you like, and we have all tastes here." She gestured to the right, where the Pearl Fairy had designed a house that greatly resembled a clamshell. "You'll want something of your own. Trust me.

"While you're on the Wishing Star, you needn't worry about budgeting your magic. It's different from Esperia. Here, all you need do is ask, and what you've requested will come. Same with your meals, unless you prefer to cook yourself. Once we're in Esperia, it'll be a different story. You won't have magic until I give you your wand. Until then, the dust will do."

"The dust?" Chiara repeated.

"Stardust, of course." Agata chuckled. "It's the stuff of hope and dreams and joy. The whole house is made of it, and some goes into our magic, too. Go on, try it. Ask for something."

"I . . . I wish for a cup of juice, please," said Chiara slowly. She wasn't sure to whom to address her request. "Orange, with a hint of lemon, like Niccolo makes."

To her astonishment, a cup of juice appeared in her hand.

"Stars, Chia. You haven't conjured a ghost." Agata laughed as Chia jumped, startled. "Try it."

Taking a breath to calm herself, Chiara tipped the cup to her lips. "Tart and sweet." Her eyes misted, and she had to set the juice down on a table before she dropped it. "Just like my brother makes. It's delicious."

"Of course it is."

The cup suddenly weighed like lead, and Chiara couldn't take another sip. She'd only been gone from home a few hours, and already she missed her family fiercely.

Agata touched her shoulder. "It'll get easier, Chia. Every day.

"Are you ready for your first lesson, or do you want to rest and finish unpacking?"

Chiara had forgotten about the bundle of belongings she'd brought with her. She didn't have much: some sheet music, the quilt her grandmother had made her long ago, a few small paintings, the dove Geppetto had carved her, and the food her mother had packed.

"I'm ready to learn."

The Violet Fairy led her to a door with a silver knob shaped like a star.

The door led to Chiara's Wishing Well in the garden. As soon as she came near, a pale blue light fanned from the well, and in the light emerged a map of Esperia.

"Once you receive your wand," said Agata, "this map will show you the areas that you have been assigned to observe. But for now . . ." She clapped, and thousands of golden dots appeared on the map.

"What are those?"

"A gold light indicates people who've made a wish recently. Your duty will be to listen to each one, and to deem whether or not they are worthy of our attention and magic."

"There are so many!"

Agata chuckled. "The life of a fairy is a busy one."

Chia folded her arms over the lip of the well, studying the gold lights. "How will I know whether a wish is worthy of my attention?"

"That is tricky," Agata admitted. "There are many kinds of wishes: selfless ones, selfish ones, and all the sorts in between. You'll hear people asking all the time to become richer, cleverer, or more beautiful. You'll hear couples wishing to have a child, widowers wishing to find love again, and children wishing that their parents' business would improve. All of them, we listen to, but we tend to listen most closely to the wishes that come from the heart."

"Then we grant their wish," said Chiara.

"To an extent," allowed Agata. "You'll find it's best not to grant someone's wish in its entirety. Take your sister, for instance. Ilaria. She wants to be a famous opera singer, doesn't she?"

It shouldn't have surprised Chiara that the Violet Fairy knew. "Yes."

"Has she asked you to help her on that journey?"

"No."

That seemed to surprise Agata. "Well, she might in the future. And if she does . . . firstly, it cannot be you, Chiara. Fairies are not permitted to consider the wishes of anyone they used to know. Secondly, if another fairy *were* to help her, it wouldn't be by granting her fame or even admission into the conservatory. That would be unfair, you see. We would simply give her the tools to use what she already has—her voice, her charm, her ambition—to the highest of her ability."

"What sort of tools?"

"A train ticket to Vallan, for instance," said Agata sensibly. "A coat so she wouldn't catch cold during the winter months; mittens and a hat, too. Perhaps a bottle that never runs out of water, for a touch of magic. Singers need to stay hydrated, or so I'm told."

Ily would have wrinkled her nose and said, *That's all?* Chiara merely blinked. "A train ticket and winter clothes?"

"What, did you think we'd give her a ball gown

covered in rubies and have butterflies fly out of her sleeves whenever she sings?" Laughing, Agata shook her head. "You've been reading too many fairy tales. Those stories are fluff made for the romantics. We mostly give a nudge in the right direction." She paused. "But every now and then, we do encounter a situation that deserves special attention. That would be when you consult with your fellow fairies."

"I see," mused Chiara. "What about wishes we don't listen to?"

"We listen to every wish, but we *never* respond to wishes that intend ill harm toward another. Those are wicked, and we do not pay them any heed."

"Why listen to them, then?"

Agata's voice went tight. "Because there are other fairies, who dwell in the arena of evil. And it is our duty to undo as much of the damage that they cause as possible."

Upon Chia's look of confusion, Agata went on, "We call them the Heartless. They're led by Amorale the Gray and Larissa the Green. They and their kind specialize in fostering wickedness and envy, wrath and hatred. They take the seeds of a malevolent thought and plant it in a human's heart, nurturing it until the heart turns rotten."

Chiara did not like the sound of Amorale and Larissa. "Why would they do that?"

"Excellent question," Agata said, leaning forward. "Just as we fairies gain power from the joy we bring, the Heartless gain strength from the misery they sow. Once we begin our lessons, you'll find it can be challenging to encourage people to be kind to one another, or to bring joy when there's pain, sadness. In those cases, it's far easier to do the opposite, to plant seeds of misunderstanding and cause people to be angry and cruel to one another."

Agata grimaced. "Larissa and Amorale were two of us, but once they found it was easier to gain power by preying upon weathered hearts . . . they formed the Heartless."

"Hearts that are bitter or angry or in grief are the most vulnerable," Chiara said, understanding.

"Yes, and that's not even the worst of it. After they've heaped misery upon someone's life, they'll offer to take their pain away. But there's always a cost, and rare is it the case that anyone can pay."

"It's a game to them," Chiara murmured.

"Indeed, and those who lose become shadows of their former selves . . . and their misery fuels the Heartless's future ploys. It's a vicious cycle, but fortunately, most of their work can be undone."

"Most," Chiara repeated.

Agata's tone darkened. "On rare occasion, Larissa and Amorale offer someone the chance to be like them. But to prove themselves, they must destroy their hearts—for good. That's why they're called—"

"The Heartless," Chiara realized in horror.

"Once done, the damage is irreversible." Agata stared into the well. After a sigh, she clapped once, and the map floating above the Wishing Well shuttered.

The Violet Fairy regarded Chiara. "I told you that granting wishes is only a small part of what we do. I believe that the people who need us most are those who are vulnerable to the Heartless's influence. It doesn't mean they are bad—or wicked, even. After all, most people crave something they cannot have: fame, money, power . . . but these temptations are often a gateway to attracting the Heartless's attention."

"How can we help them?" Chiara asked.

"For a start, we help them listen to their conscience."

Conscience. Agata had used that word before, when they'd first met.

"I mentioned before that you have a strong sense of empathy, Chiara. It keeps you attuned to how others are feeling and gives you your compassion. Something all potential fairies must exhibit, for it is our empathy that keeps us from being cold and merciless like the Heartless.

"But what I also noted was that you have a powerful conscience as well, Chiara. Empathy without a conscience is like living with only half a heart. Your conscience is what motivates you to act. It is our compass, guiding us in the direction of doing what's right.

"Unfortunately, not everyone chooses to follow theirs. We fairies try to give a nudge in the right direction, but we can only do so much. No magic can make someone's mind up for them, and we have no control over a person's will.

"Which brings me to you, Chiara. You must know—becoming a fairy will require certain sacrifices that you may not be willing to make." Agata's smile turned tight. "At the end of your training, I will explain fully. Once I do, you will have one week to decide whether you wish to stay with us. When that time comes, there is no right or wrong answer. No good or bad decision. Listen to your heart, and make your decision without any regrets. Understood?"

"Yes."

But as Agata continued with the lesson, Chiara's thoughts were full of wishes and questions and broken hearts.

CHAPTER FIFTEEN

Lessons with the Violet Fairy were nothing like going to school and learning from books and reciting sums and figures. Every day, Chiara shadowed the Violet Fairy across Esperia, learning firsthand what it meant to attend to the wishes of the brave, the truthful, and the selfless. They helped reunite a father and son lost in the forest by dropping a ball of twine that would lead them to each other. They showed a young woman how to brew a soup that might help her and her husband conceive a child. They helped a young man with no family find employment in town as a cook.

Chiara loved every moment of it.

She especially loved learning to use the magic in her Wishing Well. When she approached it, within its waters would appear a map of all Esperia, with countless bright lights dotting the land.

"Each one represents a person's heart," Agata explained. "See the different colors? White symbolizes people currently contented. Blue, people with wishes or needs to be attended."

"What about red?" asked Chiara.

"Red lights are causes for immediate attention."

A pang of worry struck Chiara, and though Agata couldn't read her mind, the older woman could certainly sense her concern. "You miss your family, don't you? Especially your sister. Why don't you ask to see them?"

Chiara spoke into the Wishing Well. "Will you show me my family—the Belmagios in Pariva?"

Almost immediately, a tall wave of water rose from the well, and her hometown emerged on the map. A watery outline of her family's house appeared along Constanza Street, and to Chiara's great relief, the four lights within were bright and white.

Mamma, Papa, Niccolo—and Ilaria. They were all happy.

That cheered Chiara, but the Violet Fairy's face had gone somber.

"What is it?" Chiara asked.

"Nothing," said Agata, before she quickly amended, "Nothing that I won't explain in due time." She smiled warmly. "Your family will be fine, Chiara. You have nothing to worry about."

The Violet Fairy's somber mood had vanished, but Chiara still ached with curiosity. She had a feeling whatever Agata was keeping from her had to do with the sacrifice she was supposed to make. Her mind had been reeling about it for days, trying to imagine what it could be.

In the silence that followed, Chiara observed the lights around her home. Niccolo's was the most radiant, which she sensed meant his courtship with Sofia was going well. Mamma's and Papa's, too, were clear, which warmed Chiara's heart to see. But Ily's—Ily's had been bright an instant ago, yet it made the barest flicker now—from white to blue.

Chiara frowned and leaned forward to get a closer look. But Ily's light went steady once more. "Agata, did you see that—?"

The Violet Fairy waved over the map, bringing Chiara's home closer into view. But as she focused the corner of Pariva on Ilaria, a faint speck of red appeared along the edges of the Lyre Sea.

Agata gasped.

"It's Monstro," she exclaimed. "Come, we must ring for the others. This might be our chance to deal with him once and for all!"

Within an hour, the Wishing Fairies had cornered the great and terrible Monstro in the Lyre Sea. On their way there, Agata had explained that he was no ordinary whale, but a monster born of the cruel wishes the Heartless had granted. Then the fairies jumped to their task while Chia observed. It impressed her how efficiently they worked together. Peri and two other fairies immediately set to rescuing the fisher-men who had encountered Monstro, and sent them sailing home safely on a raft.

The rest of the fairies concentrated on restraining the whale.

"All together now," Agata cried to her colleagues as magic sizzled from their wands. Their powers braided into a thick ring of light that encircled the beast, trapping him so he could not escape.

As the only one without a wand or wings, Chiara stayed on a floating cloud that Agata had conjured for her. She leaned over the edge of the cloud, watching intently as Monstro struggled against the fairies.

"He's teeming with anger and the need to wreak havoc,"

said Peri, catching his breath on Chiara's cloud after he sent away the fishermen's raft. "It makes him an incredible source of power for the Heartless."

"What do you mean, a source of power?"

"That's how Monstro grew so large to begin with. Ever since the Heartless created him, he's been full of wrath and hunger. The more he devoured, the larger he became. The fear he inspires benefits the Heartless, you see, for they're able to wield it as power."

"The same way we wield hope," Chiara murmured, remembering Agata's lessons.

The whale was powerful, that was no question. Even against twenty fairies, he held his own. The battle would be close.

As the braids of magic intensified and wrapped around him, Monstro leapt up from the sea, jaws wide.

Chiara's instincts were on fire. Seconds before Monstro would have devoured her mentor, she jumped off her cloud. "Agata!" she cried, pushing the Violet Fairy out of harm's way.

"That was close," Agata muttered, catching her protégé by the arms so they stayed afloat. "Thank you, my dear."

One after another, Monstro attacked the fairies.

"It seems twenty of us aren't enough," Agata told Chiara. "Will you help?"

"Can I?"

Agata nodded. "Hold my wand with me, and think of your fondest dreams. We want to put Monstro to sleep—ideally, for a long, long time."

A tingle shot up Chiara's spine as she grabbed one end of Agata's wand. Power coursed through her and out the wand, joining with the other fairies' magic.

What was more, as she held Agata's wand, she could *feel* the fear and awesome wrath coming from Monstro. It was a taste of wild power, so intense and strong she felt she could do anything with it.

Now she understood why Monstro was so valuable to the Heartless. His wrath was never-ending, and it took little effort for her to sense that his wells of strength were immense.

Chiara pushed Monstro's power aside and focused on Agata's instructions. She was supposed to wield the wand while thinking of her fondest dreams. She thought about all the mornings she had spent with Ily, making music together, making messes in their parents' bakery kitchen, tossing pistachio cookies and chocolate cakes at each other.

Was it her imagination, or did a stream of pale blue magic course out of Agata's wand? She couldn't tell, but it didn't matter.

Monstro's cold green eyes began to close. The fairies' spell was working!

It felt like forever before Chiara could be sure, but at last, the whale went still. He was asleep, and he sank deep into the sea until Chiara couldn't see him at all.

The fairies all let out a jubilant cheer.

"It's done!" Mirabella exclaimed. "Finally! Let's all return to the Wishing Star. We have much to celebrate today."

Even Agata let out a whoop of joy. "Well done, Chiara. You helped us."

"Only a little."

"More than a little." Agata hid a smile, and Chiara wondered if she'd seen that hint of blue that had shot out from her wand. "It'll be a blow to the Heartless when they learn that Monstro is missing and that his fury has been silenced."

Agata turned to leave with the other fairies, but Chiara still had questions. "What if they find him?" she asked.

"They will eventually," said Agata through her teeth. "But let's hope that's quite some time from now."

"Peri said that Monstro is a source of power for the Heartless."

"Sneaking in a lesson, are we?" Agata smiled at her fondly. "Yes, he's their most precious creation. But it's thanks to you that we've been able to track him. I would never have guessed his den would be so close to Pariva."

Chiara lowered her voice. "I felt his power, when I took hold of your wand. It was . . . unlike anything I've ever experienced. That ruthlessness and hunger . . . there was so much, I . . ."

As her voice trailed, Agata touched Chiara's arm. "I'm glad you had a taste of what the Heartless can do. It'll serve you well in the future . . . but as your mentor, I must caution you not to get too close."

"I won't."

"There will be days when we have to make difficult decisions—whom to help with our magic, and who to trust will be fine without it. Our powers are finite and have limits, Chiara. One of the reasons those limits are put into place is so we do not stray toward the path of the Heartless. A young fairy not too different from yourself made that error many years ago. He was trying to help an old woman who had fallen sick, but he'd run out of magic and there was no time to seek more, so he thought he could borrow some of the Heartless's power."

"What happened to him?"

"As you know, we have strict rules about our inter-actions with the Heartless. His wand was taken away, and he was sent home. Banished from the Wishing Star forever."

Chiara swallowed hard. "But his intentions were good."

"They were, but rules are rules, Chiara. Put in place for a reason, especially since you know how the Heartless themselves came to be. We must be careful."

Agata chuckled at Chiara's anxious expression. "Don't worry, it won't happen to you—if you do end up joining us. Now come on. If we don't head home soon, all the celebration cake will be gone. And it's got blackberry jam, which I hear you love." She stifled a yawn. "After that, all of us fairies will need a nice long nap ourselves. You'll have to excuse us all for being in a kerfuffle the next few days. That slumber spell's a strong one, and it's drained most of us. I suspect even I won't make it through today's celebration."

Agata extended a hand, but before taking it, Chiara glanced down at the Lyre Sea, taking in the slow ripples that swept across the water.

Something about the banished fairy's story had unsettled her. Chiara had never had trouble following rules. She'd never had trouble sorting whether decisions were right or wrong. After all, even Ily liked to tease her about it:

Not everything's good or bad, Chia, Ily had said to her. *You can't rely on some fairy voice to tell you what to do.*

But what if, one day, good intentions led her to make a decision that the fairies didn't agree with?

Look at you, thinking about this when you haven't even decided to become a fairy yet. Chiara laughed silently at herself. *Worry about it if and when the time comes.*

Shrugging off her concern, she took Agata's hand. As the two flew back to the Wishing Star, a last ripple brushed across the Lyre Sea.

Then the water went still.

CHAPTER SIXTEEN

Geppetto whistled as he put on his hat, doffed his apron, and strolled to the Belmagio Bakery to pick up lunch. Usually, he could afford only a small cookie or a slice of bread rather than a full lunch. But today, he was going to buy an entire sandwich. Coffee, too.

Why was he in such a jolly mood?

Because of the music box he'd been making for Ilaria. After weeks—no, months—of tinkering with it whenever he could, he'd mostly finished carving and smoothing out the exterior of the box. But he'd had trouble making it, well, musical.

Setting the melody of the Nightingale Aria into the box had been the bulk of his difficulty, but last night, he'd managed to inscribe the first two notes. A promising breakthrough. If his progress continued at this rate, he might even finish it before Ilaria's birthday, two short months away.

Still whistling to himself, he approached the main part of Pariva. Autumn was here, and crisp golden leaves showered down from the trees, landing on Geppetto's hat and shoulders.

As he swept them off his shoulder, he cast a glance at Mrs. Tappa's hat shop. Ilaria was inside, tying ribbons around the latest designs. When she saw him, a bright smile touched her face, and she waved.

For once, Geppetto wasn't shy about waving back. And when she poked her head out of the door, shouting, "Geppetto!" his smile widened and he went to greet her in person.

"Heading to the bakery?" she said. "Let me guess, another square of shortbread?"

"A sandwich today," said Geppetto.

"Ah. You're branching out. What's the occasion?"

Geppetto felt himself growing taller. "Can't say. It's a surprise."

Ily raised an eyebrow. "A surprise?"

"You'll see . . . in a few months."

"A few months?" Ilaria tilted her head. "Will Chiara be back in time to witness this surprise?"

Ily's voice had the faintest strain as she spoke her sister's name. In the weeks since Chiara had left, Geppetto noticed that Ilaria tried to bring her up whenever she could in a conversation. Those were the moments he could tell just how much she missed her sister.

"I would expect so," Geppetto said, not knowing how else to answer. "She did promise to be back in time for your birthday, didn't she?"

"This surprise is related to my birthday? Now my curiosity is piqued, Geppetto."

Geppetto's eyes widened. "No . . . no . . . that's not what I meant."

Ily laughed. She clearly enjoyed tormenting him. "At least give me a clue."

He shook his head.

"What about . . ." Ily ducked inside the shop and returned with a young yellow rose. "What about for this?"

Geppetto took the rose, almost dropping it because his hands had mutinously begun to tremble.

"Now, will you give me a hint?"

"It . . . it . . . it sings," Geppetto stumbled. "Or at least, it will."

Ily offered her most winning smile. "Then I'm sure I'll like it, whatever it is. After all, I trust my friend's taste in music." She started back into the shop. "Have a fine day, Geppetto."

"You, too."

The shop door closed, and Geppetto could have done a little dance in the middle of Pariva's square for joy. Ilaria Belmagio had called him her friend!

He twirled the little rose in his hand, then opened his innermost pocket to store it carefully inside. There, inside his coat, the rose would go wherever he went.

And he was certain he would treasure it forever.

CHAPTER SEVENTEEN

One might think that since Monstro had been found, cast into a deep slumber, and safely hidden from the Heartless, the fairies of the Wishing Star might take a break from their hard work. But on the contrary, there was little time for rest. The next day, Chiara's lessons resumed.

"With Monstro asleep, the Heartless will be endeavoring to find a new source of power," said Agata. "No doubt they're already spread across Esperia trying to make mischief and misery. That means no time for rest! Off we go."

Chiara was ready. "I saw a few red lights by the southeast coast. Is that where we're headed?"

"My, you are a bright pupil," said Agata with an approving hum. "I had a feeling you'd be. Yes, that's where we'll start. Come now; they'll be quick visits and won't require too much magic—or talking."

By then, it was no surprise to Chiara that Agata turned to magic only as a last resort, and rarely did she physically manifest before those she was helping—but Chia hadn't thought to ask until today: "Why don't you like talking to those you help?"

"Precious minutes are wasted with idle chitchat," Agata explained, holding onto Chiara's arm as they flew. "It's better to remain unseen. Fewer questions that way. People are always astounded to see you, and ask if you're real or if you're their fairy godmother, and all that. It gets tiresome after a while, trust me."

Chiara flushed. She had asked the same questions.

"But sometimes our visits do require some face time," Agata went on. "Take our next wishers, for instance." She held her wand horizontally, and it became a scroll listing the names and locations of the people they were to visit today. "Rosa Leo—the Heartless turned her fiancé into a bear a few days ago. We ought to go see her."

Agata waved her wand, and the two popped into the Hallowed Woods, the largest forest in Esperia. Chia had never been before, but every tree was gray, with leaves shaped like curved daggers.

"Now where is that girl?" muttered Agata, picking up her skirt to cross a muddy puddle. She pointed her wand at a nearby tree, which had been slashed by a bear claw. "She and the bear are supposed to be right here."

Chia shivered as her breath steamed into the air. She whirled, taking in the desolate woods. Everything was gray, and even Agata's usually vibrant purple cloak looked drabber. "It feels like despair," she murmured.

"You're picking up on the bear's sentiments. Poor thing." Agata tapped her wand on another tree. "Let's hope we break his curse before dark."

"Will the Heartless be back for him?"

"Unlikely," replied Agata. "They gleaned all the misery and despair they needed from the pair already. More likely they'll go back to Vallan or the like."

"Why Vallan?"

"The Heartless prefer big cities where there are more people to prey on, and a missing soul here and there can easily go unnoticed."

Chiara didn't like the sound of that. Ilaria wanted to live in Vallan; she'd have to warn her.

"Ah, there you are," said Agata, approaching a young woman riding a great brown bear. When Rosa saw Agata and Chia, she raised the stick in her hand fearfully.

"There, there," said Agata, putting away her wand.

"There's no need to be frightened. We're fairies here to help you, not harm you. The Heartless turned your fiancé into a bear, yes? Not to worry, his curse is quite breakable."

"It is?" Rosa Leo nearly collapsed with relief. The stick dropped from her hand, and she slid off the bear's back. "Thank the stars, you heard my pleas. I thought for sure that no one would."

"A little patience will go a long way, my dear," said Agata. She held out a handkerchief. "Now don't you two ever take a shortcut through these woods again."

Rosa Leo nodded, and the bear let out an affirmative growl.

"Brilliant. My apprentice will give you the instructions on how to break the curse."

Rosa took the handkerchief and wiped at her eyes. Then she looked at Chiara expectantly.

"Hello, Rosa," Chiara said warmly. She dipped her head at the bear beside Rosa. "And Mr. Bear." She touched the journal she kept in her pocket—every morning, she reviewed the wishers she and Agata would visit and cross-referenced their requests with similar ones that had been made before. She'd been up since dawn looking up the way to break a bear curse. Agata assured her that such spells and their remedies were like recipes and would become second nature to her given time and experience.

"Climb to the top of Mount Reve and take nine leaves from the crooked tree that grows there," said Chiara from memory. Reading off her notes wouldn't instill confidence in Rosa or her ursine betrothed. "Brew a tea from the tree and have him drink it. By the morn, he will be born again."

"Oh, thank you!" cried Rosa. "I'll do that. Thank you."

"This cloak will keep you warm," offered Agata, waving her wand. A velvet cloak fitted over the girl's shoulders. "The weather's getting cold, and the climb to the mountain will be an arduous one. Take care. And here, a bottle of tea that will never run out."

Chiara hid a smile, recognizing the very items Agata had hypothetically offered to give her sister. So practical.

As the young woman gushed with thanks, Agata took Chiara by the arm, and outwardly they vanished in a flash of light. But really, they simply became invisible once again.

"I think you've gotten the hang of the wish-granting business," whispered Agata. "I'll leave you in charge of writing up the shard this time. "

"Shard?"

"Every time we come to Esperia on business, we make a record of the magic we used and the people we visited. Oh, you know what I'm talking about. Peri tells me you've been spending all your free time in the Archives, reading shards."

"Oh, the reports!" Chiara said.

"We call them shards, affectionately. One of the more bureaucratic and painful parts of being a fairy," said Agata cheerfully. "But now that you're my apprentice, I can take a break from them." The Violet Fairy winked. "Take care not to spend *too* much time in the Archives, Chiara, or Peri will have *you* become the Archives manager within the year."

The Violet Fairy dusted her hands. "Now that all that's been taken care of, we'll finally take lunch—"

Just then, Agata's wand chimed. Once. Twice. Thrice.

An emergency.

"Mirabella needs help," Agata said, drawing furious loops with her wand. Within the circle, the Golden Fairy appeared, looking alarmed. "Just as I feared, a death curse. Quickly, Chia, take my hand. She isn't far."

Usually Agata gave Chia a chance to catch her breath before the two flew off in a beam of starlight, but not this time. It was an emergency.

They followed the sound of Mirabella's wand to the other side of the Hallowed Woods, where, beside a narrow snaking brook, awaited the Golden Fairy—and a girl who'd been turned to a tree. Her legs were roots, already deeply entrenched into the earth, and her arms branched out toward the sky, her cotton sleeves transforming into crisp green leaves. Her hair and face had already turned into wood, and all that was left were two eyes, a nose, and a mouth. But within minutes, they too would be gone.

It was the most horrible thing Chiara had ever seen.

"Agata, Chiara! Help!"

Sparks flew from Mirabella's wand; the Golden Fairy wielded it with both hands, as if she were lifting a boulder, not a slender stick of magic.

For once, Agata didn't explain the situation. She rushed to Mirabella's side and pointed her wand at the girl. A violet rush of magic burst from Agata's wand, braiding with Mirabella's golden power.

Chiara didn't know what she could do. She didn't have a wand yet, so she went up to the girl. Fear clouded her pale brown eyes, and Chiara reached for what remained of her cheek. She touched it, wishing she could do more than sense someone's emotions and could lend the girl courage. "Don't be afraid," she said gently. "Mirabella and Agata are here. They'll break your curse. I promise."

"Will you stay with me until they do?" said the girl, sounding very young.

"Of course. I'll be right here."

The gold and violet light from Mirabella's and Agata's wands twined together into a cord that wrapped around the tree, slowly extracting the Heartless's curse. Little by little, the branches turned into arms, the bark into smooth, freckled skin, and the leaves into curled, unkempt hair.

The girl fainted into Chiara's arms. She was human again.

As Chiara laid her gently on her lap, Mirabella wiped sweat from her brow and collapsed herself.

"Despicable," she said. "Absolutely despicable."

"The Heartless?" asked Chiara.

"Who else?" said Agata through her teeth. "There was a time they wouldn't attempt such death curses, but they're growing bolder. Cleverer, too. This sort of spell takes more than one fairy to break. A minute or two later, and it'd have been too late. This girl would have been a tree . . . forever."

Chiara brushed a leaf from the girl's forehead. "How long until she wakes up?"

"It could be hours," said Mirabella. "Seems like her horse ran off, and it's a good hour's walk until she reaches home."

"We can't send her through the woods alone," Agata said.

"Quite right." Letting out a tired grunt, Mirabella stood to survey the area, then crouched and collected a handful of pebbles. Using her wand, she stacked them until she created the shape of a man. Then she took a step back and touched her wand to Agata's.

"Little stones at once combine," began Mirabella. "Until the stroke of nine, awake; the gift of life is thine."

Chiara watched in awe as sparks of life glittered across the pebbles, and they burst to life, wobbling on uneven legs.

"Escort the young lady home to her family," Mirabella instructed the tower of stones.

It spread its arms in agreement, for it could not nod without its head falling off. Then, obediently, it lifted the young lady and carried her home.

"Watch out for foxes and wolves!" Agata called after them.

Chiara followed the pair with her eyes until they disappeared into the forest. Then she turned to Mirabella in amazement. "You gave life to a pile of stones!"

Mirabella chuckled. "Magic can do wondrous things, my dear. As I'm sure Agata has shown you."

"What will happen to the stones at nine?"

"They'll become as they were again. But that should be plenty of time for the poor girl to return home to her worried mother and father." Mirabella yawned, and Agata quickly followed. Both of the elder fairies had dark circles under their eyes that hadn't been there minutes before.

"It takes powerful magic to undo the wickedness of the Heartless," said Agata, reading the questions on Chiara's face. "Mirabella and I will be fine after some rest."

"I wish I could help," said Chiara.

"You will, in time," Mirabella assured her. "But for now, consider yourself lucky you haven't come across a Heartless."

"She's come across Monstro," said Agata. "Many would say he's worse."

Chiara shuddered, remembering how all the fairies had battled the great whale and finally cast a slumber spell over him.

"Have the Heartless found out?"

"Of course," replied Agata. "They're already searching for him."

"It'll take them a while," Mirabella added. "Though it's best to be on your guard. Amorale must already be planning her revenge." She eyed Agata. "Larissa, too."

Chiara swallowed hard. Something in her gut told her that she wouldn't have to wait long before meeting one of the Heartless.

CHAPTER EIGHTEEN

A week later, in the middle of the night, a domed tent appeared outside the bustling town of Miurin. No one noticed it, for a dense fog shrouded all the town and did not clear until the morning.

A dense fog with the slightest hint of green, not that anyone would notice. Anyone, that was, except the fairies.

Chiara and Agata arrived to investigate, cloaked by an invisibility spell. Mist curled about the tent, leaving tracks of dew over its wide burgundy stripes. Agata pointed at the mist with her wand.

"See the trace of green in the air?" she murmured to Chia. "That's not natural, I can tell you that. The Heartless leave a trail wherever they go."

The mist hissed at the Violet Fairy viciously, but it

didn't dare come near. Instead it stretched toward Chiara, growing claws that brushed against her cheek.

Such a bright heart, it whispered into the crevices of her mind. *Full of hope and strength and courage.*

Chia recoiled, but she wasn't afraid, and she only dug her heels into the moist grass to steady her balance. "It's hungry," she observed as the mist crawled down her face and past her neck.

"It's trying to seep into your thoughts and into your heart," said Agata. "It latches on to fear, anger, and greed. To envy and hate and anything that causes pain—and grows it inside one's heart. Green is Larissa's color. Go on, greet her."

Larissa, Chiara spoke in her mind, greeting the Heartless's mist. *Agata's told me about you.*

Naturally she has. Larissa snickered. *What a fairy you'll make, so kind and fair and . . . gullible. Having second thoughts yet? No, I take it from your bright little heart that you've yet to see the darkness I weave. Aren't you curious about your family? Your poor, darling sister in particular. Would you like to see how miserable you've made your dearest Ily?*

Chiara's blood chilled. Yes, she did want to know how Ily was faring. Every day, she wondered about her family. She wanted to know that they were well, to ask the Wishing

Well for a glimpse of her sister. But Agata had discouraged using the Wishing Well to check on her family again, at least until her training was over. Agata had promised to let her know if anything terrible was happening. Chiara wouldn't break that trust. Especially not for a liar like Larissa.

Begone, said Chiara.

Ah, there it is. That prick of doubt. So you do *worry about your sister. I thought so.* The mist curled up at the ends, like a faceless smile. *Why don't you ask your mentor what price you'll have to pay to become a fairy?*

Chiara inhaled. *I'll find out when Agata deems me ready. Now begone.*

As you wish. Have fun with Remo. He's been drinking my poison ever since he was young. He rather likes it.

Who's Rem—

Before Chiara could finish her question, the mist flew out of her in a rush, dissolving before her eyes. Then, suddenly, the air was clear.

Agata was watching her curiously. "Larissa spoke to you."

Chiara nodded.

"She warned you of the sacrifice you'll have to make to become a fairy?"

Chiara stared at the ground. "Yes."

"Don't you want to know what it is?"

"You said you'd tell me when I was ready."

A sad smile touched Agata's mouth. "So I will, Chiara. So I will. Come now. Our mission today shan't be an easy one."

Ignoring the twinge in her chest, Chiara followed Agata around the tent until they approached the front. There, they found a young boy pasting posters along the side of the tent, and on the wagon parked against a tree. Thanks to Agata's spell, he couldn't see Chiara or the Violet Fairy, or the green mist that flew behind him.

Chiara approached the posters. They illustrated a man posing in an extravagant blue coat, with purple tassels and a gaudy gold buckle. On his shoulders were six monkeys in matching blue capes and hats.

Remo the Extraordinary Showman, read the flyer. *Dancing monkeys and singing crickets. Feast your eyes on something incredible.*

"Remo's a depraved soul if ever I knew one," Agata remarked with disgust. "The Heartless got to him long ago. Thankfully there's still hope for his sons. Vito is the elder, and Stromboli is the younger. I want you to speak to them."

"All right," agreed Chia nervously. "But what will I say?"

"Listen to your conscience," said Agata, gesturing at her heart. "It'll guide you. Go on, Chia. You can do this."

Taking a deep breath, Chiara turned her attention to the young boy who'd been putting up posters along the tent: Vito, Remo's older son. He certainly didn't look wicked, and if anything, a cloud of melancholy hung about him, casting over his heavy steps and the downward slope of his shoulders.

She'd start with him.

He'd finished with the posters and entered the wagon by the tree. Still invisible, Chiara followed quietly, but she wasn't prepared for the sight that awaited her inside the wagon.

A large wooden cage hung from the ceiling, five thin-limbed monkeys crammed inside.

Vito hurriedly opened the cage door, letting them out. "Don't make too much noise," he warned them. "Papa's nearby."

As the monkeys ran and jumped about the wagon happily, Vito reached into his knapsack for a bunch of bananas. He peeled them deftly, one for each monkey—and an additional banana.

"Where's Odi?" he asked.

The monkeys grunted and pointed behind them at the tent.

Vito gritted his teeth. "Stromboli has him?"

One of the monkeys nodded.

This did not make Vito happy. "Hurry, eat, eat."

While most of the monkeys nibbled on their bananas, the youngest, smallest one crept for the door. Vito stopped him, blocking the door with his body.

"I wish I could let you go," he said, falling onto his knees. He stroked the young monkey's head affectionately. "I really do. But Papa has Odi . . ." His voice trailed. "He'd be furious . . . and when he's furious . . ." Vito chewed on his lower lip.

Chiara's heart tightened. Anyone could see the terror on young Vito's face. Just what had Remo done to him?

In the near distance, coins jangled inside the domed tent. Vito's shoulders instantly tensed. "Papa's coming. Quick, back into the cage."

"Vito!" Remo roared for his son. "Vito, get back here! And bring the crickets!"

Hurriedly, Vito locked the monkeys back into their cage. "I'll try to get you all extra food tonight after the show." He swallowed. "One day, I'll set you free. I promise."

Then he grabbed a box labeled SINGING CRICKETS and stumbled out of the wagon.

Chiara followed him into the domed tent, where Remo the Showman was pasting on a black mustache and combing his wig in front of a long mirror. Behind him, his younger son, Stromboli, counted coins from their last show. The resemblance between Stromboli and Remo was strong—same thick eyebrows, deep-set eyes, and pronounced jaw. The same glittering greed in their laugh.

The sixth monkey squirmed under Stromboli's heel, and the boy stepped hard on its tail, making it screech in pain.

"Shut up, I'm counting," Stromboli said, flicking coins into a pile. "Ah, here it is!" He plucked out a gold band from the sack of profits. "There's the ring I told you about, Papa! Look, I slipped it off a lady's finger." He snickered, and green mist curled about his fingers. "She didn't even notice."

"Well done, my boy." Remo chewed on the ring, then made an approving whistle. He patted Stromboli's head. "Tonight we'll have to work even harder. That includes you, too, Odi." Remo pointed at the monkey. "I expect this pile to double, or else you and your brothers aren't getting food for a week!"

The monkey squirmed out of Stromboli's grip and raced out of the tent, but he didn't get far. Remo and Stromboli had bound his arms with string. Stromboli yanked, and the monkey flew back, screaming.

"Look, Papa, he's a puppet!" Stromboli howled with laughter as he forced the monkey's arms behind his back.

"That's enough," Vito cried, rushing to Odi's aid. "You're hurting him!"

"Hurting him?" Remo threw up his arms. "I'll show you what hurt is."

The showman thrashed his son's face with the back of his hand. The impact made Vito stagger back.

"Don't think I don't know what you've been doing, feeding the animals behind my back." Remo raised a ringed hand and shook a banana at his son. "Maybe I should make you go without food, too! Then that would teach you some respect!"

Vito cowered in the corner. "Yes . . . yes, Papa. I'm sorry, Papa."

"Sorry, Papa, yes, Papa," Remo mimicked cruelly. "How do I have such a spineless boy?"

"A sheep!" Stromboli taunted. "Vito's a sheep."

Remo cackled. "And we are wolves."

"Stop that!" Chiara cried, stepping out of Agata's invisibility spell. She pulled on Remo's coat from behind before he struck his son again.

Remo whirled on her. "The tent is closed. Can't you read?" he growled.

When he saw her, he relaxed. "Ah, it's a fairy. It's been a while since one of you has come. I'm flattered you haven't forgotten about the majestic Remo." He puffed out his chest and put on his wig. "Have you come to grant my wish at last?"

Chiara was starting to understand why Agata chose to remain invisible for most of her visits, showing herself only when necessary. She loathed the way Remo was looking at her, clearly calculating what he could get out of their encounter.

"I have not come to grant wishes," she said as calmly as she could. "I have come to give you a chance to redeem yourself. Return the money you and Stromboli have stolen, free the animals you have in your captivity, and treat Vito with respect."

Remo blinked at her as if she'd spoken in a foreign language. Then he guffawed, the sound booming across the cavernous tent. "Ah, I see, you must be new. No wand. No wings. In that case, our business is done. I have a show to prepare for." He put on his wig, adjusting the black hair in front of the mirror. "Come, Stromboli."

"We aren't finished," said Chiara, an edge to her voice.

"Will you punish me? I think not. Ho, ho!" Remo laughed. "I know your kind. You won't use your magic to punish me. You don't even have magic yet."

A wand suddenly appeared in Chiara's hand. Agata's wand. *Thank you,* she gestured with a glance up, knowing that the elder fairy was watching her.

Stromboli's eyes lit, and he tugged on her skirt. "I want a wish!" he said. "I want a wish!"

"Let the monkey go," said Chiara to the boy. "Let him go free."

Stromboli kicked the monkey away. As it scampered to Vito's side fearfully, Stromboli turned back to Chiara. "There, I let him go. Now give me my wish."

She shook her head. "Wishes aren't transactions, paid for doing something that's right. You should act with kindness for your own sake as much as for the sake of others."

"What a load of baloney," said Stromboli, yanking angrily on her skirt. "You lied!"

Chiara stepped back. "I did not. I never said I would grant you a wish."

"You'll be sorry!" Stromboli wagged a finger at her. "Papa! Did you hear what she did?"

"Yes, yes, I heard." Remo stroked his false mustache. "It seems Ms. Fairy has much to learn, doesn't she?" Chiara had no idea what the father and son were scheming, but she was immediately on her guard.

Cackling with delight, Stromboli gamboled toward the box of crickets Vito had brought. He shook it. Hard.

While the crickets slammed against the wooden walls, Stromboli parted the lid and plucked one of the poor creatures up by the wings. The cricket was as large as his tiny fist, and he cupped it with both hands so it couldn't escape. The cricket chirped in distress.

"You seem like the caring sort, Ms. Fairy," Stromboli said in a singsong voice. "So I'm going to try again."

His voice turned into a growl: "Give me a wish, fairy." He raised his hands threateningly. "Or I'll smash this cricket into smithereens."

Chiara could hardly believe such wickedness from a young boy. "Don't do that, Stromboli."

"Or what? You'll teach me a lesson?"

Ever patient, Chiara knelt beside the boy. "I'd like to teach you to listen to your conscience. It's a voice inside your heart that tells you right from wrong. Do you hear it?"

"Conscience? What rubbish are you spewing, fairy?

She glanced at Vito, who had put his hand on his chest and was frowning as if trying to listen. At least her words were reaching *someone*.

"Will you let the cricket go?" she said to Stromboli, offering him one last chance. "And promise not to hurt it again? You ought to treat others the way you wish to be treated, Stromboli."

Stromboli blinked, and like his brother, he put his hand over his heart. He sniffed. "Oh, I understand now. Of course I promise, Ms. Fairy."

Chiara almost let out a sigh of relief. "Very good, Stromboli. I'm glad you—"

A sneer came over the young boy's face. Without

warning, he dropped the cricket and pushed Chiara as hard as he could, snatching her wand, and then ran across the tent.

"Look, Papa, I've got her wand!" Stromboli flaunted it over his head. "Make me rich. I wish to be rich. Rich as a king!"

Chiara rose to her feet, shaking her head at the boy as the cricket raced to Vito for safety. She wasn't hurt, and she wasn't angry; she only regretted that she'd had to become involved so impulsively, without having had more time to consider how she might approach Vito and Stromboli.

So what was she to do? Instead of heeding her advice to listen to his conscience, Stromboli had tricked her. Lied to her.

The first way you begin to lose yourself is with a lie, Mamma had taught her. *A lie keeps growing and growing until it's as plain as the nose on your face.*

"Mamma's wise words," Chiara murmured to herself. "If only they would help Stromboli, too."

As soon as she uttered the command, the wand in Stromboli's hand began to glow. The boy laughed and laughed, thinking gold was about to rain from the ceiling and that his wish would soon come true.

But the magic gathered around his nose . . . which began to grow.

"Papa!" he screamed, coming to a halt.

Remo seized his stool, raising it high and threateningly. "What are you doing to my son?"

"Teaching him something that you would also do well to learn," Chiara replied. Outwardly, she maintained her composure, but her heart raced as she witnessed the wand's power. *Let it be temporary*, she commanded it silently. "You will treat others the way you wish to be treated. And a lie will not get you what you want."

"Get out of here, you witch!"

"Very well." Chiara started to lift her wand.

"Wait," Stromboli cried. "Turn my nose back!"

"No," said Remo. "We don't beg. We don't bargain." He whirled to face Chiara. "This fairy's heart is as weak as a bird's. She'll do anything to save even a cricket's life."

Stromboli sneered. "What do you care about a stupid cricket? It's going to get eaten soon enough, anyway. Or stepped on."

Remo grabbed his elder son. "You want to prove yourself to me, Vito? Smash the cricket. Show the fairy who's king around here. Go on!"

Vito cringed and cowered in fear of his father. "I . . ."

"Do it! You weak sap, do it now!"

The cricket made a pleading chirp.

Chiara lowered her wand. "You don't have to do that, Vito," she told him warmly. She knelt beside him. "Have courage. There's strength in you. When you're unsure of what to do, follow the voice in your heart: your conscience. It will guide you."

"I . . . I can't kill it," Vito stammered. He gave the cricket to Chiara.

"Why, you treacherous . . ." Remo raised his hand to strike his son, but Chiara intervened—such that when he grabbed Vito's arm, his sleeve was hot as a burning poker.

He jumped up in pain.

"You must never strike your sons again," she warned Remo firmly, "and you must teach them not to lie."

"You mean not to be like me?" Remo's sneer was identical to his younger son's. "Even if I did all those things, beautiful fairy, blood is thick. My boys will end up like me no matter what anyone teaches them."

"We'll see," Chiara said.

She had hope for Vito, but to be honest, she was troubled about Stromboli. From what she'd seen, his father rewarded him for cruelty, and taught him that acts of kindness were weak and worthy of punishment. She wanted to help him further, but she didn't know how. Agata had taught her how to bring out the good in people's hearts and show them to trust their conscience, but not everyone's goodness could be unearthed after one or two visits. How did she guide someone like Stromboli?

Hiding her uneasiness, she winked at Vito, then scooped up the box of crickets and tapped her wand on the box. Instantly the crickets were free; the monkeys in the cage, too. As the former flew out of the tent and the latter scampered to freedom, she, too, made her exit.

Only after Remo had painted over his posters to announce that the night's show was cancelled did Stromboli's nose return to what it had been before.

"You did well," congratulated Agata.

"Was I too harsh?"

"No, but however did you come up with the idea to make Stromboli's nose grow longer?" said Agata. "You're smiling. You have a story. Do tell."

Chiara smiled wanly, thinking of the memory that had popped into her head while she'd held the wand. "Well, it's just that when my mamma caught us lying, she'd say, 'A lie keeps growing and growing until it's as plain as the nose on your face.'"

"Oh, I love it!" Agata exclaimed. "Sometimes one has to be tough to get a message across, as you were with Stromboli.

Show the profound effect the truth—and untruths—have on the world."

Chiara sighed. "I worry about Stromboli, Agata. He's just a child. One visit from a fairy surely will not undo the lessons his father has taught him. You saw the way Remo goaded him." She pursed her lips. It'd be naïve to think that freeing the monkeys and crickets would lead Remo to choose a more honest profession, or that he might suddenly change overnight and decide to become a good father. Chiara's shoulders fell. She no longer felt like she'd done well at all. She felt like she'd failed. "Is there some way we can help them choose a different path? The boys, especially?"

"I will speak to Mirabella about it," said Agata. "Perhaps we can have one of the senior fairies keep an eye on the two boys."

Chiara nodded. "Vito will need help finding his way, if he ever leaves home. And Stromboli . . ." Her voice trailed off. "If the Heartless came to Remo, they will certainly be after Stromboli, too. I saw green mist about him. It didn't follow him everywhere, like it did with Remo, but—"

"I won't forget about Stromboli," Agata promised. "There is one thing you must learn, Chiara, and this is not about Remo's boys, but about humans in general. No two hearts are the same. And the same heart might look very different depending on the day. Humans have thousands of choices all of the time. They do not always get it right, and sometimes they do not wish to. There will be days when our work seems futile, days when we'll encounter people who act without a sense of right or wrong. We can only provide guidance and help those who want to be helped. We cannot force our ways, even on someone like Remo."

"Larissa mentioned that she'd been visiting Remo for years. Is that why he's so . . ."

"Heartless? It certainly helps." Agata sighed uneasily. "I should have known that Larissa would be here today. Did she say anything about a new apprentice?"

"No."

"It's only a matter of time, then," mused Agata. "She'll be looking, now that I have you. If I were to guess, Larissa already has her sights on someone to pit you against. They're always recruiting people to their side; Larissa and Amorale are obsessed with not being outnumbered by us."

"All the people they recruit . . . do they take their hearts?"

"Only the ones who become fairies like them," Agata replied. "That fate is, fortunately, reserved for a select few."

She touched Chiara's shoulder. "Don't look so worried, Chiara. I won't lie—we can't save everyone from the Heartless. Sometimes we are too late, or sometimes their hearts are too far gone rotten. But it makes a world of difference to those we can help. I'd say that's what makes our job so difficult, and so fulfilling."

"After today, I see what you mean," Chiara replied. Not being able to help Stromboli and Remo left an unsettled feeling in her gut. She could only hope that a more experienced fairy would help Stromboli—before Larissa's influence found him, too.

A new apprentice. Agata's words haunted her. That would mean a Heartless devoted to interfering with Chiara's work.

Chiara couldn't help wondering whom Larissa was trying to recruit.

CHAPTER NINETEEN

"Ilaria!" cried Mrs. Belmagio. "Mail for you."

Ilaria flew down the stairs. This was it: the letter she'd been waiting weeks for.

She reached for the letter with shaking fingers and nearly tore the envelope in half instead of opening it. The paper was thick and creamy and smelled like hope. She held it to her chest, then shook her head. "You read it for me, Mamma. I don't dare."

"My hands stink of yeast. You sure you want that all over your mail?"

"Yes. If it's bad news, I'll burn it."

Mrs. Belmagio chuckled at her daughter. "Let's read it together."

Holding her breath, Ilaria unfolded the letter. Her head had started spinning, and she had to fix her eyes to the paper to read properly: "Dear Miss Belmagio, it is our profound pleasure to inform you that—" Ilaria didn't need to go on. She let out a screech that frightened off the jays perched outside the kitchen and immediately raced up the stairs to shout out the news.

"I've advanced!" she cried. She clambered up to the third floor, taking two steps at a time to the attic—

"Chia, Chia! You'll never guess—I've advanced to the audition in Vallan! I'm going to sing for Maria Lin—"

As she burst through the door, she stopped midsentence. In her excitement, she'd forgotten. Her sister wasn't there anymore.

All at once, Ilaria deflated. She kicked at the door. "Stupid me," she muttered.

Three months. It'd been three months that Chiara's room in the attic had been empty. Still, the sun shone brightest in her room, and everything was left the way it'd been before. The neat stacks of books, the ribbons hanging on a hook across her mirror, the picture Ilaria had drawn of the two sisters when they were little girls.

Swallowing the lump that had formed in her throat, Ilaria held the letter to her chest and closed the door.

———

Ily didn't want to share the good news with her friends, but Simona's father was the postmaster of Pariva, which meant she knew everyone's business.

"Heard you got a letter today," said Simona. Her so-called friend was waiting outside Mrs. Tappa's hat shop for Ily to open up. Beatrice was there, too, and the two followed Ily into the shop like unwanted shadows.

"Are you going to tell what it is?"

Ily ignored her friends. The only reason she even consorted with Simona and Beatrice anymore was because, now that Chia was gone, Ily had no other choices in female companionship her age. Still, all Simona and Beatrice liked to do was gossip and speak ill of others, even of each other when one wasn't around.

But bad company was better than no company, wasn't it?

Ily ignored the pang of loneliness that sharpened in her chest. Niccolo had started seeing Sofia Farrio, the miller's daughter, which meant he was head over heels and even less fun than usual to talk to, and Mamma and Papa were busy with the bakery. Beatrice and Simona were weak replacements for her brother and her parents, but it was better than talking to the wooden mannequins that stood in front of the shop window.

Or so Ily told herself.

"It was a letter from the Madrigal Conservatory," boasted Ily. "I'm going to Vallan."

"Really?" Beatrice's eyes widened. "When?"

"Tuesday. It's going to be wonderful. I haven't gone to the city in years."

"Think of all the new boys you can flirt with," said Beatrice enviously. "Maybe I should come with you."

"Niccolo's taking me," Ilaria lied quickly. "Sofia, too. They're inseparable these days."

Beatrice's expression soured. Ily knew that was exactly what she hadn't wanted to hear.

"You'll need something new to wear," Simona said, clearly envious. "Your old dresses will be out of fashion in Vallan, but something in vogue will be expensive. Maybe Chiara can send you a new one."

Not even Simona's backhanded insult could ruin her mood. "I already have a new dress," Ily said giddily. "Mamma went with me to have it made in Nerio last week."

Thanks to the money Chiara had given her, Ily had toured Nerio's garment district and treated herself to the loveliest red gown.

Even if I don't make the Vallan round, she'd told herself, *it'll be something beautiful to have and look at.*

But as it'd turned out, she *was* going to Vallan!

Ily's smile widened. "It's got lace on the sleeves and

rosettes along the neckline. Wait until you see it." She reached for a hat on display. "Mrs. Tappa's even letting me borrow a hat for the occasion. The red velvet one that's worth a small fortune."

Beatrice made a humming sound, which Ily knew meant she was searching for something else to poke at. Her so-called friends were like hens; Ily only wished she could throw them some feed to make them go away or lock them up in a pen like real chickens.

"I'm glad for you, Ily—about Vallan . . . but I thought the letter would be from Chia." Simona clicked her tongue. "It's been three months, hasn't it? Papa says there hasn't been any word from her."

Leave it to Simona to find the one way to storm in on her good mood. Ily raised her chin high. "Why would a fairy write letters when she has magic? She can send messages over beams of starlight or have butterflies bring gifts from the Wishing Star."

"Has she?" said Beatrice. "Or has she forgotten about you?"

"Watch yourself, Beatrice. My sister would never forget about me."

"I'm only asking because of what *my* papa said."

"What did your papa say?"

"That she won't be the same." Beatrice cast Ily a pitying

smile. "Don't you know? There's a girl from Benoita who became a fairy, what, twenty years ago? Hardly anyone even remembers her." Beatrice leaned closer conspiratorially. "They say the fairies cast a spell over the family. Over the whole town. They either make you think she's dead, or they make you forget her completely."

A chill bristled down the back of Ilaria's neck, but she ignored it and pretended to huff with disdain. "I've never heard this before. Where did your papa hear this rubbish?"

"He was a librarian in Benoita for twelve years," Beatrice replied. "He heard things."

"The books talk?" Ilaria snorted.

A glare from Beatrice. "I think it makes sense. Why else don't we remember anything about the fairies? All we know is they once were human. Don't you think someone would have tried to ask by now?"

Ily said nothing. She had no good answer for that. During her short meeting with Agata, the fairy had been unresponsive to nearly all her questions. Chia, too, had been secretive.

Simona flipped her hair over her shoulder. "I guess we'll all find out when Chia's back. She *is* coming back, isn't she?"

"For my birthday," said Ilaria, hoping the extra air she pumped into her voice would hide her uncertainty. Her birthday was in a month, and she knew that Chiara wasn't supposed to write, but still—every day she didn't hear from her sister, she worried that Chiara had lost track of time and had forgotten.

Stop worrying, Ilaria thought, tying the ribbon on her hat a little too tightly. *Next you'll be believing those stupid tall tales Beatrice made up because she's jealous that we have a fairy in the family. She's always been jealous of Chia and me because she and her sister don't get along.*

Taking a deep, calming breath, she set aside the hat and drummed her fingers on the table. "Why don't you two watch the shop for a while?"

"Us?" Beatrice exclaimed. "It's not our job to—"

"I'm going to ask Mamma for some cake," Ilaria lied. "I'll bring you each a slice."

Simona smacked her lips. "The blood orange one with chocolate?"

Ilaria sweetened her tone. "Of course."

"I don't want anything," said Beatrice, crossing her arms. Ever since Niccolo had turned his affections to Sofia Farrio, she refused to even talk about him, let alone patronize the bakery where he worked.

"Don't take too long," called Simona after her. "What will we do if there's a customer?"

Ily pretended not to hear and flitted out the door. She

needed air. Needed to get away from the same old faces, the same old clock tower with its spindly arms, the same old crooked welcome sign in front of the flower shop and the same old smells of lemon and cheese and grass and pine.

She hadn't had a good practice session in days, and she needed to get in shape before her audition. She certainly couldn't practice in the shop with Beatrice and Simona there. They talked over her singing and made unwanted commentary, and when she took her music outside, former beaus came by to flirt and other townspeople constantly interrupted her songs with greetings and questions about Chiara. Well-intentioned, but irksome, all the same.

I'll make for the pastures, she thought. She'd climb one of the low hills to the top—the way she used to with Chiara—then sing and sing. Rare was the errant eavesdropper, and the birds would make a finer audience than anyone in Pariva.

Anyone, that was, except Geppetto.

As soon as she thought about him, her gaze found the young luthier as if she'd conjured him—wandering the middle of the town square.

He pushed his wind-tossed black hair—in dire need of a trim—out of his eyes. Her stomach fluttered as he ambled through the square, carrying two long loaves of bread under each arm and nearly bumping into Mr. Vaci in the middle of the road. Ily smothered a laugh at the sight.

How strange. She'd never thought shy Geppetto handsome before. He certainly didn't have the strapping build of the young men she was used to flirting with, or the chiseled jaw and dark, mysterious eyes that infatuated most girls her age. But there was something sweet about him. Something sincere, too.

Sweet and sincere? She laughed at herself. *You must be lonely, Ily.*

Still, unlike Simona and Beatrice, at least he didn't try to provoke her with every other sentence. Everything about him was straightforward and honest; she could even tell from the way he fidgeted with his hat and how his feet pointed toward Mrs. Tappa's door that the hat shop was where he was heading—so Ilaria intercepted him with a tap from behind.

"It's a fine afternoon to shop for hats, isn't it, Geppetto?"

To say he was startled was an understatement. He jumped, and practically tripped over one of the uneven cobblestones under his shoe.

"I . . . I was going to see you, actually."

"Me?" Ilaria pretended to be surprised.

Geppetto spoke in a flustered rush, "I . . . I heard that

you advanced to the final round of auditions at the Madrigal Conservatory. And I . . . I wanted to . . . to . . ."

"Who told you that?" Ilaria asked, genuinely surprised.

"Uh. Um. Your mother?"

"You don't know?"

Ilaria liked how pink his ears turned. It was adorable.

"Yes, I do. It was your mother, Mrs. Belmagio. She said that I ought to . . ."

"To congratulate me?"

A deep breath. "Yes."

"That's very sweet," said Ilaria, meaning it. "Thank you, Geppetto."

Maybe she really did have a magic power. There Geppetto went again, his face turning redder than a tomato. Ilaria had to smother a giggle. She couldn't help being amused—and even charmed.

"I'm on break from work," she said. "Walk with me."

"Oh, no, I couldn't. I have to get back to—"

"A short walk," interrupted Ilaria. "Come on, Geppetto. It'll be too cold for strolls soon."

Geppetto relented, and Ilaria couldn't walk fast enough. Only when the bell tower ringing eleven o'clock was but a faint chime in the distance did she slow down. She glanced at Geppetto, still at her side but falling a step or two behind.

He was trying hard not to sound out of breath as he wiped his face with a handkerchief.

She forged up a low hill where dozens of pine trees grew. "Hurry, we're almost there!"

"Where?" Geppetto called.

"Here," said Ilaria, fanning out her skirt before she plopped under the shade of a tall old pine tree on the top of the hill. "My favorite spot in Pariva."

That was a lie; she didn't have a favorite spot. But at least here, she could see more of the world than anywhere else in this sleepy little town. She could make out the corners of Elph touching Mount Cecilia, and when she stretched her gaze far, she imagined the iron spires of Vallan beyond the clouds.

Geppetto tumbled down beside her and wiped at his forehead again. He folded his handkerchief before returning it to his pocket. "Some would say the journey is the best part," he said belatedly.

"Not me," replied Ilaria. "I want to get to where I'm going as fast as I can."

"Like Vallan?" said Geppetto pensively. He leaned against the tree and watched the clouds. "What will you sing for your audition?"

"They asked for one song," said Ily, sinking onto the grass. She didn't care if she stained her dress. It *was* old, as Simona had pointed out, and the pink stripes had faded until they looked practically white. "You have one guess."

Geppetto considered. "The Nightingale Aria?"

"It does seem to be a crowd pleaser. And it's my favorite."

"Mine, too. Are you nervous?"

Ilaria hesitated. "Yes," she confessed. "It'll be the most important day of my life. Five minutes that can change everything."

"I thought you didn't believe in fate."

Was he teasing her? Ilaria couldn't tell behind the twinkle in his eye. She hugged her knees to her chest. "I believe we make our own choices, and we shape whatever future may come."

"But sometimes, out of the blue, something might happen."

"Like what? Chiara becoming a fairy?" Ilaria scoffed. "She could have said no."

"She could have," Geppetto agreed. "But I think it was always her secret longing to help people. It brings her joy unlike anything else."

How could Geppetto, who had only known Chiara for a few months, see more clearly into her heart than Ilaria?

Ilaria bit down on her lip. "That's what she told me before she left."

"Don't you have a secret longing?"

Ilaria thought of the wish she'd made on the Wishing Star. She thought of her music, and how wonderful it would feel to hear her voice echo across the walls of Esperia's grand opera houses, to become a prima donna and sing with an orchestra. To see stars shine in the eyes of everyone she met, and have fresh roses and flowers tossed at her feet wherever she walked. To have grown men and women swoon whenever she blew them kisses.

"Of course I do," she said.

"Music," said Geppetto, reading the lift in her expression. "I can hear it in your voice when you sing. You love music."

"It makes me feel alive," she said, repeating what she'd told Chia. "When I sing, I'm no longer Ilaria Belmagio. I'm a princess or a revolutionary, I'm a milkmaid who's just had her heart broken—or a fairy who's lost her wand."

"Or a nightingale who's been found by a lost boy."

"Figaro," Ilaria said, naming the character. "Together, they help each other find their way home. I've always liked that story."

"Me too. It's one of the happier operas. I always cry when they're sad."

"I didn't take you for a weeper," Ilaria teased. "Or a dreamer."

"I listen to too much opera, I guess. Blame my father. He doesn't seem like the sentimental sort, but he is."

There weren't many other boys in Pariva who loved opera. Plenty listened. It was hard not to, given that the melodies spread across Esperia, carried on the wings of good gossip. It was just that most of the other boys spent their evenings at the Red Lobster Inn or playing cards. Even Niccolo had been playing his violin less these days.

She kicked at the dirt and the grass. Before Geppetto could respond, she said, "What is *your* secret longing?"

Geppetto took a deep breath. In his quietest voice, he professed, "I want to make toys."

That surprised Ilaria. "Toys?"

The light in his eyes sparkled. "Toys for every child in Pariva. Toys that delight the heart and tickle the fancy. Toys they can pass to their children and their children's children."

"But what about your father's shop? I thought you loved music, too."

"I do. But repairing guitars and violins . . . that's my father's passion, not mine. They bring their own kind of special joy to the children." Geppetto stared at his hands. "Papa won't be pleased when he finds out."

"He doesn't know?"

Geppetto hung his head. "I haven't been brave enough to tell him. But I will, soon."

Ilaria could sense Chiara's handiwork in this. She didn't know how she knew, but she did. It irked her, just the tiniest bit.

"I want to make my own music, my own way," Geppetto went on. "Clocks and singing boxes and dolls and puppets."

"And you want children of your own, I'm guessing."

It was impressive how instantly Geppetto's face turned red. "Who . . . who doesn't love children?" he stammered. "They are the future. They have their whole world in front of them, and they're free to dream."

Ilaria couldn't agree. To be stuck in Pariva for the rest of her life, living a street away from her parents, bouncing children on her knees . . . Such thoughts did not bring her joy.

Geppetto was eager to change the topic. He cleared his throat and said, "Have you hired a carriage to Vallan?"

She nodded. "Niccolo helped me. Mr. Muscado is bringing me in Monday morning."

"Is Niccolo coming with you?"

"No." She shrugged. "I don't mind. He doesn't like the city anyway."

"What about your parents?"

She tried to hide her disappointment, but Geppetto saw the flicker of discontent that crossed her face.

"They can't come," he realized.

"I asked," said Ilaria miserably, "but it's an entire day's trip. Mamma and Papa can't leave. Oh, it's not because they don't want to, or they can't afford to, but the whole town depends on the bakery . . . and Niccolo won't come, because it's Sofia's birthday—"

"So you'll be going alone?"

Ilaria tipped her chin up, mustering enthusiasm. "It'll be a great adventure."

"The audition is the most important event of your life," said Geppetto. "You shouldn't be alone." He bit on his cheek, then sucked in his breath. "Would your parents . . . would they allow me to accompany you?"

Ilaria's eyes widened. "You would do that for me? It's a whole day's trip, Geppetto."

"I don't have much work right now," said Geppetto, raking his hand through his hair. He wasn't a good liar. "Business has been slow."

"Would your father be angry? I know he relies on you to—"

"He'll understand," Geppetto assured her.

Would he? Ilaria wondered. Mr. Tommaso certainly wouldn't understand his son spending a day escorting Ilaria Belmagio—of all girls—to Vallan. She knew her reputation.

"I wouldn't miss being there for you," said Geppetto,

his voice shaking. But his meaning was firm. "I'll pick up some chocolates for Papa and work extra hard these next few days. It'll be all right."

Ilaria was touched. A rush of warmth overcame her heart, and without thinking, she reached for Geppetto's hand and laced her fingers in his. "Thank you," she said.

She'd nearly forgotten she'd come to the hill to practice.

Summoning the song inside her, she parted her lips to free the first note, a *la*. She'd never sung with an orchestra before, but in her mind, she imagined violins sustaining the tender chord of the nightingale, and flutes fluttering an impression of wings and wind. Once their introduction was finished, she began her song in earnest.

Geppetto listened. Not once did he yawn or pull out a book to read, and she knew from his expression that her song moved him.

One true listener is worth a hundred idle ones, Chia used to say when Ily declared she wanted to sing before thousands in the Accordo Opera House.

For once, Ily agreed. And as Geppetto listened to her practice for her audition for the rest of day, she didn't think once about what an awful place Pariva was.

CHAPTER TWENTY

It was a morning of disasters. Ilaria tore a button off her dress and couldn't find it, so she had to sew on a new one that didn't match, and the carriage she had spent three months saving for was little more than a hay wagon—pulled by donkeys, no less. Not even horses!

"Nothing can be done, Ms. Ilaria," said Mr. Muscado, observing her disappointment. "There was a crack on the front carriage wheel. Wouldn't be safe to take it out."

"I paid twenty oros for a carriage—" Ily spluttered. "I'm not going to take a wagon!"

"Then I wish you luck finding another ride at this hour," said Mr. Muscado sharply.

"You're a swindler."

"Your brother hired me to take you safely to Vallan by

noon. Doesn't matter if it's in a wagon or a carriage pulled by horses or sheep. You'll get there on time."

There was an edge to Mr. Muscado's tone, and Geppetto touched Ilaria's arm, urging her to accept.

She gritted her teeth. It was a good thing Geppetto was with her. If he hadn't come, she would have thrown a fit right there and then. But when Geppetto offered his arm to help her climb aboard, she put on an air of nonchalance—for his sake.

The ride was rough; the donkeys kicked up dust from the road, which dirtied Ilaria's hair and clogged her throat. And the smell! She knew by the end of the four hours she would smell like straw and hay, if not dung.

It was so awful she wanted to cry. She couldn't stomach the idea of arriving in Vallan caked in dust. Worst yet, nausea crawled up to her throat thanks to the bumpy roads and thick air. How would she sing at her best like this?

"A game of cards?" Geppetto offered, trying to distract her from her misery.

She shook her head and reached into her satchel. Out came six sheets of parchment—the music to the Nightingale Aria—but Geppetto frowned.

"You've sung the aria a thousand times," he said gently. "You don't need to sing it again. Let your mind and voice rest."

"How can I rest when I'm practically choking on dust?"

"Look there," he said. "We can't even see Pariva anymore. When was the last time you journeyed so far from home?"

She swallowed. "Three years ago. Chia and I came to Vallan to see our first concert together. There was a famous duo I'd wanted to see—a soprano, and her sister at the harpsichord." Ily's voice went low with longing. "They performed together across Esperia. I always thought that might be Chia and me one day."

Geppetto's shoulders fell. His lips were parted, and he was clearly trying to find some way to comfort her. "What an adventure you'll have today," he said at last. "No matter what happens, it'll be something worth remembering."

She couldn't quite summon Geppetto's optimism, but she did smile. "I hope so."

"I know so."

Ilaria inched closer to him, reveling in how her nearness made Geppetto lean nervously against the edge of the wagon. If he moved any more to the left, he'd fall out.

Then he reached into his coat pocket. "For luck," Geppetto said, passing her a small box wrapped in newspaper that had been carefully painted red, her favorite color.

Ily looked up at him. "A present? But my birthday isn't until next month."

"I know. I meant it as a birthday present, but I finished it early. Last night. Thought I'd bring it in case you needed a smile, and it looks like you do."

That did make Ilaria smile. She loved presents.

She undid the paper, not even minding when some of the red paint smudged her fingertips. Geppetto's gift was a heart-shaped box, its dark wood intricately carved with a nightingale on a tree bough, the leaves etched with a vibrant yellow paint.

"It's beautiful," she breathed. "Did you make this? I'll put all my jewelry inside. It's perfect!"

"It's a music box, actually." The young man blushed. "Here, you'll see. Let me help you wind it up."

Geppetto wound the crank on the side of the box, and a song tinkled like little bells. Ilaria recognized the tune immediately.

"It's my aria!" She stared at him in amazement. "How did you do that?"

"I read a bunch of books," he said shyly, "and took apart my mother's old music box. Papa would have killed me if I hadn't put it back together, so I found a way."

"I'm glad you did."

He ventured, "It doesn't sound as pretty as you do."

It was Ilaria's turn to blush. Mostly because she knew

he meant it. She held the music box close. "Thank you, Geppetto. I'll treasure it always."

She played the music box over and over until her fears subsided and her worries fell to the back of her head. This time, when she moved closer, Geppetto went still. She leaned on his shoulder and closed her eyes, letting her mind drift to the music of Geppetto's steady breathing and the tinkle of her favorite song.

"Ily, Ily!" Geppetto shook her awake. "We've arrived."

Ilaria jolted, and instantly sprang up. They were in Vallan!

Ilaria forgot about her shame over arriving on a cart. She forgot about the dust in her curls and how her throat tickled when she breathed in. Before her, only a hundred steps away, was the city.

She practically ran, and poor Geppetto had to sprint to catch up with her.

"We're late," he said, though Ilaria was hardly listening. "Mr. Muscado will be waiting for us to take us home—"

"Do you see that, Geppetto?" she breathed as she looked up.

Geppetto craned his neck. "What are you looking at?"

"The sky," she exclaimed. "I can hardly see it. The

buildings—there're so many of them. And they're so close together. It's marvelous, isn't it?"

"Ily, did you hear me? We're running—"

She darted down the street. There was a restaurant on every corner, and how fashionably the men and ladies dressed! She adjusted her hat and brushed invisible dirt off the ruffles along her neck. How fine she'd thought her dress when she'd bought it in Nerio. Here it looked like an old frock twenty years out of date. No one had rosettes on their waist, and it seemed that ruffles were only for grandmothers or babies.

Still, everywhere she turned, there were sights that dazzled and mesmerized her. Acrobats in the middle of the streets, surrounded by a crowd tossing coins and flowers at the performers; opera singers in masks who sang along the street corners.

"You've ten minutes . . . t-to reach the c-conservatory," said Geppetto between breaths.

"Ten minutes!" Ilaria exclaimed. She hiked up her skirt. "Why didn't you tell me?"

"It's this way."

Together they dashed down the streets. Ilaria had no idea where she was going, but Geppetto had studied a map of Vallan while she'd napped, and he led her on turn after turn until she saw it.

The Madrigal Conservatory.

It occupied its own block on the street, with the names of Esperia's great composers carved into the white stone facade, just under the roof. The very sight stole away Ilaria's breath. It was the grandest building she had ever seen.

There was only a minute until she was expected, and she hastily patted at her perspiring temples and tried to iron out the wrinkles on her dress.

"No need for that," said Geppetto. "You'll dazzle them with your voice." He offered her the last of his water.

While Ilaria drank deeply, Geppetto sat on a bench beside a lamppost.

"I'm a bit too dusty from the road to accompany you into a place like the conservatory," he said sheepishly. "I'll wait for you out here."

Ilaria wanted to tell him that she wanted him there with her, but she didn't want to make him feel out of place. "Don't you want to explore the city while you wait?" she asked. "It might be a while."

"A scoop of ice cream costs half an oro here," replied Geppetto sensibly. He took out his half-eaten sandwich from his bag. "I'll wind up penniless simply from walking around."

Ilaria laughed. It wasn't meant to be a joke, but she found it funny anyway.

She licked her lips and returned his canteen to him. "Thank you."

"You are the music, Ilaria. Show them that, and there is no way you can fail."

The words warmed her. She leaned forward and kissed Geppetto on the cheek.

Without looking back to see his reaction, she straightened her posture and strode into the conservatory. The school's interior was even grander, with lush burgundy carpets and a winding staircase with marble railings. She could practically smell music being made; the walls were the same color as parchment, embellished with gilded symbols that looked like clefs.

After a few minutes, she was taken into a narrow hall on the second floor. There, another girl was already waiting. She had perfect golden curls, a spotless white dress with lace so delicate it looked knitted by spiders, and dainty silk shoes with embroidered roses on the sides and an elegant heel that gave her extra height. A matching parasol rested at her side, and as Ilaria approached, a fragrance tickled her nostrils. The girl smelled like . . . like flowers from Mamma's garden.

No one in Pariva indulged in an extravagance such as perfume. Ilaria hadn't even thought of it! But suddenly she became all too aware of the sweat prickling under her arms and the odor that followed. She grew conscious of the loose button on her bodice, the dust stains on the ruffles over her shoulders—only noticeable if you looked closely, as this girl seemed to be doing from behind a curtain of thick black lashes.

"Are you Ilaria?" said the young lady, her voice far too honeyed to be sincere. "I'm Carlotta. Carlotta Linda."

Ily's eyebrows flew up.

"Yes, Maria Linda's niece." Carlotta bowed her head demurely. "They're waiting for you inside."

"Oh. Thank you." Ily hurried toward the door opposite Carlotta. In her haste, she didn't watch her step, and Carlotta's parasol shot out of nowhere.

Ilaria tripped and fell flat on her face.

"Oh, I'm sorry!" Carlotta said, extending a hand to help her up.

Were she Chiara, Ily would have gratefully accepted the hand. But Ily knew the face of a devil when she saw one.

"You tripped me!" she cried.

"Pardon?" Carlotta tilted her head. "I was sitting. My parasol must have fallen."

Ily gritted her teeth as she leaned against the wall to get up. *Don't make a scene,* she told herself. Her dress was fine; she wasn't hurt. She'd go in for her audition as if nothing had happened.

She had started to pivot for the door when Carlotta plucked a piece of straw from her skirt. She flicked it to the ground, giggling. "Figures you came here by wagon, Ily Bumpkin. Break a leg."

Ilaria's shoulders squared. She shot Carlotta a glare that usually unsteadied even the most resolute of souls, but Carlotta didn't even flinch. She put on a smug simper as if she knew something that Ilaria did not.

Ily whirled away, but inside, her heart was hammering, and she felt suddenly lightheaded, her stomach whooshing as though she had eaten something disagreeable.

Stop it, she rebuked herself. *You can't let a silly girl ruin this.*

She had imagined this moment a thousand times. Walking confidently into the room, where a mahogany harpsichord, a ceiling-high arched window, and a bookshelf of music awaited.

Aglow with energy, she'd sing her best. Her voice would be velvet, and every note would be smoother than the chocolate Mamma spread onto their toast.

But in reality, she could hardly speak. Maria Linda was there, seated beside an elderly gentleman with a gray velvet coat and brass-buckled shoes: the conservatory director, Maestro Lully.

All Ilaria could focus on was Maria Linda. Her idol.

The diva was as beautiful as Ilaria had heard, with raven black hair plaited into a long braid at her side, and pearls as large as marbles dangling from her ears. While her white gown had a scandalously low neckline, the fur stole over her shoulders added just the right touch of modesty. Even the way her gown fell, into a satin silk pool at her feet, looked luxurious. The entire effect was a picture of glamor and elegance; she looked like a goddess, the goddess of music.

"Ilaria Belmagio?" said Maria Linda.

"That's me," Ilaria replied, almost trilling in her excitement.

Maria Linda barely looked up. She fluttered a hand at the harpsichordist. "Start at the recitative."

The accompaniment began without any warning, giving Ilaria only a second to compose herself and step into character. She was a bird, a lonely nightingale that had lost her way, but she'd come across a kind young man, Figaro, who was also lost in the forest. She would appeal to him to help her go home.

Maria Linda closed her eyes, listening with a far-off expression.

Excitement bubbled to Ilaria's toes. She didn't expect to learn the results of her audition immediately after singing, but from the notes Maestro Lully was furiously scribbling into his book, she knew she was making an impression.

"That will be all."

Maestro Lully waved his notebook, and the accompanist abruptly stopped playing. Ilaria didn't understand what was happening, so she kept singing, certain it was a test to see how she sounded unaccompanied.

"I said, that will be all."

Lully's tone was sharp this time, and Ilaria's song died in her throat. She couldn't move. She blinked, certain she had misheard. "That'll be all? I hardly finished the recitative. I haven't even begun the aria—"

"Had you arrived on time, you would have been allowed to sing more."

Anger burned in Ilaria's chest. "Do you know what it took for me to get here?"

"We judge on the quality of your voice, Ms. Belmagio, not the hardships you face getting to your audition on time."

"But I've practiced—"

"For months? Years?" Maria Linda spoke this time, and she uncrossed her ankles. "Yes, and you are not alone in that. You are a fine actress, I'll give you that, and your voice is lovely. But a star is far more than that. How many languages do you speak?"

"One," said Ilaria, pursing her lips. "But I can sing proficiently in five—"

"Who was your teacher?"

"Ms. Rocco."

"Rocco?" Maria Linda frowned. "I'm not familiar with the name."

"Valeria Rocco," Ily supplied. "She sang in the Vallan Opera for years before she retired."

"She was an *alternate* for the chorus," corrected Maestro Lully. "I remember the name. Quite a scandal at the opera . . . she was dismissed for coming to rehearsals drunk."

Shame heated Ilaria's cheeks. Ms. Rocco had enjoyed the occasional drink, but . . . Ily swallowed. "Please, let me try again."

"When you are onstage, they will not let you *try again*," said Maria Linda. She stood and circled Ilaria, her heels clicking against the wooden floor as she walked.

"You're a lovely girl with a lovely voice, Ms. Belmagio, and you have a decent ear as well as a fine sense of drama. But that's all it is. Lovely. A prima donna cannot afford to be lovely. She must make the stars themselves bow down when she enters."

Maria Linda leaned in as if she had an invisible monocle with which to scrutinize Ilaria's clothes. Then her nose made a disdainful wrinkle. "Yes. Yes. It is as I say. Your unfortunate ensemble can be rectified with a visit to a proper clothier and your deplorable pronunciation are things that can be worked on and trained, but your presence? The

Nightingale Aria is about more than a bird who is lost in the forest. The nightingale is angry, she is miserable, she is in pain. It is a song of transformation, of transcendence. You see, when her melody returns, it transcends into something new. She finds love amid despair and wretched loneliness; it is this new transformation, this change in her song, that allows her to finally find her way home. It is meant to make the listener weep and feel joy at the same time. I sensed none of that spark from you."

Maestro Lully nodded in complete agreement. "I couldn't have said it better." He set down his book of notes. "We thank you graciously for your time, Ms. Belmagio, but unfortunately the conservatory is not a fit for your efforts. You may go."

You may go.

In three words, Ily's thirteen-year-long dream came to an end.

Her world spun, and she didn't remember storming out. But in the next dizzying minute, she was outside in the narrow hall once more, the heat of tears held back blurring her eyes.

To make things worse, Carlotta held out a handkerchief. "The washroom is that way." She pointed. "First left and down the hall."

Any other time, Ilaria would have snapped that she

didn't need directions to the washroom and that she was fine. But the tears were already starting to fall, and she would *not* cry in front of Carlotta Linda.

She ran into the washroom and leaned against the wall, slumping down until she was on the ground. Years of dreaming—of practicing until she sang even in her sleep, of walking miles to the next town where a new aria might be sung, of training her ear until she could transcribe a melody after hearing it only once—all of it had distilled into a few minutes in a dimly lit room.

She pounded her fists against the wall, furious at herself, angry at Maria Linda and Maestro Lully.

She *was* the nightingale. Lost and miserable and in pain. But she'd find her way home. She'd *make* her way home.

"I'll march right back there and make them accept me," Ilaria determined. "I won't give up."

Determined to snatch back the fate she knew she deserved, Ilaria inhaled a shaky breath and strode back toward the audition room.

But she didn't get very far. Even one hall down, she could hear someone singing from the room. Carlotta Linda.

Carlotta's voice was a light and airy soprano, completely unexpected and different from her speaking voice. The aria she'd chosen was a difficult one, a showstopper requiring a four-octave range and difficult leaps that were barely supported by the harmony in the harpsichord's accompaniment. Yet Carlotta glided through the song fluidly, masterfully.

Every note was wrought with passion and emotion, and even if Ilaria hadn't understood a single word that Carlotta sung, she wouldn't have been able to wrest her ears away.

There she stood, her palm pressed to the door, half-miserable, half-riveted. Spellbound. If she'd thought Maria Linda had made a mistake about her, she didn't anymore.

Carlotta had it all: the voice, the presence, the power.

Ily's knees went weak with realization. Maria Linda hadn't tried to be cruel; she had simply conveyed the truth. Ily wasn't good enough.

Tears welled around the rims of Ily's eyes.

I won't cry, she said, blinking furiously. *Stop it, Ily! Stop it!*

A violin student turned the corner into the hall, and Ilaria ducked her head before he noticed her crying. Tilting her hat over her head, she hurried out of the conservatory, her heart thundering against her steps.

Geppetto was there, as promised, waiting for her. He hadn't brought a book to read or purchased even a newspaper to occupy his time, and when he saw her, he lifted his hat and started to wave—only to drop his hands.

"Ilaria, what's wrong?"

Ily didn't even have the energy to lie. "It was stupid," she said sourly. "All of it was stupid. They didn't even let me finish my aria, or ask me my range, or ask me to sight-sing." The words hurt; each one was like swallowing a needle. "Come on, Geppetto. Let's go home."

Bless him, Geppetto didn't question her. "You should eat something."

"I'm not hungry."

"I tried looking for your favorite cookies, but the bakeries here don't have them. . . ."

His voice trailed when he noticed her bleary eyes. Geppetto's shoulders fell. He looked as crestfallen as she felt. "I'm sorry, Ily." He pursed his lips. "You'll have another chance, I'm sure."

"I won't."

"Fate is kind. She'll see your dreams through. Maybe not in Vallan, but there are other cities in Esperia."

He took her hand, clasping it in both of his, and Ilaria shook her head. She couldn't help it, but a flare of irritation rose to her chest.

Fate wasn't kind, no matter what Geppetto said. Ilaria knew that in her heart. She'd always known it. First it had taken Chiara from her. Now her dreams.

If she wasn't good enough for Vallan, then she'd always be second rate. There was no use in trying somewhere else.

Ilaria drew her hand back and turned on her heel. "Let's go home," she said, with her back to Geppetto. "I never want to come back to this awful place again."

"How was it?" Mrs. Belmagio asked when Ilaria returned home. It was well past her mother's bedtime, but she was still up, sitting beside two plates of Ilaria's favorite cake with matching forks. One for Ilaria, one for Mamma.

When Ily and Chia had been little, they used to sneak slices of cake before bedtime and share with their mother. Any other day, the sight would have melted Ilaria's heart, but not tonight. Tonight, Ilaria's heart was stone.

Inwardly, she thought the truth: *I'm tired, Mamma. It's been a long day. My dreams were shattered and I have nothing left. I just want to be left alone and go to bed.*

"Ily?" Mrs. Belmagio's tone leaked concern, and the brightness on her face dimmed. "Ily, is everything all right?"

Mamma handed her a square of chocolate cake—speared on a fork, which Ily accepted numbly.

"Thank you."

She said it automatically; ate the cake automatically, too. But inside, her dreams of traveling the world, of singing in the great opera houses—crumbled like the cake under her fork.

She couldn't tell that to Mamma. "It's delicious," she said as brightly as she could.

"Are you all right?" Mrs. Belmagio asked again.

Taking the plate from Mamma, Ilaria started up the stairs, the creaks in the wood sounding louder than they ever had. Then she forced her most brilliant smile. "Of course I'm all right. I'm going to be a star, Mamma! The brightest star that Esperia has ever known."

Mamma's hand flew to her mouth. "The audition was a success? From the way you sounded just now, I thought . . ."

"That they rejected me?" Ily threw back her head and laughed. "I was acting. They took me, Mamma! I'm going to Vallan!"

"You devious girl!" Mamma pinched Ily's nose, then hugged her close. "To the theater for you. What an actress you've become. I did believe you."

Ily struggled to keep her voice even: "Were you disappointed?"

"No. Your papa and I would have been just as content for you to stay in Pariva with us forever. We're selfish that way."

"I won't be staying," said Ilaria, the words rushing out before she could think. "I'll leave for Vallan as soon as winter is over."

Mamma wiped at her eyes. "First Chia, now you. It

seems Fate has grand plans for both my girls . . ." Her voice trailed. "Your hard work has paid off. Soon, your dreams will come true."

Ily's smile faltered, and she pushed her mother away. Regret filled her chest, but she didn't dare take back the lie. She'd tell Mamma the truth in a few days. When her head and her heart hurt less and every word she uttered didn't taste so bitter.

Mamma caught the hitch in Ily's composure, and held on to her hand. "What brings you joy brings us joy, Ily. Are *you* happy, my darling?"

"Why wouldn't I be?" Ily said airily. "This is what I've dreamt of my entire life." She took a step up the stairs toward her room. She had to get away before her mother saw through her lies. "I should get to bed, Mamma. It's been a long day."

Without saying good night, she practically flew up the stairs into her room and closed the door. She leaned against the wall, sinking inch by inch until she fell onto the ground, her toes curling against the soft, knotted rug her mother had made her when she'd been a girl—back when dreams were as distant and bright as the stars hanging in the sky, and reaching for them wouldn't turn them into dust.

"Where are you, Chia?" she whispered, searching for

the Wishing Star. But only the moon peered back at her, a sliver in the sky. "Can you hear me? I miss you. I need you."

They were only a year apart, and almost like twins. They'd spent their whole lives together, and Chiara's not being here was like missing a part of herself.

How unfair it was that Chiara, who would have been happy staying in Pariva for the rest of her life, was out exploring the world! No doubt she was flying with silly gossamer wings and meeting every sort of person, important and not.

All while Ilaria was stuck here. Talentless, unwanted, and never good enough.

"Fate isn't kind," she repeated to herself. "Geppetto was wrong. She isn't kind at all."

Over and over she repeated this to herself as she cried herself to sleep.

Little did she know, someone was watching. Someone with the power to change her fate.

CHAPTER TWENTY-ONE

Esperia had crossed winter's threshold, and even the stars were cold. But Chiara hardly shivered as she hurried down the silver-dusted path to the violet house across from her own.

Five months under Agata's tutelage, and her resolve to train with the fairies had only strengthened with every mission, every wish granted, every visit to Esperia. Until today.

Today, when she'd woken and looked outside her window, the sight of the kaleidoscope of fairy homes, the glimmering brooks, and the argent trees brought a pang to her heart. She missed seeing the sun crawling over her sill. She missed seeing Papa sweeping the old cobblestone road outside their home, missed hearing children screech that they were late to school, missed resting her eyes on the ever-blue Lyre Sea.

Before coming to the Wishing Star, she had never spent more than a day away from her family. Now she had spent the entire autumn without seeing them. Occasionally she would steal a glimpse at Pariva through the map over her well, but it could not show her parents, her brother, or her sister as anything other than specks of light. Every day, Ily's grew dimmer, and Chiara couldn't let go of Larissa's taunts:

Would you like to see how miserable you've made your dearest Ily?

Chiara's hands closed into fists at her side. Branches of wisteria swayed above the Violet Fairy's crystal door. Carved along the edges were canal boats drifting down a narrow river. Such hints of Agata's past were present throughout her home, and in the months Chiara had resided on the Wishing Star, she had just begun to notice them.

She thought of the wooden dove she kept in her bedroom, the sheet music she'd brought to remember Ilaria, and the slice of almond-blackberry cake she asked for every morning to think of her mamma's baking. She wondered whether one day soon, she'd sprinkle traces of her own past into her home. Whether it'd make being away from her family harder—or easier.

Or whether she'd never come back to this place again, and it'd become only a distant memory.

Her hand trembled as she lifted it to knock on Agata's door.

One rap was all it took before the Violet Fairy appeared. She seemed to be expecting her.

"Well, good morning, Chiara. You're early for your lesson."

Chiara entered Agata's home quietly, taking her usual seat beside the window. Agata's home always smelled like the sea, with a hint of orange—and chocolate, if Chiara inhaled deeply enough.

"Something's on your mind," Agata observed. "I take it we should address it before discussing the itinerary for today."

Chiara gathered her courage. "I haven't seen my family since coming here," she confessed. "It's been five months as of yesterday, and today is my sister's birthday. She turns seventeen."

"You're right," said Agata, clucking her tongue. "It has been five months. You've acclimated so well to our ways I half forgot you were an apprentice, Chiara. I suppose this means it is indeed time for you to go home."

Chiara gave a nervous nod.

"That isn't all, is it?" Agata sensed. "There's more."

Chiara pursed her lips, wondering how Agata had read her so easily. Then again, the woman was a fairy—skilled at reading one's heart and emotions.

"Do you wish to *stay* at home?" Agata asked gently.

"I don't know," she confessed. "I miss my family more than anything, and yet . . . I feel like I belong here."

Agata settled into the seat across from Chiara. She said, kindly, "It's natural for you to feel at war with yourself. I would be concerned if you didn't."

"I don't know how I'll be able to make a decision when the time comes."

"Then perhaps it's time I tell you everything," said Agata quietly. "What you'll have to give up before becoming a fairy."

It was a thought that had occupied her mind these last few days. "I have some idea." Chiara spoke as quietly as Agata. "Fairies don't age or die. You've served for centuries. Mirabella even longer than that." Chiara folded her hands over her lap. Every spare moment she had, she spent in the Archives, reading about the fairies before her. Her very first time there, she'd noticed the years and dates of Agata's reports.

"If I become a fairy permanently, my age will become suspended until I decide to give up my wand. My family will pass on, as will my friends and everyone I know. I'll never see them again."

"That is one way to put it," Agata replied. "But there is more. I want to be truthful with you about this, for it is not easy on the heart. Should you choose to stay with your family, you will forget your time here with us on the Wishing Star, and all will be as it was before."

"What if I choose to come back with you?"

"Then after your week at home, you will cast a spell upon everyone you know—so that they will forget *you*."

A hard lump rose to Chiara's throat, and she suddenly couldn't breathe. "I have to make everyone forget me? No. No! I couldn't do that."

"The choice is yours. No fairy is forced into their decision."

"Why didn't you tell me earlier?" Chiara said, feeling a stab of betrayal.

"Because you wouldn't have come with me," replied Agata. The words were the plain truth, but she flinched as she spoke them. "Am I wrong?"

Chiara's throat closed. "No."

A cup of coffee appeared in Agata's hands, and she dropped an extra scoop of sugar into it before sipping deeply. "I deserve your anger, Chiara. All of us do. We did not want to mislead you, but the truth of the matter is, the Heartless grow powerful, and there are not enough of us to reverse their wickedness. Magic is particular and does not speak to everyone. Yet it spoke to you—it led me to you long before you saved Geppetto. We need new fairies such as yourself. . . ."

Agata pursed her lips. "But a fairy's love must be unconditional. You should not form attachments, even to your family—your love for them should be as great as your love for a stranger."

Chiara's voice shook. "Are you saying I can't see them?"

"You may observe them from your Wishing Well, but you aren't to help them. That will be another fairy's duty, should it be fitting."

"I see."

Agata touched her arm. "This is the hardest rule for us all, but it's also the most important. I don't expect you to stop mourning the loss of your life back home overnight, or even over a year. It takes time . . . a long time, and all of us have gone through it.

"It was difficult for me, too," confessed Agata. "My parents died when I was young—of a fever that swept my town. But I had an older brother I looked up to. He was my whole world."

"What happened?"

"As you can see, I became a fairy later in life," Agata replied, gesturing good-naturedly at the wrinkles along her eyes, "after my brother married and had children of his own. It was easier for me to leave. But you're still a young woman with many years ahead. Perhaps I've asked too much of you."

"It is much to ask of anyone," Chiara said honestly. Not long before, she'd been sure that she wanted to be a fairy. But now a war raged in her heart, and she did not know which side she wished to win.

"Coffee, Chiara?"

"No." A mug of hot chocolate appeared in Chiara's hands instead. Its warmth comforted her, and she took a long drink. Her eyes fell on the boats along Agata's door, the purple wisteria petals that gathered outside the fairy's home. "Do you miss your brother?"

"Every hour of every day," said Agata softly. Her coffee disappeared in a puff of stardust. "There won't be a lesson today. Take the morning off. Spend some time thinking about what I've said. After you finish your cocoa, I'll take you home."

CHAPTER TWENTY-TWO

Half past noon, Ilaria tossed on her coat and wrapped her new fur stole around her neck.

It was her seventeenth birthday, and she'd wasted enough of it huddled in the corner of Mrs. Tappa's shop, rubbing her hands by the meager fire waiting for customers while the lady napped upstairs in her bedroom. Winter had arrived, and snow dusted the road outside, and everyone was crowded around the market to buy last-minute groceries. No one, absolutely no one, was going to buy a hat today.

Ilaria plucked a red feather off one of the caps and wriggled it into her chignon. Then she buried her face in her fur. She'd left work early yesterday when Mrs. Tappa was at the market and hired a wagon all the way to Nerio to buy it. An exorbitant purchase, but it was her birthday, and she deserved nice things. Nice things that would take her mind off the future that'd been stolen from her.

A bell chimed at the door. Mrs. Tappa was back.

"Just where do you think you're going?" she demanded as Ilaria buttoned her coat.

"Out. It's my birthday."

"I don't care what day it is," Mrs. Tappa said. "I've had quite enough of your insolence, Ilaria Belmagio. Day after day I let you come in late, let your friends loiter about my shop without buying anything. Don't think I didn't notice you leaving the store yesterday, unlocked and open for thieves to steal all my wares. And now you want to—"

"If you care so much about your shop," interrupted Ily, "maybe you should try tending it yourself."

"Why, you impertinent, ungrateful little wretch! Get back here. Don't you go to the door, or I'll—"

"Fire me?" Ilaria whirled. "I'm going to be famous, Mrs. Tappa. So famous you'll be engraving my name by the door to tell everyone that I used to work here, because it's all people will remember you for."

The words spewed out of her lips before she could control them. Every word was a lie, but Mrs. Tappa didn't know that. How good it felt to see the old woman's jaw fall agape!

"I'll take this as a gift," said Ilaria, plucking a velvet hat off the nearest mannequin. It was scarlet, matching the red feather in her hair. "It's the only one here that isn't hideous."

She didn't know where her audacity was coming from, but it felt wonderful. She felt free.

Ily sauntered out the door, ignoring Mrs. Tappa's threats to tell her mother. What did Ily care? She hated working at the shop. The hats were overpriced and ugly, the ribbons were of shoddy quality and frayed after a week, and she didn't need the money for tuition anymore.

She hated Pariva, too.

Mrs. Tappa was kind to you. A little voice poked into her head. *She gave you a salary for doing practically nothing. Is this how you repay her?*

Like I said, Ilaria told the voice stolidly. *She'll get to engrave my name on her door.*

Snow crunched under her shoes, and the sound quickly grated on her nerves. The past few weeks, she'd moped about town, trudging her way to the shop and watching the clock hands tick slow second after second. Simona and Beatrice had stopped visiting her at the shop—she'd been brusque to them upon returning from Vallan.

"So, what happened?" said Simona. "We heard Mr. Tommaso's son went with you to Vallan. Gius—"

"Geppetto," said Ilaria.

"Geppetto," Simona repeated. "He's poor. And not particularly handsome or charming."

Ilaria pretended not to hear and twirled the ends of her hair. "The director of the conservatory practically dropped his baton once he heard me sing," she lied. "He's famous, you know. Conducts the Vallan Symphony as well as the opera orchestra."

"You actually got in?" Simona said.

"Did you ever have any doubt?" Ily scoffed. "Of course I did, and I'm counting down the days until I leave this backwater."

"When do you leave?" asked Beatrice, raising a skeptical eyebrow.

Ilaria lifted her chin. "First thing in the spring. I'm going to be a star, and I'll never come back to this paltry little town again."

"That's funny. Your eyes look puffy, Ily dear. And Pietro said he saw you crying when you came back with Geppetto."

"They were tears of joy."

They hadn't believed her. Ilaria couldn't stomach their pitying looks and I-told-you-so glances at each other. Worse yet was keeping up her lie at home. Ily knew Mamma was starting to grow suspicious and sensed she was keeping something from her. She could tell, too, from how nice Niccolo was being to her, and how Papa's morning kisses on her forehead felt like a sympathy stamp. As if they were waiting for her to tell the truth.

Deep down she wanted to, but her pride wouldn't let her. If she told them the truth, her dream would be gone forever. Better to cling to the illusion as long as she could, better to pretend to be *someone* than to go back to being no one, even if it was just for a little while. Someone more than a baker's daughter in Pariva, someone people admired and dreamt of meeting.

Better to pretend than face the truth and have to nurse the wound that Maria Linda's words had carved into her soul.

And so Ilaria pretended, and the grander her lies grew, the deeper she buried the sorrow in her heart. Until today, on her birthday, she woke remembering something very important. Something that made her stop feeling sorry for herself.

A wide grin spread across Ily's face, and the ache in her heart turned into a fierce burning. No one would ever have to know that she'd lied. Just let them wait. She might be unworthy now, but soon enough she'd return to Vallan and show everyone—*the world*—just what she was capable of. Maria Linda, Maestro Lully, Carlotta. All who doubted her would witness her soar.

"Shouldn't you still be at work?" her mother inquired as Ily entered the family bakery. "It isn't even two o'clock yet."

"Mrs. Tappa let me out early for my birthday," lied Ily. "Are there cookies for me?"

"You're in luck. Papa just pulled them out of the oven. Careful, they're a bit hot."

Ily reached greedily for the sack and inhaled. Cinnamon, with a hint of dark chocolate. Her favorite.

"There's seventeen of them," said Mamma, counting one cookie for each year Ily had been alive. "Plus one extra for luck." She winked. "You might want to share them with your young man."

Ilaria rolled her eyes. "Geppetto isn't my young man."

Her mother shrugged. "If you say so." She swept aside Ily's dark bangs and pressed a kiss to her daughter's forehead. "Happy birthday, my love."

"Mamma," Ily protested at the show of affection. But for the first time in weeks, she didn't cringe or twist away. She took the drawstrings over the sack of cookies and tied a bow. "I suppose eighteen cookies *would* be too much for me to eat alone."

"Cookies taste better when they're eaten with friends," said Mrs. Belmagio. "Especially good friends. You two aren't courting, are you?"

"Mamma!" Ily cried, but her cheeks heated. "I said we weren't."

"You've been seeing an awful lot of each other ever

since he took you to Vallan," said Mamma with another shrug.

That was because Geppetto was the only one who knew the truth. At first, she thought he would judge her for lying to her family, the entire town, even to herself—but he never said a word about it. Nor did his eyes, clear and blue as before, ever waver when they held her gaze. In these weeks, having Geppetto believe in her and stand by her meant more to her than she could have imagined.

He was her truest friend. And like Mamma said, maybe more.

"Thank you, Mamma. You're the best." She grabbed the bag of cookies, then, humming happily to herself, hurried for Mr. Tommaso's workshop. She had a proposal for Geppetto that she knew he wouldn't be able to refuse.

Geppetto was sitting by the window, so intent on his work that he didn't even notice Ilaria at the door. A good thing. She took a moment to fluff her hair and rub color into her cheeks. Then she paused before the other side the window, craning her neck to see what he was working on.

To her surprise, it was a toy. Geppetto didn't usually work on toys in the middle of the day—what would his papa say?

She stood on her tiptoes to get a better look at the

figurine. It was still roughly hewn, the shapes of two people beginning to take form. Ilaria could make out the outline of a girl with her arm outstretched, and a nightingale—same as the one Geppetto had chiseled onto the music box he'd made for her—was perched on her fingers.

"Is that supposed to be me?" she greeted coyly.

Geppetto whirled, startled by Ilaria's appearance. He tossed a cloth over his workplace, trying in vain to hide the figurine. "Ilaria! I wasn't expecting you so early. What are you—"

"I left work," she interrupted, not wanting to explain herself for the second time. "Is your father here?"

"He stepped out for a walk. I was going to come find you after I finished—"

"I beat you to it." She flashed him her most winsome smile, then dropped the cookies on his worktable. "And I brought snacks. Cinnamon chocolate cookies. My favorite. Smell."

She raised the bag to Geppetto's nose, and he inhaled deeply.

He said, gently, "You shouldn't be the one bringing me cookies on your birthday."

"Who would I bring them to, then? Simona and Beatrice?" She snorted. "You're supposed to eat sweets on your birthday for a sweet year ahead—with your sweetest friend." She paused. "That's you, Geppetto."

Before he could respond, she broke a cookie in two and offered him the bigger piece. Geppetto took it, and they ate together, sitting side by side on a bench in comfortable silence. She'd kissed dozens of boys in her seventeen years, yet sharing a cookie with Geppetto felt like the most romantic thing she'd ever done.

"Thank you for coming with me to Vallan," she said quietly. "And . . . for keeping my secret. It's meant a lot to me these last few weeks. Chiara was right about you—and I'm glad we're friends."

It was his cue to kiss her, but as before, Geppetto was so oblivious that he didn't seize the opportunity.

"I am, too," he said, just as quietly. Over the last weeks, he'd grown less anxious in her presence, though he still fidgeted with his glasses when she was close. He did so now, then offered her his handkerchief. "To wipe your hands," he explained.

Ilaria laughed. "How considerate. But I'm having another cookie."

As she reached into the sack, Geppetto observed, "You're happy. You haven't been happy in weeks."

"That's because I realized something today." Ilaria

rose from the bench. "You were right, Geppetto. There *are* other big cities in Esperia aside from Vallan. Who needs the Madrigal Conservatory? If I studied with Maria Linda, I'd waste an entire year in school. Better I go out and make my own future. Chia will help me."

As soon as she said it, the many clocks on Geppetto's wall announced that it was one o'clock. Still no sign of her dear fairy sister.

But Chiara had promised to be back for her birthday, and she never broke a promise.

"Is she allowed to do that?" Geppetto asked belatedly.

"Why not? She's my sister." Trying to hide her dwindling confidence, Ily grinned. "She could help you, too." She plucked a violin off a rack on the wall. "Why repair instruments when you can *make* them? You could become the most famous violin maker in Esperia, Geppetto. A legend! Think of all the masterpieces you'll craft. Violins for the greatest virtuosos of our time, for kings and princes and dukes! Instruments that everyone in Esperia would clamor to buy. Everyone would know your name. Wouldn't that be marvelous?"

Geppetto picked up a cookie, but he didn't take a bite. "It would be something," he said at last.

"Your father wouldn't have to worry about this shop anymore. You'd make plenty of money. Just imagine! After a few years, you could retire and carve all the toys you want."

Geppetto picked up his whittling knife and wiped it clean with his apron. "My heart isn't in music the way yours is, Ilaria. I love listening to it, being surrounded by it, but I . . ." He spread his arms at the walls of violins, violas, cellos, and guitars. "This isn't my dream."

Ilaria frowned. "It'd only be for a few years." She remembered the figurine he had been carving. "What, you want to waste your youth making trinkets? Little toys that people admire from the window but don't come in to buy? Your father wouldn't approve."

"Our workshop has been in our family for generations," Geppetto deflected good-naturedly. "But I've thought long and hard about it, and even if Papa is upset with me, I can't lie to him anymore. Or to myself."

His gentle gaze fell on her, and suddenly Ilaria stiffened. "Is this your way of lecturing me about my own lies?"

"No, I would never lecture you. It's not my place."

"Then?"

"I only wonder if you should tell your family the truth. Don't live a lie, and don't run away."

Ily's mood soured. Geppetto, too? She couldn't believe it. "I thought you of all people would understand," she said. "But you're just like the rest."

"Ilaria . . ."

"At least my dream is worth lying for," she said harshly. "Any peddler on the street can sell toys. Why do we need a shop dedicated to them? There's no future for a toy maker in Pariva."

Geppetto's face fell, and she knew she ought to take her words back. But she didn't.

Instead she stormed out of the workshop, ignoring Geppetto's shouts behind her.

"Ilaria! Ilaria!"

Her heart screamed at her to turn back, to reconcile with the young toy maker and make things right with him, but Ilaria shut it out. She hurried faster, sprinting back into town before Geppetto could follow.

She didn't look back once.

"There you are!" exclaimed Nico as Ilaria stalked through the town square. She was tired and out of breath from walking so fast, and she had nowhere she planned to go.

"Ily!" her brother said again, chasing after her. "You've got to come home, now."

"Leave me alone. I don't feel like talking to anyone."

"Not even Chia?" Nico grinned as Ilaria's eyes flew up from the ground. "Yes, she's back. She's home!"

CHAPTER TWENTY-THREE

It was fortunate that the cookies on Mrs. Belmagio's tray had already cooled, for when she spied her eldest daughter enter the bakery, she dropped the entire batch on her feet.

The cookies crumbled on the ground, and Mrs. Belmagio burst into tears. Her tears, of course, had nothing to do with the ruined cookies.

"Chia," she choked out. "My dearest dove. You're home."

Mrs. Belmagio would have scooped her daughter up into her arms if she could, but Chia was a grown woman. So mother and daughter embraced, and for once Mrs. Belmagio didn't care that her hands smelled of dough or that there was chocolate all over her apron.

"I missed you," whispered Chia into her mamma's hair. "I missed you so, so much."

Mrs. Belmagio lifted Chia by the shoulders to have a look at her. "You've gotten thinner," she said, pinching her cheeks. "No good bread in fairy-land?"

"Not like yours."

"You've come to the right place, then." Mamma hugged her again, and Chiara took the deepest breath she had in months. Notes of cinnamon and almonds and oranges sharpened the air—the smells of winter at the Belmagio Bakery—but behind them was the absolute best smell in the world: that of Papa's freshly baked bread and Mamma's cookies.

Mamma only then noticed the fallen cookies. "My stars!" She clucked her tongue. "It's all right, those were extras. Niccolo!"

Niccolo poked his head from behind the kitchen doors. When he saw Chiara, he threw off his baking hat. "You're back!" he cried.

Mamma turned to the door, turning away the hungry customer who had appeared. "We're closed for the day," she said without explanation.

Papa pushed through the shutter doors from the kitchen. His long face revealed no surprise at the sight of Chia, standing in front of the cake counter as if she were an afternoon customer and not his daughter, but his eyes danced with the same merriment that touched his wife's.

"Back in time for the cookies, I see." He tugged at the

end of his mustache and wagged a finger at her. "Aren't you cold in that?"

Startled, Chiara looked down at what she was wearing. For the last five months, her uniform had been the same gauzy white dress with a silver cord at the waist. She hadn't changed come summer, autumn, or winter. She hadn't even put on a scarf or mittens or a cloak.

Come to think of it, she hadn't felt cold in months. Hadn't felt goose bumps rise on her skin, or a shiver, except when she was near the Heartless.

"Here," said her father before she could answer. He plucked a cloak off the rack behind him and settled it over her shoulders. "Seems being with the fairies has made you forget how to take care of yourself. That's what parents are for."

Chiara hugged her father. As always, he smelled like basil and rosemary. "How's the herb garden?"

"Shriveled up for the winter," he replied with gusto. "But it'll be back." He showed off his jars of dried basil, harvested from his garden. "This'll be enough for now!"

Chiara's stomach grumbled. She couldn't wait to eat. "Have you all had lunch yet? Is Ily working?"

"No." Mamma rapped Niccolo on the shoulder with a towel. "What are you standing there for?" she said. "Go fetch Ily. She's at Mr. Tommaso's."

Chiara tilted her head. What was her sister doing at the luthier's workshop? "Is she seeing—"

"Geppetto," Niccolo finished for her slyly. "They've been spending every day together. Guess he's her last fling before she moves to Vallan."

Chia gasped. "She . . . she's moving? The conservatory accepted her? That's wonderful news."

"Isn't it?" Nico said. "Should I bring Geppetto, too?"

Mamma rapped him again. "Family only today. It's Chia's first day back."

As her brother left the bakery, her parents steered her home. "Walk faster, Chia," Mamma said over and over. "You'll catch cold in that dress. What were the fairies thinking, dressing you in a summer shift like that?"

Once they turned onto Constanza Street, Chia's breath caught in her throat. There it was. Home.

Snow and frost rimed the yellow roof, and frost gathered at the eaves. But inside, nothing had changed. The cat-shaped rug by the door, its eyes scratched off by a puppy Niccolo had brought home when he was five. Stella, they had called her. She'd died three years ago, and Ily had cried so hard she'd come down with a fever.

There was a line of mugs she and her siblings had sculpted and painted; they hung on the wall above the grandfather clock that had been in their family for a century. The harpsichord in Chiara's beloved Blue Room hadn't moved. She didn't need to touch it to know that its keys were probably still in dire need of tuning.

Her whole life, Chiara had spent in this house, and she could have navigated every corner with her eyes closed. She still could, yet something . . . *something* about it all was different.

That something was her.

"Your sister will be thrilled to see you. And just in time for her birthday!" Her mother chattered nonstop, something she did when she was nervous. Until finally she looked at Chiara and asked, "Will you only be back a week?"

"Yes, Mamma," replied Chia.

"And then?"

Chiara bit her cheek. Of course her mother remembered what Agata had said. That after the week, she'd have to make up her mind whether she'd stay in Pariva or return to the Wishing Star for good. Of course, she didn't know that if Chia chose to go back, she'd have to make everyone forget her. . . .

Stop thinking about that, Chiara rebuked herself. She wouldn't let anything put a damper on her precious time home.

Why? she couldn't help asking herself. *Because it could be my last? It doesn't have to be. I don't have to go back to the Wishing Star. . . .*

Coming home had only magnified her doubts about becoming a fairy. Seeing Mamma, Papa, and Niccolo, she was happier than she'd been in months. She wasn't homesick anymore; she was home surrounded by the people who knew and loved her best. Already her months on the Wishing Star were a faded memory, and she was slipping back into her old life.

"Don't ask her that," said Mr. Belmagio. "She's got seven days to figure it out."

"Seven days!" Mrs. Belmagio was exclaiming. "That's hardly any time at all." She elbowed her husband. "Luckily we knew you'd make it home for Ily's birthday. We have some of your favorite dishes prepared."

"Mamma . . . it's Ily's birthday. Not mine."

"Ily isn't the one who's left home to become a fairy," tsked her mother. "Let me spoil you a bit, Chia. You never let me spoil you."

That was when Ilaria appeared. She wore a new coat, black and furred at the collar, and held a red velvet hat at her side. Her dark hair was pinned up at her nape, a red feather stabbed into the middle of the chignon.

Her sister looked different, but in a way only someone

who hadn't seen her in months would notice. Her cheek-bones were sharper, her mouth was harder. And her eyes—her eyes that always glimmered with mischief and merrymaking—held a secret sorrow.

Thanks to her fairy's gift, Chiara could practically taste Ilaria's sadness. It was like tea left too long to steep, chocolate without any sugar, olives that hadn't been cured.

Ilaria put on a bright grin. "Knew you wouldn't dare break your promise," she said, a bounce to her step as she greeted her sister. "Aren't you going to wish me a happy birthday?"

"Happy birthday, Ily."

"What's the matter? You're staring. Has my nose grown a nest?"

Mamma laughed. "Go on, Ily. Help your sister into something warmer."

"Shouldn't we help with dinner?" asked Chia.

Nico snorted. "Only you would volunteer for chores during your first hour home. Relax, Chia. Papa and I will set the table."

With that, Ily tossed aside her coat and dragged Chia up to the attic. "See, your room's exactly the same. I took up some of your closet space, though. You don't look like you'll miss it. Did you not bring anything back? What about a gift for me?"

Chia's breath hitched. "I didn't get a chance—"

"It's all right," Ily interrupted. "Birthdays are about more than gifts. I'm simply happy you're back. Now, what should you wear?"

While Ilaria rummaged through her clothes, Chia sat on her bed. "I heard about the conservatory. You must be so happy, Ily."

"Mmm-hmm," replied Ily, still flipping through Chia's dresses.

That wasn't quite the reaction Chia had expected. She changed the subject. "Is your coat new?"

"It's a present to myself."

It looked expensive, observed Chiara, and she held back a frown as her suspicions about Ilaria rose.

"This one!" Ily said, selecting Chiara's old favorite dress. It was pale blue like her eyes, with a matching blue bow at the waist and sleeves.

"Yes, that will be much better than that nightgown you're wearing."

"It's my apprentice's gown."

Ily wrinkled her nose. "You always sounded like you were a hundred years old, but now you dress like it, too."

Her fairy's gown *was* rather old-fashioned, with its long flowing skirt and straight sleeves. But Chiara hadn't minded it. Without complaint, she shrugged it off and put on the dress Ily had selected. The cotton was soft against her skin, and the soft stripes were a pattern she didn't see much of on the Wishing Star.

"Now," said Ily excitedly as she jumped onto Chiara's bed. "Tell me everything. What kind of magic can you do? Will you show me?"

"I can do magic when I'm on the Wishing Star. Otherwise, I need to borrow Agata's wand."

"You don't have your own?" Ily cocked her head. "What have you been doing these last five months?"

"Honing my sense of what is right and wrong—it's what the fairies call your conscience. And visiting people across Esperia who might need extra guidance."

Ilaria stifled a yawn. "What about wishes? Don't you have to listen to people's wishes?"

"It turns out that's only a small part of what fairies do." Chiara hesitated. "Mostly I look after people's hearts. I have a map I can access that shows me how someone's faring."

A flicker crossed Ilaria's features. She got up quickly and fiddled with a crinkle in the curtain. "Oh?"

"It showed me yours," Chiara said softly. "You've been . . . sad."

"Sad? Why on earth would I be that?" Ily picked up a

mirror on Chiara's desk and gazed at herself approvingly. "Everything is going just the way I want it to. I got into the Madrigal Conservatory, and—"

Chiara didn't need to hear any more. Ilaria's emotions told her all the truth she needed. "Don't lie to me, Ily. Please."

"I'm not."

"That coat you wore downstairs must have been over a hundred oros. Money you would have used for rent in Vallan, for food, for coal . . ."

Ily's expression hardened. "You *would* notice that."

"What really happened?"

Ilaria turned down Chia's hand mirror. "I didn't get in." She pursed her lips tight. "It's fine. It's not like I really *wanted* to go. Who wants to be a stupid opera singer anyway? You know what they say: fame is a poisoned chalice."

A lump formed in Chia's throat. That explained everything. Her sister had dreamt of going to the conservatory for years. "You don't believe that."

Ily's lips thinned. "Maybe not. But still."

"You mustn't give up—it's been your dream forever to sing."

"Why shouldn't I give up?"

Her sister was staring at her expectantly. For what,

Chiara couldn't possibly begin to guess. "Tell me what went on in Vallan."

"Maria Linda said I didn't have presence. Whatever that means." Ilaria laughed as if she didn't care. "This other girl, Carlotta, got the spot instead. You should've seen her—she had swan feathers sewn into her dress and pearls as big as grapes in her hair! It looked awfully gaudy, and don't get me started on her perfume. One whiff of her and I thought I'd lose my lunch. Guess that's the sort of girl they're looking for in Vallan."

So that explained the expensive coat, the feather in her hair, the dramatic antics. Ily was pretending everything was all right.

Chia reached for her sister's hand. "It's time to tell everyone the truth."

"Can't it wait until after my birthday?"

"Ily . . ."

"It's been a horrible day, Chia." Ily's lower lip trembled. "Mrs. Tappa fired me from the shop, Simona and Beatrice have been cold and cruel, and I had a row with Geppetto . . ."

"What?"

Tears heated Ily's eyes. "If you hadn't come home, this would be the worst birthday ever. But you're back, Chia. And you'll make everything right again, won't you?"

Ily flew into her arms, catching her off guard.

Chiara held her sister and tipped her chin over Ily's head. "I'll do whatever I can, Ily."

Ily sniffled. "Really?"

"Yes. I'm your sister, and I love you."

Ilaria wiped her eyes with the back of her hand. A smile tugged at the corner of her lips.

"Did you really have a row with Geppetto?" Chia asked quietly.

"A small one," she admitted. "We've become friends since you left."

"Good friends?" Chiara teased.

"He's in love with me," said Ilaria. "He just hasn't been able to tell me so. I have to show you what he made me."

Ily towed her downstairs to her room, where Chiara noticed a beautiful wooden box on the vanity. It was unmistakably Geppetto's handiwork. The craftsmanship was on a different level from the simple figurines he had carved. The box itself was shaped into a heart, and on the top was a finely etched nightingale. She lifted the lid and gasped as it began to tinkle the Nightingale Aria. "Your favorite song, Ily!"

"Not anymore," said Ilaria with a shrug. "He made it for me to bring luck for my audition, but obviously it didn't work."

Ily paused in front of the small hearth in her room, lifted

the brazier's lid, and tilted the music box toward the hungry flames within. "Now it just stirs up bad memories."

"Ily!" Chiara cried, grabbing her arm. "Don't. It's his gift to you."

"Seeing it brings me no joy."

"Then I'll keep it." Chiara took the music box before her sister threw it into the fire. She cupped her hands over the heart-shaped wood. Maybe it was best if she held on to it—for safekeeping—until her fickle sister made up with Geppetto.

"I don't know what you two fought over," Chiara continued, "but it's obvious he cares for you—and you for him."

"What are you, a fairy in training or a matchmaker?"

"Fairies bring out people's joys. Love happens to be one of the great ones." Chiara tucked the box into her pocket. "I'll keep this until you two make up."

Ilaria made a face. "What makes you think we will?"

"My special fairy sense."

Her sister snorted, but didn't resist when Chia enveloped her in a hug.

"I'm glad you're back," Ily finally said, her shoulders softening as the rest of her did, too. "It really feels like all my dreams have come true."

"That's my job," replied Chiara.

"So it is." Ilaria flashed a grin, and there was something

so sly about it that even Chiara couldn't pinpoint what it meant.

She had no idea that she was playing straight into Ily's hands, and that was exactly what her sister was counting on her to say.

CHAPTER TWENTY-FOUR

Over the next seven days, Chiara became her old self again. A daughter, a sister, a neighbor, and a friend. She went ice-skating with her family; even convinced her mother—who was scared of falling—to join. She and Niccolo held Mrs. Belmagio's hands as she nervously toed across the frozen pond while Ilaria and Mr. Belmagio chased the ducks. Then they spent hours playing cards and laughing over countless mugs of hot chocolate and slices of almond cake.

She checked in on the townspeople of Pariva. Many shyly asked if she could grant their wishes, but all she could promise was to listen. For most, that was enough.

She baked with her papa again, kneading dough with her fists as he chuckled at her side. "You've still got the muscle," he said approvingly.

"I won't lose it," she promised.

She played chamber music with Niccolo and his quartet and caught Ily stealing by the Blue Room to listen. *Join us,* she mouthed. But Ily shook her head.

One entire week home, and Ily hadn't sung once. Chiara couldn't remember the last time Ily hadn't sung, or at least hummed, everywhere she went.

But her sister had changed. Worse yet, she still hadn't told the truth about what happened in Vallan. The last time Chia prodded her, Ilaria's response had been cutting: "When are you telling us what *you've* decided? Are you leaving us for the Wishing Star, or are you going to stay?"

Distress leaked from Ily's tone, and Chia pursed her lips. "I don't know," she admitted.

"This could be our last week together, Chia. I won't ruin it by telling everyone I lied." Ily flipped her hair over her shoulder. "I'll tell the truth when you make up your mind."

What could Chia say to that? One minute, she was certain she would stay in Pariva with her family. But the next, when she looked up at the stars and remembered her time with the fairies, there came a twinge in her chest. The fairies needed her help against the Heartless. No matter how much she wanted to be with her family, if she forsook her duty to the fairies, thousands could be harmed.

Yet how could she hurt those who loved her most? Her mother, her father, her brother—and sister?

That's why they'll forget, she thought. *They won't hurt if they can't remember. Only I will.*

It was all she could think about, and on the morning of her seventh and perhaps last day at home, she tried to focus on her breakfast, but she couldn't. She stole a glance at Mamma, gripping her knife so tensely she scooped up half the jar of jam on her blade. Papa, who had taken off his spectacles and was pretending to stare at the newspaper. Niccolo, who was sipping nervously at his coffee as if it were grappa.

"Where's Ily?" she asked. "She's usually awake by now."

Her mother gave her a glazed look. *Stay with us,* her eyes read, even if her lips wouldn't speak the words. Chia couldn't see them without guilt prickling her conscience. "She's probably in her room . . . doing her hair. She's been doing that a lot lately. Why don't you bring her down to eat?"

Every step up the stairs reminded Chiara that she had only hours left to make her decision. When she reached the top, she took a deep breath.

Heavens, she hoped her sister wasn't in her room sobbing. If there was anyone who could convince her to stay, it was Ily.

Ilaria sat beside the window, watching snow fall outside as she brushed her hair. Dark and lustrous, her hair had grown long and nearly touched her waist.

"Ninety-eight, ninety-nine." Ily lifted her brush for one last stroke. "A hundred."

Chiara took that as her cue to step into her sister's room. "Are you coming to breakfast?" she asked softly. "Everyone's waiting for you downstairs."

Ilaria slid to the edge of her bed, but she didn't hop off. She sniffed the air. "Smells like yesterday's leftovers. I'll bet Mamma and Papa didn't want to bake on your last day here."

"I haven't said it's my last day," said Chia, quietly.

As if she hadn't heard, Ily prattled on, "Doesn't matter. I'm not in the mood for coffee or pastries. Sit with me, Chia. Let me brush your hair. A hundred strokes every day and night will keep it glossy and bright."

"I thought you gave up on that when you were seven. Said it took too much time and effort."

"Seventeen's a good time to pick up new habits. Stop moving so much. Sit still."

Obediently, Chiara sat and let Ily brush her hair.

"You have such pretty hair, Chia. I've always envied it, you know? The way it curls at your shoulders and every hair seems to be in place. Niccolo says it looks like noodles—like angel hair. What a silly name for pasta. I think fairy hair is more fitting."

A chill bristled against Chiara's nape. This wasn't the conversation she'd imagined having with Ily today. She twisted to face her sister. "What are you saying?"

"I'm saying . . ." Ily eyed the crack in the door and lowered her voice. "I'm saying, I've decided to let you become a fairy."

Chiara was certain that she had misheard. "Come again?"

"I know it's your dream to help people and to spread good across all corners of Esperia and all that nonsense," said Ily, wheeling her hands. "I mean, obviously it's not nonsense. But the point is I know it's what you've already decided, and I could kick up a fuss about it, but I'm going to be an adult. I'm seventeen now, after all."

"Thank you for your permission," said Chiara, still rather dazed. "You . . . you *want* me to go?"

"Mamma and Papa won't agree, but I think it's the best for Pariva. For the family, too. Everyone's been pestering us about you ever since you left. Think of what a disappointment it'd be for the town if you changed your mind about the fairies and stayed?"

Chiara couldn't sort through her emotions. She didn't know whether to be relieved that her sister was giving her blessing to become a fairy, or disappointed. Or flabbergasted.

"It would be nice if you gave me a farewell gift, though," Ilaria went on, twirling her hair the way she did when she was about to make a request that she knew had a high chance of getting rejected.

Chia was instantly on guard. "What sort of gift?"

"For weeks after my audition I was despondent. Yes, I lied—I told everyone that Maria Linda wanted me. That I was going to be her sole student in Esperia's most prestigious conservatory. I wished I hadn't lied. It was miserable, because I didn't know what I was going to do. But then I remembered—my sister is a fairy!" The morning sun hit Ilaria's green eyes, making them sparkle. "A fairy who promised to make all my dreams come true."

Chiara didn't like where this was going. "Ily, that's against the rules—"

"Make me a great opera singer." Ilaria leaned forward. "Make me as great as Maria Linda. Think of it: I'd be able to take care of Mamma and Papa, and Niccolo, too. Think of how many people would hear about our bakery, and how everyone's lives in Pariva would be changed. For the better."

"You aren't listening to me," said Chiara, as gently as

she could. "Even if I wanted to help you, I can't. It's against the rules for me to help you. You're my sister."

"I *am* your sister," Ily repeated.

"I can't be seen bestowing favors to my family or my friends."

"I won't tell anyone."

Chia shook her head. "No, Ily."

Ilaria's face darkened. "You promised. I'm not asking much, Chia. All this time you lived in Pariva, you helped everyone you knew. Now help the person you love the most. The person who loves you the most."

The words stung, and Chiara flinched, but she wouldn't be swayed. "I can't."

"Music is all I have," persisted Ily. "The conservatory doesn't want me. There will always be someone better. Unless you help me. I'll waste away if I stay here my entire life."

"No, you won't." Chia touched her cheek. "You're strong, and you work harder than anyone I know. You'll make your way."

"I'll make my way?" Ilaria recoiled from her touch. She scoffed. "Mamma and Papa don't make enough money to send Niccolo to university. Did you know that? His heart isn't in becoming a baker, but he has to. You have the power to make our lives better, and you won't. I thought fairies were supposed to stand for goodness and compassion. You pretend to care—"

"I *do* care."

"Then do something for us. Help *me*. Music is all I have that's my own. I'll die without it, Chia. I'm happiest when I sing."

"Then sing," said Chia. "Why do you need fame to be happy? Why not spread your love for music by teaching the girls and boys in Pariva? They adore you, Ily. They always have, but you never pay them any heed."

"I don't want to be a teacher. I want to be heard."

"You want to be adored," said Chiara. "And you already are. You just can't see it yet."

"What would you have me do?" Ily said. Her tone turned cruel: "Marry Geppetto and help him paint toys?"

Chiara drew a breath. "What's gotten into you, Ily? This doesn't sound like you."

"Maybe this is who I'm destined to be. What did you expect, after living in your shadow for seventeen years? You've always been the perfect one. Not everyone's life is as charmed as yours."

"You think my life is charmed because I'm going to be a fairy?"

"Isn't it? It's always Chiara *this* and Chiara *that*, what a beautiful and brilliant and kind sister you have. It's such a shame she's gone. I guess there's Ilaria."

"No one says that."

"They do," insisted Ily. Her shoulders shook as she began to weep, and her heart was so full of anguish that Chia couldn't tell whether she was acting.

Chiara drew her close, and squeezed her sister's hand. Once again, she began to understand why the fairies made their loved ones forget them. To save them pain. Pain that she alone would bear.

"They'll forget me, Ily," said Chiara softly. "Everyone will."

Ily went still in her arms. "What are you talking about?"

Chiara swallowed, realizing her mistake, but she wouldn't lie to her sister. "If I go back to the Wishing Star tonight, I'll cast a spell over the town. Everyone will forget me, even Mamma and Papa."

Her sister drew a sharp breath. "Do they know?"

"It'll be easier for them if they don't."

"You weren't going to tell us?" Ilaria pushed her away roughly. "You would abandon me, your whole family, the life you've had—everyone's always said you were the selfless one, Chia. But now I see. Eternal youth, magic, you can go anywhere you want, do anything you want. And you'll live forever. All you have to do is leave behind your little mortal family."

"Ily, it's not like that. . . ."

Ilaria was in disbelief. "I thought you'd at least be able to visit. That I'd at least see you . . . but you'll be leaving for good. I won't even know you."

Chiara wrung her hands. There was nothing she could say without feeling awful. "It'll be easier that way. For both of us."

"Easier that way?" Ilaria's anger returned, and sunlight ignited her eyes, turning them gold. "Easier on your precious conscience, maybe. You won't have to fret about leaving us behind."

"That isn't it," Chiara pled. "Fairies love everyone unconditionally. We don't favor someone over another. Even if that someone is my sister."

"So you'll throw away your family. Eighteen years of memories." Ilaria wiped her eyes. She was crying. "How could you?"

Chiara faltered. She wanted to comfort her sister, but she didn't know how. She didn't even know how to defend herself—or the fairies. "It's for the good of—"

"The good," Ilaria rasped. "It's always about the good. Not everything is good or bad, Chia. Not everyone has a diamond heart like you, fit to discern who is deserving and who isn't."

Chiara flinched, trying to overlook the vehemence in her sister's voice. Ily was angry; she was hurt. And she deserved to be. Chia wouldn't deny that.

"You'll have a good life, Ily," said Chia gently. "Mamma, Papa, and Niccolo, too. The fairies promised me this. Even if I can't watch over you, others will."

Ilaria didn't give her a chance to explain further. There was a tremor in her sister's voice as she spoke again: "I hate you."

They were words Ilaria had said to Chiara hundreds of times when they were little girls. But this was the first time Chiara knew that Ily actually meant it.

"Go on, cast your spell. Make me forget now." Ilaria's voice was venom. "Do it. Better now than tonight. What difference will it make, anyway?"

Stricken, Chiara stepped back toward the window. "You have the right to be upset. I'm sorry, Ily."

"Go ahead and cast your spell." Ilaria seethed. "I hate you, and I wish I'd never had a sister."

"Ily . . ."

Ilaria turned her back to her.

Swallowing hard, Chiara reached into her pocket. "You

can have this back," she said, setting Geppetto's music box on Ily's vanity. Though she hadn't wound the lever, the Nightingale Aria tinkled, filling the silence between Ily's clomping footsteps. If once the song had melted Ilaria's heart, now it did the opposite.

Ily angrily snatched the box from Chiara and threw it across the room.

The box hit the wall, then landed on the rug with a thump.

"I said, leave!"

Chia bit the inside of her cheek so her own tears wouldn't fall. Then, with a silent apology to her sister, she exited the room.

Her mother was waiting for her at the bottom of the stairs. "Your mind is made up," said Mrs. Belmagio astutely. "You're not staying."

Chia couldn't lie. "I'll leave tonight."

"I had a feeling. I think Ily did, too." Mamma tilted her head, the way her daughters did. "It'll be hard on her."

"I know."

"Don't feel guilty, Chia. It's your calling. I've always felt you had one that would take you far away, and on a grand adventure. I think I've known it since you were a little girl."

Chia's lower lip trembled. "I wish I didn't have to leave."

"I know, my dove." Mamma brushed her fingers against Chia's cheek. "But no matter where the stars take you, I'll always be your mother. I'm content knowing that."

Tears of sorrow and relief welled in Chiara, and she wrapped her arms around her mother, hugging her. After her bitter fight with Ilaria, she couldn't begin to describe how much she needed to hear her mamma's words.

"Your sister will come to understand," Mrs. Belmagio said, stroking Chia's hair. "Give her time. In the meantime, do as much good as you can. Our world can be an ugly place. But you, my Chia, you will make it brighter for every life you touch."

"I hope so," Chia whispered.

Chiara stood alone outside her home, leaning against the old lemon tree in her courtyard, and held her wooden dove close. "I can't do it," she whispered to it, as if it could listen. "Ilaria hates me, and I can't cast the spell on my family when we're . . . broken."

"Then speak to her," Agata replied from behind. "Reconcile with your sister, and cast the spell tomorrow."

Chiara practically jumped. She didn't think she'd ever get used to the fairies materializing out of thin air, even when she became one herself.

"Sorry if I startled you." Agata took Chia's arm and

guided her down the street. "But I sensed you were distraught."

"Why are we not allowed to grant the wishes of our loved ones?" Chia blurted, instead of greeting her mentor.

Agata let out a sigh. She held out her wand, and in a wave they had left Constanza Street and stood on the top of Pariva's bell tower. There, the Violet Fairy sat on the roof and finally answered Chia's question: "We were permitted to, once. But a few errant fairies took advantage of the privilege and made their families rich and powerful. Larissa and Amorale—they led a rift among the fairies and formed the Heartless.

"That is why we must uphold our rules. Should you break them, your wand will be taken away, and you will be cast out."

"Are there no exceptions?" asked Chiara.

"The fairies would never punish you for having compassion, Chiara. But there is a reason certain spells are forbidden, and that is to uphold a balance in magic, and to keep it from tipping into the Heartless's favor." Agata paused. "Spells that would benefit you personally, for instance—or those that you know and love. In Ilaria's case, you know that your sister's desires are not selfless."

"Yes, I know. But she's my sister, and I love her."

"As she loves you. She will forgive you in time."

"She won't remember me."

The Violet Fairy lowered her arm. "In her heart, she will. It may seem cruel, what we have to do, but it is the responsibility we bear."

"I know," whispered Chiara. She'd known from the beginning. "Thank you for explaining. Now I understand what I have to do."

"You are certain that this is what you wish?" said Agata. "There's still time for you to change your mind."

All it would take was a simple no, and Chia would return in time for lunch with her family, then spend the afternoon making music with Ilaria and playing checkers with Niccolo. Everything would be as it had been.

But deep down, she knew she couldn't ignore the tug on her heart. That if she didn't take this chance, she'd always feel like she'd let herself down.

"Yes, I'm sure."

Agata reached into her sleeve and drew out a slender wand. "Then this is for you."

Chiara gasped as her mentor passed her the wand, and a small star appeared at its tip. It should have warmed Chiara's heart to see it, but she could barely muster a smile.

"The reception of a fairy's wand is often a bittersweet occasion. Let that be a reminder for you that magic can bring great joy as well as sorrow, hope as well as fear. May you use yours to shine light upon darkness."

"I will," Chiara vowed.

As soon as the words left her lips, the star on her wand came aglow and a pair of iridescent wings bloomed from her back.

"What name will you take, Chiara Belmagio?"

The answer was one she had toyed with ever since she'd considered the fairies' invitation. "The Blue Fairy."

Blue was the color that brought her joy. The color of the walls of the music room where she and Ilaria had spent countless hours laughing and chasing each other and making music; the color of her father's eyes, like hers; the color of the sea where she and Niccolo took their little boat out when the weather was fair.

Her dress shimmered with stardust. The pale color deepened into a warm and rich blue, and the fabric softened into gossamer silk. The threads stitched themselves into a gown worthy of a good fairy, turning her long sleeves into iridescent swaths of starlight. A beautiful yet understated uniform. Perfect for the new fairy.

Only the ribbon she wore in her hair was the same as before. A reminder of Chiara Belmagio, daughter of Pariva.

"Go on," encouraged Agata. "Cast your first spell."

Chiara hadn't thought of what that would be. She looked to the wooden dove on her palm and gently touched its head with the tip of her wand. "Awaken, little bird. Have life."

Once the words left her lips, the dove purred and its wings trembled at its sides. But the dove was still made of wood, not of feathers and flesh as Chiara had imagined.

Chiara's brows knit together in confusion.

"A beautiful spell, Chiara," said Agata slowly, "but the gift of life is not yours to give."

Chiara held the wooden dove close as she swallowed hard. "I didn't know. I'm sorry."

"I hadn't told you, so it is not your fault. You recall when Mirabella enchanted the stones in the Hallowed Forest to life?"

When Chiara nodded, Agata went on, "That was a temporary spell. You see, no fairy has the power alone to give life fully where there is none. It is a spell too great, and disrupts the natural balance of things."

The Violet Fairy tapped the end of her wand upon the dove, reversing the magic that Chiara had cast. The dove went still once more.

Heat pricked the edges of Chiara's eyes, but she managed a smile as her mentor returned the dove to her.

"Magic that manipulates life is forbidden, Chiara. If you were to attempt such, you would be stripped of your powers."

"I understand, Agata," whispered Chiara. "Thank you for the lesson."

Agata's expression softened. "I know you'll make a wonderful fairy, Chiara." She squeezed her shoulder. "It is hard, what we ask of you, but you'll see it's for the best. As for the forgetting spell, come back tomorrow, make up with your sister, and cast it before sunset."

"Before sunset—tomorrow?"

"The sooner you cast the spell, the better," said Agata. "It will hurt less." A pause. "For you and for your family."

Chiara gave a nod. "All right."

"Good." Agata's smile was bittersweet. "Now let us go back to the Wishing Star. Everyone is waiting to welcome our new Blue Fairy home."

CHAPTER TWENTY-FIVE

Ilaria waited until Mamma and Papa were asleep. Niccolo, too. The house was never quiet at night. Papa and Niccolo snored and whistled in their sleep, while Mamma occasionally mumbled the bakery's menu for the following day. Tonight, though, she let out a quiet sob. Hearing it made Ily falter, and she almost gave up on her plan. But no, she couldn't. Not even for Mamma.

She put on her coat and red velvet hat—and at the last minute, picked Geppetto's music box up from the floor. With a rueful sigh, she thumbed the dent she'd made on the edge and wheeled the crank round and round, but the song came out fractured, the rhythm off-kilter and more than a few notes off pitch.

It was broken, like her. And she didn't know how to fix it.

I don't need to be fixed, she thought as she stuffed it into her pocket. As quietly as she could, she crept downstairs.

Lifting one of Papa's bread bags, she threw in a handful of matches and candles, a loaf of bread and a jar of honey, and the money her father kept behind the atlas he displayed on the wall above their dining table. It'd be enough to get her to southern Esperia, or maybe even out of the country altogether. She had no idea where she was going, only that she had to leave tonight.

Before Chiara returned to tamper with her memories.

Once she stole out of the house, she hurried down Constanza Street for the other side of Pariva. It was a cold night, and the air bit at her nose and fingers. She thought about going back to get her gloves, but she didn't dare risk it. Within minutes, her fingers were stiff with cold and her teeth chattered. Still, Ilaria didn't turn back.

She snatched a lantern off a neighbor's fence, not knowing whether she'd ever return it, and held it close for warmth.

She paused, trying to think. At this hour, there'd be no carriage she could hire, and she didn't dare sail a boat on her own. Where would she go?

Geppetto's, she thought, her feet changing direction for the luthier's workshop.

The hour was late, and as she cut through the town square, fear rattled her heart.

Mamma always said that Pariva wasn't safe after dark. Their little village was situated between Elph and Nerio, two important port towns, and many travelers came through Pariva on their way. Most visitors were genial and warm, but every now and then, the town would get an unpleasant character or two—especially at the Red Lobster Inn.

"Only hooligans frequent that tavern," Mamma said once. "Thieves, drunkards, liars, and conmen."

"I've seen Niccolo there once or twice," Ily had replied tartly. "Papa, too."

The glare Mamma shot her was withering.

"Mamma was exaggerating," Ily muttered to herself now. Yes, she'd heard about a few brawls breaking out in front of the tavern, but she wasn't about to avoid taking the fastest route across Pariva simply because she was afraid of a few drunk fishermen.

The guttering streetlamps did little to quell her fear, and Ily walked as fast as she could. She was a street away from Geppetto's corner when she realized that her footsteps had an echo.

She was being followed.

A rush of fear washed down her spine, and as she picked up her pace to turn the corner, a carriage wheeled in front of her, almost ramming her in the side. Startled by the horses, Ilaria stumbled and fell off the pavement into a bush.

"Guess I was wrong about the lack of carriages at this hour," she muttered to herself.

Then came the sounds of someone leaping out, and a shadow darkened the already dim street. A man leaned over her. His smirk was shaped like the sickle moon, but the rest of his face was cloaked in darkness.

"What's a pretty minx like you doing in this part of town?" he said, making a low whistle. "Isn't it past your bedtime?"

"Get away from me," Ilaria muttered.

"No need to be rude," said the man, advancing with one long stride. "What have you got in that bag there?"

He reached down to grab her, but Ilaria was faster. With all her might, she slammed her heel into his knee and sprang up, running. But a second man grabbed her from behind—the one who must have been following her. A hand went over her mouth.

"That wasn't very nice," said the man with the smirk as his partner brought Ily around. "Hey, I've seen this lass before. She's that girl who knocked me on the head!"

Moonlight fell upon the man with the smirk, and Ily recognized him now. The gray hair, the uneven beard, the faint markings of an old bruise on the side of his head.

Alarm spiked Ilaria's pulse. "Help!" she shouted. "Help!"

She swung her elbow back, feeling her bone hit against a jaw. The arms around her waist slackened, and she started to wrest herself free—until a knife slashed into view.

Ilaria went rabbit still. Her anger dissolved immediately into fear as the man with the gray beard pointed the knife at her throat.

"Well, now I'm angry," he said with a growl. "Stupid donkey. Bray all you want—that's going to be the last sound you ever make. I'm going to pay you back."

His friend held her by the arms, twisting them behind her back until she yelped with pain. A blow came to her head, knocking her senseless. The world went black, then the guttering streetlamps appeared again. Another hit was coming. Ilaria had to fight! Her legs were still free, and she kicked and kicked, but it was no use.

Her vision went blurry with the effort, and darkness started to close in.

Then suddenly the knife dropped from the man's grasp as his hands went to his throat. His partner, too, was choking on what seemed to be nothing. Within seconds, they were on their knees.

A woman loomed over Ily. Her green gown was far too thin for the wintry night, but she didn't look cold at all.

Tiny emeralds glittered on her skin in place of freckles, and vines and leaves that couldn't possibly thrive in this weather were entwined into her long black hair.

She extended a hand to help Ilaria up. "That was no way to treat a rising star such as yourself, Ilaria Belmagio.

"Tell me, wouldn't you like to punish these ruffians?"

CHAPTER TWENTY-SIX

Ilaria caught her breath. Her coat was ripped; her skirts, too, and there was snow and mud all over her boots and hair. But somehow, she was calm. She turned to the two men quavering in the snow, their hands still scrabbling at their throats as air left their lungs.

"Yes," she said shakily. "They deserve to be punished."

"Do you like animals?" A magnificent ebony wand appeared in the woman's hand, spiraling almost to the ground. At the top was a dark and gleaming emerald. "I think they'd make a nice pair of billy goats. Or rats, perhaps."

Ilaria gawked in astonishment. Magic emanated from the woman's wand in streams of smoke and shadow. Could she be a fairy? She didn't seem anything like Chiara's old and frumpy mentor.

"What do you say, Ilaria?"

Ily eyed the men who'd nearly killed her. A stupid donkey, they'd called her. "Turn them into donkeys."

"Interesting choice." A dark eyebrow lifted in amusement. "As you wish." A tap of the fairy's wand, and the men began to change. First went their hands and feet, which became hooves that thumped against the ground as they screamed and flailed. Fur bristled over their skin, and tails sprouted from their backs as their pants ripped and their shirts stretched until the buttons popped and the fabric shredded onto the ground.

They brayed and brayed, pleading and whining. Ilaria staggered back, horrified.

"You look dismayed," observed the fairy in green. "Should I change them back?"

A part of Ily pitied the men's fate, and then she saw the cuts on her hands, remembered the overwhelming wave of fear as they'd hit her. "No."

"I thought not." The fairy's wand flashed into a whip. Raising it high, she lashed at the donkeys' backs until they bolted away. "Get!" she shouted. "Get!"

Once the donkeys were gone, Ilaria whirled back in the direction she had come—for Geppetto's workshop. She was no fool. The fairy who'd helped her was even more dangerous than the two brutes who'd attacked her.

"Rather ungrateful, aren't we? No thank-you for the help?"

"I'd sooner thank a devil," retorted Ilaria.

"That can be arranged." The woman smiled wickedly. "Aren't you forgetting something?"

The fairy held out her music box.

Impossible! The box was in Ilaria's pocket. Except . . .

Cursing to herself, she turned and seized her music box back, wiping off the snow with her sleeve. When her fingers fell upon the dent in the heart-shaped box and the scratches on the nightingale, she swallowed. She wanted to hug it close, make it good as new.

Why did that make her heart hurt? She didn't care about him or about the stupid song in the stupid box. They were all reminders of her terrible life in Pariva, anyway. She wanted to lift the box and hurl it into the snow, but she couldn't.

"Something the matter, my star?"

"I'm not your star," spat Ilaria.

"You wish to be a great diva," said the fairy, taking Ily's arm. Her nails were sharp, and Ilaria recoiled from her touch. "I can help you."

"Everyone says that. Everyone's lying."

"Your *sister* lied," the fairy in green corrected. "Very unbecoming of her. But also unsurprising."

The fire in Ilaria's lantern went out, leaving her cold. Within seconds, she could hardly feel her nose. Meanwhile, the fairy at her side seemed as comfortable as ever, even in her gown with no sleeves and a scandalously low neckline.

"Cold is a human weakness," said the stranger, noting Ilaria's bewilderment with a smile. "Not a fairy's."

"A fairy?" Ilaria repeated, alarmed. "*You're* not a fairy."

"I am," she confirmed, glancing back at the smoky wings that flickered behind her. "But not like any you've known. My name is Larissa the Green."

Larissa's voice multiplied, becoming a chorus of itself, low and reverberant. "I am a mistress of the night."

With a wave of her wand, they were no longer in the streets of Pariva. They were on the shore, steps from the ocean. Ilaria felt the hairs on her nape prickle. The beach was empty, no one would hear her shouts. She staggered back, trying to twist toward the road, but her feet were rooted to their spot.

"I can't move!" she cried.

"Red suits you, my star." Larissa touched the blood on Ilaria's lip. "It's full of passion, just like you. You could be far more than a simple stage singer, should you wish it."

Little by little, Ilaria's fear disappeared, replaced by a cautious curiosity. "You're going to grant me a wish?"

"No, no, I'm not in the habit of wish granting. I think of it more as making a deal."

"What sort of deal?"

"You want to be a famous opera singer, don't you?"

"I did." Ilaria stared at her hands. "But it seems Fate isn't on my side."

"Fate has many faces," replied Larissa, drawing closer. "*I* can help you change yours."

Ilaria's eyes narrowed. She told herself to trust her instincts. "Go away. I know better than to make deals with someone like you."

"Who else can help you, Ilaria? You've been betrayed by the person you loved most, and abandoned by her, too. You are meant for more, Ilaria. Your sister couldn't understand that."

"What does this have to do with Chiara?"

"Do you want the truth?" said Larissa. "She's worried that you'll outshine her."

Ilaria snorted. "Chia doesn't even know what envy is. She's only following rules."

"Rules that *you* would have broken for her, had you been in her place. Wouldn't you?"

Ilaria's laugh died in her throat, and soured into resentment. "I would have."

"That's because you love your sister. If she loved you,

wouldn't she want you to be happy? Wouldn't she have lent just a crumb of her great power to help you, the dear sister she loves most?"

Ilaria's lower lip began to tremble. She knew the words were poison, triggering the simmering anger in her chest, yet she couldn't help nodding. It was true, all of it.

"It isn't even as if you would have needed much," continued Larissa, stepping closer to Ilaria. "You have the talent and the beauty, the drive and the charisma. All you needed was a bit of luck and it would be you studying under Maria Linda's tutelage, not that overdressed peacock Carlotta."

Ily couldn't disagree.

"I can give you the power to make all your dreams come true," Larissa purred.

"You don't look like a fairy."

"I'm in a different circle than your sister. One that actually cares. I know you want to be the greatest singer in the world. You want to step into a room and have it go silent with awe, to have people fawn over you, to be famous and loved—even more so than Maria Linda."

Shivers tingled down Ilaria's nape. It was all true. She yearned for her music to have the approval and attention of everyone who heard her. But Larissa's offer was too good to be true, and she knew it. "In exchange for what?"

A smile, and those flat eyes lit afire. "Your heart."

"What!" Ilaria staggered back in shock. "Never."

She tried again to turn away, but it was in vain. Her feet wouldn't move. "Chiara!" she cried. "Chia, help me!"

"Your sister is preoccupied on the Wishing Star with her fairy induction," said Larissa, tittering as if the event were a pathetic joke. Her smile widened. "But I'm here. You've impressed me, Ilaria Belmagio. It appears my offer is not enough. So I shall make it sweeter."

"There's nothing you can give me that would change my mind. I'll never give you my heart."

"Then don't," said Larissa. "Keep it yourself. In a box."

Now Larissa had her attention. "A box?"

"You saw what I did to those men. I turned them into donkeys. Not once did you beg for their lives."

Ilaria shrugged. "Because they're criminals."

She regretted it as soon as she said it, for her answer pleased Larissa greatly. "You have taken the first step to your destiny, my star. How would you like a taste of such power? Not just fame and glory, but *magic* as well—magic that will rival your sister's in every element imaginable."

"I'm not evil."

"Is it evil to take what you deserve?" Larissa said. "Some would call it wisdom, strength. Your heart gets in the way. It is a weakness."

Ilaria's hand went to her chest. It was true, there was a

pain in her heart she couldn't shake. Was that the weakness Larissa spoke of?

"It won't hurt, I promise," said Larissa. "You won't even miss it."

"No," Ilaria said, still unable to move. "Let me be."

"All right, if that's what you want. In a few days, you won't remember who I am, anyway. Fairies will merely be a bedtime story. Your sister, too."

They were just the words Ilaria didn't want to hear. She pinched her eyes shut. "Go away," she said, but her mettle had withered, and her words were a mere whisper.

Ilaria found she was able to move her feet again. Her mind in a fog, she started back onto the road, but Larissa followed her, a tendril of green mist grazing her ear: "Do you know why fairies make their loved ones forget them? Why your sister is not allowed to grant your wishes?"

Keep going, Ilaria's conscience pled. *Don't listen.*

But temptation preyed on Ilaria's resolve. She slowed, and twisted back to Larissa ever so slightly. "Why?"

"Because of me." Larissa advanced toward her. "Long ago I was one of them. Young and innocent, not so different from your sister. I had a mother whom I loved, and even after I became a fairy, I visited her often. But about a year after I earned my wings, a gang of bandits ravaged my hometown and burned my mother's house and farm. She lost everything and became ill with grief, but she had no money—not for medicine or food. I asked the leader of the fairies, *Mirabella*"—Larissa uttered the name as if it were poison—"to help."

"She refused you," murmured Ilaria.

"Fairies are not as compassionate as they pretend. Mirabella was vexed that my time with my mother was distracting me from my duties. She forbade me from helping her."

"What happened?"

"That winter was harsh, and her illness grew worse. I had no choice, so I used my magic to bring her silver and gold and whisked her to a warm place where she could heal from her fever. Because of that, I was cast out from the fairies. They broke my wand." She held it forward so Ilaria could see that wedged into the black wood were two broken pieces of a fairy's silver wand.

"So who is crueler, them or us?"

That answer, Ilaria found, was not so easy.

"I won't give you another chance to consider my offer, Ilaria. Refuse, and you will go back to your pathetic life in that pathetic little town. Over time, your youth and beauty will fade; your voice, too. Maybe you'll marry that toy maker in the village, pop out half a dozen brats."

Geppetto's music box reappeared in Larissa's hand.

Ilaria lunged for it, but Larissa held it out of reach. "Stay here and you'll wither. You'll always wonder if you could have done more." A deliberate pause. "Been more."

Without warning, Larissa touched her wand to Ilaria's forehead, and suddenly, she saw the future she'd craved. A future where her mother gushed to her friends about Ilaria's successes as the finest singer in Esperia, where her parents lived in the grandest house on Vallan's richest streets, where Geppetto awaited her in the wings of the theater every night with dozens of roses. He was dressed finely—like a prince.

"The prima donna of Esperia," shouted her adoring fans. "And her husband, the most famous toy maker in Vallan."

All too soon, that future vanished into mist.

All of Ilaria's defenses crumbled. She drew back her hand, resting it over her heart once more. How it ached, still trying to piece itself together after her fight with Chiara.

"Your sister will do wonders for the world at the cost of neglecting her family," Larissa said. "But you, Ilaria. You can uplift your whole town. Reward everyone who's been good to you, and punish those who didn't think you were worthy."

"In exchange for my heart," Ilaria whispered.

"You won't miss it." The emerald on Larissa's wand glinted, emitting a cloud of mist. Within, Ilaria's most painful memories resurfaced. Maria Linda telling her she wasn't good enough to enter the Madrigal Conservatory, Geppetto chiding her for lying to her family, Chiara abandoning her to become a fairy . . . the hurt Ilaria had tried to bury from each of those moments rose to her heart, sharper and keener than ever before.

"Your heart will only hurt you," said Larissa. "You see?"

Pain stabbed Ilaria's heart, cutting off her breath and knocking the wind from her lungs. "Stop," she pled, but the pain mounted until she couldn't breathe.

"If I stop, you'll die, Ilaria. The pain of a broken heart will kill you. Do you want that? Do you want to die?"

Ily squeezed her eyes shut, refusing to answer.

"Life is short, Ilaria," pressed the Green Fairy. "Even if your dreams come true, you'll enjoy them only for a few short years at most. Come with me, and you'll live as fairies do. You'll not age, and you'll not die. You'll be young and beautiful. Forever."

"Forever?" whispered Ilaria. She was delirious; the pain was too much.

"Yes," Larissa purred. "All I need is your heart. Shall I take it?"

"Yes," she rasped, before she could regret the words. "Take it."

Green mist snaked around Ilaria's body, taking the shape of claws that looped about her shoulders and neck. Ily screamed as the claws tightened over her neck. She couldn't breathe, couldn't move. Couldn't change her mind even if she'd wanted to.

The claws pierced into her chest, and Ilaria's world splintered. Darkness turned into light, and light into dark. Magic tore her apart, shattered her with its fist, then put her back together again . . . but changed. In a flash of light, it was done—and Larissa ushered Ilaria's heart into the wooden music box, shutting it tight with a cackle.

"How do you feel?" asked Larissa.

Empty was the only word Ilaria could think of. Hollow. No pulse throbbed inside her chest, no beat drummed in her ears as she breathed. But that wasn't all. The world— all the voices, the memories, the regrets and hopes and fears she had held tight in her heart—faded away into a misty haze.

All was gloriously quiet.

"I feel . . . free," replied Ilaria, staring at her hands. Her nails were varnished a dark crimson, the tips so sharp they drew blood when she pressed against her arm. But her skin healed immediately. "I'm . . . I'm . . ."

"You have taken the first step to becoming a Heartless," said Larissa. "Welcome, Ilaria."

Larissa passed her back the music box. It was heavier

than it had been before, and Ilaria cringed at the faint beam of light trapped within the seams of the lid.

"What am I to do with this?"

"Destroy it," said Larissa. "That will be your oath to the Heartless, and you will be one of us forever."

Destroy it? Ilaria drew a sharp breath as she looked down at the box in her hands. From the cracks in the wood, it glowed against the black night, radiant with the heart she had just lost.

"Here," said Larissa, passing Ilaria a black wand that twinned her own, except it had a sparkling scarlet ruby instead of an emerald at its head. "This will help."

Ilaria gripped the wand tight, and a wave of icy seawater swept up to her ankles. It should have been freezing, but she felt nothing. A realization that almost made her drop her wand.

"Nervous, are we?" Larissa laughed. "Or are you having second thoughts?"

Ilaria gulped. "No. No second thoughts."

"Good. I would hate for you to lose everything that I've so generously offered," said Larissa. "But I know it isn't easy."

The Green Fairy tilted her head, considering. "How about this? Your sister is casting her forgetting spell tomorrow at sunset. Why don't you settle your business with your friends and family before then?"

"What do you mean?"

"Offer your parents the riches they deserve," said Larissa, encouraging Ily with her wand. "Whatever you can think of, you imagine it and point."

Ilaria looked at her wand in awe.

"Yes," encouraged Larissa. "Gather your friends and family to your side—and not Chiara's—then destroy your heart before your sister casts her spell. Your place will be waiting for you among us once it's done."

Ilaria held her box closer to her heart, suppressing a shiver.

"I'll do it," she said quietly.

"Marvelous," Larissa said. She patted Ily's shoulder. "You'll feel so much better once it's gone, my star. Hearts are the worst kind of pest, after all. They're no good until they're dead."

CHAPTER TWENTY-SEVEN

"You fixed the bridge on the Vaci girl's viola?"

Geppetto nervously pushed his spectacles closer to his eyes, hoping his father wouldn't see how his brow twitched. "Yes, Papa."

"The broken neck on Mr. Gusto's guitar?"

"Yes, Papa. The loose braces, too. You can take a look if you'd like."

With a harrumph, Tommaso set his candle on the worktable and leaned over the instruments. Though his old hands could no longer work with the precision required to perform his craft, his eyes were sharp—even in the shadows and gloam. They scrutinized his son's work; no crack or blemish, no excessive space between strings—no matter how tiny, no slanted fret or even bridge would get past. Geppetto knew that. Which was why, when Tommaso exhaled through his nose with a satisfied grunt, Geppetto nearly collapsed with relief.

"All your years of apprenticeship are finally coming to fruition," said Tommaso with a rare approving nod.

Geppetto's father untied the apron around his waist and hung it on the rack against the wall. His voice turned soft, and he took a tone Geppetto hadn't heard since his mother had been alive. "I know I've worked you hard these last few years, Geppetto, and I know I've been stern. But I had no choice."

"I know, Papa."

As Geppetto began putting away his tools, his father picked up an inspection mirror and a set of clamps. Anyone could see in the older man's misting eyes that he missed his craft.

"I thought these hands would have many more years of work," Tommaso said, uncurling his fingers. "Unfortunately, Fate has had other ideas, and since I cannot repair a violin with my toes, it falls to my son to learn." Tommaso took a cloth and dabbed at a drop of varnish on the work-table. "One day soon, this workshop will be yours."

"Papa . . ." Geppetto was at a loss for words. More than anything, he wanted to tell his father about his true dream. That he did not wish to become a luthier, but a toy maker.

And yet, to finally see the approval in his father's eyes . . . he could not ruin this moment.

He hung his head. "Thank you, Papa."

With a nod, Tommaso took his candle. "Don't work too late."

He ascended the stairs to his bed, leaving Geppetto alone in the workroom.

Once the young man heard his father snoring, he put aside the shop's work. These were the precious hours when he could chase his own dream and hone the craft he truly loved. A new toy or clock that would make a child's heart sing. Or a present for the woman he secretly loved.

Had it been a mistake for him to carve that music box for Ilaria? He'd hoped the gift might bring her luck at her audition, but it seemed it had only made her unhappy. Ever since their trip to Vallan, she no longer sang, and she rarely smiled. The last thing she would want to hear was the Nightingale Aria tinkling from the little box he'd made her. It would only stir up unpleasant memories.

That afternoon, Chiara had visited him in his workshop. She'd come earlier in the week, too, with Ily. The two had filled his workshop with their laughter and teasing, making the afternoon a cherished memory. But on her last day in Pariva, she had come alone. To say goodbye.

She'd decided to leave with the fairies. It wasn't a

surprise to him, but the sadness in her eyes was unmistakable. He wasn't one to prod, but when he'd tried to ask if something was wrong, Chiara only replied that everything was as it should be—and that she would leave that night.

She'd asked him, then, for a favor:

"My sister is fond of you. She trusts you. And you . . . you love her, don't you?"

Geppetto's heart nearly stopped. He took his glasses and set them on the table beside him. "Yes," he said softly. "Yes, I do."

"I know you two will be good to each other," said Chiara. "Watch over her while I'm away. Help her stay true to herself. It won't be easy, but you can do it."

Geppetto swallowed hard. "I see. I would only wish for Ilaria to be happy."

"Thank you, my friend. Remember, Geppetto, stay true to your dreams, too. Bring joy to those around you."

"I will," he promised.

Then she was gone.

Geppetto couldn't get the conversation out of his head. If Chiara hadn't succeeded in cheering Ilaria up, what chance did he have?

"I still have to try," he told himself. And so he had spent the night modeling his new project. At the moment, it was a simple carving, the shape of two young sisters side by side. One would be holding a sheet of music and a fan, and her arms would open when the music played. The other sister would be at the harpsichord—which would be a music box. It was an ambitious undertaking, one that would likely take a month to put together, then another week to paint. Maybe more, if things got busy at the shop. But Geppetto prayed it would make Ilaria smile again—and remember her sister.

He became so absorbed in his work that the night grew late, and the candle on his desk burnt to a tiny stub with at most a few minutes remaining. The fire in the hearth had long since gone out, and his fingers were stiff with cold. He rubbed at his eyes, feeling fatigue set upon him, but still he kept on working.

"Geppetto," whispered a voice in his head.

It sounded so close to his ear that he jerked up. But there was no one.

"I must be dreaming," he muttered to himself. He returned to his work.

Then one of the windows flew open, and the wind blew out his candle entirely.

As Geppetto rose to fetch a new one, there came the voice again, louder and clearer:

"Geppetto?"

He whirled, recognizing it instantly. "Ilaria!"

She stood at the door, cloaked in the shadows falling

from the oak trees outside. It was so dark he couldn't even make out the whites of her eyes.

"It's . . . it's late," Geppetto stammered. He found a new candle and tried to light it, but his match wouldn't strike. "What are you doing here at this hour?"

"I'm leaving town." She dared a step forward. "Come with me, Geppetto. We can have the future we dreamt of—together. Come with me. I won't ask again."

Geppetto set down the match. Ilaria sounded different. Her voice, usually rich with warmth and color, was flat. Cold, even. "Leaving town? What's the matter?"

Light appeared, but Geppetto couldn't make out its source. It was red and vibrant, casting streaks across Ilaria's dark hair.

Her eyes, too, were turning red. Geppetto staggered, a tingle of fear making him step back. "Ilaria, what's happened? Are you in trouble?"

Ilaria drew close, the feathers on her coat brushing against his arm. Her nearness usually made him heady with nervousness, but tonight, he could focus only on how different she appeared. Funny, he didn't remember her having a coat with feathers. She'd bought a new one recently, with black fur. It looked nothing like what she wore now.

"No, I'm not in trouble," said Ilaria with a laugh. "No one can ever trouble me again."

Her hand wrapped over his wrist. Her fingers were cold; her nails were long and painted with a dark crimson varnish. When she let go, he shivered, watching as she picked up the figurine he had been working on. "You want to make trinkets for children? So be it. I'll make you the most famous craftsman in Esperia. You'll be rich beyond your dreams."

"I told you," said Geppetto gently, "I don't do this for money. I don't want fame."

"Then what *do* you want?"

He reached for his jacket. "I want to walk you home, Ilaria. It's late. Your parents will be worried."

For an instant, the old Ilaria he'd known flickered back. He started to reach for her hand. But she twisted away and her expression turned hard. "Foolish Geppetto. Then you shall forget. You shall forget we were ever friends."

Geppetto blinked, but Ilaria had vanished. He blinked again. Once. Twice.

He could not remember why he had put on his coat and hat. Or why the door was open on such a cold night, letting in the wind.

In the corner of the night sky, a pale star flickered, and the frigid draft blew out his candle.

Curious; the door was closed.

He reached into his pockets, trying to find a hint of

what he'd been planning. But there was only a dried-up old yellow rose. He tossed it out the open door before closing it.

Then he sat at his worktable and frowned at the chunk of wood before him. It was a roughly hewn outline of two young women, one singing and one seated at the rough makings of a harpsichord.

For the life of him, he couldn't remember who they were supposed to be.

CHAPTER TWENTY-EIGHT

Who knew that even fairies could have trouble sleeping? Chiara tossed and turned in her bed, catching only scraps of slumber. She couldn't close her eyes without revisiting her last fight with Ilaria.

Go ahead and cast your spell, Ilaria had said. *I wish I'd never had a sister.*

She'd never forgive herself if those were the last words they exchanged as sisters.

It had been only a day since she took her fairy's vow, but she visited the Wishing Well in her garden, anxious to have a glimpse of her hometown. Surely Ily's anger had cooled by now.

"Show me Pariva," the Blue Fairy instructed the waters of the Wishing Well.

A tall wave rose, and her hometown appeared in the form of a map. Hundreds of bright lights dotted Pariva—each one representing a person's heart.

"I'd like to see Ilaria Belmagio," Chiara told the map. "Show me her heart."

The map of Pariva flickered, and in a rush, all the lights vanished.

Leaving none.

Chiara frowned. Red she had dreaded, even expected. But nothing?

She focused on the little house on Constanza Street with the yellow roof and door. "Show me Ilaria's heart," she repeated.

The map didn't budge. It couldn't lie, couldn't deceive.

Which could only mean Ilaria's light was gone.

"The last trace I can find of her heart is in the Lyre Sea," said the Orange Fairy. Peri was the Wishing Star's most experienced archivist, and during Chiara's apprenticeship, he had become a friend. He was a jovial fellow, always with a cheerful thing to say to everyone. Even when she'd woken him this morning with pleas to help her at the Archives, he'd risen without complaint.

But now, as he also couldn't find Ilaria's light, his expression turned grave. Not a good sign.

"In the Lyre Sea?" Chiara repeated. "When?"

Peri peered through his spectacles at the wall-wide and ceiling-tall map of Esperia. "Last night."

Chiara gripped the side of her chair. "What would her heart be doing in the middle of the sea?"

Peri glided his wand across the Lyre Sea, scanning the facsimile of its emerald-blue waters a second time. The Archives' map was a more expansive version of the one in her Wishing Well, and it glittered with magic, showing in synchronous motion the clouds that actually drifted across the world, the boats that currently sailed, even the waves rippling the sea.

"I don't know," Peri replied honestly. "It is peculiar."

Try as she might, Chiara could not smother the fear growing inside her. Where had her sister gone? Had she taken a boat into the sea, then gotten lost?

"What are those dark clouds?" She pointed on the map. "Is a storm coming?"

"Those are pockets of dark magic," replied Peri. "Not even our maps can penetrate what lies beneath them."

"There are so many."

Peri chuckled. "This is actually the fewest we've seen in decades. If you'd looked a year ago, half the sea would have been dark. Because of Monstro. Before he was put in his slumber."

Apprehension made her chest tight as she pointed at the dark clouds. "Do you think . . . do you think Ilaria could be there?"

"It's possible," said Peri. His expression turned even graver than it'd been before, and new lines creased his already furrowed brow. "There are usually two reasons that a heart goes missing. I'm sorry, Chiara . . . but either your sister's heart has been captured by the Heartless—or she's dead."

Dead.

No, Ilaria was alive. She would have known, would have felt . . . Chiara didn't know why the fairies couldn't locate her sister's heart, but there had to be a mistake.

In a rush, she flew off the Wishing Star, making for her parents' bakery. Maybe there would be answers there.

"Mother," she said, appearing before Mrs. Belmagio in the middle of the kitchen.

Mamma started. "Goodness me!" she cried. "You startled me, Chia. I don't think I'll ever get used to you popping in and out like that."

Mrs. Belmagio set down her dough scraper and covered the loaves she was about to bake with a clean cloth. "I didn't expect you back so soon. Let me look at you. How splendid your dress looks! And your wings . . . oh dear, why the long face, Chia?"

Chiara drew a deep breath. She wouldn't worry her mother until she was absolutely sure what had happened. For now, it wouldn't hurt to ask: "Have you seen Ilaria? I wanted to set things right with her."

"Ilaria!" Her mother chuckled and turned to kneading the rest of the dough. "I thought you fairies were all ears. Didn't you hear? Ily's gone to Vallan."

"To Vallan?" Chiara repeated. "When did she leave?"

"Yesterday evening." Mamma frowned. "Or was it the day before? I can't seem to remember."

Couldn't remember? Chiara's frown mirrored her mother's. Mamma had a memory sharper than a bread knife.

"You'll have to find her in the capital. But don't ask for Ilaria—she'll be using a new name. Cleo del Mar, or something silly like that."

"Are you sure?"

"Why wouldn't I be?" Mamma laughed. "A letter came by this morning. I still have it in my pocket. Here."

The letter smelled like cinnamon, and Chiara unfolded it hastily. "'I've arrived safely in Vallan,'" she read aloud in disbelief. It *was* Ily's handwriting—she recognized the round loops and flourishes. "'Come visit soon—I'll send tickets for my first performance.'" At the bottom, signed so large it took up half the page, was *Cleo del Mar*.

"This arrived in the morning by post?"

"Beatrice brought it herself. Her father's the postmaster, you recall."

Chiara did, but it just wasn't possible. The timing made no sense. She'd spoken to Ilaria only last night—she couldn't have packed and left for Vallan in a matter of hours.

Something was amiss. Something that made apprehension crawl across the pit of Chiara's stomach.

"I'll find her," said Chia.

"Take a cookie for your travels," called her mother. "Even fairies have to eat."

Chiara searched all day for her sister. As the sun began to sink beneath the horizon, she began to lose hope. She'd promised to cast her forgetting spell by sunset.

Her heart heavy with disappointment, she decided to try the last place she expected to find her sister: home.

The Belmagio house was empty when Chiara slipped inside. Niccolo was out with Sofia, and her parents were at the Vacis' playing cards.

"Ily?" she called, searching room by room.

Her sister wasn't in the Blue Room. Not in the kitchen, either.

There was a faint hiccup of light coming from upstairs. Chiara couldn't imagine Niccolo being careless enough to leave a candle burning, but she went upstairs to inspect it anyway.

The light was coming from Ily's room!

She went inside, holding her breath. Her sister's bed was made, the pillows neatly arranged in a row—and on top of the blanket was the music box Geppetto had made for her.

Chiara thumbed the nightingale etched on the top. It looked not too different from her own wooden dove, and she fished it out of her pocket, setting the figurine beside the box. They were made of the same wood by the same maker. Almost like sisters.

As she set her dove on her lap, a glint of light leaked out from the music box.

"What could that be?" she said aloud, picking up the box. Strange; it was warm. Alive, almost.

Her brows drawing together, Chiara opened it slowly, expecting to hear the tender melody Geppetto had scored in honor of her sister.

What she saw instead made her gasp.

"Oh, Ilaria, what have you done?" she whispered. "What have you done."

She shut the box, so distraught she didn't even notice her wooden dove fall off her lap as she stood.

"Ily," she said, summoning her magic with an urgent wave of her wand. "Ilaria Belmagio, show yourself."

The air had gone still, and not even the wind blew. Then she spied a scarlet mist, curling outside the window like a ribbon.

The mist slid into the bedroom and materialized into a familiar form.

Only it wasn't the sister Chiara had known and grown with all her life. This Ilaria was different. Her green eyes were wickedly vibrant, the pupils dull and flat with no reflection. She wore a long one-shouldered gown decorated with rubies and matching red feathers, and wrapped around her neck was a choker of black pearls.

"Why, if it isn't the esteemed Blue Fairy herself." Ilaria made a mock curtsy. "How might I serve you, Your Honorableness?"

Chiara was too distraught to pay attention to her sister's sarcasm. "No," she whispered. "Tell me you didn't. . . ."

"What?" Ilaria finally noticed the music box and made a loud titter. "Oh, good, you found it. Did you scream when you saw my heart inside?"

The light in Chiara's wand flickered, mirroring the sudden skip in her chest. "Your heart?"

"Yes," murmured Ilaria. "You see, I've beaten you. I cast my own little spell."

"What spell?" Then it dawned on her. Ilaria, moving to Vallan. Taking on the name Cleo del Mar.

"No, Ily," breathed Chiara. "Please don't tell me you made a deal with the Heartless."

"You told me my dreams wouldn't come true. But I found a way." Ilaria laughed smugly. "All Pariva will remember me as the most famous prima donna in the land."

"It isn't real."

"Jealous, aren't we?" Ilaria clucked her tongue. "I wouldn't have expected that of you."

"I'm not jea—"

"You are. Our parents will always remember me, and think of me fondly. While they'll forget everything about you. Everyone always says I'm the selfish one. Chia could never be selfish, Mamma says. She's doing good for the world. We're all *so* proud of her." Ilaria rolled her eyes. "Did you know Mamma would cry herself to sleep at night? She thought Nico and I couldn't hear, but we did. Oh, I'm sure your little forgetting spell will make everything all better."

Chiara's voice was small. "Don't do this, Ily. I know there's good in you still—"

"Enough with the good and the bad," Ily said sharply. "Not everything or everyone can be sorted into heroes and villains."

"By choosing to be a Heartless, you are going down a bad path."

Ilaria released a bitter laugh. "Would a villain offer Mamma and Papa riches . . . Niccolo power, and Geppetto fame? I say no. I wanted the best for them, but they all turned me down. They'd rather cling to their poor little lives here than come with me. Well, it'll be their loss. I have a new family now."

"The Heartless aren't your family. Their magic comes from making people suffer."

"I know what they do." Ilaria smiled. "Like you taught me, there's a price for power. This is the one I chose to pay. It's about balance. Not 'chosen ones.'"

"Then they've tricked you," Chiara said. "Take your heart back, Ily, before you do something you'll regret. Please. It's not too late. Don't leave Mamma and Papa and Nico. And Geppetto. They love you so much."

She reached out and touched her sister's arm. She felt Ilaria stiffen suddenly, then look up as if a spell had been broken. The rancor in Ily's eyes vanished, and her shoulders drooped. Her lower lip trembled, and she hung her head low with remorse. "You're right. I can't do this. What was I thinking?"

Chiara let out a silent exhale. Thank the stars she'd found Ily in time. A glance out the window, and she saw she had only minutes until sunset.

"I don't want us to be mad at each other, Ily," she said quietly. "I only want you to be happy." She placed the music box in her sister's waiting hands, then stroked her hair. "Here."

The Blue Fairy stepped back to give her sister room, and Ily held the box close, her shoulders still trembling. But as she looked up, a cunning smile smeared the remorse on her face, and she laughed cruelly. "There's one good thing about my not having a heart. You can't tell anymore when I'm lying."

Ily held up the box. "Burn!" she said, and a hiss of fire spurted from her ruby wand.

"No! No, Ily!"

As the music box burst into flames, Chiara lunged, knocking it out of her sister's hands and putting out the fire. Before Ily could snatch it back, Chiara shuttered the charred box away with magic. She wouldn't trust her sister to take it again.

In retaliation, Ily pointed her wand at Chiara's wooden dove, still on the ground. Sizzling scarlet light shot forth, magic no doubt intended to destroy the bird, but Chiara reacted in time. Her own magic poured out of her wand, meeting Ilaria's right before it struck the wooden dove.

And the strangest thing happened.

The dove came alive, its wooden feathers turning into

real, white ones. It purred and warbled, and the two sisters watched in astonishment as it quickly fled the room and flew out of the window.

What just happened? Chiara wanted to ask, but after one look at Ilaria, she wisely kept quiet.

Ilaria couldn't have cared less what their two magics had accomplished. Her eyes were bloodshot, and she demanded, "Give me my heart."

"No. Not until you're ready to receive it."

Ily gritted her teeth in annoyance. Chiara worried that her sister might attack her with her wand, but the Scarlet Fairy made a sharp turn.

"Keep it, then," she said, seeming not to care. "Sooner or later, I'll get it back. You'll hand it to me yourself. You see, I already am one of them. And I'm excited to learn what my power can do."

Ilaria laughed and laughed before she disappeared in a plume of red mist.

"Ily!" Chiara cried. "Ily!"

But her sister was gone.

A silent sob racked Chiara's chest, and she sank onto Ily's bed and conjured the music box back in her hands.

The dove she and her sister had enchanted to life suddenly soared back into the room and perched on her shoulder. Chiara marveled at it, both joy and sadness heavy in her chest. The dove stroked her hand with a comforting wing, and Chiara touched it gently. She knew she ought to turn it back into a wooden figurine as before—those were the rules, after all. But she couldn't, not without Ily's help. And truthfully, she wasn't sure if she wanted to.

"I guess you'll have to stay with me, little dove," she said. "At least until we get Ily back her heart again."

The dove purred, and Chiara offered it a sad but hopeful smile. The light of her sister's heart still glowed from within the box, and it was warm.

"We will?" she said, responding to the dove's sounds. She tucked the box away, promising she'd safeguard it no matter how long she needed to. She wouldn't give up the faith that one day, things between her and Ily would be right again. "I hope so. I hope so."

CHAPTER TWENTY-NINE

Evening crept across Pariva, and as the sun sank behind Mount Cecilia, there was only one final thing for Chiara to do.

Numbly, she left her sister's bedroom and trod up the nine steps to her own bedroom, taking one last look. It was the smallest bedroom in the house—meant to be an attic, then Ily's room after she was born, only she'd been too afraid. "There's spiders up here!" she squealed, so Chiara had insisted on sleeping there instead. She didn't mind spiders.

Over the years, Ilaria would overcome her fear of the attic. She'd come up into Chia's room, and they'd tell each other stories while lying down on a mound of pillows. Papa had worked a window into the ceiling to let in more light, and the two girls would stare at the moon until they fell asleep.

Chiara approached her old bed, tucking in the corners of her sheets one last time. Then she dusted the top of her dresser with her handkerchief, letting her hand linger on the blue and purple hearts she had painted on the sides when she'd been a girl, the neat stack of books beside her window, full of her favorite stories and adventures. Then she turned to the window, to the painting she had made of her family. Mamma, with a long braid, carrying a loaf of bread under her arm and flowers that she held together with Papa. Niccolo, with a toy boat in his hands and two little sisters on his left.

Her, and Ilaria. Hands held, arms linked. Inseparable . . . until now.

She pressed her cheek to the windowpane. It was cool, almost cold. Outside was a starless night, guarded by a slender moon.

It was time. She had to move through the heaviness in her heart to do what she'd come to do.

"Little town of Pariva," she whispered to the village outside, "you have my heart forevermore. Now sleep, for we must part. Forget me."

The light from her wand swelled out of the star, fanning over the house and across the town. She could feel the edges of the past being sanded off, her name and face washing away from the minds of the hundreds of people she had met in her lifetime.

Before her eyes, her room began to change. The floral blue canopy over her bed, the matching curtains and the lace doilies on her dresser—all disappeared. So did her books and sheet music and set of paints, even the pot of violets she'd kept in the corner. In their place were sacks of flour and sugar, a broken chair and Niccolo's first violin, boxes of old toys and books and memories that no longer included Chiara. Dust grimed the beams along the ceiling, and cobwebs slung over the corners of the windows. Her bedroom had become the attic it was always meant to be.

Chiara choked back her tears, and she held her wand to her heart. Slipping under her guise of invisibility, she tip-toed down the stairs and visited her family. Niccolo first. He was snoring, a pirate novel half covering his face. Chiara tugged on his blanket, raising it so it covered his shoulders.

"Be good, be well, my dear Nico," she told him tenderly.

Then she visited her parents and kissed her mother's cheek, then her father's. Her father smiled in his sleep, almost as though he could feel her presence.

Mamma, Papa, and Niccolo wouldn't know her even if they saw her. For the last time, tonight, they would dream of having a daughter with soft curls the color of uncooked pasta—as Niccolo liked to tease. A girl with a gentle laugh and a love for playing the harpsichord. A girl as bright as her name, Chiara.

When they woke, they would remember only Ily—but the details of where she had gone would be like smoke in their memory. A little unclear.

"I'm sorry," she whispered to her parents. "I'll find a way to bring Ilaria and her heart together again. I'll bring her home. I promise."

And Chiara folded into the stars.

CHAPTER THIRTY

Forty years later

The years passed, and though Pariva remained the same quiet and sleepy town, the world around it changed. Railroads tracked across Esperia, connecting its great cities, and trains pumped from day to night, traveling at ten times the speed of even the fastest carriage. Along Esperia's five seas, steam-powered boats as large as whales ripped down the coastline. The world grew smaller every day thanks to such innovations, but certain things did not change. Hearts, dreams, and hopes.

Envy, anger, and hate.

In the towns and villages surrounding Pariva, dozens of boys had gone missing over the past few months. At first it seemed like a stroke of terrible misfortune, and the parents wept, and the towns grieved. But little by little, the numbers of missing children grew, and the fairies themselves were called to investigate.

Chiara was one of those fairies. It'd been a long time since she'd been called to duty near Pariva, and as she searched its surrounding areas for the missing boys, she found clues of dark magic, of an island that came alive at night and disappeared in the day.

The Wishing Fairies had no idea what to make of such information, and though they tried, they couldn't find this mysterious island—or its connection to the lost children.

Chiara became certain that the tragic disappearances were the work of the Heartless. Since the Wishing Fairies had put Monstro to sleep, the Heartless had lost a great source of dark magic, and over the years, they had unsuccessfully tried to recover their power through waves of wickedness. All had failed, until now.

Time was running out. With every boy that went missing, they harvested more despair and more anger and fear, and Chiara didn't know how to stop them.

Little did she know, her troubles were only just beginning.

CHAPTER THIRTY-ONE

Under the shroud of mist and shadow, twenty-odd Heartless fairies hovered above the Lyre Sea's still waters in a circle. At last, after years and years of searching, they had found him.

But before his spell could be broken, a late arrival made her entrance known—through a flare of scarlet light.

"Oh, look, it's our bright shining star," huffed Amorale as the Scarlet Fairy appeared. "I'm surprised you even deigned to show up."

Amorale's displeasure with Ilaria was becoming increasingly worrisome. Ilaria bowed deeply, and in her most formal tone, she said, "I'm sorry, Madame Gray Fairy. It won't happen again." She tried to take her place in the circle, but Amorale blocked her.

"Another concert in Vallan?" said the Gray Fairy. "I

would've thought after four decades, you'd tire of the hollow praise, the mindlessly adoring audience, the—"

"I'm not," Ilaria interrupted, only regretting her rudeness a beat too late. "I mean to say, I'm not tired of it."

It was true, mostly. Ilaria *wasn't* tired of the singing. Yet. The rare evening she took off from the Heartless to sing and make music was the only thing that brought her even a glimmer of joy these days.

What she *was* tired of was the lies, and the glamor cast upon her audience that made them acclaim her, no matter what she crooned from her lips.

At first, she thought it would make her happy to be famous and idolized and loved, but she was wrong. None of it was real, and she could tell from the glazed eyes and too-wide smiles that she faced in the audience whenever she performed.

The Heartless made no secret that they had expected her to outgrow her yearly performance in Vallan and eventually give it up, but Ilaria couldn't. Empty as the experience made her, she still looked forward to it. It was the only night every year she could forget about the misery and fear she sowed daily—to prove herself worthy of being a Heartless to Larissa and Amorale. Ironically, the very fact that she wouldn't give it up made Amorale increasingly doubtful of her commitment.

"I question your dedication," Amorale said, stating her thoughts. "Could singing in some frivolous concert be more important than the reawakening of our greatest ally?"

"That's enough," Larissa cut in, coming to her protégé's defense. "Singing makes our little star feel powerful, and look, she teems with energy from the city. We'll put it to good use in breaking Monstro's sleeping spell."

Amorale glared at the Green Fairy. "You're always coming to her defense."

"It's only natural that Ilaria still has ties to her old life," said Larissa sensibly.

Indeed it was. Ilaria was the only one among them who still had a heart. It might not be in her, but it was out there— in her sister's clutches. So long as it still beat, she would always have doubts; she'd always *feel*.

She was desperate to get her heart back from Chiara. As soon as she reclaimed it, these seedlings of doubt would go away. She wouldn't even need her annual concerts. And Amorale would finally accept her as a true member of the Heartless.

"When will she get it?" Amorale said. "It's been decades. No one else has taken so long."

"No one else's has been stolen by a Wishing Fairy," Ilaria cut in. "I'll get it soon. I swear it." She held out her ruby-tipped wand. "Now may I join?"

"You can stand guard for those Wishing Fairies," Amorale said shortly. "Your pest of a sister has been seen poking about the area looking for the missing boys."

"And for Monstro," added Larissa. "Word spreads quickly on the Wishing Star."

Their decision made, Amorale and Larissa turned their backs to Ilaria and instructed their fellow fairies to begin the spell. As one, they descended closer to the water. Power sizzled from their wands and met in the center in one brilliant burst of energy. Then, in a thunderclap, the magic struck the water.

It was silent at first.

Ilaria dared hope, in her secret and conflicted mind, that the silence meant the spell hadn't worked.

Then the sea rose in one great wave, and an enormous black whale emerged.

Monstro!

The Heartless clapped with glee as the whale's eyes peeled open, the spell of slumber cast by the Wishing Fairies broken.

"Welcome back, old friend," said Larissa, patting the whale's side with a green-gloved hand. "You're freed at last."

The whale let out a terrifying low hum.

"Yes, yes. You'll have your revenge," Amorale assured him. "Now quickly, into the water. Swim for the bright lights west of Mount Cecilia. We have much to catch up on, but for now—you'll find haven there . . . and a few fishing ships." She chuckled darkly. *"Dinner."*

As Monstro tunneled his tremendous body back into the sea, Ilaria bit down on her lip, trying to push away that prick of discontent that arose in her.

What do you care if the Heartless wake Monstro up again? she scolded herself. *What do you care if he terrorizes the coasts and sinks every boat he comes across?*

You obey Larissa and Amorale. They've given you everything—sisterhood, power, fame. In exchange, you do as they ask.

That was the deal she'd struck with the Heartless, and it was too late to go back.

Far too late.

But Ily was a clever girl. Given how scornful Amorale had been toward her recently, she knew she needed to work hard to prove herself. Specifically, she'd need extra magic to get her heart back from Chiara.

Before Monstro disappeared completely into the water, she pointed her wand at him. When the Heartless were not watching, she channeled power away from him ever so furtively—power grown by the fear that was already beginning to spread across the sea.

She had a feeling it would come in handy very soon.

CHAPTER THIRTY-TWO

In the morning came news of two missing fishing boats and three drowned men.

"Oh, my stars," Geppetto exclaimed after hearing about the tragedy from people passing by his shop. "Did you hear that, Figaro?"

He stroked his kitten absentmindedly. "Three men drowned. We'd best stay away from the sea." He tickled Figaro's head affectionately. "I guess it's a good thing you don't like to swim, anyway."

With a sigh, Geppetto closed his pot of paints. After such awful news, he was hardly in the mood to work.

"Your mouth will have to wait," he said to the puppet sitting in front of him.

Geppetto had followed his dreams and become Pariva's

beloved toy maker. He was an old man now. His hair had turned white, his mustache too, and he walked with the slightest lean forward, mirroring his dear puppets. But his fingers were still nimble, and the years had honed his artist's eye into one that could bring life to even the dullest block of wood.

That he had proven with his latest toy, affectionately named Pinocchio.

The puppet sat against the wall, its painted eyes innocently round and curious. Geppetto had put off giving the boy a mouth for days. Perhaps because he wasn't ready to sell Pinocchio yet. He'd grown oddly attached to the wooden boy.

"Maybe I'll keep him," Geppetto mused. "What do you think, Figaro? You and Cleo could have a new brother."

Figaro wrinkled his nose.

Geppetto chuckled. "You don't think so?"

He picked Figaro up and set the kitten by the kitchen, where he'd cut some bread and sliced some meat. While Figaro ate, Geppetto also fed his goldfish, Cleo, and he watched his two companions tenderly.

After Geppetto's father passed away, the house had grown colder, the small rooms too big for Geppetto alone. For years, loneliness had snaked its way into Geppetto's heart, and he spent most of his time making toys. Unless he was helping a customer, he went days without speaking to anyone, so he began speaking to his figurines as he made them. It wasn't until he had chanced upon Figaro alone and abandoned in the pasture that he had realized just how lost he'd been. He'd whisked the young cat into his home and fed and nourished him until he'd become the pampered prince that he was today. A few short weeks later, he'd adopted the goldfish Cleo.

Their names had come to him instantly, as though they had always been there. They became his family, and he couldn't imagine his life without them. Yet every time a child came into his shop and left smiling and laughing with a new toy, Geppetto's heart ached just a little for what could have been.

He'd always wanted a son or daughter of his own. Since Fate hadn't willed it for him, he instead tried his best to make the children of Pariva happy through his toys. Still, deep down, he couldn't let go of his secret longing. He traced an invisible smile over Pinocchio with his finger.

Every night he searched the sky for a Wishing Star, but he'd always missed it. Watching the children outside his window laugh and run to school, Geppetto hid a gentle smile.

He would try again tonight. Maybe one day soon, his wish would finally come true.

CHAPTER THIRTY-THREE

Not far from Pariva was indeed a secret island that came alive at night. It lay cloaked behind a veil of shadow, so entrenched in dark enchantment that not even the fairies of the Wishing Star could find it. Yet sailors and fishermen who erred too late and far from home sometimes heard the raucous music of a carnival and the shouts of young boys. If they listened long enough, they even heard donkeys braying.

Spooked, they returned home and told their wives and mothers what they had heard. *Ghosts*, word immediately spread. Ghosts congregated behind the mountains, and now with that monster whale sighted in the waters . . .

Such stories amused the Heartless. They encouraged them, in fact, and soon the pathetic humans were so frightened by the tales that none dared sail too close. None, of course, except the wicked men and women the Heartless kept in their employ.

The Scarlet Fairy drummed her long nails against her wand. She was tired of overseeing this far-off island. Tired of listening to donkeys braying well past midnight, and of having to play a glorified shepherdess as they were herded off into carriages and carts that would take them back onto the mainland to be sold. Night after night of donkeys and screaming little boys and puddles of popcorn and melted ice cream wasn't what she'd envisioned when she'd pledged herself to the Heartless.

The truth was, she didn't like coming to this part of Esperia. It was too close to Pariva, and she didn't like being so near to the home she once had known.

She couldn't complain. Pleasure Island was thriving, and supervising its success was the first responsibility Larissa had given her. It'd been Ily's idea to turn the boys into donkeys, inspired by the night she'd first turned into a fairy, and the misery and suffering that emanated from the place had made the Heartless more powerful than ever. And it was profitable, it turned out.

Still, she loathed the place. She had better things to do than be tied down to a carnival, such as locate her heart. For forty years, Chiara had done an admirable job avoiding her. Try as she might, Ilaria hadn't been able to goad her sister into an appearance. Not even by sabotaging the lives of the people Chiara tried so hard to help, or by causing mischief everywhere she went.

Every rip she made in the world, Chiara patiently patched. Every life she ruined, Chiara made even more joyful than before. All while somehow avoiding Ilaria altogether.

It was terribly frustrating.

But tonight, fortune smiled upon her. As Ilaria stared up into the night, bored with her watch, she caught a shimmer of magic headed toward Pariva. It was Wishing Star magic, and she tilted her head, curious.

On a whim, she trailed the light, but she was to be greatly rewarded for her efforts. For lo! She found none other than her sanctimonious sister dipping into Pariva—a place Chiara wasn't supposed to loiter, and what had the perfect Blue Fairy done?

In one swoop, she'd broken all of the fairies' cardinal rules: she'd granted the wish of someone she once had known and cherished, she'd given life to a wooden puppet when life was not hers to give, *and* she had done it all in secret—without congressing with her elder fairies.

Ilaria nearly cackled with delight.

She'd have to play her cards carefully. The Blue Fairy

was clever, and if Ilaria wanted her heart back, she'd have to offer something Chiara wanted in return.

As she spied on her sister, waiting for the perfect moment to intercept her, Ilaria descended upon an old house near Pine Grove.

It was a workshop, tables and walls filled with toys and clocks.

Old Mr. Tommaso's home. Now Geppetto's.

Something about seeing Geppetto as an old man made her breath catch, only for a fraction of a moment. Then she recovered.

What did she care about Geppetto? The memories from her life as a girl in Pariva might as well have belonged to someone else. She cared nothing for the town, nor the people in it.

All she cared about was getting her heart back—so she could destroy it. She couldn't lose this chance: after all these years, she'd finally cornered her sister into the perfect opportunity to get it back.

"Still making promises you know you can't keep," she mused from behind Chiara. "Some things never change."

Chiara spun, and her blue eyes went wide.

"Speechless, I see," murmured Ilaria, relishing her sister's stunned silence. "Well, it *has* been a long time."

It was always fun putting Chiara on edge. She let herself have some fun and taunted Chiara about sneaking into Geppetto's workshop, breaking the Wishing Star's rules, and giving the puppet life. She piled guilt and distress upon her sister's ever fragile conscience, then—at the right moment, when Chiara was about to leave for home to confess her egregious transgressions—Ilaria said:

"Prove to me that your little Pinocchio can spend three days out of trouble. *If* that chirping conscience of his helps him be a good boy, I will help you turn him into a real boy."

The Blue Fairy looked up. "That sort of magic is—"

"Against the rules? But not impossible." Ilaria eyed the small white dove that they'd given life together, many years ago. The sight of the bird made the hollow in her chest ache, but she pushed the feeling away. "We can do it, together."

The Blue Fairy faltered, and Ilaria hid a smile, gleeful that she'd managed to put her unflappable sister on edge.

"I don't need to hear the rest of your proposal," Chiara said, shaking her head. "My answer is no."

Ilaria wasn't surprised. "I didn't think you'd say yes," she purred. "It wouldn't be like the noble Blue Fairy to accept such a wager—especially from a Heartless like me."

Chiara flinched at the word *Heartless*.

"But then again, that same noble Blue Fairy *has* broken all her sacred rules." Ilaria put her finger to her lips before

Chiara could interrupt. "I know, I know. You're going to go straight home and tell Agata and Mirabella that it was out of love that you did what you did. But while the fairies will sympathize with you, the rules are the rules. One stray step off the road might make you fall. After all, Mirabella still remembers what happened to Larissa. . . ." Ilaria paused delicately. "She'll make you reverse your spell on Pinocchio."

Ilaria gave a low chuckle. "I can already hear what she'll say." Ilaria put on her most pompous voice: "'A boy who won't be good might just as well be made of wood.' You know it, I know it. And think of how sad poor Geppetto will be when his little son turns to wood once more."

Chiara was only half listening. Behind Ilaria, Geppetto had woken. Unaware of the two fairies' presence, he stumbled down the stairs only to discover, happily, that his beloved puppet had come alive.

"You do talk!" he cried in astonishment.

"Yes," said Pinocchio. "The Blue Fairy came. And someday . . . I'm going to be a real boy!"

"A real boy!" Geppetto cried. "It's my wish. It's come true!"

Geppetto danced in celebration, winding up his toy music boxes and collecting toys to show his new son.

Ilaria stole a sidelong glance at her sister, who was

practically dancing along. Trust Chiara to see the beauty in the moment of the father and his new son. *How happy they look,* she was certainly thinking. *What good work I've done.*

Good work, indeed. Well, Ilaria was going to remind her how short-lived their joy could be. Soon everyone would know what she had all along—Chiara wasn't the "good" sister after all.

"You know what they say about wood," she murmured, tilting her wand toward one of the candles in the room. Her dark eyes became bright from the flame. "He burns . . . with curiosity."

At that moment, Pinocchio noticed a candle burning at his side. His eyes rounded with curiosity. "Ooh, nice."

"Ilaria . . ." Chiara warned. "Don't you dare!"

Still smiling, Ilaria spoke into the ruby glowing on the top of her wand. "Bright and burning, what could it be? Touch the flame, and then you'll see."

Before Chiara could intervene, Pinocchio stuck his finger into the candle. The puppet didn't even flinch as his finger caught on fire.

"Look!" he said, eliciting his father's attention. "Pretty!"

In a panic, Geppetto dropped the toys in his arms. "Oh, help!" He tried to blow out the fire on Pinocchio's finger, but Ilaria had her wand raised, and the flame wouldn't go out.

"Stop it!" Chiara cried. "Ilaria, stop it!"

"Why?" said Ilaria. "Isn't it better that he burn now, before father and son grow too close? You'll only break Geppetto's heart otherwise."

"Ilaria!"

"Water!" Geppetto was shouting. "Where's water?" Desperate, he plunged Pinocchio's finger into the goldfish's bowl. The fire went out instantly, and Geppetto let out a sigh of relief. "That was close. Maybe we'd better go to bed before something else happens."

As they left, Chiara crossed her arms. "That was cruel of you, Ilaria. You could have hurt him."

"Was it me?" Ilaria feigned innocence. "Or was it the boy's curiosity? He has no strings—and no heart."

"He has a conscience." Chiara glanced down at the cricket, who had settled into a matchbox and was already asleep.

"A conscience won't make up for his lack of a heart. He'll end up like me. Depraved, wicked, and delightful."

The Blue Fairy shook her head. "Pinocchio will be a good boy. I have faith."

"If you're so sure, why not accept my wager?"

Chiara inhaled and raised her chin. "I already said—"

"No?" Ilaria finished for her. "But you haven't heard the sweetest part of the deal. If you win, Chiara, I'll also give you what you desire most."

"There's nothing I desire."

Ilaria almost laughed aloud at how serenely Chiara replied. "Now, now, *sister,* we know that isn't true." She spoke over her, slowly and dramatically: "There is one thing you desire more than anything." She paused, relishing how Chiara's pale blue eyes flickered.

Ilaria whispered, "My heart, Chiara. If you win, I'll take my heart back."

CHAPTER THIRTY-FOUR

It was the last thing the Blue Fairy had expected Ilaria to offer. The words startled her, and she drew an involuntary gasp. "You'll take back your heart?"

"That's correct; you heard me. If you win, I'll take my heart back."

"No tricks?"

"I'll swear it on my wand."

Chiara's pulse thundered in her ears. Every ounce of reason told her not to accept, that Agata would disapprove and that if she were found out, she'd be cast from the fairies forever.

But for forty years, Chiara had sought a way to turn her sister away from the dark path she'd chosen. Deep down she knew there was no way for Ilaria to turn back into the girl she once had been—unless she chose to do so herself. Still, every day there was a part of her that mourned her sister and blamed herself for what Ilaria had done. Their parents had passed without ever seeing their daughters again, and though their brother had a family of his own now, everything he knew about the one sister he could remember was a lie.

Was all the good she had done in the world worth the pain she had brought to her family? It hurt Chiara more than anything to ask herself that question, but she forced herself to, every day.

What do I do? she asked herself. Her conscience had never led her astray, and she expected it to tell her to follow the rules, to be the honorable and noble Blue Fairy all had come to know.

But here, her conscience was just as torn as she was.

She could not give up this chance to redeem Ilaria.

And her sister knew it.

"But if you lose," went on Ilaria, twirling a strand of hair around her finger—the way she had when they were sisters—"you'll give me *your* heart."

Chiara tightened her grip on her wand. "My heart?"

"It's only fair. A heart for a heart. You'll become a mistress of despair like me. We'll finally be on the same side again. Isn't that what you've always wanted?"

Chiara's muscles tensed. "No, it isn't."

"Then I guess this is where we say goodbye."

"Take your heart, Ily," Chiara said. "It's too late to go back to the life you could have had with Mamma and Papa. . . ." Her voice cracked. "But there's still time for you. Nico has a family now. They would welcome you. And Geppetto . . . he was your friend. He might have been more, had you stayed. He still could be more."

Ily was unmoved. "You think I care about them?"

"Then what do you care about? You've lost your family, your friends, your music." Chia paused. "You used to love singing. It was your life. How long has it been?"

"I still sing," Ilaria replied. "Every year at the Vallan Opera. People pay fortunes to hear me."

"They pay to hear Cleo del Mar, and she is only a figment of your vanity. A lie that you created with Heartless magic. Every year you dread the concert more and more. Your audience *hears* you, but they don't listen to you." Chiara's voice, still a whisper, fell even softer. "And the music, Ily . . . music used to be your greatest joy. But now when you sing, you feel nothing."

"I feel magnificent," snapped the Scarlet Fairy. "I've sung on the greatest stage in the world, thanks to Larissa and Amorale. They kept their word to me. Unlike you."

That stung, just as Ilaria meant it to.

"Larissa was right," Ily went on. "You fairies *are* cruel. You wouldn't break your precious rules for your own sister, but you'll break them for a stranger."

"Geppetto isn't a stranger. And his wish comes from a place of good—"

"So did mine!" Ilaria barked. "So did Larissa's."

In the decades Chiara had been a fairy, she'd learned a great deal about the Heartless. She knew where they had come from.

"They lied to you," she said solemnly. "You think Mirabella denied Larissa's mother help? Larissa was the one who hired the bandits to burn down her town. She planned it with her mother's blessing so her family could pray to the Wishing Star for riches."

"A likely story," said the Scarlet Fairy, crossing her arms. "Twisted from the *good* fairies' point of view."

"It's the truth," said Chiara. "Listen to me. I know the fairies aren't perfect. But the rules were made to deter us from abusing our power."

"Only you would defend the rules as you break them," retorted the Scarlet Fairy. "Why didn't you ask your precious council to review Geppetto's wish before you cast your spell? Because you knew they'd reject it. We're not so different, you and I. At least I don't try to pretend to be so high and mighty."

"I'm not afraid to beseech the council for help, Ily,"

Chiara said softly. "I granted the wish out of compassion. What I am afraid for—is you." She swallowed. "Geppetto used to love to hear you sing. He cared about you. Would you hurt him?"

Ilaria stared at her sister. "You never give up, do you? Still trying to appeal to my nonexistent heart. Still trying to save me."

"There's still hope for you," said Chiara.

"But I'm not *good*," Ilaria said mordantly. "No one is. Not truly, not as you believe they should be. That makes me a villain in your book, doesn't it?"

Chiara swallowed. It was supposed to. After all, the Heartless were the Wishing Fairies' adversaries—and, by definition, *evil*.

So why did she still believe in Ily? Why was she tempted to make a wager with her sister, a Heartless?

The answer was clear: for the same reason she'd broken the rules to bring Pinocchio to life. Because maybe, maybe the Wishing Fairies had been overly harsh in judging what was good and what was evil, and didn't always consider the many shades in between. Chiara, during her years as the Blue Fairy, had found herself guilty of that plenty of times, and was still learning.

"I have your heart," Chiara tried again. "If you take it back now—"

"If I take it back, I'll destroy it."

"You'll remember."

"I already remember," the Scarlet Fairy replied. "I remember that Geppetto had his chance to come with me and become greater than his wildest dreams. But he turned me down, and now he's an old man, at most a handful of years from death." She sneered. "Whatever fate I wrought upon his son, he deserves."

Chiara shrank back. *Ilaria truly is lost.*

"I tire of your company, sister," said Ilaria. "I have places to be, and things to do. If you'll take your chances with your fairies, then—"

"I accept your wager," said Chiara, so softly she almost didn't hear herself.

The Scarlet Fairy turned slowly, a smile forming on her painted red lips. "I have your word, on your honor as a fairy?"

"You do," Chiara said.

Ilaria blew her sister a kiss. "Then I'll see you in three days."

The words echoed in Chiara's mind even as Ilaria disappeared, filling her as much with hope—as with dread.

The good fairies of Esperia were meeting on the Wishing Star, and for the first time since she had joined their ranks, Chiara was the last to arrive. Thirteen chairs carved of moonstone were arranged into a circle, and Chiara took her seat, grateful to rest. She hadn't felt so tired in years.

It'd barely been half a day, and already maintaining the magic to keep Pinocchio alive taxed her energy. Such an enchantment was meant to be temporary—Chiara wasn't even sure if she could keep it up for three days. But she had to. Or else she would have to turn him back into a puppet.

"Are you all right?" whispered Agata, who sat on her right. "You look pale."

Guilt weighed on Chiara's conscience as she folded her hands over her lap. She had gotten to know each of the fairies during her tenure, but the closest to her was still Agata, who had moved from being her mentor to being her friend.

In no world would Chiara ever lie to her, but she wasn't ready to tell anyone about the bargain she'd struck with Ilaria.

"I'm worried about Monstro being so close to Pariva."

It was a deflection, but also the truth. Monstro had been asleep for forty years. A week earlier the Heartless had finally found him. They awakened him, and now he was possessed by an unquenchable hunger and rage. Seven ships had already fallen to his wrath, but the whale's fury was not limited to the surface. He terrorized all creatures in the sea, and countless carcasses floated adrift on the surface. All the fairies were on high alert, yet whenever someone came close to tracking him, he mysteriously disappeared.

"I can't blame you," said Agata kindly. "But we'll find him. Are you ready to give us your report?"

With a numb nod, Chiara rose and cleared her throat. "I've returned from scouting the Lyre Sea. I observed the Lake of Mount Cecilia as well as the shores of the Saffiar Beach, and the townships of Elph, Pariva, and Nerio. I warned the fishermen not to enter the waters, but most didn't need the warning. It seems they already know of Monstro."

"It isn't natural," mumbled Mirabella, who headed the discussion. "He was bad before, but nothing like this."

"Were you able to locate him?" asked the Rose Fairy.

"I didn't sense him in the Lyre Sea," Chiara replied, "or anywhere near the northern coast."

"Then we'll have to double our patrols," said Mirabella darkly. "He'll be hungry. Monstro is a hunter, and preying on the fish in the sea will occupy him only for a short while. Soon, he'll look for a new challenge."

Chiara suppressed a shiver. Monstro was strong enough to manipulate the seas. One swing of his great tail would destroy an entire village.

"No one who lives near the water is safe," Mirabella

went on. "Take care watching the sailors and fishermen and guide them to safety away from Monstro's clutches."

The fairies chimed their agreement.

"Chiara, why don't you continue monitoring the Lyre Sea?" suggested Peri. "You know that part of Esperia."

"Would that be advisable?" began Chiara. "It is rather close to my hometown."

"All the better," Peri said merrily. "We trust you, Chia. When's the last time you've ever broken a rule?"

As the fairies chuckled, Chiara could not laugh. Guilt sharpened in her chest. She looked at her wand, as if it might give away what she had done. But it sparkled as it always did, shining as true as the stars in the night sky.

Say something, her conscience urged her.

But if I tell them what I did, Geppetto might lose Pinocchio . . . and I might lose Ilaria.

The stakes were too high, and she knew this was exactly what Ilaria had planned—pitting Chiara against her conscience and her friends.

Yet if she could help Geppetto, Pinocchio, and her sister . . . wouldn't it be worth it? Her heart and her conscience were at odds, and she didn't know which one to listen to. No matter what decision she made, there would be consequences.

The fairies were awaiting her response.

It's my fault for bringing Pinocchio to life, Chiara thought, *but in my heart, it was the right thing to do. I know this. Just as I know that if I give up on Ilaria, no one else will give her a chance.*

She dipped her head. "It would be my pleasure to watch over the Lyre Sea."

"There will be storms across Esperia next week," said Mirabella. "You'd best be careful. You know how cruel Larissa and her kind can be."

CHAPTER THIRTY-FIVE

The next morning, Geppetto sent Pinocchio off to school. A shimmering blue mist watched as the father and son said goodbye, its presence so subtle that practically no one detected it. No one, that was, except Ilaria.

She stayed hidden, blending in with a crowd of gossiping women. But her eyes stayed on the mist as it followed Pinocchio and his chirping conscience down the street.

That wouldn't do. Ilaria couldn't have the Blue Fairy hawking over Pinocchio all day. Not while she had plans for him.

She tilted her head to the sky, and as soon as she commanded it, dark storm clouds loomed over the Lyre Sea. Ilaria twirled her finger around her hair, and the clouds took the shape of a whale.

"Monstro," she sang in a low voice. "Monstro is here."

Her little lie traveled into the wind, finally touching upon the pool of shimmering blue mist.

Chiara took the bait, just as Ilaria knew she would. The blue mist slowed, falling behind Pinocchio as he sauntered off toward the schoolyard. Then it floated up to investigate the sea.

This is too easy, Ilaria thought with a wicked smile.

Ilaria knew that Chiara and her fairies considered finding Monstro their mission of the utmost importance, so of course she went after him. Did she really trust an insect to protect Pinocchio from the Heartless in the meantime?

The Wishing Fairies had done plenty of ludicrous things before, but this topped them all. Ilaria was almost tempted to call the whole thing off. What fun would ruining Pinocchio be if Chiara wasn't going to pay attention?

Ilaria sighed, moving through the streets swiftly and silently. Fun or not, she needed her heart back. And she wasn't about to leave anything to fate. There was too much at stake.

How long has it been since you've sung, Ily? Chiara had asked her.

Her hand went up to her collarbone, sharp nails grazing against where her heart should have been. Sometimes she could feel the ghost of a pulse inside her chest. Then, and only then, did she miss the music she once had made. The sound of laughter and the warm embrace from a friend, a sister, a brother, a lover.

Fortunately, the feeling never lasted.

How could it, when being a Heartless had made all her dreams come true? She'd wanted fame. Everyone in Pariva thought of her as Cleo del Mar, the most famous opera singer in the world. It didn't matter that Cleo del Mar didn't actually exist; in the end, memories were all that remained anyway.

Ilaria had wanted out of her small town. As a Heartless, she'd seen the world. She'd dined in palaces and danced with kings, she'd skated across mountaintops and sailed the Five Seas. She'd rained doom upon more towns than she could count.

But what she loved most was that no one dared look down on her. No one dared upset her, criticize her, or say anything terrible behind her back.

All eyes fell to the ground in her presence, all spines curved and knees bent as if she were an empress. A flick of her wand, and she could make kings weep with despair; she could ignite wrath as if it were kindling and set it ablaze. She could turn an idea into a war.

Music had had no such power. Oh, she had made her grandmother shed a tear or two, and inspired a few girls enough that they'd wanted lessons from Ms. Rocco just like her. But behind her back, everyone had always doubted she'd achieve greatness. Even Chiara.

No longer.

Well, that wasn't quite true. She dug her nails into her palms. She was a fairy with magic, but she wasn't a full Heartless—immortal and near invincible like Amorale and Larissa. They wouldn't accept her into their inner circle until she finally destroyed her heart. She could tell, after all these years, they were starting to doubt her commitment.

I'll prove myself, she thought. In two days, she'd crush her heart with her heel and smash it into a thousand bits.

The Scarlet Fairy moved out of the crowd of gossiping women—thanks to her powers, none of them even noticed— and resumed her usual guise. Her mud-stained cotton skirts turned into the reddest silk, and the straw hat upon her dark locks became an ebony crown studded with rubies and feathers. No one would notice, though—unless she wanted them to. And she had two in mind to visit.

She leaned on her wand as she approached the Red Lobster Inn, its half-painted facade still an eyesore on the outskirts of town. After forty years, it'd become even seedier than when it first opened, and its den of delinquents was something she'd learned to count on.

A low whistle escaped her lips. It didn't take long before

Honest John and Gideon appeared. Her eyes flashed as she scrutinized the pair. Honest John was suavely dressed—if one neglected the subtle patch on his knee—with a bright blue cape, a jade-colored suit, and matching hat. His side-kick, Gideon, however, was an even worse eyesore than the tavern. His clothes were rumpled and ill fitting, and his hat had a hole large enough to fit a fish.

By the Vices, she could not wait until she no longer had to deal with such gormless henchmen. But for now, they would be perfect foils for Chiara's precious wooden puppet. Honest John was as gentlemanly as a criminal could be, but behind his smooth lies and twisted words was a most dishonorable fox. Pinocchio would fall for his charm immediately.

And Gideon? Well, Gideon was a mean cat. He would make sure Pinocchio didn't get away.

"Milady," said Honest John. He swept a bow. "Lady Scarlet, how might I serve your unworthiness?"

Gideon reached for her hand to kiss, but Ilaria moved it swiftly away, so focused that she didn't notice the white dove landing on the tavern's signpost, observing her quietly.

"Boys, boys," she said, in her most lilting tone. "No need to fawn. Now listen carefully. I have a job for you two."

CHAPTER THIRTY-SIX

The Blue Fairy.

Geppetto chuckled as he tidied up the toys he had excitedly scattered across the workshop last night. Pinocchio must have been dreaming, to speak of fairies and such. Why, there hadn't been a fairy spotted in Pariva in over a hundred years.

But then again, what other magic could have brought his "little wooden head" to life?

"Maybe it *was* a fairy," Geppetto mused. "She must have listened to my wish." He smiled, remembering how wonderful it felt to have Pinocchio beside him. "Just think: Pinocchio will become a real boy. He already feels that way to me."

He was sanding a new set of eating utensils for

Pinocchio. A fork and spoon and a knife. A bowl and plate, too. While Geppetto's deft fingers worked, he whistled to himself, feeling happier than he had in years. His father had passed away some years ago, and Geppetto couldn't remember the last time he'd prepared a meal for two.

Oh, he couldn't afford a grand feast on his humble livelihood, but that didn't mean he couldn't splurge on their first meal together. He didn't know yet what Pinocchio liked to eat—or even if he *had* to eat, given he was made of wood. No matter; Geppetto would buy some of everything. Some tuna, perhaps—that was fresh around this time of the year—and bread from the Belmagio Bakery, carrots and potatoes and some leafy greens to help the boy grow strong.

"What else might the child need? Some books to feed his brain, some milk to feed his bones, and a new jacket for winter so he doesn't get cold."

Figaro eyed him skeptically.

"Don't look at me like that. I don't know if the boy will get cold, but he did say he would become a real boy one day. Perhaps by winter, Figaro." Feeling giddy, Geppetto patted the cat's head, unable to believe that Fate had smiled upon him and given him this chance to be a father. He wouldn't take it for granted, and he'd do his best to give Pinocchio a good home and provide for him.

He mused aloud, "Imagine that. It'll be nice to fill up this old house, hear singing and laughter bounce off the walls." He turned to Cleo. "What do you think?"

Cleo folded her fins and twisted to the side as if she were scoffing. Geppetto had cleaned her water first thing in the morning, but she was understandably still irked at him for using her home to put out the fire on Pinocchio's finger.

With a chuckle, Geppetto opened a cupboard drawer and withdrew a drawstring pouch filled with his savings. "He'll need his own room when he gets bigger. I suppose that can wait. For now, some new clothes. And food to feed his belly!"

Whistling as he put on his hat, Geppetto set out for the town square to do some shopping.

Within an hour, he was carrying so many groceries that he did not see his little boy pass him on the other side of the street, flanked by two beastly men and chased by a tiny cricket.

"Mr. Geppetto! Oh, Mr. Geppetto!"

Geppetto turned, spying two young girls chasing after him as he headed to the marketplace. He brightened, recognizing Dafne and Nina Belmagio. Dafne was eight, Nina seven, and the two were the sweetest girls in Pariva. Geppetto sorely hoped they would be friends with Pinocchio.

"Shouldn't you young ladies be in school?" asked Geppetto.

"Not today! We just got back from Vallan. Papa went for work, and he brought us."

"We went to a toy store," added Nina, "but we didn't want anything."

"No one's toys are as nice as yours, Mr. Geppetto."

Geppetto beamed. "Your parents are doing well, your grandfather Niccolo, too?"

As Dafne nodded, she peered into his empty basket. "No Figaro today?"

"He's at home watching Cleo."

"How is Miss Cleo?" piped Nina. "Does she still like her name?"

Geppetto chuckled. Little Nina was getting so tall, it felt like only yesterday she had run off from her sister and dipped into his shop to hide.

"When'd you get a fish, Mr. Geppetto?" Nina asked, her hands behind her back as she peered at the glass bowl on Geppetto's work desk.

"Just yesterday. I thought Figaro could use some company."

"Cats eat fishes, Mr. Geppetto. They aren't friends."

"My Figaro is the friendliest kitten." Geppetto scratched Figaro's ears. "Aren't you?"

Nina looked skeptical, but she shrugged and turned her attention back to the goldfish. "She's pretty. Look at those long and elegant fins! Does she have a name?"

"No . . . not yet."

"You should name her Cleo," Nina declared. "After Cleo del Mar. She looks like a diva."

For some reason—and he didn't know what—the name made Geppetto's breath hitch. "The opera singer?"

"Not just any opera singer," Nina cried. "Cleo del Mar is the most famous prima donna in Esperia. And she's my great-aunt, did you know?" Nina puffed up with pride. "Grandpa's going to take me to hear her sing one day."

"You don't say." Geppetto's brows drew together in confusion. "If she's Niccolo's sister, why doesn't she visit?"

"She's too busy touring the world. You must have known her when you were young, Mr. Geppetto. She lived here."

The words struck a chord in Geppetto, making his throat close. Yes, he could picture Niccolo's sister. Dark raven hair that curled past her shoulders, and green eyes that sparkled when she laughed. Was she an opera singer? Geppetto couldn't remember her song. Time had faded the memory, and whenever he tried to think of her, his focus grew hazy.

"Old age will make you forget even your name," he joked, trying to hide his uneasiness.

Back in the present, Geppetto's smile faded. Strange

that he could not remember Niccolo's sister at all—they must have been about the same age, and yet his memory of her was as elusive as that song she used to sing. A tune from an aria that had been popular when he was younger, but was hardly ever sung these days. Every time he tried to parse the melody, it slipped between the cracks of his memory.

It was about a bird; which type, he couldn't even remember.

"Does she still like her name, Mr. Geppetto?" Nina prodded again when he didn't answer.

Geppetto blinked. "Ah, yes. You should come ask her sometime. She would love to see you."

"I will!"

"So will I," added Dafne. "Grandpa says he'll buy me a new toy if I get good marks in school. I've been studying very hard."

"I'm sure you have. Come to think of it, you two should stop by soon and meet Pinocchio!"

"Pinocchio?"

"That's my son," said Geppetto proudly. "The fairies brought him to me. He's about your age, Nina. Shorter than you, though." His shoulders shook merrily. "Pinocchio's at school right now. It's his first day."

"Wow! The fairies brought him? And to think we weren't at school today of all days," lamented Dafne. "We're

going home now. But we'll see him tomorrow and say hello."
She winked at Geppetto's basket. "If you're going to our
bakery to get Pinocchio dinner, pick up some cinnamon
cookies. Grandmamma made a batch just now, and they're
divine."

"I'll do that," said Geppetto, waving as the two girls
skipped off, and he headed into the bakery to buy some
bread.

It was nearly sundown, and the grand meal Geppetto
had prepared for Pinocchio sat on the table, untouched and
growing cold. Flies buzzed over the cinnamon cookies, and
Figaro pawed at the plate of sliced meats, his belly growling
with hunger.

Geppetto swatted the cat's paw away. "No, no, we sit
together. It's rude not to wait."

Figaro let out an anguished moan. He was hungry, and
Geppetto couldn't blame him. They'd been waiting for over
an hour, and Pinocchio still hadn't come home.

Unable to sit still any longer, Geppetto rose from his
chair and paced in front of the window. Never had he been
more aware of the *tick tick tock* of the clocks on his wall, of
the vibrant shouts of schoolchildren outside on the road.

"Relax, old Geppetto," he told himself. He forced

himself to chuckle. "It is his first day. Maybe he made friends and is playing ball in the fields. Nina and Dafne did say they'd look for him. I'll bet they're all getting along wonderfully."

The thought calmed him, but only for a moment. No matter how he tried, he couldn't banish his worries.

"What could have happened to him?" he said. "Where could he be at this hour? I'd better go out again and look for him. And remember"—he wagged a finger at Figaro– "nobody eats a bite until I find him."

Figaro let out a whimper, but he nodded dolefully.

"Good." With his chin up, Geppetto grabbed his coat and set out into town again.

There were plenty of children in the fields, playing ball as he imagined. But Pinocchio wasn't among them.

"He must be in town, then," Geppetto reasoned. "He's a curious boy, like his father. I'll bet he's at the bakery sampling all the cookies. Or with Vito petting the horses."

But Pinocchio was not in either the shop or the stables. Nor was he anywhere in the town square. In fact, when Geppetto stopped by the school to ask the teacher, the young woman replied, "I'm sorry, Mr. Geppetto, but Pinocchio never came to school."

"That can't be!" Geppetto exclaimed. "Are you sure?"

"Yes," replied the teacher. "I hope you find him. I'll let you know if I hear anything."

It was a greater anguish than anything Geppetto had ever experienced, not knowing where Pinocchio was, and not being able to ensure in his mind that the boy was safe and sound.

His stomach dropped. One day as a parent, and he'd already failed his son. Forgetting to say goodbye, he turned away from the school and began to search the rest of Pariva.

"Pinocchio?" he called, searching desperately. He asked everyone he encountered, "Have you seen my boy? Black hair and a yellow hat? Are you sure? He's a wooden boy without strings."

"No," all would reply.

What had he done by sending Pinocchio off to school? He'd been so overjoyed to have a son, he hadn't considered the boy's safety. He hadn't prepared him, hadn't made sure he'd known about the world.

And now he'd lost him.

"I'll find my son," Geppetto swore. "He'll be okay." He had to be.

His voice was hoarse and his legs were tired by the time he returned home. Figaro had fallen asleep on the table; the food was still untouched. It had begun to rain furiously, and thunder rumbled across the sky.

Cleo was still awake and hadn't eaten. "No, I didn't find him." Geppetto swallowed hard. "Come, Cleo. Time to eat. We'll save some food for Figaro, hmm?" He inhaled a ragged breath. "We'll need our strength to keep looking again tomorrow."

CHAPTER THIRTY-SEVEN

Chiara didn't notice the white dove racing over the Lyre Sea, crying out for her attention. It was night, the world illuminated only by a slender moon, and she was channeling every bit of concentration she had on finding Monstro. The sea writhed with dark magic, and simply searching past its barriers made her lightheaded with effort.

Her wings wilted as she coasted the clouds. She'd been searching all day, and it was time to return to the Wishing Star. She needed rest.

Just one more try, she thought, not wanting to give up yet. She was more tired than usual because of the magic she'd lent to Pinocchio. But she wouldn't allow any idleness in her duties.

Dipping into her reserves of strength, the Blue Fairy

pointed her wand at the shroud of Heartless magic fogging over the sea. It was no use. The mist wouldn't clear.

Chiara dropped her wand to the side. Monstro was hiding somewhere in these waters, and no one would be safe until he was found. But there were countless pockets of such dark enchantment scattered across the Lyre Sea.

It would take months to search them all.

"There has to be another way," she murmured.

At that moment, her dove landed on her shoulder with a cry.

"Pinocchio?" she said, alarmed. "What's happened to him?"

She touched her forehead to the dove's, and in flashes, she saw into the bird's memory. After she had left Pinocchio in Pariva, two of Ilaria's henchmen—Honest John and Gideon—had lured him away from school. They looked like ordinary village folk, but Chiara's wand showed her their true colors. They were part of the vast network of cronies the Heartless called upon to do their bidding on Earth—happy to get paid handsomely for their trouble, while the Heartless reaped the magical benefits of their subterfuge. And Ilaria had heaped them on Pinocchio.

Horrified, Chiara watched as the men led the boy to none other than Stromboli's theater. The dove showed her Honest John and Gideon presenting Pinocchio to

Stromboli, who rubbed his hands with glee and passed the two swindlers a generous pouch of oros.

"My little gold mine," Stromboli *purred, ushering Pinocchio into his wagon.*

It was all Chiara needed to see.

Her heart hammering, she spun back for Pariva. In any other circumstance, she had faith that the cricket would guide Pinocchio in making sensible decisions.

But she knew Stromboli's ways. Over the years, she'd visited him countless times and tried to guide him, but the Heartless claimed him, and he'd grown up to be a duplicitous conman like his father. Now he traveled across the country to perform with his marionettes, robbing his audience when they were enthralled by his show, and even cheating his own brother, Vito.

Poor Vito. He'd run away soon after her visit when he was a boy and had retreated to the countryside, where he'd settled in Pariva. For years, he'd been happy and free from the influence of his father. Then one day he'd noticed Stromboli's traveling wagon, and he'd called out to his brother—naively forgetting that Stromboli had been as cruel as Remo. Stromboli proceeded to steal Vito's hard-earned savings, which forced him to take a second job at the Red Lobster Inn at night. What was worse, Stromboli circled back to Pariva at least once a year, extorting his brother for money and free lodging.

To Pinocchio, he would do far worse. He would woo Pinocchio with empty promises of money and fame. With temptations that the poor young puppet wouldn't be able to resist.

Chiara flew faster, thinking of all that could go wrong. The rain did not touch her, but the lightning and thunder cut into her nerves. Not a good portent. Trouble brewed below.

She hurried, gliding down toward Stromboli's wagon. Inside was Pinocchio, trapped in a wooden cage.

A rare flash of anger bubbled to the Blue Fairy's chest. The poor puppet was helpless, and every second the wagon trundled farther and farther from home.

It took all of her restraint not to spirit Pinocchio away from Stromboli's clutches and whisk him back to Geppetto's home. But Pinocchio's predicament was partially his fault. He hadn't listened to his conscience and gone to school.

For him to have come across Honest John and Gideon and Stromboli all in one day . . . Her hands shook at the unfairness of it all. The poor boy stood no chance against the Scarlet Fairy. Not without some help, anyway.

Taking a deep breath, she composed herself. Freeing

Pinocchio wouldn't be enough. She needed to teach him how to handle such situations. Otherwise, Ilaria would certainly sway him off the right path again.

"Take it easy, son." Jiminy Cricket was consoling Pinocchio before he noticed a beam of light entering the wagon. "Hey, that star again! The fairy!"

"What'll she say?" Pinocchio asked worriedly. "What'll I tell her?"

"You might tell her the truth."

Good advice, Sir Jiminy, thought Chiara as she materialized before the pair. She smiled, not wanting to give away how worried she'd been. "Why, Pinocchio! I didn't expect to find you here. Why didn't you go to school?"

"School?" Pinocchio repeated. "Well, I . . ."

"Go ahead," Jiminy encouraged. "Tell her."

"I was going to school till I met somebody. Two big monsters with big green eyes!"

Chiara paused, waiting for Pinocchio to go on. It was hard not to be charmed by the boy's already vast imagination. But in order for him to understand the consequences of his actions, she'd have to teach Pinocchio to be honest. Luckily, Chiara had a feeling it would be more successful with this sweet boy than it had the last time she'd tried it.

As Pinocchio continued to tell his story, magic sparkled

around his nose. It suddenly grew an inch longer. His eyes widened. "Why, I . . ."

"Monsters?" Chiara inquired, allowing herself the smallest smile.

In a way, Honest John and Gideon *were* monsters. Not the seven-eyed, three-headed monsters with scales and claws and flaming tails that Pinocchio was envisioning, but monsters of a different sort. The kind that wore masks of friendliness and charm—and seemed harmless to his child's innocence. Harmless as, say, a fox and a cat.

"And where was Sir Jiminy?" Chiara asked.

"Leave me out of this," Jiminy instructed Pinocchio in a whisper.

"They put him in a sack," Pinocchio replied, ignoring the cricket.

By now, Pinocchio's nose had grown so long that it had become a tree branch with flowers sprouting from the end.

"How did you escape?" Chiara inquired.

"I didn't," Pinocchio replied. "They chopped me into firewood!"

His nose grew across the space, and leaves bloomed from the branch; a nest with two young birds appeared at the end, with poor Jiminy between them.

"Oh, look!" Pinocchio cried. "My nose! What's happened?"

"Perhaps you haven't been telling the truth, Pinocchio," observed Chiara.

"But I have!" insisted Pinocchio. "Every single word!"

The leaves on his nose wilted, and the birds in the nest flew out in alarm.

Pinocchio held out his hands in entreaty. "Oh, please help me. I'm awful sorry."

Chiara gazed at him, echoing what her mother used to say: "You see, Pinocchio, a lie keeps growing and growing until it's as plain as the nose on your face."

Jiminy Cricket raced across Pinocchio's nose to tell the boy, "She's right. You better come clean."

"I'll never lie again. Honest, I won't."

"Please, Miss Fairy," Jiminy entreated. "Give him another chance for my sake. Will you?"

She nodded, her heart full of everything she wanted to say, of all the protection and help she wished she could offer the both of them. "I forgive you, but remember . . ." The Blue Fairy paused, borrowing the words Ilaria had spoken: "'A boy who won't be good might just as well be made of wood.'"

"We'll be good, won't we?" Pinocchio and Jiminy said to each other.

"Very well," said Chiara. She tapped her wand on the cage, breaking its lock and setting Pinocchio free. His nose returned to its normal size, and Pinocchio beamed at the fairy.

"Thank you, ma'am."

"Remember to listen to your conscience, Pinocchio."

With that, she faded into the starlit night, turning herself invisible so she could observe the pair a while longer. She watched as Pinocchio and Jiminy slipped out of the wagon. Stromboli helmed the mules, unaware that his precious "gold mine" had escaped.

Chiara let out a quiet sigh of relief, but her hands were clenched at her sides. What would have happened to Pinocchio if she hadn't sent her dove to look after him? Did Ilaria expect Stromboli would turn the boy's heart rotten like his? That his greed for coin and fame would spread to Pinocchio?

Already she'd proven Ilaria wrong. But she hadn't proven that Pinocchio was worthy of the magic it would take to make him a real boy. *Two more days.*

So long as Ilaria kept interfering and putting Pinocchio in situations of danger and temptation, there was no way he could win.

Pinocchio wasn't far from home, but this time, Chiara wouldn't leave his safety to chance. She trailed him and Jiminy Cricket—until a dark presence blocked her way.

"You found him," greeted Ilaria. "I was starting to

worry. The game can't end when it's only just begun. That would be no fun at all."

"You know what's also not fun?" said Chiara. "Cheating. You put Honest John and Gideon on Pinocchio's path—"

"I never said I wouldn't interfere."

"Pinocchio could have been hurt!"

"He's just a puppet." Ilaria shrugged and leaned forward on an imaginary ledge, batting her eyes innocently at her sister.

"Pinocchio is a good boy. *You* sent Honest John and Gideon after him. You set him in Stromboli's path. He could have been *killed*, Ily! Stromboli had an ax, and—"

"Enough with the dramatics, Chia. I wouldn't get the boy killed. If he died, he wouldn't exactly be wicked, now would he? He'd only be dead."

Chiara fell silent, but her hands balled at her sides. For the life of her, she couldn't believe this was what had become of her sister. This cruel and unfeeling, *heartless* creature.

"*Stay calm,*" Ilaria taunted, pretending to be her conscience. "*Think before you react.*" She smacked her lips. "So predictable. Though you are looking weak, sister. Are you sure you'll be able to keep up Pinocchio's spell for another two days without help from your fellow fairies? I wonder how disappointed dear Agata will be, knowing her star pupil has broken the rules."

Chiara's voice was a mere whisper: "The fairies wouldn't punish me for having done the right thing."

"But you *would* be punished for bargaining with me." Ilaria fiddled with her hair, a habit she had kept from when she was a girl. It pained Chiara to recognize it. "You'll need your strength if you're going to keep Pinocchio safe. I've plenty of help on my side. Maybe I'll even ask Monstro to make an appearance."

Chiara stilled. It shouldn't have surprised her that she was involved with Monstro, but she didn't want to believe it. "You know where Monstro is?"

"Why wouldn't I?" Ilaria fluttered her hand, clearly loving that she knew more than Chiara about the giant whale. "I was part of the coven that woke him from his nap. You dear fairies have been worried sick about what he'll do." She licked her lips. "Let me tell you, it's nothing good."

"Tell me where he is, Ily," pled Chiara. "He can't be free like this. Think of how many he'll hurt—he'll *kill*."

Ilaria simply twirled her hair. "Then you'd better work fast to find him, hadn't you?" she said sweetly. She tore off one of Stromboli's posters and pointed at the illustrated marionettes. "You know, I'd have to say that Geppetto's are of much higher quality than these. Perhaps Stromboli should patronize his shop one day."

A muscle ticked in Chiara's jaw. *Don't react,* she reminded herself. *She's trying to bait you.*

"Will you promise not to interfere with Pinocchio again?" she asked, getting back to the matter at hand.

"Would you believe me even if I did?" The Scarlet Fairy snickered. "I can see you're going to help him each time. He'll never learn that way."

Slowly Chiara lowered her wand. A part of her wondered if Ilaria was right. At what point would she need to let go? Pinocchio would never learn to follow his conscience if she always stepped in to save him.

"By the Vices, you're actually listening to me?" Ilaria cackled with delight. "Time's made you into even more of a gullible fool than I remembered."

Chiara clasped her hands together, trying her best to summon her calm. During her years as a fairy, she'd answered the wishes of those whom she'd deemed worthy— people, like Geppetto, who had shown kindness and compassion and were noble of heart. Her sister, after all the terrible things she'd done, did not fall in such a category. So why did Chiara still have hope for her?

Why had Chiara broken the fairy's rules, even though she knew the risks?

Because not everyone is all good or all bad, she realized. *It might be easy to label them as such, but it simply isn't true. Even if Mirabella and Agata disapprove, I know this is what I have to do.*

She regarded her sister. "I have faith that Pinocchio's heart is worthy, and he'll show that he deserves to be a real boy—even without my help. Just as I have faith in you, Ilaria. Your heart is true, and it's waiting for you."

The smile on her sister's face vanished. "I have places to be. Monsters to feed, and souls to reap. I'll see you soon enough, Chia."

Ilaria vanished in a puff of red mist, leaving Chiara alone once again.

The storm thundered on, and the Blue Fairy looked to the starless sky, wishing with all her might that she was right about Pinocchio—and her sister.

CHAPTER THIRTY-EIGHT

Geppetto wished he'd brought an umbrella. Rain streamed down his spectacles, and he took them off, wiping them against his damp scarf. He was cold, wet, and exhausted, but he had to forge on. The only question was where. He'd already searched every last corner of town and knocked on every door, but his son was nowhere to be found.

As he put on his glasses again, he leaned against the side of a house for a moment's rest. It was the Belmagio house, it turned out. He recognized the yellow door, the lemon trees, and the garden of herbs and violets in the front yard. The soft strain of a violin wove through the rain. He lumbered closer to the window; inside the house, Niccolo Belmagio was playing the violin while his wife read a book.

At the sight of Geppetto, Niccolo lowered his instrument

and waved. "Come inside, old man," he mouthed. When Geppetto resisted, Niccolo disappeared from the room. A few beats later, the front door was flung open.

"This is the third time you've circled our street looking for your boy," said Niccolo, ushering Geppetto inside. "You need to eat. And look! You're soaked. Dry yourself before you catch cold."

"I can't. There's no time to waste. Pinocchio needs me—"

"Yes, and you won't be able to find him if you die in this storm. You're wetter than a fish. Come inside before I reel you in."

Niccolo wasn't a man who took no for an answer, and Geppetto reluctantly entered the house.

"I always took you for a man of good sense," Niccolo said, shaking his head as Geppetto's teeth chattered. "How long were you out there in this storm? Careful of your boots on the carpet. It was my grandmother's, and Sofia just cleaned it last week."

Geppetto nodded, numbly removing his boots before he followed his friend inside the house. He hadn't been to the Belmagios' in years, but something about being back here jogged his memory, as fragments of his past—that he hadn't remembered in forever—resurfaced.

On his left was the music room; its blue walls were more faded than he remembered, and the old harpsichord was still there in the corner by the window, next to a wooden music stand in the shape of a lyre. The famous chamber where Cleo del Mar had practiced singing. Geppetto could almost hear laughter and music from years past. How odd that she never visited Pariva.

He followed Niccolo down the hall into the small parlor, where a fire crackled in the hearth. There, he greeted Niccolo's wife, Sofia, who offered him a blanket and a mug of hot chocolate. The drink and the fire tickled the chill out of his blood, but not the sorrow in his heart.

"You've looked everywhere? The docks, the fields, the—"

"Everywhere," replied Geppetto morosely. "I can't find him. I'm afraid he's . . . he's . . ." His voice faltered. He couldn't bring himself to say it aloud.

"There, there," Sofia said, patting him gently on the shoulder. "You'll find him. I'm sure of it."

Niccolo scratched his head, his brows knitting. "To be frank, I didn't even know you had a son, Geppetto. The children mentioned something about the fairies bringing him to you, but I thought it was just one of their imaginary games."

"No, Pinocchio is real," replied Geppetto. "Well, as real as he can be . . . for a boy made of wood. He's a puppet I wished to life, you see. A puppet without strings."

"A puppet?" Sofia exclaimed. She and Niccolo exchanged incredulous looks. But old Geppetto certainly was not one to misspeak, so after a moment passed, Sofia nodded. "It's about time Pariva had its own touch of magic, I suppose. It's been a while."

Her husband, on the other hand, was frowning. He looked deep in thought. "A puppet without strings, you say?"

"What is it?" said Geppetto.

"Nina and Dafne went to the theater tonight," Niccolo replied. "They saw the marionette artist who comes by every year. I always forget his name."

"Stromboli," Sofia provided. "The Master Showman."

"Ah yes, Stromboli," Niccolo said thinly. "More like master conman. His ticket prices are extortionate, and every time I've gone to see him, I swear his monkey picks my wallet. But you know how my son is, always spoiling his children. My parents would never have indulged in such a thing." He sipped his drink, the chocolate turning his white beard brown. "Anyhow, the girls were enthralled—they keep singing this song about having no strings. I thought it was some ditty they'd picked up, but now that you tell me your son is a puppet without strings . . .

"You might want to talk to them about it—their parents let them stay up until an ungodly hour on theater nights. Dafne! Nina!"

The two sisters scampered down the stairs, holding hands and swinging them high as their footsteps thumped across the wooden floors. As soon as they came fully into view, they composed themselves.

"You called, Grandpa?" said little Nina. Her green eyes widened. "Oh, Mr. Geppetto! How pleasant to see you!"

"Mr. Geppetto wants to know about the dancing puppets you saw tonight," said Niccolo.

Geppetto cleared his throat. "Was Pinocchio there?"

"I don't know, sir. There were so many children there. I didn't see—"

"No, Dafne. On the stage."

Dafne's eyes went as round as marbles. "You mean . . . oh gosh, that was *him*?" She elbowed her sister. "The puppet without strings!"

Nina let out a squeal. "He was amazing!"

Geppetto didn't dare to hope. He slid off his chair and knelt on the carpet beside the two girls. "You saw him? He was there?"

"He was the star!" Nina exclaimed.

"Shush," said Dafne, clapping her hand over Nina's mouth. The older girl had noticed the urgency in Geppetto's demeanor—or perhaps the worry in his eyes. "Did something happen to him, sir?"

"He's missing." Geppetto felt his gut rise to his throat. "Did you see him after the show?"

Dafne gave a doleful shake of her head. "Sorry, Mr. Geppetto. If we'd known he was your son, we would have looked for you. But we went home."

"I'd bet a pretty oro that Stromboli took your boy," said Sofia with a scowl.

Geppetto swallowed, already knowing it had to be true. Poor Pinocchio. He was so new to the ways of the world. He rose. "Then I'll find him. No matter how long it takes, I'll bring my Pinocchio home. Thank you for your help, Niccolo, Sofia. Dafne and Nina. I'd best be going—"

"Try the tavern," Niccolo interrupted. "Vito works nights there, and I've seen Stromboli at his house before. He might know where he's gone."

"Take this," said Sofia, passing him an umbrella.

Emotion clogged Geppetto's throat, and all he could do was pass them a grateful look. Then into the storm he returned, making for the Red Lobster Inn.

Geppetto had never been inside the tavern before. It was a gloomy establishment, with so few candles lit inside that he could barely make out his own feet as the door behind him swung shut. A handful of patrons sat inside, almost all men he had never seen before. As he passed their tables, most eyed him with suspicion. One or two cast him carnivorous glances, as if he were meat to be carved.

The old toy maker was not a brave man, and in any other circumstances, he would have quailed and whirled for the door. But entering a nest of hoodlums and hooligans was only the beginning of what he'd do to find his boy.

Thank goodness Vito saw him bumbling through the dark tavern.

"Are you lost, Mr. Geppetto?" greeted Vito, grabbing him by the arm before Geppetto walked into a bucket and a pile of shattered glass. "Didn't take you as someone with a taste for spirits."

"Vito," Geppetto said, relieved. "You're here."

"I work here every night except Sundays," said Vito cheerfully. He was a pleasant fellow whom Geppetto knew more as the keeper of Pariva's stables, where he worked during the day. Geppetto had never understood why he worked in a place like the Red Lobster Inn past dusk, but he supposed that Vito was a large man, his broad shoulders easily twice Geppetto's width. Geppetto doubted anyone would give him trouble.

Someone behind him let out a loud belch, and Geppetto shuffled nervously toward Vito. "I'm looking for my son. Niccolo said you're . . . you're acquainted with Stromboli."

As soon as Geppetto mentioned the name, Vito's expression hardened. He pulled Geppetto to a shadowed corner, and his voice went low. "What business do you have with my brother?"

"Your brother?" Surprise etched itself onto Geppetto's brow. He'd never seen Stromboli in person, but he'd noticed his posters pasted throughout town.

"We don't look anything alike, I know." Vito scoffed. "It's because of all his makeup and that wig and sham accent. Embarrassing, really, the show he puts on."

"Oh, that's wonderful news."

"Wonderful?"

"That he's your brother." Geppetto's knees nearly knocked with relief. "Have you seen him? He has my son. Pinocchio—"

"Pinocchio?" Vito spluttered. "You mean to tell me your son is that puppet? He's the talk of the town! An extraordinary, magical sensation!"

It seemed everyone in Pariva had witnessed Pinocchio's performance at the theater.

"Yes," replied Geppetto, "and now he's gone."

"Gone is right," Vito said thinly. "No wonder he was furious."

"Who was?" Geppetto asked, confused. "Pinocchio?"

"No, no. Stromboli." Vito gestured at a pile of shattered

glass he had swept into a corner. "He came back an hour ago, accused me of stealing your boy. Broke every glass he could get his hands on. Took four men to put him down. I was worried he'd set fire to the place. Probably would have, if not for the rain."

"I . . . I don't understand."

"I didn't either until now. Seems like your Pinocchio's left."

"Escaped!" Geppetto drew a breath, daring to hope.

"It was, hmm, an hour ago. Maybe more." Vito glanced at a patron who'd fallen asleep or unconscious among a pile of drinks, as if using the number of empty bottles to gauge the time. "He hasn't come home?"

"I . . . I don't know," said Geppetto, suddenly feeling light in the head. All this time he'd been out, Pinocchio could have been at home waiting for him! "I need to go!"

Vito yanked off his apron and whistled at his colleague. "I'm taking the night off," he told him. Then, to Geppetto, he said, "I'm coming with you."

Geppetto hastened home, but the moment he saw his house, with the lone candle he'd kept lit for Figaro and Cleo, all the hope he'd let flood into his chest went out again. He hardly had the strength to pull open his door.

Only silence greeted him, then the mournful *meow* of

his cat. Figaro crept out from behind the stairs and nuzzled Geppetto's leg.

"He's not here," said Geppetto, collapsing to his knees. "Oh, Figaro, what could have happened to him?"

Geppetto spun back for the door. "Don't close it, Vito. I have to go back out."

"At this hour?" Vito looked at him worriedly. "It's still raining."

"Something's happened to him. I know it."

"It's late, Geppetto. Better you wait until the morning, when you've had some rest. You don't even know where Pinocchio could have gone."

"It doesn't matter. I'll search all of Esperia if I have to."

Vito grimaced. "Something isn't right about all this. Your boy would've come home by now if he'd escaped."

"That's why I have to keep searching."

"No, Geppetto. Listen. There's dark magic afoot, I can feel it."

"Dark magic?"

"It used to follow my papa wherever he went—like a shadow. Comes with Stromboli, too. Lately, it's been around Pariva an awful lot." Vito frowned. "I heard some of the men at the tavern talking . . . about boys who've gone missing."

"Missing boys?"

"Yes, there's been a slew of them gone. Mostly from villages down south, a couple from Elph. Or so they say."

"What else did they say?"

"It's just a rumor, Geppetto," Vito said uneasily, as if unsure whether he should go on. "You can't believe everything drunk men say."

"Tell me."

"He said that there's an island behind Mount Cecilia, and that several boats have sailed to it these past few weeks. Boats all filled with young boys—who disappear and never come back. It's possible Pinocchio was taken there."

"What is this place called?"

"I heard someone say . . . Pleasure Island."

A chill shivered down Geppetto's spine, and he swallowed. "Okay." He moved toward the door.

"Wait until dawn," Vito urged. "The sea's not safe, especially at this hour. Monstro's destroyed every boat that's sailed the last few weeks."

"I don't care about a whale."

"Wait until dawn," Vito repeated. "Get some rest so you can search for your boy with fresh eyes. You can take my boat. It isn't much, but it's small enough that it might not attract Monstro's attention. It'll get you to the other side of the mountains faster than if you ride or walk."

What choice did he have? "Thank you, Vito."

———

At first light, Geppetto settled Figaro and Cleo onto Vito's boat and slipped out into the waters. All was quiet. The past few weeks, hardly anyone had dared sail out into the sea. Even Geppetto had heard the warnings; the first time he'd heard the name Monstro, his heart had jumped with fear, as if he'd encountered the whale before. But that was silly. Even an absentminded old man like him wouldn't have forgotten such an event.

It didn't matter, anyway. Geppetto would gladly sail into the jaws of Monstro himself if it meant a chance of finding Pinocchio.

The sky was still gray from the last night's storm, and Figaro shrank under a blanket as Geppetto prayed, "Blue Fairy, if you're listening, please help me find Pinocchio in time. Please let me bring him home safe."

He would need all the luck and guidance that the fairies could offer. The sea was vaster than he remembered. Within an hour, Pariva's coastline disappeared from sight, and in every direction was only blue sea.

He was alone.

"Not *all* alone," he murmured to himself. He patted Figaro's head and tickled Cleo's fins. "It could be worse," he told them. "The water's calm, and we have Vito's boat." Though Vito had said it was small, it was almost as big as

Geppetto's humble abode; it even had a cabin with a bed and desk.

Figaro made a skeptical meow, and Geppetto drew him close. "You'll see. We'll find him."

For all the comfort his friends brought him, Geppetto could not banish the apprehension creeping into his heart.

And he did not see the whale lurking under the waves, waiting to devour him.

CHAPTER THIRTY-NINE

Wicked as she was, even Ilaria thought it supremely gauche to have a celebration marking the disappearance of one thousand boys. The Coachman, who headed Pleasure Island, clearly disagreed.

"That's a thousand souls gone into the Heartless's bank of evil," he said gleefully, rubbing his hands together as one of his shadowy minions delivered a bottle of red wine. "One week earlier than predicted."

"You've done well, Coachman," said Larissa, clapping politely.

"More will arrive tonight." The Coachman peeled a black whip off his belt and wrapped it meticulously—once, twice, thrice—around the bottle's neck . . . as if he were tying a noose. Then he gave the bottle a good, hard slap. "Shall we celebrate?"

A pop of the cork punctuated the question, and the Coachman roared with laughter as red wine exploded out of the bottle. By the Vices, he had a face that begged to be punched. His nose was round and bulbous like a target. All Ilaria wanted to do was sock it.

He whistled obliviously while filling the four bronze goblets on the table in front of him.

"To new blood," he said, passing Larissa and Amorale their goblets first. Then Ilaria.

Ilaria took it and pressed her cheek to the window. The glass was one way, and no one outside could see her. An unnecessary precaution. The boys on Pleasure Island were so spellbound by the island's offerings they wouldn't have noticed the three fairies gathered at the top of the House of Mirrors, spying on them like vultures.

"To another heinously cruel venture," Larissa toasted.

"And its brimful payoff," added Amorale as wine dribbled off the sides of her goblet.

Ilaria tipped her glass for an imaginary clink, but only because she knew it'd raise Amorale's suspicion if she didn't. Trying her best not to look bored, she swirled her wine, then pretended to drink. The claret pool in her cup was one shade away from her signature scarlet. But it made her ill to look at it. Tonight, the longer she stared at her glass, the more she thought of one thing: blood.

You're not feeling bad about all the boys you've doomed, are you? she asked herself. *Or about one boy in particular . . .*

She knew Pinocchio was on the island. He'd arrived one boat earlier, and he'd gamboled into her trap like the other boys in his crowd. Just like she'd planned.

Then why this tickle in her throat? This sour note on her tongue?

Did she regret it? Was she secretly hoping her sister might swoop onto the island and save him again? Even Chiara wasn't powerful enough to break through Pleasure Island's barriers to do that.

"The wine not fine enough for you, Ily?" said the Coachman, interrupting her thoughts.

The Scarlet Fairy glared. No one called her Ily. For the Coachman to dare such familiarity was a symbol of the favor Larissa and Amorale had granted him. She despised it.

"I've had better," she said hotly.

"Why don't you sing for my boys?" he said, pretending not to hear. "Larissa says you're quite the little star in Vallan. Clara del Mar?"

"*Cleo* del Mar," she corrected.

"Pardon, Cleo," said the Coachman, lifting his hat in apology. "I spend all my time dedicated to the works of power and wealth. Not much time for going to the theater. Or the opera. Might make for quite the treat for my boys though, what do you say?"

She'd rather pick fish bones out of Monstro's teeth than diminish herself by singing on Pleasure Island.

"Opera is a high art," she told the Coachman haughtily. "It has no place in a carnival."

"Ilaria," warned Amorale. "Your manners."

"No offense taken," the Coachman said with a wave. "She's right. No boy here would pay attention to some dame crowing her lungs out. Not when there's fights to be picked and mischief to be made."

The three laughed, while Ilaria finally forced herself to take a drink. The wine burned down her throat.

"Sixty-six new boys tonight," the Coachman declared. "A new record that should tip the balance of magic in your favor. We're going to need an extra wagon at this rate for the poor blokes."

Another sip. Her throat shriveled, and Ilaria clawed her nails into her glass as the walls began to quake. A gang of boys had entered the House of Mirrors with wooden anvils and begun shattering the mirrors. It was chaos. Knives, hammers, and wooden bats being handed out along with candy and soda and ice cream—a perfect den of encouraging violence alongside pleasure.

The whole place was the Coachman's idea, of course. Larissa had loved it. Amorale, too.

But Ilaria?

Obviously, she didn't trust any of the depraved souls that the Heartless collaborated with, but the Coachman was in a special category of wickedness.

Larissa and Amorale had recruited him a decade ago. He'd been an architect working in Vallan—an ordinary, unremarkable citizen, designing homes and buildings and such. Or so he'd appeared.

At first glance, he didn't look so different from her grandfather, when her grandfather had been alive. He had a wide face that entertained wide smiles, soft white hair that poofed like a goose's bottom, and round, marble-shaped eyes that seemed to bulge with kindness.

Yet behind the gentle and harmless mask was a face carved of cruelty.

He'd already begun a career of kidnapping children before he met Larissa and Amorale. He'd cart young boys and girls across Esperia and sell them to the highest bidder. Ilaria rarely spoke up against the Heartless, but when they'd considered recruiting him, she'd been against it. Not that her opinion mattered.

What mattered was that his methods generated results, which greatly pleased Larissa and Amorale. And when they were pleased, they paid handsomely, which in turn pleased the Coachman.

He would have made a perfect Heartless, and more often than not, Ilaria worried that Amorale would convince Larissa to replace Ilaria with him. And now that he was the mastermind behind Pleasure Island, the bringer of a thousand souls that the Heartless would reap for more magic . . . he was a compelling recruit.

He also still had his heart, rotten as it was. Even without hers, Ilaria could sometimes feel traces of regret and compassion, fear and even hope. Ilaria hated hearing the wails of three-dozen-odd little boys, night after night, calling for their mothers. The moment their throats closed up and their words turned into brays and snorts never failed to chill her.

She hid her unease perfectly. Her life and position with the Heartless depended on it—she'd gone too far to turn back now. But every now and then she swore Amorale could read her mind. If not for Larissa, who had taken her in and mentored her, Amorale would have cast her out long ago. Or killed her.

Until Ilaria's heart was crushed completely, she'd always have this weakness. This softness in her that would keep her from becoming as powerful as Larissa or Amorale.

The Coachman had no such weakness.

Envy reared its ugly head. *Once I get my heart from Chiara, everything will be fine,* Ilaria tried to reassure herself. *It'll be fine.*

But that little voice in her head—that *conscience*—had gotten infuriatingly louder over the years. *Will it?* it asked now. *Or will you only lose what's left of yourself?*

"Here it is," the Coachman announced as some of his shadowmen came forth carrying a veiled painting. "Behold, a gift for the Heartless, in honor of our ten years together."

The Coachman lifted the veil, and Larissa gasped in delight. "My mother!"

Indeed, the woman in the painting did look like Larissa. The same darkly arched eyebrows and dark green eyes, the sheet of black hair—only with gray entwined along the temples.

"To the woman responsible for inspiring the Heartless," said the Coachman. "Shall we give her a place of honor? Perhaps in the House of Mirrors? Or right here, where she can overlook all of the glory we shall bring."

Uneasiness prickled Ilaria. How odd that the story Larissa had told of her mother's plight against the Wishing Fairies was coming up again. "Why would we celebrate Larissa's mother?" Ilaria asked.

"Don't you know your own lore?" The Coachman chuckled.

"Ilaria's not fully one of us yet," said Amorale with a dismissive wave. "Her heart's always been . . . soft."

Ilaria seethed. For Amorale to think she wasn't dedicated enough for the Heartless was bad enough, but to be humiliated in front of the Coachman . . .

Amorale tipped her dark wand up at the painting of Larissa's mother in a motion of respect. "I guess it's time you honored this clever woman yourself, Ilaria. Without her, the Heartless would never have been born. It's because of her we discovered the power of hate and despair."

Ilaria spoke slowly. "What happened?"

"We burned down my hometown," said Larissa, with a wistful smile that made Ilaria's blood chill. "When my mother prayed to the Wishing Star ever so convincingly for aid, it was Amorale who answered. Mirabella was suspicious from the start, and it was rather brazen of us to try the same with Amorale's village—but you know what we discovered? As people screamed and begged for mercy, we fairies could drink their fear and misery. That was how the Heartless were born."

The Coachman cackled with them, and Ilaria suppressed the anger flaring to her chest. Larissa had lied to her all along. If she'd known the truth, she'd never—

Never have joined them? she asked herself. *Is that really true?*

If she was honest, she couldn't answer that. While the three kept laughing, she clenched her wine, forcing herself to drink.

"Serves the Wishing Fairies right," said Larissa. "Them and their ludicrous rule about not using magic for your own personal advantage. Why not improve our family's life and station if we have the talent for magic?"

Why not indeed? Ilaria asked herself. After all, that was what had compelled her to join the Heartless in the first place, wasn't it? Wanting what was best for her family?

Or was it wanting what was best for herself?

Another sip, and the wine was done. She needed to share her own piece of celebratory news—before she lost her nerve.

She spoke while her throat burned: "Your Malevolences," she addressed Amorale and Larissa, "I have news to report— in private."

Amorale lifted a thin gray eyebrow. "Not now, Scarlet. Can't you see we're celebrating?"

"It has to do with my . . . my former sister," she forged on. "You'll like it."

Ilaria so rarely brought Chiara up that Amorale's eyes immediately flared with interest. "All right, but make it quick. There's too much fear to waste."

Just a whiff of fear gave her power, and it wouldn't be long before the first boy would transform. After that, it was only minutes before terror spread across the island. That was the Gray Fairy's favorite part of the night.

"The Blue Fairy has been assigned to search for Monstro. She's tracking him."

Amorale tossed a sheet of silvery hair behind her shoulder. "Exactly how is this good news? Or news at all, for that matter?"

"Because I know for a fact that the Blue Fairy, my former sister, has recently committed a mortal error."

Amorale frowned. Her interest was piqued.

"Go on," said Larissa.

"She granted the wish of an old friend and brought his puppet to life." Ilaria paused for effect. "He's a wooden boy named Pinocchio, and he's now on Pleasure Island, thanks to me."

Larissa leaned forward with interest. Amorale, too. "You mean to say that the Blue Fairy has broken the most sacrosanct of fairy rules?"

"She did," Ilaria confirmed. "I caught her in the act and offered to help her—for a price." Ilaria summarized the wager her sister had accepted.

"Well done, Ilaria," murmured Amorale. "Your sister's

heart would be a worthy prize indeed. You say the puppet is here?"

Amorale's recognition was so rare that Ilaria forgot her guilt and preened. "Yes, he arrived tonight."

"She'll be distracted as she looks for him," Larissa murmured, exchanging looks with Amorale. "We'll have to act fast."

"What must we do?" asked Ilaria.

"It seems misfortune is on our side," Larissa said. "First Monstro, now your news."

"What has Monstro done?"

"You'll soon find out." Larissa and Amorale indulged in a knowing chuckle. "Bring the wine, Ilaria."

"What for?"

"To trap Chiara inside." Amorale and Larissa exchanged nefarious glances.

"Coachman," Amorale said brusquely. "Go and find this puppet boy, Pinocchio. Make sure he doesn't escape while we're gone."

"Oh, they never escape, ma'am," said the Coachman. He rubbed his hands gleefully. "Not the way they came, anyway."

Gathering his whip, he lashed it on the ground, and Larissa and Amorale cackled in delight. Ilaria laughed too, but she felt no humor.

Only a chill in her blood that she couldn't shiver away.

There was a boulder in the middle of the Lyre Sea the size of a small island. It was smooth and dark as obsidian, and half-submerged in the water. Tired birds dove onto the rock to rest their wings, and the moment their webbed feet landed they realized something was wrong. But it was always too late to escape. Too late to leap into the air and fly away.

For the boulder came alive, and Monstro swooped down into the sea, taking the birds with him and drowning them before their next breath. Then his giant maw roared open, and he devoured them in one gulp.

Without missing a beat, he surfaced again, lying still as he had before. Maw shut; eyes, too. Monstro reveled in death—and his hunger knew no bounds.

As soon as he sensed the Scarlet Fairy and her elders approaching, Monstro's eyes flew open, filled with the smug satisfaction of a pet who knew he was about to be fed.

Larissa never disappointed. She blew a cloud of emerald magic into the water, illuminating the path toward a small boat a few leagues ahead. Ilaria's sharp fairy vision spied an old man aboard, his face obscured by the white sail he was attempting to adjust against the gathering wind. He and his boat stood no chance against Monstro.

"That rusty old dinghy?" said Ilaria with a scoff. "You're going to send Monstro after that? There's only an old man aboard. How much suffering and fear can we get out of him? He'll probably die soon enough anyway."

"You'll see," said Amorale with the smile Ilaria didn't like. "Fate is kind indeed, and she's brought us an old friend."

As if on cue, Monstro turned on his belly and ripped back into the sea. While he sped toward the boat, Amorale dusted her hands.

"You see, little star, that rusty old dinghy belongs to Pinocchio's father," said Amorale. "I believe you knew him. Once upon a time."

A knot of dread started to tangle in Ilaria's stomach.

Once upon a time. Amorale's voice dripped with mockery. As if Ilaria's life before becoming a Heartless had been a fairy tale. She shrugged it off, pretending she hadn't heard, and fixed her gaze on the little boat. It juddered against the roaring waves, a speck in the water, completely unaware of the great whale torpedoing its way.

In a minute, Geppetto would be gone.

But what could she do? What did she care? He was probably searching for Pinocchio. Helping him only hindered her cause.

And yet . . . guilt needled her.

"Why so silent, little star?" said Amorale, poking at Ilaria's silence. "I remember Geppetto was a beau of yours, long ago. Don't tell me you still care about him."

"I don't," Ilaria said flatly.

"Good. Then you can be the one to seal his fate."

Ilaria bit her cheek before she expressed surprise. But Amorale was sharp. She always had been. "You look stricken, little star. All these years, Larissa's spoiled you by letting you get on without having to dirty those pretty little hands. You wanted more responsibility; you wanted to show how devoted you are. Show us."

Show us.

It *was* the chance Ilaria had been waiting for. She plastered on a smile. "It would be my greatest pleasure."

Unlike her mentors, never had she taken a person's life. Oh, she'd done cruel things. Made toads leap out of a girl's mouth when she talked, turned half a dozen boys into stone, and even cursed a king to turn everything he touched into silver. But in the back of her mind, she knew Chiara and her fellow fairies would undo each of those spells within time.

Killing someone was final. Irreversible. A scar on her soul she wouldn't be able to wash away.

And to kill Geppetto of all people . . .

"Do this, and I will help you take your heart back from your sister," whispered Amorale. She patted her on the shoulder. "You'll be one of us in earnest, my darling. Isn't that what you've wanted most?"

Ilaria swallowed hard, ignoring the hollow pang in her chest.

Monstro was on his way, coursing unseen across the sea. But he was waiting for her blessing to take the ship.

Yes, that is what I want.

She had always been good at lying. Best of all, to herself. And as a Heartless, she'd mastered squashing that tiny conscience in her head. *Don't do this,* it begged her.

It's too late for Geppetto, she thought back. *I have to.*

Don't, Ily.

If he doesn't die, then I will. Larissa and Amorale will kill me.

At least let him live.

Ilaria made the slightest pause. It was hesitation, but she bore it outwardly with a smile, knowing Larissa would read it as pleasure. "I bid you devour that ship," she commanded Monstro through the ruby on her wand. Then, hoping the whale would obey her exact words, she added, "Swallow it whole."

Monstro opened his tremendous jaws, the sea roaring into his mouth. Geppetto and his ship disappeared into the whale's belly, like a flame gone out.

Had she killed him? The ghost of her heart thundered

in her head, loud enough that she could barely hear herself speak. "It is done."

"He's still alive," said Amorale, looking into the black diamond shining upon her wand. Within flickered an image of Geppetto crumpled on the deck. The impact of Monstro's attack had slammed him against the wall of his ship, but he was breathing and starting to rise.

Larissa scowled. "You didn't kill him."

"If I killed him, then he wouldn't suffer the loss of his son," Ilaria replied evenly. "Let Pinocchio turn into a donkey first, and let us claim my sister's heart for our own. Then we can deal with Geppetto."

Her words were convincing enough even for herself. But Ilaria knew she was only buying time. Time for Geppetto, and time for herself to untangle just what she had done. If the Heartless knew she had listened to her conscience, the consequences would be . . . fatal.

She'd seen Amorale with her own apprentice, about two decades before. Amorale had been going through a phase where she trapped her victims in mirrors, and her apprentice made the mistake of accidentally breaking one and thus freeing the souls she had imprisoned within. Before he got a chance to set things right, Amorale had tapped him on the head with her black diamond, and the boy shattered like the mirror he had broken.

A gruesome, horrible fate. Amorale kept the remains in her Vallan mansion; the boy's mournful dead eyes were the first thing you saw when you entered.

Larissa was more patient. But that didn't mean she was more forgiving. The last Heartless who dared cross her she had trapped in a champagne bottle, wandless and power-less, and cursed to float forever across the ocean and never be found.

"I see," Amorale murmured. "I wasn't sure you had it in you."

"I told you my apprentice was well chosen," said Larissa. "There's not a chance Pinocchio will redeem himself now. He's doomed his father."

No, thought Ilaria mournfully.

I've *doomed his father.*

CHAPTER FORTY

A cloak of dark enchantment hid Pleasure Island from Chiara's detection. Its threads were fear and misery manifest, woven from the powers of all the Heartless combined.

Mist frothed over the sea, and Chiara would never have found the island if not for her dove.

"Pinocchio's there?" she asked, spying only water.

The dove insisted. It shook a wing, demonstrating that there was an invisible string linking it to Pinocchio. After all, they shared a creator in Geppetto—in a way, the bird and puppet were linked like siblings.

"I trust you," Chiara murmured. "Show me where he is."

The dove touched its forehead to hers, allowing her to see through its eyes. Then, folding its wings to its sides, it plunged through the mist and landed on top of the island's high wooden gate.

At the dock, a boat unloaded dozens of young boys from across Esperia. They rushed through the entrance giddily, lured by its spectacular sights—a Ferris wheel as tall as Esperia's grandest cathedrals, a carousel that never stopped, floating balloons shaped like bears and tigers.

Not one boy noticed the faceless shadow creatures lurking behind the gates. Chiara had never seen one before, but she recognized what they were: poor souls that had made bargains with the Heartless—and lost. As punishment, they lost their hearts and were forever doomed to serve Larissa and Amorale.

There had to have been hundreds of them on Pleasure Island. Some wore the masks of normal human beings, and acted as caretakers of the amusement park, food vendors, and even janitors. The rest loitered about the island coast, waiting.

Waiting for what?

"Right here, boys!" cried a food barker. He was tossing out candies and ice cream like a farmer tossing feed to chickens. "Get your cake, pie, dill pickles, and ice cream. Eat all you can. Be a glutton, it's all free!"

Music piped loudly, drowning out the boys' excited squeals. They hurried deeper onto the island, a few dipping into the so-called brawl houses where everyone picked fights with one another, and everyone grabbing axes and hammers that the island staff handed out, using them to smash anything and everything in sight—all for the fun of it. The dove picked out Jiminy Cricket weaving frantically through the crowds, trying not to be squashed by the stampede of boys.

The crack of a whip startled the dove. As it jumped off the gates, the boat that had carried the boys to the island departed, and the gates began to close.

"Hop to it, you blokes," said the Coachman, lashing out his whip at the shadowmen. "Come on! Come on! Shut the doors and lock 'em tight." He laughed wickedly. "Now get below and get them crates ready."

Chiara didn't have to wait long to learn what they were getting them ready for.

It was something of an event at Pleasure Island—a twisted, grotesque celebration—when the first boy lost himself. Bells rang and sirens sang from every attraction and restaurant and building, though few paid attention to the noise. The music in the place was nearly deafening, and a few extra sirens were hardly cause for alarm.

But Chiara saw. She wished she could look away, but horror—pure, resounding horror—froze her in place.

Gray-brown fur coated the boy's arms, spreading

quickly to the rest of his skin, and a tail sprouted out from the back of his pants. He screeched in terror, but the music piping over the island muffled his cries as his hands and feet became hooves and he fell onto all fours. "Mamma!" he cried. "Papa!"

They were the last words he uttered before his words turned into brays.

And the boy turned into a donkey.

Terror gripped Chiara. *Pinocchio,* she thought immediately. If he turned into a donkey, he'd be lost—just like Ilaria wanted. *We have to help Pinocchio.*

Her dove was already searching the island, swooping through room after room for the young puppet. To her relief, the cricket had figured out the island's scheme, and her dove tailed the pair making their escape. Together, cricket and boy dove into the sea, and as they swam to shore, Chiara let out a shaky breath.

"That was close," she said when Pinocchio and Jiminy had untangled themselves from the thorny mists that cloaked Pleasure Island.

Too close, she thought, watching Pinocchio wring his donkey ears and tail dry as they scampered through Pariva for Geppetto's workshop.

"The fairies need to know what's happening here," said Chiara, suppressing a shudder. There *had* to be a way to reverse the curse over the boys and return them to their families.

She lifted her wand, about to chime the Wishing Star's bells for an emergency meeting—when her dove let out an emphatic cry.

"Monstro?" she said.

The dove held out a wing, urging Chiara to follow. Together they flew down toward Pleasure Island. A handful of leagues outside the Heartless stronghold rested a figure so still Chiara had taken it for a boulder in the sea.

"So this is where he's been hiding," she breathed. "He's guarding the island. Only at night, you say? How on earth did you find him?"

The dove let out a sorrowful coo.

"Because Geppetto's trapped inside," she said as she understood.

It only just happened, the dove confirmed. *While Pinocchio was on Pleasure Island.*

"We need to send Pinocchio a message," said Chiara. A feather quill appeared in her hand, and quickly she wrote:

Your father went looking for you and has been swallowed by a whale named Monstro. He's alive, but you must find him quickly. Save him, while I recruit the fairies to help the boys on Pleasure Island.

She had to hurry.

Tomorrow would be the third and last day of her bet with Ilaria. If Pinocchio couldn't prove that he was a good boy by dusk, he would turn into lifeless wood again, this time forever.

And she would owe her heart.

CHAPTER FORTY-ONE

Deep in the belly of the whale Monstro, Geppetto tried to count his blessings. For one, he was alive; Figaro and Cleo, too. Two, his ship was still mostly intact, having been swallowed whole down the giant whale's gullet. He had a bed with a blanket—a bit threadbare, but it was better than nothing—a table and two chairs, even a stack of spine-bent books to pass the time.

"It's almost like home," he said aloud to his pets, trying to remain cheerful.

Who was he fooling? He was trapped in the cavernous belly of a whale. His situation was hopeless, his fate was fixed. There was no way to escape Monstro's jaws. Not a sliver of daylight pierced the cracks between his enormous teeth, and the whale had been asleep ever since he had swallowed Geppetto's ship. Had it been only a day? It felt like more. Geppetto had no sense of time anymore.

Worse yet, he had run out of food.

All day he'd spent fishing, but every net came up empty. Hard to stay cheerful in such conditions.

For Figaro's and Cleo's sakes, he masked his desperation and hummed whenever he could—slivers of his favorite tunes. But not even music could raise his company's morale.

"Not a bite for days," he mumbled miserably. "We can't hold out for much longer." He sneezed. "I never thought it would end this way, Figaro . . . starving to death in the belly of a whale." He sniffled. "My poor little Pinocchio."

His stomach growled, and he leaned over the railing of his ship, staring into the empty water that pooled over Monstro's gut. "It's hopeless, Figaro. There isn't a fish left. If the monster doesn't wake up soon, I . . . I'm afraid we are done for."

Geppetto heaved a sigh, about to rise from his chair and give up on fishing. But lo, something rattled against the top of Monstro's head, and the whale lurched.

He was awake!

His jaws began to part. Wind and ocean spilled inside, rocking Geppetto's boat back against Monstro's throat. Geppetto clambered to the edge of his ship for a better look. His eyes watered from the bright light that fanned across the ship, but as he squinted, the most beautiful sight came thrashing across the waters.

Tuna! Hundreds and hundreds of tuna!

Seizing his net and his fishing rod, Geppetto raced to catch as many as he could. "Here they come," he cried. "Tuna, tuna fish! Here's a big one. Get them in there, Figaro!"

The cat leapt with joy, and Geppetto would have done the same if he hadn't been so busy. There wasn't a second to waste. He hauled tuna onto the boat, hurling them onto the floor, onto the cargo boxes and the barrels behind him. It didn't matter, so long as they were aboard.

He was so absorbed in reeling in fish that he did not hear the voice that suddenly cried out behind him.

"Hey! Hey!"

"Here's another one," Geppetto shouted, winding another tuna into the barrel. He had to hurry. Oh, he'd caught maybe a dozen or two fish, but Monstro's jaws were already starting to close, and who knew how long it would be until he woke again? He hurled his net into the water again.

"Hey, Father!" cried the voice once more. "Father!"

"Don't bother me now, Pinocchio," Geppetto dismissed, one beat before his eyes went wide with realization. "Pinocchio!"

What a wondrous turn of events! He must have reeled the boy onto his ship and not have noticed it! The father ran toward his son, scooping him up into a delighted embrace. "Pinocchio, my boy. I'm so happy to see you!"

Pinocchio sneezed, and Geppetto's heart immediately leapt with worry. "You're soaking wet. You mustn't catch cold."

"But I came to see you!"

How Geppetto warmed at the words. He knelt so he was eye level with his son. "Let me take your hat." He started to pat the boy's black hair dry and slid off Pinocchio's hat.

A gasp caught in his throat, and he nearly fell backward.

"What's the matter, Father?" asked Pinocchio.

"Your ears!" Geppetto whispered, pointing at the two gray donkey ears that curled up from Pinocchio's head. "What's happened to your ears?"

Pinocchio reached up above his head, suddenly remembering with a good-natured smile. "Oh, these. That's nothing. I've got a tail, too." He laughed, but the sound quickly morphed into a beastly hee-haw. His humor vanished, and he covered his mouth with his hands and stared at the ground.

Sensing his son's shame, Geppetto exhaled quietly. His alarm melted, and emotion heated his eyes and throat.

"Never mind now," he said tenderly. He scooped up the boy into his arms. "Old Geppetto has his son back. Nothing else matters." He laughed, touching his nose to his son's. He sat Pinocchio on his lap. "Are you hungry? Have you been eating, sleeping?"

He didn't give Pinocchio a chance to respond. "We'll cook a feast! We've plenty of fish now. You can tell me where you've been, and how you found me." His voice turned stern, an echo of his father's. "Though you really shouldn't have come here, Pinocchio. It's dangerous, you know."

A wave of emotions overcame him, and his rebuke trailed, and he hugged the boy close. He couldn't muster any more words of reproach at Pinocchio; he was too grateful and relieved to have him back.

Even if he had to spend the rest of his life trapped in Monstro's belly, it wouldn't be so bad now that he had Pinocchio with him. They would find a way to survive, one day at a time.

CHAPTER FORTY-TWO

Chiara navigated a low-hanging cloud, advancing as close as she could to Monstro. But every time she ventured near, a net of dark enchantment threatened to ensnare her. She tried sending her dove, but Monstro was fast asleep. Her bird couldn't even slip through the gaps between the whale's teeth, or fly through his blowhole.

So she waited, and she rang the Wishing Star's bell thrice, over and over. Help was on its way, but did it always take this long for the fairies to come? Every second mattered, and there weren't many left.

The day aged, and the sun pinched into a corner of the world, about to begin its daily descent.

"Still holding out hope for Pinocchio?" Ilaria said,

materializing on Chiara's cloud. "It's time to gracefully admit defeat, sister. You've lost. The wager is over."

"It isn't sundown yet," said Chiara, acknowledging her sister only with a glance.

"It might as well be. Pinocchio's actions have doomed Geppetto. Look at them. They're trapped inside Monstro's belly, perishing together in a cruel twist of fate, as Geppetto would've done as a young lad if you had not intervened—oh, what an opera this would have made." Ilaria bent backward and pretended to swoon. Then she chuckled darkly. "I can't think of another production with such delightful agony. It's time to face the truth: Pinocchio will never prove himself worthy of being a real boy. Not in the hour that you have left."

"I have faith in Pinocchio," said Chiara. Her voice, though calm, betrayed her with a hitch. Ilaria was right—Pinocchio couldn't redeem himself while he was trapped inside Monstro. "Pinocchio is brave. He will follow through."

"Brave, perhaps," Ilaria allowed. "But unselfish? Truthful?" She snorted. "It's your fault, really, if you must know the truth. If you hadn't made Geppetto forget his past, he wouldn't have sailed into the Lyre Sea in the first place. He would have remembered what Monstro did to him."

"Geppetto would have gone anyway. His love for Pinocchio is true, just as mine is for you." Chiara held out her hands to Ilaria. "That's why the Heartless haven't been able to reach you, Ily. There is no greater power than love, and there is nothing I wouldn't do to bring you home."

Ilaria turned rigid. "You're delusional, Chiara. Concede and give me your heart, and I'll let Geppetto go free."

"No."

"I give you this chance to come with me," said Ilaria. "Larissa and Amorale will make it much more painful for you than I will."

"I have faith in Pinocchio," Chiara repeated. "And in you."

"Then you're about to be very disappointed." Ilaria tipped her gaze upward at the sky. "You're waiting for your friends." The red feather in her dark hair shook as she tittered. "I regret to inform you, sister dear, that they have been . . . detained. But don't fret. *My* friends are here."

Green and gray mist permeated Chiara's cloud, and in a flash, Larissa the Green Fairy and Amorale the Gray Fairy appeared at Ilaria's sides.

Chiara didn't even get a chance to take out her wand. Together, Larissa and Amorale stirred their wands into her cloud. Lightning sizzled, and shadowy arms of magic shot out to wrap around Chiara's ankles.

The Blue Fairy couldn't move. When she tried, the Heartless's spell gnawed deep into her flesh, dark magic sinking into her bones. The pain was unlike anything she had ever felt.

"Hurts, doesn't it?" said Larissa, stroking Chiara's cheek. "That's just the beginning. Like you said, you still have an hour until the wager's up. We can deal a lot of pain in one hour—before we kill you."

"You didn't say you were going to kill her," said Ilaria. She conjured a wine bottle and held it out. "I thought you were going to trap her—"

"We changed our minds," said Larissa. "Do you take issue with that, little star?"

It was a challenge, and Ilaria knew it. Her breath hitched. "I thought you couldn't kill a fairy."

"Normally, we can't," Amorale agreed. "But since the two of you have a binding contract where Chiara will owe her heart when she loses, it is yours—*ours,* to destroy."

"That would make her one of us, a Heartless," said Ily, trying to understand. "Wouldn't it?"

"You think she'd become a Heartless even without a heart?" Amorale chuckled. "Oh, poor dear. Only the truly wicked can survive when their hearts are obliterated, my star. Your sister Chiara is all heart. She will die."

Ilaria shrank. "I never agreed to—"

"You do as we say," Amorale growled. "Unless you think we should question your commitment."

"No." Ilaria faltered. "No."

"Good," said Larissa, stabbing her heel into the cloud. "Your bond has always held you back. With her gone, the time will come for you to join us, as *our* sister."

Chiara flailed, but the chains over her ankles only shot fire into her veins. The pain made her crumble to her knees. *Ilaria, please.*

Ilaria pretended not to see. "I'm ready."

"Wonderful," said Amorale. "Then we begin."

Larissa brandished her wand, and its emerald glowed, searing the sky with its brightness. Two green claws extended from the emerald and reached, tauntingly, for Chiara's heart.

Chiara wasn't looking at Larissa or her wand. "Ily," she whispered, reaching out to her sister. "Ily . . ."

Then the claws wrapped around her heart, cold as ice.

Chiara's entire body spasmed, and as hard as she tried to hold in her scream, it boiled out of her throat. She felt like a piece of glass being shattered again and again. Each time her heart dared to beat, Larissa's powers dug even deeper, and pain exploded inside her, threatening to rip her apart.

Through it all, Chiara kept her eyes on her sister. Ily's lips were pursed, and she floated off the edge of the cloud. But at her sides, her fists were curled, and she was holding her wand.

"That's enough," Ilaria said harshly.

Chiara lifted with hope until Ilaria stepped forward, her face an unfathomable mask. "I'll deliver the final blow."

And yet, Chiara did not quail. She would not give up her faith in her sister. "I believe in you, Ily."

"Your hopes are in vain," said Larissa, making way for Ilaria to approach. "That's it, my star. Remember all the Blue Fairy's broken promises, her lies and betrayals. Without her, you'll be one of us. Finally."

"I never lied to you," said Chia staunchly. "I love you, Ily."

Energy crackled from the ruby on Ilaria's wand, and she drew tiny circles in the air, gathering the darkness that emanated from Monstro's aura. The ruby turned obsidian black, heavy with enchantment.

"Goodbye," Ilaria said, pointing it at Chiara.

In a cascade of red light and shadow, magic surged out of Ilaria's wand, but at the last instant, she whirled and cast her spell instead upon Amorale and Larissa.

There was no one word that could encapsulate the look on their faces. Terror, outrage, shock, and fury. All those twisted the Heartless's features before Ilaria sent them reeling into smoke.

"Begone!" Ilaria cried, seizing Larissa and Amorale's wands before the two fairies began to funnel into the bottle.

"You stupid, stupid girl," Larissa whispered as she

fought off the spell, trying desperately to take her wand back. But her fingers were already smoke, and she could not grasp it. "What do you think will happen to your dreams when you betray us?"

"No one will remember Cleo del Mar," hissed Amorale. "You'll be back where you started."

Ilaria's chest tightened, only for a second, and then her expression hardened. "Good." Holding all three wands, she banished her former mentors into the glass bottle and conjured a thick round cork to shut it tight. Without bravado, she dropped the bottle into the sea—listening intently for a splash.

"Good riddance," she muttered.

Then she aimed her wand at Chiara's shackles. They fizzled into the air.

The Blue Fairy's voice came out as a rasp. "What . . . what did you do to them?"

"Trapped them. They can't cast magic without their wands, and certainly not while they're locked up in that tiny space. It will probably take a century or two for them to get out." Ilaria rubbed a spot of dirt off her ruby. "They had it coming."

Ilaria's back was to her, but Chiara's heart welled with warmth. *You're back,* she thought, tears pinching the corners of her eyes. *You're finally back.*

"Ilaria . . ." she began.

"Don't say anything," grumbled Ilaria as she snapped Amorale and Larissa's wands in half over her knee. "I don't need you gloating."

"I never gloat," said Chiara.

Ilaria whirled. "Yes, you do. When your left eyebrow lifts—like it is right now, it's the I-was-right look."

"It's more of an I-am-relieved sort of look." Chiara rose slowly to her knees. "Thank you for saving me."

"You're—you're all right?" said Ilaria. "Did they . . . hurt you?"

Chiara's body still tingled from the lightning shackles Larissa and Amorale had bound about her ankles, but the pain had already faded. "I'm fine. How did you do that?"

"They've been channeling most of their magic into cloaking Pleasure Island and Monstro from the rest of the world. I stole back some of that energy from Monstro— to use it against you." Her smug air faltered. "I suppose I ended up putting it to better use. Wasn't sure it would actually work . . . but Larissa and Amorale sure didn't expect it."

Chiara clapped. "*I* didn't expect it."

"Yes you did. I knew you were gloating."

"Not gloating, Ily. Proud."

"Whatever you say," Ilaria mumbled, but the edge in her voice was sanded off. "I couldn't let them take you, too."

Chiara reached for her sister's hand. "Thank you."

Ilaria looked down at their hands, then spun toward Monstro. "We better hurry if you're going to win our wager. You only have a few minutes left. Here." She passed Chiara the snapped halves of Amorale's wand. "You throw Amorale's, I throw Larissa's. Aim for his eye."

"Monstro's head?" Chiara asked as Ilaria flung the wand. Chiara threw, too, matching her sister's strength. The wands skimmed the side of Monstro's head, then bounced into the sea.

"It was worth a try. No magic will touch Monstro—not yours, not mine. All we can do is wait. And hope that he wakes up soon."

CHAPTER FORTY-THREE

Geppetto wrapped his son with a blanket and sat with Pinocchio in the ship's hold. It was the warmest spot he could offer, and the poor boy was drenched from swimming. Geppetto had so many questions, but the sight of Pinocchio safe and with him made him decide they could wait.

"Is this your boat, Father?"

"Mine? No, it's from a friend. I borrowed it."

"Does that mean we have to give it back? I like the water. There's a lot of fish inside."

"When we go home, I'll get us a boat. We can go fishing together."

"I'd like that!"

"But first we have to get out of this whale," said Geppetto

sadly. "You know, it's funny. I feel like I've met Monstro before. But that's impossible, isn't it?"

Geppetto leaned back against the wall, trying with difficulty to recall when he might have met the whale, but he couldn't.

With a sigh, he hummed a song as he stroked Pinocchio's long ears. A song he hadn't heard in many years. The first notes came tentatively, and he made the winding turns and leaps of the melody like navigating to a destination without a map, but he forged on, letting his heart take him from note to note. Bit by bit, the song budded and bloomed, and it was like finding a treasure he'd buried years ago under the sand. Still there. Just a little older and dustier.

"That's a pretty song, Father. What is it?"

"It's about nightingales," replied Geppetto, amazed that he remembered. "A nightingale who is lost in the forest, and in her despair, she loses her song. Only through love and hope does she find it again. Then she finally flies her way home."

"I wish we were birds and could fly out of here," Pinocchio said glumly. "There has to be a way we can escape."

"I've tried everything," Geppetto replied. He reached for his boy's hand to comfort him.

"Maybe if we had a smaller boat—"

"We do," said Geppetto. He gestured at the raft he'd built that morning. It was a pitiful-looking thing, but it floated against the water, tethered to the boat by rope.

"A raft!" Pinocchio's eyes lit. "We'll take the raft, and when the whale opens his mouth—"

"No, no, no." Geppetto gestured the impossibility of it all with his hands. "Now, listen, son. He only opens his mouth when he's eating. Then everything comes in. Nothing goes out." As Pinocchio's face fell, Geppetto took him by the arm. "It's hopeless, Pinocchio. Come on, we'll make a nice fire and cook some of the fish."

"A fire, that's it!"

"Yes," agreed Geppetto. "And then we'll all eat again." Just the thought of food comforted his belly.

"A great big fire," Pinocchio went on. "With lots of smoke!" He started grabbing items within the boat and smashing them into firewood. "Quick, some wood! We'll make him sneeze!"

"Make him sneeze?" Geppetto considered. "That will make him mad."

"Mad is what we want!"

Geppetto's heart picked up its pace as he thought this through. Maybe. Just maybe, Pinocchio's idea would work. They heaped a pile of wood on the boat, and Pinocchio shattered a lantern over it. A fire blazed over the wood, and smoke billowed high above their heads.

As the fire consumed the boat, Pinocchio and Geppetto quickly gathered Figaro and Cleo, grabbed oars, and leapt onto the raft. Together they rowed, fighting against the current with all their might.

The whale was already shuddering, holding in a sneeze as the smoke grew. He heaved over and over, trying to stifle it.

But he could not.

In a thunderous blast, Monstro sneezed. Out of his jaws Pinocchio and Geppetto sailed, racing into the open waters of the Lyre Sea. They knew they couldn't let up, for once Monstro regained control of his senses, he would be after them.

Monstro chased them across the sea, ripping through the waves as if they were paper. It was hopeless trying to flee, and their pitiful raft skated across the waves, nearly crushed by Monstro's tail alone. Both of them knew it was only a matter of time before the waves destroyed them. At the last moment, before the sea blasted their raft into smithereens, Geppetto and Pinocchio leapt with Figaro and Cleo.

The water was so cold that the chill set into Geppetto's blood and muscles and nearly froze his mind.

"Swim, Pinocchio," Geppetto cried as the sea gained strength and water rushed into his lungs. "Swim, my boy!"

He swam, too, kicking and pushing with all his might. But he was not a young man anymore, and he was exhausted and hungry. Even if he had been at his prime, there was no way he could have defeated Monstro.

Let alone a furious Monstro.

Geppetto could feel the whale's wrath in the water. As Monstro ripped through the sea, the very world tilted and shuddered. All it took was one giant wave thundering over him, and Geppetto was knocked senseless.

Seconds later, when he regained consciousness, he was hanging over a piece of floating debris. Shore was within sight, a blurry aspiration that he had not the strength to reach.

"Father!" cried Pinocchio, clutching his arm. "Father, stay awake! We're almost there."

Geppetto gazed at his young son, who struggled to keep both of them afloat. He had never felt more love for anyone. "Go on, Pinocchio," he murmured. "I'll only hold you back. Save yourself."

"No! Father, come on!"

With what strength he had in his reserves, Geppetto kicked and thrashed. Every second felt like a year, and he couldn't tell whether it was the sky growing darker or whether it was his vision growing dim.

At last, the shore was within reach, but a current tore Pinocchio and Geppetto apart. Geppetto's back slammed against a boulder, and the world blanked into nothing.

When he washed up on the shore, it was dusk.

Geppetto rose limply. His throat burned, and his eyes stung with salt. By some miracle, Figaro and Cleo in her bowl had washed up beside him. Were he not so utterly spent, he would have picked them up in joy.

As it was, he crawled across the sand, one hand in front of the other, his legs plodding after them. The world was a wash of rock and seawater; his glasses were broken, and he could hardly make out the sand from the sky.

Behind the rocks, a haze of red and yellow distilled into the outline of his dear son.

"Pinocchio!" Geppetto cried, finding his voice. His arms and legs found strength, and he hurried toward his son.

But his son's face was in the sand. The wooden boy, who had so filled Geppetto's heart with happiness—was dead.

CHAPTER FORTY-FOUR

The sun dipped behind the mountains, and night swept away the last remnants of day. The Heartless were gone, and Chiara's wager with Ilaria was over.

A song peeled out of the howling winds, and neither sister dared move. It was a song that both sisters were sure at first that they were imagining—soft, sung slightly off-key, but carrying all the heart in the world.

Geppetto. The old man wept on the beach, shadows crawling over his shoulders as he held his son to his chest and rocked him from side to side, as if he were a cradle for his fallen boy.

Geppetto cried the Nightingale Aria. The song Geppetto had immortalized in the music box he'd once given Ilaria. Once, it had been performed by every prima donna across

Esperia; its popularity had faded over the years, and now it'd become a ghost, like Chiara and Ilaria—forgotten almost completely.

Geppetto sang slowly, stretching out the words between his tears, yet his voice was so gentle, so tender, that it sounded like a lullaby.

Ilaria said nothing. She bit on her lip, trying to hold in the emotions that rose to her chest. Emotions she hadn't felt in forty years.

She wished she could comfort Geppetto. She wished she hadn't brought this misery upon him, and she regretted everything. Most of all, she regretted that she'd left home.

"You've won," she told Chiara at last. "Pinocchio is a good boy."

The Blue Fairy swallowed. "It's too late. No power of light or darkness can bring the dead back to life."

"But Pinocchio was only half-alive to begin with." Ilaria examined the ruby on her wand.

The resentment and anger she'd nursed inside her for forty years was fading, and with it, her power. She needed to hurry. She didn't want to be a Heartless a moment longer than she had to, but there was something she needed to do before she renounced her dark enchantments.

"With the last of my magic, I pledge to help Pinocchio become a real boy." She extended her hand to Chiara. "You remember what happened when our magics came together and struck your dove?"

As if on cue, Chiara's white dove flew past them and landed on Ilaria's arm.

"She came to life," Chia murmured. "Thanks to the two of us."

"It takes two to make miracles happen," said Ily. "Will you do the honors?"

Taking in a deep breath, Chiara nodded, and together, hand in hand, the sisters approached the lifeless Pinocchio.

Prove yourself brave, truthful, and unselfish, and someday you will be a real boy. She touched her wand to Pinocchio's head. "Awake, Pinocchio. Awake."

Magic brimmed across the young boy's still body, bringing him life. His cheeks turned rosy, and his wooden nose became one made of flesh, the nails in his knees and elbows turning into joints and bone and muscle. Gone were his donkey ears and tail.

"Papa!" he spoke. "Papa, I'm alive!"

Geppetto rose from the sand, unable to believe his ears. But when he saw his dearest Pinocchio a real boy, his tears of sorrow turned to joy. He scooped his boy into his arms. "My son," he whispered. "You've come home."

Chiara watched them, her heart full of relief and gladness. This was what made her love being a fairy—

the tender moments of joy, the proof that hope was never in vain.

While the father and son rejoiced, the Blue Fairy guided her sister away from the coast. Two hearts had just been reunited, but there were two more that she was waiting on.

Chiara held out Ily's old music box. "Will you take your heart?" she asked quietly.

"If I do, will I have to forget you, like everyone else?"

Chiara swallowed hard. "I don't know," she admitted. "I'll have to ask."

Ilaria slid the music box off Chiara's palm onto hers. "Even if they say yes, I want my heart back. Even if I'm only your sister, your best friend, your Ily for a minute or an hour, it'll be worth it."

Tears rimmed Chiara's eyes, and she linked her arm with her sister's as Ily opened the music box. The Nightingale Aria hummed to life, and Ilaria let out a shaky breath.

"I'm going home," she whispered to Chiara. "Like the nightingale, I've finally found home again."

She sang along, softly, as she held the box to her chest. With each note, a beam of light radiated from the music box, growing brighter and brighter until it enveloped Ilaria completely.

The light folded into her chest, and her heart was her own once more.

Warmth returned to her eyes, and she aged forty years, her dark brown hair graying into a peppery silver. But her green eyes still danced with youthful mischief.

"I thought I'd be more upset at seeing myself old," Ilaria said, staring at her hands and patting her cheeks. She cleared her throat at the sound of her voice, a good half an octave lower than it'd been only minutes ago. It would take some getting used to. "But you know, I don't look bad." She glanced at her reflection in the sea and tapped at the wrinkles around her eyes. "Almost as pretty as Mother, I'd say."

Chiara laughed and held out her arms to hug her sister. But after a long beat, Ilaria withdrew.

"I don't deserve to live again." The former Scarlet Fairy stared at her hands. "After everything I've done . . ."

Chiara wrapped a protective arm around her sister. "You've done terrible things, but many of them can still be undone. That's where you'll begin."

Bells interrupted Ilaria's chance to reply, and the two sisters looked up. A kaleidoscope of lights descended upon them: the fairies of the Wishing Star. Released from the Heartless's obstructive spell, they were coming to heed the Blue Fairy's call.

CHAPTER FORTY-FIVE

It was the first time Chiara had seen her fellow fairies assembled together outside the Wishing Star. They landed one by one on the beach, each a bright and vibrant pop of color against the pale sand and gray sky. Not one was smiling.

Chiara's heart sank, but for Ily's sake, she kept her spirits up and led her sister to greet the fairies.

Mirabella was already waiting, but her stern gaze was on Chiara, not the former Scarlet Fairy.

She spoke: "It has come to my attention, Chiara, that you were once friends with Mr. Geppetto of Pariva, and that you granted his wish to bring to life his wooden puppet, Pinocchio."

Chiara bowed her head. "Yes, ma'am."

"You promised Pinocchio that you would turn him into

a real boy if he proved himself to be brave, truthful, and unselfish."

"I did."

"Such promises are not to be made without express permission and consideration from your fairy elders and the council."

"I know," pled Chiara. "But Pinocchio . . . if only you'd seen the happiness on his face. And on Geppetto's face. It was not a wish made in selfishness."

"Manipulating the gift of life goes against our ways," Mirabella said. "Instead of adhering to the rules you've been taught, you entered a bargain with one of the Heartless, and in the hopes of redeeming the Scarlet Fairy's heart, you gambled your own—on Pinocchio's life. This is most disappointing, Chiara, and not what I would have expected from a fairy of your caliber and reputation."

Ily stiffened at her side. "I didn't give her a choice," she said. "You can't blame her."

"I haven't finished," Mirabella said, frowning at the former Scarlet Fairy. She settled her austere gaze on Chiara, then sighed. "You've made some questionable decisions, Blue Fairy, and yet . . . at the end, an old man who has spent a lifetime bringing joy to those around him has at last found his own joy, a puppet has become a real boy, and a Heartless has found her heart again."

Chiara dared to look up.

Now Mirabella was smiling. She lowered her wand. "I think some of us have been on the Wishing Star so long that we forget that the rules we set in place long ago may need reviewing. In our efforts to protect ourselves and those we love and guard from the Heartless, we forget that not every heart is only good or only bad."

The other fairies murmured their agreement.

"We forget that the sacrifices we require and make in good faith aren't always what's best for everyone, and we forget to cherish, most of all, the joys and happiness that come with compassion, selflessness, and bravery."

Mirabella drew herself tall. "By the vote of the fairies of the Wishing Star, you will remain a fairy, so long as you wish. But to admonish you for the rules that you have broken, you will be suspended from the Wishing Star for a period of one year—once our business with Pleasure Island and Monstro is finished. During that time, you will remain in Pariva with your family. You will be reinstated once the year is over."

That was hardly a punishment, and Chiara's heart rose. "Mirabella . . ." she breathed. "Thank you."

"I'm not finished." Mirabella's tone had softened, and Agata appeared at her side.

"It has never sat right with me that we must make our loved ones forget us," said Agata quietly. "As Mirabella says, perhaps that sacrifice is not what's best for everyone, and it is time we revisited that rule, and reevaluated whether it does more harm than good."

"Fairies need time with their loved ones, like everyone else," chimed in Peri. "I think those connections to our friends and family actually make our magic stronger."

"I would agree," exclaimed the Rose Fairy.

"Me too!" the Yellow Fairy said.

"It seems like there's enough desire for us to take a vote when we're back on the Wishing Star," mused Mirabella.

"A vote's perfunctory," Agata murmured to Chiara. "I have a feeling we'll have many forgetting spells to undo, shortly. It's about time, too."

"We'll take a vote," Mirabella repeated. "But first, Monstro awaits."

One by one, the fairies waved their wands and became beams of flying starlight.

Chiara was last to go. She took Ilaria's hand. "Come with us," she said.

"Are you sure I'm allowed to?"

"We'll need all the help we can get," Chiara assured her.

Side by side, the two sisters flew together—with Chiara holding on to Ily—after the other fairies, until they came upon Monstro resting in the middle of the Lyre Sea.

Joining their powers together, the fairies of the Wishing

Star pointed their wands at Monstro. "Sleep, Monstro. Sleep, and do not let your wickedness trouble the shores and seas of Esperia any longer."

In an effort to fight off the fairies' spell, the giant whale thrashed and started to dive back into the sea, but the Heartless magic that had once given him unimaginable power had weakened, and without Larissa and Amorale's help, he could no longer resist the good fairies' magic. Slowly, his eyelids grew heavy, and he began to sink to the bottom of the sea, where he would remain for a long, long time.

The fairies let out jubilant cheers, and Agata dusted her hands. As always, she was ready for the next item of business. "Next, we visit Pleasure Island," she said. "There are hundreds of boys who want to go home. Their mothers have been missing them."

"May I come, too?" Ilaria asked in a small voice. The ruby on her wand was starting to lose its luster, and soon, once she let go of all her resentment, bitterness, and anger, she would lose her power. "My magic as a Heartless contributed to building the island. Let it help dismantle the place, and reverse the curse upon all those poor boys."

"And what will you do after you help us, Ilaria Belmagio?" asked Agata. Her words did not betray any reproach, but they also carried no sign of forgiveness. "You are a Heartless no longer."

Ilaria swallowed and stared down at her reflection in her wand's ruby. "I'm an old woman now, and with the years I have left, I'd like to atone for the mistakes I've made." She held out her wand. "Imprison me, please. The way you did Monstro. I would welcome the sentence."

"It is not our place to punish the deeds you regret," said Mirabella kindly. "That is for your own conscience to bear."

"Then what must I do?" Ilaria said.

"What do you *want* to do?" asked Chiara.

Ilaria drew a ragged breath, and her eyes misted. "I'd like a second chance with my family," she said quietly, meeting Chiara's gaze. "I'd like to ask their forgiveness for my selfishness. I know I don't deserve it, but that's where I'd like to start."

It was all Chiara could do not to hug her sister right there and then, but Ily wasn't finished. "Music once brought me great joy," the former Scarlet Fairy went on. "I'd like to start a school for children, maybe even a choir in town." She paused. "The boys of Pleasure Island contented themselves by brawling with one another and destroying everything in sight. I'd like to teach them—as well as anyone who will listen—to find happiness through song and harmony."

"You always did love to sing," said Chiara, wrapping her arm around her sister. "I think it's a wonderful idea."

"As do I," said Agata.

"And I," Mirabella chimed in.

One by one, the fairies of the Wishing Star agreed, and with the fairies' blessing, Ilaria accompanied them to what remained of Pleasure Island.

It took one long week for the fairies to track down every boy who had been turned into a donkey, and Mirabella and Agata personally sought out the Coachman, Honest John, Gideon, Stromboli, and other servants of the Heartless and ensured that the villains were taught just lessons for their evil behavior. Stromboli, for instance, was plagued with nightmares that his puppets came to life and attacked him, and Honest John and Gideon dreamt that they drowned in piles of golden coins.

But for the Coachman, who was so evil that no lesson would redeem him, Ilaria used the last of her Heartless magic and turned him into a donkey. In the pastures of Pariva, he spent the rest of his days gnawing on hay and grass and braying unpleasantly whenever young boys laughed at his smell.

As for the Heartless—without Amorale and Larissa to lead them, their strength as a group waned, and many of them instinctively fell into a deep slumber, as Monstro had. Their absence wouldn't last forever of course, but it would give the Wishing Fairies time to reevaluate the rigidity of their old rules and ways.

In the meantime, the Wishing Fairies found the bottle that contained Amorale and Larissa and brought it onto the Wishing Star. There, they dropped the bottle into the bottom of the deepest well, with a sign for all there were Heartless within, and they were not to be disturbed.

When it was all done, Ily and Chia received the fairies' blessing to return to Pariva. It was unanimously voted that the fairies should lift their respective forgetting spells, and in the future, every fairy would receive one month every year to spend in Esperia—with their family, their friends, or however they pleased.

Chiara's time home would begin as soon as she set aside her wand.

Spring seemed to have arrived overnight. Daffodils and violets bloomed from the flowerbeds along the cobblestone streets, birds chirped and whistled from every tree, and the town square was busier than ever. Hardly anyone noticed Chiara and Ilaria walking along Pine Grove.

"You know what I wished, all those years ago when we were girls?" Ilaria's voice hitched, and her eyes turned wet. "You thought I wished to be an opera singer. The best in all of Esperia."

"Didn't you?"

She shook her head. "I wished that we would be together, always."

Chiara swallowed hard. She hugged her sister. "We will be together. I'm coming, too, remember?"

"Give me a moment on my own," Ilaria said, flipping her gray hair. "I've got a lot of explaining to do. Though I don't even have a room anymore. Our grandnieces have taken it over."

"They're still young," said Chiara with a smile. "I'm sure they'd be happy to share. Maybe in exchange for singing lessons."

Ilaria tossed her a skeptical look, but as if on cue, Nina and Dafne Belmagio raced each other down the road. In her haste, little Nina didn't look where she was going and nearly bumped into Ilaria.

"I'm sorry!" the young girl cried. Her red hair bow had come undone while she was running, and it fell onto the ground.

As Ily knelt to pick it up, Dafne went over to her sister's side. "Told you to look where you're going when we race. Come on, Grandpa's waiting for us to help make cookies. We should—"

"Don't forget your ribbon," said Ilaria, calling after the pair as they headed toward the bakery.

Dafne glanced over her shoulder. "You sound familiar,"

she said, her bright green eyes rounding at the sight of Ily. "Do I know you?"

Instead of replying, Ilaria knelt and gently tied Nina's bow back into her hair. Then she faced the elder Belmagio girl. "You're Dafne. Niccolo Belmagio's granddaughter?"

"Both of us are," chimed in Nina.

"Hush, Nina, we aren't supposed to talk to strangers."

"But she doesn't look like a stranger. She looks like Daddy."

Ilaria's heart swelled, feeling pain and joy both at once.

"What's your name?" asked the older girl.

"Ilaria, but friends call me Ily. Ily Belmagio."

"Belmagio?" cried Nina. "But that's our name!"

Ilaria chuckled. "Well, you see . . . I'm your grandfather's sister. That would make me . . ." She frowned, having to think about it.

"Our great-aunt Ily!" Nina staggered back, unable to believe it. "Grandpa told us you're famous—a real prima donna. But I thought your name was . . ." Nina stopped with a frown. "Funny, I can't remember anymore. All I can think of is a goldfish."

Ilaria chuckled. "I'm no diva," she said honestly. "I did like to sing when I was young, though."

"You mean you're not famous?" said Nina, blinking with confusion. "Grandpa lied to us?"

"No, *I* lied."

Dafne crossed her arms. "That's a big lie to tell."

Ilaria couldn't disagree.

"Grandpa says if you tell too many lies, your nose will grow flowers."

"My nose used to have a lot of flowers," Ilaria admitted. "It took a long time for me to prune them all off."

"They must make a nice bouquet."

That made Ilaria laugh again. "The prettiest bouquet you'll ever see."

"Grandpa told me so many stories about you. How you used to sing with . . ." Dafne frowned, suddenly remembering. "With Great-Aunt Chia on the old harpsichord. It's in the attic now, but we could bring it down."

"That'd be a good idea," said Ily. She tilted her head slyly at the invisible Blue Fairy watching from the near distance. "I have a feeling your Great-Aunt Chia is going to be visiting very soon."

"Can you give us singing lessons before she comes?"

"I'm not such an experienced teacher . . ." Ily said. "But I'll do my best."

"You'll be a natural," Chiara murmured, knowing Ily could hear. The two sisters smiled, and Ily grasped her grandnieces by the hands and skipped down the road with them.

Are you coming? Ily mouthed at Chiara.

Soon, Chiara replied. She set her wand on her palm, watching as Fate stepped in and reunited her sister with her past. For who should Ilaria come across—but Geppetto and Pinocchio?

Laughter echoed from the end of the road as Nina and Dafne befriended Pinocchio, and Geppetto shyly reacquainted himself with Ilaria.

Chiara strolled down Constanza Street for the first time in years. She didn't have wings at the moment, but how wonderful it was to walk. She paused before the house she had once called her own. Before she went inside, there was still one more thing she needed to do.

The cricket.

She whistled quietly, and before long, he appeared.

"I haven't forgotten you, Sir Jiminy." She lifted the cricket onto her finger. "You've done marvelously."

With a tap of her wand, Chiara rewarded him with an official conscience badge, and the cricket preened, admiring the shiny new addition to his suit.

"Pinocchio has proven himself to be a fine boy," Chiara said. "But your work is far from done. Will you stay on as his conscience for a little while more?"

"It'd be my pleasure, Your Honor."

Jiminy leapt onto the road, but he darted a glance back at the Blue Fairy. "Will you be coming, too? Smells like the bread's coming out fresh from the oven."

What a keen cricket. "I'll be just a minute," Chiara said with a chuckle.

As Jiminy hopped away, the Blue Fairy spun her wand for one last spell before she tucked it away for a year. In her mind, she conjured the smell of cinnamon and pistachios, of chocolate and buttery sugar. A modest plate appeared on her palm, and she inhaled. "Just like home," she whispered to herself.

With a wave of her arm, she let go of her wand and made for the humble two-storied house with a yellow door. A lemon or two still hung from the trees brushing against the back window, and a bittersweet pang overcame Chiara's heart. It squeezed inside her, filled with excitement and nervousness and wonder.

When she found her courage, she knocked.

At first, she didn't think anyone heard. Then from inside, Niccolo's wife shouted: "It's the girls! They must be back early."

Footsteps approached, and Chiara held her breath. Niccolo himself answered the door, and let out a gasp.

The expression on her brother's face was one she would

treasure all her life. Joy and surprise flooded his eyes as years of forgotten memories came back to him. When he finally cried her name, his voice choked with emotion. "Chiara?"

"I know I'm a few years late," she said, finally letting go of her breath. She smiled at her brother. "But is there room for one more at dinner tonight? I've brought cookies."